I0760822

The Dare List

(To be undertaken by Lady L, under no duress whatsoever, except perhaps that of curiosity)

1. stargaze from a roof
2. explore somewhere new and bring back evidence
3. flirt with someone
4. get rain-soaked on purpose
5. keep your eyes up for an entire gathering
6. tell someone no
7. stand up for someone who cannot stand up for themselves
8. take a midnight swim
9. smoke driftshade leaf
10. be entirely improper
11. speak your mind to someone who scares you
12. kiss someone

ALSO BY RACHEL MORGAN

THE CHARMED LEAF LEGACY

Tempests & Tea Leaves

Deals & Dream Spells

Love & Letter Charms

CREEPY HOLLOW

The Faerie Guardian

The Faerie Prince

The Faerie War

A Faerie's Secret

A Faerie's Revenge

A Faerie's Curse

Glass Faerie

Shadow Faerie

Rebel Faerie

RIDLEY KAYNE CHRONICLES

Elemental Thief

Elemental Power

Elemental Heir

CITY OF WISHES

The Complete Cinderella Story

STORMFAE

From Storm and Shadow

Love & Letter Charms

Readers may experience musical accompaniment that changes with the emotional tenor of each scene. This enchantment is undetectable by most readers but can be sensed by those with particular magical sensitivity. If you hear nothing, your magic simply lies in other domains, but should you perceive the melodies, rest assured your book is functioning properly.

ISBN 978-1-998988-32-7 (ebook)
ISBN 978-1-998988-33-4 (paperback)
ISBN 978-1-998988-34-1 (hardback)

www.rachel-morgan.com

RACHEL MORGAN

To the shy, the quiet, the anxious.
May you find your own kind of fearless.

Prologue

One Year Ago

THE CARVED WOODEN BOX SAT INNOCENTLY AMONG THE CLUTTER OF Vesper's Curiosities & Oddities, yet something about it commanded Aurelise Rowanwood's attention like a whisper in a crowded room. She'd come seeking a birthday gift for a friend but found instead what might be either folly or fate—an enchantment promising written exchanges with an unknown recipient.

The wood was dark and smooth, engraved with delicate roses whose thorny stems twisted around the edges in an intricate border, and when Aurelise opened the box, she found an elegant inscription on the inside of the lid: *To the seeker of correspondence: Place your reply within and receive an answer that may change your path.*

Intrigued, Aurelise asked her older brother Evryn if he would purchase the box for her. He frowned at first, his protective instincts clearly warring with his inability to deny her anything. She waited patiently while he questioned the shop owner, his brow furrowed with concern about his seventeen-year-old sister potentially corresponding with some unknown and possibly questionable individual. The shopkeeper, however, had assured them that the enchantment was entirely self-contained, crafted by a retired enchanter who specialized in harmless novelties. Nothing more threatening than a clever parlor trick.

And so Evryn purchased the box for her. Yet once home, Aurelise found herself staring at it as it sat upon her vanity, suddenly struck by the absurdity of writing letters to no one. What was the point of committing her thoughts to parchment when only an enchantment would read them? The novelty seemed to fade before she'd even begun, and so the box remained untouched, its promise unfulfilled.

Then came Evryn's wedding to Lady Mariselle Brightcrest in all its glorious, scandalous tumult—a love that conquered ancient grudges and swept the family through weeks of joyful preparation before depositing them, tired but triumphant, into the blissful quiet that follows a perfectly executed celebration.

Aurelise and Kazrian's eighteenth birthday passed, the Bloom Season drew to a close, and the Rowanwoods prepared to return to their country estate. And then, in a single evening, everything changed.

It happened at a quiet family gathering during their last week in Bloomhaven. A sudden, overwhelming rush of magic surged through Aurelise's veins, far more potent than any ordinary magic she'd ever experienced. The music that had always lived privately in her mind and beneath her fingertips at the pianoforte suddenly filled the room, audible to everyone present, while delicate threads of light looped through the air around her, swirling in time with the melody that poured unbidden from her very being.

For several startled moments, all anyone could do was stare at her. Then: "My dearest, you have manifested!" her mother exclaimed, delighted tears in her eyes as everyone gathered around in wonder and celebration.

But for days afterward, Aurelise felt as though she was drowning. The music that had once been her sanctuary, her private refuge from overwhelming emotion, was now the very thing that threatened to suffocate her. Worse still, it betrayed her every feeling to the world. A moment of frustration might summon the sound of discordant strings, a flicker of joy could produce unbidden harp cascades, announcing her emotions to anyone nearby. Her refuge had become her betrayer.

Evryn must have noticed her distress—or perhaps Kazrian, in whom she eventually confided everything, had told Evryn—because he'd suggested she might find relief in writing down her feelings, in giving them shape outside of herself where they might seem less overwhelming.

That night, sitting at her small writing desk with a blank sheet of paper before her, Aurelise's gaze fell upon the forgotten wooden box, its promise suddenly beckoning like a confidant who would never judge. And so, after several false starts and crumpled attempts, she finally penned:

Dear Imaginary Recipient,

I confess I am uncertain how to begin a letter to what may simply be an enchanted repository of spelled paper and ink designed to make the lonely feel heard. Though I must admit, there is profound relief in knowing no real person will ever read these words, allowing me the rare luxury of complete honesty.

Today marks three days since my magic manifested, and I find myself quite overwhelmed by it all. Everyone speaks of the joy of finally coming into one's power, but no one mentions how frightening it can be when magic suddenly flows through you like a river breaking its banks. No one speaks of the paralyzing fear that comes with being unable to control one's newly manifested power, or the guilt that haunts every moment of celebration when siblings still await their own manifestations.

My family expects me to be utterly delighted by this development, and perhaps most young ladies would be, but I find the whole business rather terrifying. I wonder … do enchantments understand fear? Or joy? Or the peculiar loneliness of being surrounded by people who expect you to be delighted when inside you feel rather like you might shatter?

The thing I once treasured above all else—my one true solace when the world grew too loud, the thing that gave me the space to breathe when I felt as though the world may smother me—has transformed into the very thing that now overwhelms me. It has broken my heart in ways I never thought possible.

Well, this is silly. I've written far too much to a box that I have been assured holds nothing but a clever enchantment. And yet … I can't help but wonder what response I will receive to these thoughts I am too afraid to voice aloud.

With uncertain regards,

A Tentative Correspondent

She closed the lid with a soft click, then immediately opened it again. Her letter was gone. Her heart performed an odd little skip. Even knowing it was only the enchantment at work, the disappearance felt thrilling somehow, as though her words had been whisked away to some mysterious recipient who might actually understand the storm of emotions she kept carefully contained behind her quiet demeanor. She checked again a few minutes later, and then again after an hour, but the box remained empty.

She looked once more before retiring for the night, lifting the lid with waning hope, only to find it still empty. Disappointment settled in her chest like a cold stone. How foolish she was being. It wasn't as though a real person was ever going to reply to her outpouring of feelings. The enchantment must be faulty, or perhaps it had languished too long in Vesper's dusty shop and simply expired.

But the next morning, when she lifted the lid without any real hope, there it was—a letter, the handwriting bold and slightly slanted, nothing like her own careful script. Her heart leaped into her throat, and a flush of warmth spread across her cheeks. With trembling fingers, she unfolded the letter.

Dear Tentative Correspondent,

I must inform you that I am disappointingly real, which means that whoever assured you your box holds nothing but a clever enchantment was either lying or had no idea what they were giving you.

Congratulations on your manifestation! Though I notice you've cleverly avoided mentioning what form it takes. Very mysterious. I approve. I do hope it has not truly broken your heart, though. Perhaps with time you might rediscover what made this gift so treasured in the first place.

As for your question about understanding fear—I'm afraid I understand it rather too well. Just last week, I was presented with a dish of boiled parsnips and felt the same chill I did as a boy when first confronted with those pale carrot impersonators.

But you also asked about the loneliness of expectations, and there I must confess you've struck upon something I know intimately. Everyone assumes manifestation means finally knowing exactly who you are meant to be. No one mentions that sometimes it feels more like being handed a responsibility you never asked for while everyone watches to see if you will drop it. Though it has been several years since I manifested, that weight of expectation has only grown heavier with time, not lighter as everyone promised it would.

I hope you do not shatter. I hope you find the space to breathe again. The world needs more people brave enough to write honest letters to potentially imaginary correspondents.

With decidedly real regards,

A Not-So-Imaginary Correspondent

Aurelise read the letter three times in quick succession, her fingers tracing the bold, confident strokes of the handwriting. She committed each word to memory, analyzing every hint about her mysterious correspondent. A man, certainly, and one at least several years her senior. The thought sent an inappropriate little thrill through her that she quickly tamped down.

She should stop this correspondence immediately. It wasn't at all proper for an unmarried lady of barely eighteen to be exchanging private letters with an unknown gentleman. Yet curiosity flared like phoenixfire. And what if this was still merely an elaborate enchantment, designed to seem real? If that were the case, there was no harm in responding.

She traced the signature—*A Not-So-Imaginary Correspondent*—and found herself smiling despite her reservations. Real or not, she wanted to write back. Just once more, she told herself. Just to see what would happen.

Dear Not-So-Imaginary Correspondent,

Your parsnip phobia was precisely the amusement I needed. I must admit I have been rather melancholy these past days, overwhelmed by the sudden change in my life, but the image of a grown man cowering before a 'pale carrot impersonator' made me laugh so unexpectedly that my lady's maid came rushing in to ensure I hadn't taken leave of my senses. I hope that doesn't make me terribly wicked, finding amusement in your culinary distress.

And I must clarify—it was not deliberate avoidance when I didn't mention my manifestation specifically. That was merely the way my thoughts flowed onto the page. But now that I suspect you may be real (though I remain skeptical), I shall be careful to refrain from mentioning specific details that might reveal my identity. One cannot be too cautious when corresponding with mysterious gentlemen through enchanted boxes, after all.

I find myself wondering what other perfectly harmless things might inspire terror in you. Embroidery hoops? Dancing lessons? The color lavender?

With amused regards,

Still Tentative

P.S. You called me brave, but I must correct this misunderstanding. I am perhaps the least brave person in all the United Fae Isles. I am shy to the point of invisibility and speak rarely in company unless directly addressed. When I attempt to initiate conversation, I somehow manage to choose topics so utterly tedious that I can practically see my companions' eyes glaze over with boredom. Then I end up stammering and flushed with mortification. Words on a page are much easier.

Dear Still Tentative,

Terribly wicked indeed! I am wounded to my core that my deepest fear—the insidious parsnip—has become a source of such callous amusement. Though the thought of bringing laughter to you in your melancholy does soothe my injured pride somewhat.

But what do you mean I 'MAY' be real? I'm thoroughly offended that you do not believe me! What can I do to prove my existence beyond these pages?

Ah! Perhaps I could send you something? A token of my reality? Let me consider what might convince you …

Perhaps a preserved parsnip, elegantly mounted and framed like a trophy of conquest? A series of dramatic sonnets entitled 'Ode to the Pale Horror That Lurks Beneath the Soil'? A trained gossip bird that squawks 'Parsnips are an abomination!' at regular intervals?

Do let me know which would be most convincing. I await your instructions with bated breath.

Still very much real,

The Parsnip Dreader

P.S. There are many forms of courage in this world. Some are loud and dramatic; others are quiet and no less significant. Perhaps you are braver than you know, just not in the way society has taught you to recognize.

It had taken all day and night for this reply to show up in Aurelise's enchanted letter box. Her lady's maid had departed hours before, having helped her into her nightgown and arranged her hair into a simple braid for sleeping. She had been drifting into dreams when a soft hum pulled her back to wakefulness. Instinctively, she knew it was the box.

She'd promised herself only one more exchange—and it was certainly improper to be sending magical notes across the realm at such an hour—but then again, she still couldn't be certain there was truly a person on the other end of this enchantment. If she was merely conversing with a clever spell designed to provide the illusion of correspondence, then propriety hardly mattered, did it?

This reasoning was flimsy at best, she knew, but it didn't stop her from slipping from beneath her covers and seating herself at her writing desk to pen a reply.

Dear Parsnip Dreader,

Your offerings are most generous, if decidedly peculiar. However, I cannot in good conscience reveal where I live. If you ARE real (which I am still not entirely convinced of), then sending items to my personal residence does not seem safe at all. I do not know you! You could be a parsnip in disguise, infiltrating polite society for nefarious vegetable purposes.

Besides, what would my family think if mysterious packages began arriving from unknown gentlemen? The scandal would be unbearable.

Your faithful correspondent,

The Cautious Skeptic

P.S. I had never considered there might be different forms of courage beyond the obvious. It sounds like beautiful nonsense, the kind that poets spin to make ordinary things seem extraordinary. And yet, I find myself wondering if there might be some small truth to it. I shall contemplate your words, though I make no promises to believe them.

Dear Cautious Skeptic,

Your prudence is admirable, if frustrating to one attempting to prove his corporeal existence. But I must ask—how am I to convince you of my reality if I cannot send anything, cannot visit, cannot provide any tangible evidence of my existence?

Am I doomed to remain forever a figment of enchantment in your mind? The thought is oddly poetic, yet unsatisfying. There must be some way to bridge this gap between enchantment and reality without compromising your safety or reputation.

Perhaps you might suggest a method that would satisfy both your caution and my desire to be acknowledged as more than magical correspondence?

Awaiting inspiration,

The Increasingly Existential Correspondent

P.S. I look forward to receiving the letter in which you inform me that you've realized I am, in fact, correct about this matter of courage.

Aurelise gazed out of her window at the moonlit gardens of their Bloomhaven residence, absently brushing the feather of her self-inking quill back and forth across her chin as she contemplated how to respond. A smile touched her lips whenever she thought of his postscript about courage—his certainty was both presumptuous and oddly charming—but decided now was not the time to rise to that particular bait. The more pressing matter was determining whether this mystery gentleman truly existed.

An idea began to take shape in her mind, centered around her grandmother's establishment. Lady Rivenna Rowanwood owned The Charmed Leaf Tea House, the beating heart of Bloomhaven society gossip. While Aurelise and her immediate family were scheduled to depart for their country estate in just two days' time, returning to the sprawling manor where they spent most of the year when not attending the Season in Bloomhaven, her grandmother would remain, overseeing her business with her customary sharp eye and sharper tongue.

Would it truly be dishonest for Aurelise to say she was not in Bloomhaven right now? By the time her mysterious correspondent could possibly act on her suggestion, it would be true. She weighed the small deception against the protection her anonymity provided, and decided that this careful obscuring of details was merely prudent caution, not truly a lie.

Dear Increasingly Existential Correspondent,

After much consideration, I believe I have a solution that might satisfy us both. Do you know of The Charmed Leaf Tea House in Bloomhaven? I am not in Bloomhaven myself, but everyone of any consequence knows of The Charmed Leaf.

Send something there. Something outrageous, something that will be certain to grab the attention of the gossip birds. News of anything truly remarkable will spread quickly and will surely reach me before long.

Oh! It must involve a parsnip somehow. That detail will be our secret signal, so I shall know with certainty it was you and not some other mysterious prankster terrorizing tea houses across the realm.

I await news of your daring deed,

Your Reluctant Conspirator

My dear Architect of Mischief,

Brilliant! A public spectacle at The Charmed Leaf? Consider it done.

I am not in Bloomhaven either, but I shall make the necessary arrangements. Within a week, The Charmed Leaf Tea House will play host to a parsnip-related incident that will have gossip birds fluttering their wings in scandalized delight for months to come. I shall spare no expense nor creativity in proving my existence to you.

Until the parsnips make their debut,

Your Conspirator in Scandal

Two days later, the Rowanwood family departed Bloomhaven for their country estate. Their trunks had been sent ahead by carriage, but the family themselves traveled via the swifter and more elegant means afforded by their status—ley line gliders. The enchanted vessels, shaped like elongated leaf-boats with hulls of impossibly thin wood, glided effortlessly along the ancient underground rivers of magic that flowed beneath the realm's surface, reaching the Rowanwoods' distant manor in mere hours rather than the several days a carriage journey would have required.

Nearly a fortnight passed after Aurelise proposed her plan, during which she exchanged several more letters with her mysterious (and possibly still imaginary) correspondent. Their topics ranged widely. She learned he had no siblings (and in turn told him she couldn't decide who she was closer to, her twin brother or her older sister), and admitted she preferred the company of fictional characters—and the ever-blooming roses in her garden—to that of real people.

Then, one afternoon, a letter arrived via magically expedited messenger pixie from her grandmother. That evening at dinner, as Lady Lelianna read the correspondence aloud with increasing astonishment in her voice, Aurelise nearly choked on her peas and had to quickly disguise her laughter as a coughing fit.

It turned out that her stern and proper grandmother had been utterly horrified when a group of performers dramatically invaded afternoon tea at The Charmed Leaf, announcing they were the 'Court of Vegetable Justice' and that they were holding an emergency session to try Lady Rivenna Rowanwood for 'egregious discrimination against the noble parsnip family.'

After recovering from her coughing fit, Aurelise had to bite her lip to keep from dissolving into helpless laughter, her cheeks flushed and her heart pounding as she realized her mysterious correspondent was undeniably, extravagantly real. She could hardly wait to retire to her chambers that night to write to him.

Dear Conspirator in Scandal,

A 'Court of Vegetable Justice' summoning Lady Rivenna Rowanwood to trial? You have exceeded my wildest expectations. I don't believe anyone has ever dared perpetrate such an outrageous prank at The Charmed Leaf in all its storied history.

Consider me thoroughly convinced of your existence.

With astonished regards,

No Longer Skeptical

P.S. I'm glad you are real.

My dear No Longer Skeptical,

I find myself disproportionately pleased by those five simple words—'I'm glad you are real.' It leaves me wondering whether you think of me at odd moments throughout your day, as I find myself thinking of you.

I imagine you'll be discussing all of this with those ever-blooming roses you prefer over the company of people. No doubt they'll be quite scandalized to hear you're corresponding with a REAL gentleman orchestrating vegetable-themed chaos across the realm instead of merely enchanted paper.

Victoriously yours,

The Very Real Correspondent

Dear Very Real Correspondent,

I feel I must correct a misunderstanding. I never claimed to TALK to the roses—merely that I prefer their company to that of most people. Though now that you've suggested it, I believe I might try it. I imagine they are excellent listeners, and unlike certain correspondents, they are unlikely to make remarks specifically designed to bring color to my cheeks.

If I WERE to discuss you with them (which I absolutely have not done and would never consider doing), I'm certain they would say you are a terrible influence.

Reproachfully yours,

The Rose Companion

Dear Definitely Talking to the Roses,

Ah, my remarks make you BLUSH, do they? That is dangerously endearing information to share. You realize, of course, that I must now slip something into every letter specifically designed to set your cheeks aflame?

Though you strike me as someone who blushes at everything. Compliments, embarrassment, strong breezes, letters from devastatingly charming correspondents …

Am I warm? (The answer is yes, you are definitely pink right now.)

Incorrigibly yours,

Devastatingly Charming

Dear Audaciously Presumptuous,

I do NOT blush at strong breezes. That's absurd. I blush at perfectly reasonable things like … well, certainly not at letters, anyway.

Since you are so insistent, however, I feel compelled to tell you that I DID, in fact, attempt a conversation with the roses. They informed me—very solemnly—that you are unnecessarily provocative, prone to mischief, and in dire need of proper supervision.

I am inclined to agree with them.

With botanical disapproval,

The Rose Companion

Dear Co-Conspirator of the Roses,

Your roses sound like elderly chaperones. Do they also disapprove of uncovered ankles and dancing too close to one's partner?

Not that you, of course, would ever be guilty of such shocking behavior. No, I picture you perfectly poised, proper to the last fingertip. Right now, you are sitting straight and elegant while reading this, perhaps smoothing your hair, most certainly blushing as your eyes move over this very sentence.

Go ahead, tell me I'm wrong. (But do it convincingly this time.)

Scandalously yours until the roses faint,

Your Devoted Tormentor

Dear Devoted Tormentor,

You grow bolder with every letter!

Fine. I will concede that I sit up straight while writing, though it is due more to the unyielding back of my chair than to my own poise. I will also admit that I did smooth my hair while reading your letter, though only because a most unruly strand had fallen out of its arrangement and across my cheek. But as for blushing—absolutely not. My complexion remains perfectly serene and untroubled.

If you could see me now, you would find me cool, composed, and perhaps even faintly disdainful at your outrageous presumptions.

With unblushing dignity (and the faintest suspicion that you will not believe me),

Your Entirely Composed Correspondent

P.S. The roses ARE elderly chaperones. They've been growing in that garden for almost forty years. They probably have opinions about everything.

The weeks that followed blurred together in a flutter of letters. Aurelise found herself checking the box multiple times each day, her heart performing that same peculiar skip whenever a new folded paper appeared. Sometimes she and her unknown correspondent fell into a rhythm so swift and immediate it seemed impossible they weren't sitting across from one another. His hastily scrawled replies would appear less than a minute after she closed the lid on her own letters.

At other times, silence stretched between them, hours turning to days before his familiar handwriting appeared again. During these lapses, Aurelise caught herself composing questions about his absence—what obligations had pulled him away, what duties demanded his attention—only to discard them. She had no right to such curiosities when she herself refused to share the particulars of her own life. Their delicate balance depended on this mutual mystery, however much she sometimes longed to breach it.

Sometimes they exchanged letters about delightfully trivial matters—debating the proper way to eat scones (cream first, then jam, he insisted, while she maintained the opposite), or crafting increasingly elaborate excuses one might use to escape the most tedious social obligations.

On other days, their correspondence delved into more significant terrain. They spoke of loneliness (his), of overwhelm (hers), and of fear (vague, yet shared between them like a bridge connecting their separate worlds). She told him about her daily practice with her newly manifested magic. The hours spent in solitude mastering its nuances, the small victories as unpredictable surges became controlled expressions. The intense joy of reclaiming something that had seemed, at first, as though it might be lost forever.

I can breathe again, she told him one day. *I am not broken. I did not shatter. I am … happy.*

It brings me more gladness than I can properly express to know that you have come to appreciate your manifested magic, he replied.

It is more than that, she wrote back. *I feel as though nothing else in life will ever compare to this. It is so precious, so perfectly suited to who I am, that I believe all other joys will pale beside it.*

Do you not think there might be space in your life for different kinds of joy? he asked. *Not greater or lesser, but simply different colors of the same light?*

Perhaps … though I struggle to imagine what could shine as brightly as the feeling of creation flowing through me. I don't believe I could ever love anything as completely or as wholly as I love this.

You cannot imagine loving anything else as completely? he teased. *What about ANYONE?*

She deftly changed the subject then, not entirely sure how to share the truth that lingered in her heart. How could she explain that the very thought of loving someone with the same intensity she felt for her music filled her with quiet terror? Her soul already overflowed with emotions that threatened to consume her daily—every feeling amplified beyond what others seemed to experience. Love—true, passionate love—would surely be the most overwhelming of all.

She had witnessed its effects on Jasvian and Evryn, her two older brothers who had been fortunate enough to find love matches. They appeared transformed by it, utterly and completely happy in a way that most people could only ever dream of. But Aurelise was not built as they were. Such all-consuming emotion would wash away whatever fragile boundaries she had managed to construct around her too-sensitive heart. Better to find a gentle companion who would give her space for her music than to risk drowning in the depths of a love she could neither control nor contain.

More weeks passed, filled with letters about everything and nothing. Complex theories about what really happened to all the missing left gloves in the world, increasingly ridiculous guesses about what Aurelise's manifested magic might be (*I've got it! You can communicate telepathically, but exclusively with parsnips! This would explain your amusement at my vegetable vendetta, as the parsnips have surely been complaining about me for years.*), and the occasional confession that he still struggled with control over his manifested ability, even years after it appeared.

And then, after three months of letters, her mystery correspondent asked:

Dear Friend Who Remains Nameless,

We have now written for the length of a full season, and I still don't know what to call you in my thoughts. Would you tell me your name? Or at least something I might call you that's shorter than 'Person Who Writes Lovely Letters and Makes Me Laugh'?

Hopefully yours,

Still Just a Mystery

P.S. Have I asked yet what season you prefer? Where I live, beyond the United Fae Isles, the seasonal transitions are less defined. More a gentle blending rather than a dramatic transformation.

She stared at his letter until the words blurred before her eyes, recognizing that she stood at the edge of dangerous territory. Their correspondence had come to mean more to her than she knew how to express. She cared for him—there was no use denying that to herself anymore. Aside from her music, his letters had become the bright points around which her days orbited, each one treasured and reread.

But it was the distance between them that made caring for him *safe*. He existed only in ink and paper, in words she kept bundled with silk ribbon in the secret compartment at the base of her dressing table drawer, cleverly concealed beneath a false panel. Words on a page were safe, she told herself repeatedly. They remained contained, controlled, unable to flood her world unexpectedly as real emotions so often did.

But to know his name, to give him hers—these were steps toward a reality she could not allow herself to contemplate.

She needed him to remain at arm's length. Or rather, at continent's length, as he apparently resided somewhere beyond the boundaries of the United Fae Isles. The very notion of what lay beyond those borders was hazy in her mind. Distant lands described in geography lessons, places of strange customs and unfamiliar magic that seemed more legend than reality.

Yet she couldn't simply ignore his request. To offer nothing felt unkind after all they had shared. But what? Even just the initial 'A' seemed as though it were revealing too much. But a random name or letter felt dishonest, a betrayal of the authenticity that had defined their correspondence.

She closed her eyes, considering, until her thoughts settled on the name her siblings still called her on occasion. The name Kazrian had first given her when they were small and his toddler tongue couldn't manage all the syllables of her full name.

Lise.

Dear Mystery,

You may call me L.

I know that's not very satisfying, but I must be honest and admit that I prefer our established anonymity. I hope you understand my caution. It is not a lack of trust in you specifically, but rather a shield I find I cannot set aside.

Mysteriously yours,

L

Dear L,

L! How delightfully enigmatic. Let me guess what it stands for: Ludicrous? Luminous? Loquacious? (Though given your admitted fear of crowds, perhaps not that last one.) Lamentable? Luxurious? Lexicographer? (I'm particularly proud of that one.)

Oh! I know. Librarian. You're secretly a librarian who's been studying ancient texts about mysterious letter enchantments this entire time.

Since you've given me a letter, I suppose it's only fair I return the favor. You may call me R.

Riddlingly yours,

R

Dear R,

R for Ridiculous, I assume, given that list of increasingly absurd suggestions. Lexicographer, honestly. As if I spend my days compiling dictionaries. (Though words ARE rather beautiful, aren't they?)

Mysteriously yours,

L (for none of the above)

P.S. I was relieved to see your reply in my box this morning. I feared my insistence on anonymity might have tried your patience beyond repair, that you might decide our correspondence was no longer worth pursuing. Thank you for understanding my need for this particular boundary, strange as it may seem.

Dear L (for Definitely Lying About the Lexicography),

Fine, you've caught me. R does indeed stand for Ridiculous. Also Remarkable, Ravishing, and almost always Right About Things.

Ridiculously yours,

R

P.S. As if I could ever cease writing to you.

Chapter One

The dressing table mirror reflected chaos. Not only Aurelise Rowanwood's wide eyes and half-done hair, but the whirlwind that had overtaken Windsong Cottage in the hours before the Season's Opening Ball. Behind her, the reflection captured her mother's hands fluttering like anxious birds over a tiny rent in the silk overlay of Aurelise's gown, her sister Rosavyn sprawled across the small bed in defiance of all propriety, and Marta, her lady's maid, rummaging through a jewelry case while muttering about pearl hairpins.

Through the open doorway, the mirror caught a flurry of activity in the sitting area. Kazrian balanced on the low table, his hands outstretched toward the ceiling faelight as he attempted to coax it back to proper illumination, while their grandmother, Lady Rivenna, swept into view, admonishing him about the flagrant indecorum of standing on furniture. She barely had time to duck as an errant spark of magic shot from Kazrian's hand, narrowly missing her meticulously arranged silver hair.

"I did express my concerns about the lack of space here," Lady Lelianna muttered, leaning closer to inspect her magical repair while drawing in her skirts as Marta passed with her newly discovered hairpins, the maid offering breathless apologies as she squeezed between Lady Lelianna and the crowded dressing table.

"Oh, nonsense," Rosavyn replied from her horizontal position. "This is *fun*, Mother! All of us here together in this cozy little—"

A crash from the other side of the cottage interrupted her. Several moments of silence followed as everyone paused. Then Lady Nirella Brightcrest's voice floated through the rooms. "Not to worry! That was merely the teapot meeting its unfortunate end. I shall brew a fresh pot in that lovely porcelain with the pink flowers instead."

"Try the silver teapot with the lumyrite base," Lady Rivenna called to her friend. "The lumyrite infuses that particular blend with more potency."

The silver teapot. The one with the lumyrite base. Yes, she should focus on that, Aurelise told herself as she swallowed past the dryness in her throat. Not this crushing anxiety pressing against her chest.

Tonight. Stars above, it was actually tonight.

The Opening Ball of the Bloom Season had always been a grand affair, but this year promised to surpass all others. With Dreamland—that miraculous piece of the dream realm brought into physical reality—finally restored and ready for visitors, the High Lady had delayed its grand opening specifically to coincide with tonight's festivities. The ball would take place within Dreamland itself.

The restoration had been Evryn and Mariselle's project, of course. Mariselle with her dream magic and Evryn with his ability to shape the required lumyrite structure that powered the operation. It was still strange, at times, to think of the two of them together: a Rowanwood and a Brightcrest.

Just last Season, a union between the two families had been unthinkable. They had maintained a very public hatred for generations. Yet there Evryn had been, bound by what everyone believed to be a soulbond to Mariselle Brightcrest herself. Only the family now knew the truth: the 'soulbond' had been a cleverly disguised magical contract, forcing them to work together on Dreamland's restoration after the two of them had accidentally activated its long-forgotten magical clauses.

They'd managed to get Dreamland functional before last Season's end, after which they'd launched into preparations for a wedding that had set every gossip bird in Bloomhaven chirping for weeks. But there had still been much to accomplish before Dreamland was restored to the breathtaking wonderland of its legendary past. Now, after months of additional work, Dreamland stood ready to enchant all of society. And every fae lord and lady whose magic had manifested within the last year would debut their new abilities within its impossible landscape tonight.

After the High Lady had made this decision, sending the news to every noble house a few weeks before the Season began, someone within the Rowanwood household had suggested they prepare for the ball at Windsong Cottage. The idea had been rather sentimental—to dress for the grand night in the very place where the original Dreamland plans had been conceived. Lady Nirella, Mariselle's grandmother, had loved the notion, happily offering her cottage for the occasion. Aurelise's mother and grandmother, however, had been less enthusiastic about the practical challenges.

They'd compromised by having the elder Rowanwoods and Kazrian prepare at Rowanwood House before joining the sisters. A complex enchantment had been required just to accommodate the preparations. Jasvian had performed the intricate spell that transported both girls' dressing tables directly from Rowanwood House into the cottage, with Aurelise's fitting snugly in the bedroom and Rosavyn's wedged against the window in the living area. Despite this clever solution, the cottage's intimate dimensions remained a challenge for readying two young ladies, especially when one was about to be the focus of every eye in fae society.

"Tea? Now?" Her mother's voice, usually so gentle but now sharp with worry, brought Aurelise's attention back to the present. "Who on earth requested refreshments at this critical hour?"

Aurelise took a breath. "I did."

Lady Lelianna's eyes met hers in the mirror, a perfect blend of concern and exasperation. "Aurelise, darling, now is hardly the moment for a leisurely tea service. We still have your final accessories to arrange, and—"

"It's the serenity blend. I asked Grandmother to bring some. I thought it might … help."

"But we've barely finished your hair, and your gown is—" Lady Lelianna gestured helplessly at the delicate layers of fine silk. "What if you spill? The High Lady will be scrutinizing every detail tonight."

Rosavyn rolled onto her side, propping her head on one hand. "Oh splendid, Mother. Remind her of the High Lady's critical gaze. I'm certain that will settle her nerves far better than any tea could."

Lady Lelianna pivoted toward her elder daughter with a soft huff. "Rosavyn, for goodness' sake! The way you're draped across that bed, one might think you were auditioning for a fainting scene in a melodrama rather than preparing for the Season's Opening Ball. Do sit properly please, before you wrinkle your gown beyond the redemptive powers of even the best pressing spell."

"Fine, fine," Rosavyn grumbled as she pushed herself upright and shifted to perch on the edge of the bed with exaggerated reluctance. "Though I fail to see why it matters when no one will be looking at me anyway. At least, not for the right reasons."

The words were light, but Aurelise caught the underlying current. Her chest tightened.

"Mother." Kazrian poked his dark head through the doorway. "Might I head on over to Dreamland? To see if—"

"Absolutely not!" Lady Lelianna's laugh held a note of barely contained hysteria. "You cannot simply *wander* into a piece of the dream realm. And before the High Lady's arrival! She would be *most*—"

"I meant the maintenance room," Kazrian clarified, leaning against the doorframe. "Where Mariselle is likely driving Evryn mad with unnecessary last-minute adjustments. I could offer my steady presence, perhaps remind them that everything is perfect, and suggest they join us for a moment before the chaos truly begins."

Lady Lelianna pressed her fingertips to her temple. "As if this cottage needs additional bodies crammed into it."

"The sitting room is practically empty," Kazrian countered, gesturing behind him.

"Kazrian, dear." His mother's voice softened though her expression remained firm. "Your brother and sister-in-law do not need another distraction right now. Please keep your grandmother company until we've finished with Aurelise. It's vital that she looks absolutely flawless tonight."

Aurelise's stomach knotted tighter at her mother's words, while Kazrian's shoulders slumped. "All right then," he muttered with a sigh.

He disappeared, but not before Aurelise caught the flash of something raw in his eyes. Kazrian should have been preparing for his own debut tonight. They were twins, after all, born mere minutes apart. All the signs suggested his magic would manifest any day now. The restless energy, the way magical objects responded strangely in his presence, the occasional stray magic that escaped him at odd moments. But 'any day' had not yet become 'today,' so while Aurelise would be presented to society tonight as Lady Aurelise, her twin would remain simply Master Kazrian, watching from the sidelines.

The unfairness of it sat like a stone in her stomach, made heavier still when she caught Rosavyn's reflection in the vanity mirror. Her older sister maintained her careless posture, but Aurelise knew better. Rosavyn had passed her twentieth birthday months ago with still no sign of manifestation. The gossip birds had barely waited for the Rowanwood carriages to stop before spreading their unpleasant screeches through Bloomhaven. *Two unmanifested Rowanwood children! Rowanwood bloodline weakening!*

Aurelise had overheard her mother and grandmother speaking in hushed tones just yesterday. Would Rosavyn's situation—and now Kazrian's—reflect poorly on Aurelise? Would potential suitors wonder if the Rowanwood magic was truly failing? Would she be considered a less desirable match?

Yet Aurelise found herself wondering whether it even mattered. Unlike her brothers, who carried the weight of the Rowanwood legacy, or Rosavyn, whose prolonged lack of manifestation had become a source of family concern, Aurelise's hopes were modest. There was no need for her to secure a brilliant match to salvage family fortunes or status. Her mother and grandmother naturally wished for her comfort and security, but their concerns went far beyond what Aurelise herself required.

She desired a husband who would be … undemanding. Someone who understood her need for solitude and wouldn't expect grand passions or constant companionship. The sweeping romantic tales that made other young ladies sigh held little appeal for her, the overwhelming emotions seeming exhausting rather than enticing. If she could find someone who would give her the freedom to retreat into her music whenever she wished, who would allow her that private sanctuary without resentment, that would be enough. Music was the only love affair her heart truly craved.

Although … there was R.

She tensed, disquieted as she always was when this particular thought breached the careful walls she'd built around it. R belonged safely on paper, a collection of clever words and teasing remarks, but nothing more than that. Already she felt too much when his letters appeared in the enchanted box, her heart racing in a way that threatened her carefully maintained composure.

She would not allow herself to imagine anything beyond their correspondence. As she constantly reminded herself, the man behind those witty lines could be anyone. Ancient, deceitful, nothing like the person she'd constructed in her imagination. Not that she could ever truly bring herself to believe that.

As Marta secured the final pearl-tipped pins into her hair and her mother smoothed the elbow-length gloves she'd selected, Aurelise allowed her thoughts to drift back to the correspondence she and R had exchanged earlier that week.

Dear R,

Indeed, the season has fully established itself here, with wildflowers carpeting every meadow and tree branches heavy with blossoms. The ever-blooming roses are being absolutely insufferable about the 'seasonal' flowers finally making an appearance. "Oh look who's decided to join us after hiding all winter," they seem to say with every petal-quivering breeze.

I wish I could properly enjoy the warmth and beauty, but I find myself unable to appreciate much lately. Anxiety has begun to claw at my thoughts with increasing persistence, for there is something rather terrifying on the horizon.

With quiet dread,

L

Dearest L,

What torment you've inflicted upon me! You cannot possibly introduce such ominous foreboding and then provide no details. My imagination is now running wild with possibilities!

Is it vegetables? A poetry recital where you're expected to perform? An offer of marriage from a gentleman whose company you can scarcely endure for more than a moment?

I shall be utterly sleepless until you elaborate.

Consumed by curiosity,

R

Dear R,

If only it were something as straightforward as vegetables, or even an unwanted proposal, for at least that can be met with a graceful refusal and the matter swiftly concluded.

No, I'm afraid it is far worse: a social gathering. Multiple social gatherings, in fact.

Woefully,

L

Ah. That is indeed more dreadful than vegetables. My deepest condolences.

Thank you. I find myself in the most frustrating contradiction. I desperately want to be included, to be part of these gatherings, to feel as though I belong. Yet the moment I am surrounded by people, I want nothing more than to dissolve into the wallpaper. Conversation eludes me entirely. My mind empties of all clever thoughts, and I'm left with nothing but painfully dull observations about the weather.

I have the perfect solution. When conversation fails you, simply look the other person directly in the eyes and ask, with complete seriousness: "Do you think plants have opinions about us?" I promise you it will be memorable.

I imagine such a question would be met with nothing but stunned silence and raised eyebrows.

Exactly! That blessed silence gives you the perfect opportunity to elaborate on your theories about those ever-blooming roses you speak with. Perhaps share their thoughts on proper tea service or their opinions on the latest fashions.

At which point they will determine I've completely lost my senses.

Perhaps. I imagine you'll receive one of two outcomes with this approach. Either they will light up with unexpected delight, revealing themselves as a kindred spirit who has secretly wondered the same thing about judgmental flora, in which case you've discovered a companion worthy of conversation. Or they will decide you're utterly mad and will be desperate to extract them-

selves from the conversation, leaving you free to retreat to a quiet corner. I see no flaws in this plan.

When you explain it that way, it does seem like surprisingly sound advice.

You're most welcome. I am, as always, still right about everything.

R … I feel I should clarify that the roses do not actually speak to me. I wouldn't want you to think I've genuinely lost my wits. (Though I do sometimes find myself assigning them personalities when I'm alone in the garden for too long.)

L for Ludicrously Concerned I Had Misunderstood,

Yes. I am aware of the sad reality that the roses do not truly speak to you. But I suspect they would have excellent opinions if they could.

Aurelise had written nothing further, settling into bed with a small smile on her lips. But barely a half hour later, the distinctive hum of the enchanted box had pulled her from the edge of sleep. Inside, she'd found a hastily scrawled note:

L,

I told myself not to ask. I promised myself I wouldn't. But I find I cannot sleep with the question burning in my mind. Are you referring to the Bloom Season? Will you be in Bloomhaven? I know you manifested since the last Season began … Does this mean you will be debuting your magic?

Please forgive the intrusion,

R

Aurelise's fingers had trembled as she read his words. Did this mean he would be there too? Hadn't he claimed to live beyond the United Fae Isles? What if he was planning to travel to Bloomhaven, hoping that the two of them might … meet? The thought sent a wave of panic through her chest. And so, for the first time in their long correspondence, she had deliberately lied.

Dear R,

Your intrusion is forgiven. I could never hold your curiosity against you!

Alas, my family's circumstances prevent us from traveling for the Season this year. Such is life. Full of disappointments both small and large.

I do hope this satisfies your midnight curiosity enough to allow you peaceful slumber.

Sleepily,

L

"There," Marta declared with a final adjustment to one of the pins. "You're ready, my lady."

Aurelise turned slightly, rising with care as the silk layers of her gown whispered against the stool. For a moment, her eyes swept her reflection in the dressing table mirror. The rose-pink silk fell in graceful lines beneath the empire waist, drifting into gauzy layers that shimmered when she shifted. Gold embroidery traced tiny blossoms across the bodice, and a sash of ivory silk was fastened with a delicate rose-gold rosette.

She turned from the mirror, lifting her chin and lacing her fingers together, standing still beneath the careful scrutiny of three pairs of eyes.

"Oh, darling," her mother breathed, her eyes misting. "You look absolutely beautiful."

"Truly lovely," Marta agreed with a proud smile.

Rosavyn, still sitting on the edge of the bed, tipped her head to one side. "I suppose you'll do," she said with mock indifference.

Aurelise smiled at her, while Lady Lelianna pressed a hand to her chest in horror. "Really, Rosavyn—"

"I have no doubt, dearest sister," Rosavyn said, a wide smile stretching her lips as she stood, "that you will be the loveliest creature in all of Dreamland tonight."

Aurelise drew a deep breath that did little to ease the tightness in her chest, her smile fixed like fragile porcelain that might crack at the slightest pressure. Being the focus of attention was precisely what she dreaded most about the evening ahead. She looked around for her gloves, seeking something to do with her trembling hands.

"Aurelise, dear!" Lady Nirella's voice called out. "Your tea is ready."

Lady Lelianna sighed and shook her head. "I still think this is most irregular timing. I shall see what mischief is transpiring between the grandmothers. Oh, the rose water! Is it—"

"My dressing table, I believe," Rosavyn said.

Lady Lelianna turned to Marta. "Could you look for it please?"

"Of course, my lady."

As her mother and Marta left the room, Rosavyn flicked her fingers, sending a gentle current of air to nudge the door closed with a soft, deliberate click. "Now," she said, turning back to Aurelise and taking her hands, "how are you *really*—"

"Do you hate me?" The words tumbled from Aurelise's lips before she could stop them, cutting across her sister's question.

Rosavyn blinked. "Hate you? Whatever for?"

"Because my magic has manifested and yours hasn't. Because I'll be presented tonight and you won't. Because they're all fussing over me when it should have been you first. I *wish* it had been you first." The words rushed out in a torrent now that the dam had broken. "I know what they're saying about our family, about the Rowanwood bloodline weakening, and I know it must be the most hurtful thing in the world to—"

"Lise, darling, I suspect it hurts you a great deal more than it hurts me."

The ache beneath Aurelise's ribs deepened and spread, the familiar guilt and worry for her sister expanding until her chest was so tight she could barely breathe. *Inhale*, she reminded herself. *Exhale.*

"But I—"

"Stop." Rosavyn's voice was gentle but firm as she squeezed Aurelise's hands. Her eyes—warm brown instead of the stormy gray that marked the rest of the Rowanwood siblings—moved over Aurelise's face with such open affection that not even a shadow of resentment could be found in their depths. "Not for a single moment have I ever resented you for manifesting. Not once. My lack of manifestation is not your burden to carry. Whatever my magic is doing—or not doing—has nothing to do with you."

"But the gossip—"

"Gossip birds will always find something to screech about," Rosavyn said with a dismissive toss of her head. "Last Season it was Evryn and Mariselle's unexpected engagement and their scandalously over-the-top public affection for one another. The Season before that, it was 'the half-blood who dared to think she could be part of proper society.' And now it is the unmanifested

Rowanwoods." She shrugged. "Next Season, it will be something else entirely."

Aurelise swallowed the secret fears that pressed against her throat, unwilling to give them voice. What if Rosavyn's magic never manifested? What if the whispers followed her sister for years to come, narrowing her prospects with each passing Season? "You're not even a little jealous?" she asked in a small voice, needing to be certain.

Rosavyn's lips curved into a wry smile. "Oh, I'm terribly jealous of your hair. Mine never holds those pearl pins properly." When Aurelise didn't smile, Rosavyn's expression softened once more. "Yes, I wish my magic would hurry up and make an appearance. But that has nothing to do with you. Your magic is beautiful. It's perfectly, wonderfully *you.* I would never begrudge you that joy for even a moment."

Tears pricked at the corners of Aurelise's eyes. "That is a relief indeed. I couldn't bear it if you resented me."

"Well, fortunately, you don't have to bear it." Rosavyn released Aurelise's hands and reached across the bed for the gloves Lady Lelianna had laid out. "The only thing I resent is the system that makes manifestation such a public spectacle in the first place. But that's hardly your fault, is it?"

"No, but—"

"Enough about my lack of manifestation," Rosavyn said firmly, laying the gloves across Aurelise's palms. "Tonight belongs to you, regardless of how much you may wish to shrink from the attention. You will meet it with the same quiet grace and poise with which you always weather these sorts of overwhelming occasions."

"That is not the way I feel inside."

"I know. But your music brings you closer to that serenity, doesn't it? Even if only while the notes linger in the air."

Aurelise allowed herself a small nod.

"Then anchor yourself there. When you're standing in front of everyone, close your eyes as you always do, and let everything else fall away until there is only the music flowing through you. The rest of us will simply disappear."

Aurelise smiled and nodded. "Thank you."

A commotion from the sitting room drew their attention—new voices joining the chorus. Voices belonging to Evryn and Mariselle.

"We should go," Rosavyn said, moving toward the door, "before Mother starts wondering what mischief we're getting up to in here."

Rosavyn opened the door, and their private moment of peace vanished like a popped bubble as the cottage's cheerful chaos rushed in to reclaim them. Rosavyn crossed the room toward the newly arrived couple, while Marta approached Aurelise with the delicate crystal bottle of rose water. Aurelise extended her wrists one at a time, receiving a carefully measured drop on each pulse point as Evryn greeted his mother and Mariselle's squeal of excitement rose above the chatter: "Can you believe it's finally happening?"

"I know!" Rosavyn exclaimed in response. "I cannot *wait* to walk on actual clouds!"

"And inside champagne bubbles!"

"Yes!"

The two of them grasped hands and jumped up and down in small, excited hops, completely disregarding any semblance of proper decorum. They fell against each other in a tangle of silks and laughter, their foreheads nearly touching as they dissolved into the kind of unrestrained mirth that always made Aurelise's heart lighten.

"Ladies!" Lady Rivenna's stern voice cut through their excitement. "Must I remind you that we are preparing to attend the High Lady's Opening Ball, not a village harvest festival? Such displays are entirely inappropriate for young women of your standing."

Both women straightened immediately, assuming expressions of exaggerated propriety that lasted little more than a moment before breaking into poorly concealed giggles behind gloved fingertips.

Sighing through her nose, Lady Rivenna turned with a small shake of her head, posture remaining impeccable, to survey the cottage's disheveled sitting area. With a brisk sweep of her hand through the air, every cushion snapped to attention, while the woolen blanket that had slipped to the floor folded itself into neat thirds and draped itself over the back of the nearest armchair. Even at the end of a long day, Lady Rivenna moved with the same crisp energy Aurelise had seen her display during early mornings at The Charmed Leaf.

The family had expected her to begin transferring more responsibilities to Iris by now, but with recent developments, that transition had been postponed. Aurelise suspected her grandmother was secretly thrilled to remain fully in charge for a while longer. What would someone with Lady Rivenna's inexhaustible energy do with herself if she weren't orchestrating the daily theater of Bloomhaven society from her kingdom of teacups and gossip?

"Your tea, dear," Lady Nirella said to Aurelise, gliding into the room carrying a small silver tray, which she placed on the small side table between the armchairs. "Oh, Mariselle, dearest, you are here! You've become quite the phantom these past days, flitting about Dreamland and leaving your poor grandmother to wonder if you still remember her face."

"You can hardly blame me for that, Grandmother," Mariselle said, stepping past Rosavyn. "I feel as though I've made at least a dozen last-minute adjustments to the dream core in just the past half hour."

"Is Jasvian coming tonight?" Evryn asked, turning to his mother while straightening his cravat.

Lady Lelianna shook her head. "No, dear. He wanted to stay home with Iris."

A flicker of disappointment crossed Evryn's face. "Ah, I was hoping he might want to attend."

Mariselle swatted her husband's arm. "Of course Jasvian is staying with Iris. If it were me, I would expect you to be nowhere else except by my side."

Evryn's expression melted into something tender and devoted as he leaned toward his wife, clearly forgetting their audience. "That is precisely where I will be, darling." Before his lips could reach hers, something small struck his cheek. He jerked back, hand flying to the spot as indignation replaced romance. Aurelise's gaze followed the tiny object as it dropped to the floor and rolled to a halt. A dice.

"Kazrian!" Evryn bellowed, glaring across the room where his younger brother had already ducked behind Lady Rivenna's stately form.

"For goodness' sake," Lady Rivenna muttered, not bothering to step aside as Kazrian crouched behind her skirts, his laughter barely contained. "I would have thought you both might have outgrown using me as your battlement by now."

It was then that Mariselle caught sight of Aurelise standing in the bedroom doorway. "Oh, Aurelise! You are simply radiant!"

Another wave of nervous energy washed over Aurelise like a cold tide. "Thank you," she breathed, hoping the tremor in her voice wasn't noticeable to anyone else.

But Mariselle knew her well by now. She crossed the room and gently took one of her hands. Aurelise realized she was still clutching the gloves in her other hand, the delicate fabric surely acquiring creases that would earn her mother's dismay and require yet another round of pressing spells.

Mariselle leaned in closer, her voice dropping slightly. "I added a pink bow to the sky, just for you. It's one of the cloud formations I've enchanted to take shape once the magical demonstrations begin. When you stand before the High Lady and your courage wavers, look for that bow in the dream-sky. It's my promise that you're not alone, even when you feel as if the whole world's gaze is upon you."

Aurelise nodded, pressing her lips together as she fought against the tightness in her throat. She could do this. It was just one night. One singular, nerve-wracking night. Tomorrow she could return to her comfortable position at the edges of ballrooms, watching rather than being watched. Or perhaps, she thought with a flutter in her chest as she recalled R's letter, she might even attempt some ridiculous conversation about opinionated roses.

"Darling," Evryn said, appearing at Mariselle's side and touching her arm. "I believe we should go. The High Lady will be arriving any minute now."

With a final squeeze of Aurelise's hand, Mariselle turned away.

"Perhaps the rest of us might join you in a few minutes?" Aurelise suggested, desperately grasping for any excuse to delay the inevitable. "My tea—"

"There's no time for that now," Lady Lelianna interjected, her voice bright with poorly disguised relief. "Come, dear, put your gloves on. We cannot keep the High Lady waiting."

The family began to move as one toward the cottage door, a flurry of final adjustments and chatter filling the air. Lady Lelianna fussed over Kazrian's waistcoat buttons, which had been fastened in the wrong sequence, while Lady Rivenna issued crisp instructions to Aurelise and Rosavyn's maids about tidying the cottage and taking the waiting carriage back to Rowanwood House.

With a final wistful look at the abandoned cup of serenity blend still steaming invitingly on its tray, Aurelise followed.

Chapter Two

A SHORT DISTANCE AWAY FROM WINDSONG COTTAGE, DREAMLAND rose from the earth like the last blush of sunset caught and woven into silk, its vast tented pavilion shimmering. Its walls arched high into peaks and curves, the fabric shifting fluidly between rose pink and burnished gold with each wandering breeze, as if the whole creation inhaled and exhaled on some unseen breath. Along every seam and edge, veins of rose-gold lumyrite pulsed with a slow, hypnotic rhythm, tracing the structure in radiant lines that suggested a beating heart beneath its surface.

Months ago, Aurelise had glimpsed the original drawings of the tent—all midnight blues and twilight purples, a vision plucked straight from slumbering minds. But when the High Lady sent word to Evryn and Mariselle informing them of her intention to host the Season's Opening Ball within Dreamland's enchanted walls, the palette had transformed in her honor.

Now its splendor mirrored Solstice Hall's regal warmth, the golden-hour glow that had graced royal celebrations for generations. Mariselle planned to return Dreamland to its dreamy nightscape once the Season concluded, but secretly, Aurelise found herself captivated by this incarnation, drawn as she'd always been to the gentleness of soft pinks and rose hues.

But as beautiful as the magnificent structure was, she couldn't keep her composure from cracking a little more with each step she took toward it. Her throat constricted as though invisible hands tightened around it, each swallow becoming a deliberate act she could no longer perform naturally. Inside her gloves, her palms grew damp, and she resisted the urge to tug at the fine fabric, knowing it would only draw attention to her discomfort. The music that lived perpetually within her threatened to spill out, a discordant symphony of anxiety she fought desperately to contain.

The crowd pressed closer around the Rowanwood and Brightcrest families—both assembled close to Dreamland's main entrance—as more carriages arrived, depositing their elegantly dressed occupants onto a long crimson-rose carpet. It stretched from the grand archway right up to the gold-veined marble platform upon which Dreamland sat. Excited chatter filled the air, punctuated by gasps of wonder as newcomers caught their first glimpse of the magical pavilion. The crush of bodies, the rustling of countless silk gowns, the overwhelming mixture of perfumes—it all pressed against Aurelise like a physical weight.

Her chest tightened further. She tried again to swallow.

Without thinking, she stepped closer to Kazrian, her shoulder brushing against his arm. He must have sensed her distress, for his hand found hers immediately, giving it a gentle squeeze.

"You're ready," he whispered, not looking at her but keeping his gaze fixed on the pavilion ahead.

"I'm not." The words barely escaped her constricted throat.

"You are."

She turned to look at him then, tilting her chin upward to find his face. "You ought to be at my side for this. We've shared almost every moment since we were born. This shouldn't be any different."

He hesitated before answering, eyes still pointed forward. "Sometimes one must step forth alone. Perhaps it is for the best that we did not manifest together."

"Then it ought to have been you first."

He shook his head, finally turning his gaze toward her. "No. My magic is quite untamed. Sparks and surges without rhyme or reason. It doesn't yet feel ready." He paused, then added in a quieter tone, "I'm not concerned about when I'll manifest. I know it will come." His gaze drifted ahead to where Rosavyn stood arm-in-arm with their mother. "Rosavyn, though …"

The memory of that raw look in his eyes back at the cottage suddenly made sense. It hadn't been disappointment for himself but worry for their sister. Aurelise's heart ached with a different kind of tightness.

A sudden hush fell over the assembled crowd, rippling outward from the main approach like a stone dropped in still water. The High Lady's golden carriage had arrived, gleaming in the twilight as if it had been carved from a single piece of sunset amber.

With a swift gesture and a near-invisible flicker of magic from the footman, the carriage door swung open. The prince stepped down first, turning at once to offer his arm. A moment later, the High Lady placed her gloved fingers in his and descended with fluid elegance, pale blue hair cascading freely down her back. Her gown of bronze silk seemed to hold stars within its folds, shifting and glimmering with each graceful movement.

She moved to stand beside her son, and Aurelise found herself frowning as her eyes moved to the prince. Midnight-blue hair fell in artful disarray above ink-blue eyes alive with mischief. His skin, darker than his mother's alabaster complexion, reflected the golden hues of sunset against sand.

As they began their procession through the parted crowd, his eyes caught on a small cluster of young ladies standing near the Rowanwood family. His smile turned decidedly roguish as he winked at them, causing an immediate outbreak of fan fluttering and poorly suppressed giggles. One young lady actually swayed slightly, as if the mere acknowledgment might cause her to swoon.

Aurelise suppressed the urge to roll her eyes. Though she had not attended many society events yet and had seen the prince only a handful of times, his reputation as an incorrigible flirt was legendary. Every gossip bird in Bloomhaven seemed to have a story about Prince Ryden's romantic entanglements and scandalous flirtations. There were also rumors that the High Lady endeavored to keep him confined to Solstice Hall for much of each Season, yet for someone supposedly under his mother's watchful eye, he certainly cultivated an impressive collection of dalliances for society to dissect.

The High Lady climbed the stairs onto the raised marble platform and stopped before the pavilion's entrance. She turned to address the gathered fae elite.

"My dear friends, we stand at the threshold of a most extraordinary evening. Tonight marks not merely the opening of a restored Dreamland, but also the dawn of a new Bloom Season, bringing with it the promise of new magic and new possibilities. You have journeyed from all corners of the United Fae Isles, while my son and I have crossed the veil from the royal realm in the Shaded Lands beyond the northern borders. All of us drawn to Bloomhaven, where the land is infused with potent magic unmatched anywhere else. Tonight, all eyes will witness our young lords and ladies debut their manifested gifts before society—a moment that transforms private talent into public identity, forever shaping their place among us."

And naturally, Aurelise's magic chose that precise moment to betray her.

A delicate trill of flutes escaped into the evening air as the High Lady finished speaking. The sound lasted barely a heartbeat before Aurelise clamped down on it with desperate force, but she'd already sensed several heads turning in search of the sound. Heat flooded her cheeks as she gripped Kazrian's hand so tightly that her knuckles ached.

"Steady," he murmured without looking at her, squeezing her hand in return, and there was something anchoring in his firm hold, a familiar weight that drew her back to herself. She exhaled slowly, deliberately, feeling the restless magic within her settle like disturbed water gradually returning to stillness.

"Lord and Lady Rowanwood," the High Lady said, gesturing gracefully toward where Evryn and Mariselle stood, "would you do us the honor of officially opening Dreamland?"

Pride swelled in Aurelise's chest as she watched her brother and sister-in-law step forward. Evryn's usual playful demeanor had been replaced by something more solemn, more worthy of the moment. Mariselle practically glowed beside him.

Together, they approached what appeared to be a curtain of pure golden light stretched across the pavilion's entrance. They joined hands and, in perfect synchronization, pressed their palms against the barrier. The light responded immediately, fracturing into thousands of golden butterflies that burst outward and upward, dissolving into sparkles that rained down harmlessly on the delighted crowd. Applause erupted around them, and even Mariselle's typically sour-faced parents allowed their pinched disapproval to soften into something that might, with generous interpretation, resemble admiration.

"Your Majesty," Evryn said with a deep bow, while Mariselle curtsied beside him. "Dreamland awaits."

The High Lady inclined her head graciously and entered first, Prince Ryden at her side. The crowd surged forward after them, and Aurelise found herself pressed ahead of Kazrian, swept along in the tide of silk and excitement.

The moment she crossed the threshold, wonder momentarily eclipsed her anxiety.

The interior defied all logic. They stood in what appeared to be a garden made entirely of spun sugar and starlight. Crystalline flowers bloomed along paths of rose-gold that shimmered with gentle radiance, while above them, the ceiling had vanished entirely, replaced by a sky that couldn't possibly exist—swirls of pink and gold clouds that moved like living paint across a canvas of deepening twilight.

"Oh, look at it all!" Rosavyn breathed, appearing beside Aurelise and linking their arms together. "This is extraordinary."

Despite her nerves, Aurelise couldn't help but agree. Everywhere she looked, impossible beauty beckoned. They continued along the shimmering path and discovered fountains of liquid pearl spilling over tiered basins of mirror-polished stone. Trees with bark of polished rose-gold bore leaves of delicate glass that chimed sweetly in a breeze she couldn't feel.

The path carried them through a succession of ever more fantastical scenes. Soon they came upon the champagne bubbles—vast, shimmering spheres large enough to contain entire rooms of magical delights, while countless smaller bubbles drifted through the air, as though they were strolling inside a glass of freshly poured champagne.

Then came the cloud bridge, appearing to be made of nothing more substantial than compressed cumulus, white and impossibly fluffy, stretching across a chasm filled with swirling mists of gold and silver. Tentatively, Aurelise and Rosavyn stepped onto it, giggling with childlike wonder as they found it solid beneath their feet, though it compressed slightly like the finest carpet.

Rosavyn's eyes lit with mischief. "Shall we test it properly?" Without waiting for an answer, she gave a small experimental hop. The cloud beneath her feet bounced her slightly higher than expected, and she laughed with pure delight. "Oh, you must try this!"

Propriety warred with curiosity for all of three seconds before Aurelise joined her sister. The sensation was unlike anything she'd ever experienced, similar to jumping on her bed as a child but somehow softer, more magical. They clasped hands and jumped together, their laughter ringing out across the ethereal space.

"Ladies!" Their mother's scandalized voice called from behind them. "Such behavior is entirely inappropriate for—"

"—young women of refined breeding," their grandmother finished.

But even their synchronized scolding couldn't dim the joy of the moment, especially when Kazrian appeared at Aurelise's other side, linking his arm through hers with a grin that matched Rosavyn's for mischief.

"If we're to be scolded anyway," he said, and gave an enormous leap that lifted all three of them higher than before.

Aurelise's shriek escaped before she could contain it as she found herself momentarily weightless. Then the three of them descended in a tangle of laughter and limbs, and for one perfect moment, she forgot about her impending presentation, forgot about the watching crowd, forgot everything except the pure magic of sharing this impossible wonder with her siblings.

I must remember every detail, she thought suddenly. *I'll write to R tonight and tell him—*

But she caught herself before the thought could proceed any further. She'd told him she wouldn't be in Bloomhaven. She couldn't share any of this with him. A different kind of anxiety twisted in her stomach as she glanced around the crowd. What if he had been planning to come anyway, regardless of whether she was able to attend the Bloom Season or not. What if he was *here*?

Her eyes swept the assembled faces, as if she might somehow recognize him by instinct alone. But every gentleman looked like a potential correspondent. Or … none of them did. Though she lacked even the vaguest notion of what R looked like, she carried within her a sense of who he was—his wit, his warmth—and not a single face in the crowd seemed capable of containing such qualities.

No, she told herself firmly. He wouldn't have come without telling her. While she guarded her secrets with careful precision, R seemed constitutionally incapable of containing his enthusiasm. His letters always brimmed with his plans and thoughts, spilling across the page in that bold, slanting hand.

Had he intended to visit Bloomhaven, she doubted he could have resisted telling her.

The path finally opened into the grandest ballroom Aurelise had ever imagined. The floor beneath their feet sparkled like sun-caught water, each step sending ripples of light radiating outward. Along the ballroom's edge, fountains poured cascades of glittering butterflies that tumbled downward in shimmering streams. Their wings caught the light as they fell, dissolving into sparkling golden liquid before reaching the basins below.

High above, the ceiling was a dream of endless twilight sky—soft watercolor washes of pink melting into lavender and deepening into periwinkle blue. The colors drifted, sometimes mingling in feathery wisps, sometimes separating into distinct layers that folded back upon themselves in hypnotic patterns. Delicate cloud formations had begun to take shape against this painted infinity, though Aurelise couldn't yet spot the pink bow Mariselle had promised would appear during the presentations.

The High Lady proceeded to a throne that appeared to have been carved from a single, enormous pearl, its surface gleaming with subtle iridescence. She seated herself gracefully and gestured for Prince Ryden to take the smaller throne beside her. He slouched into it immediately, one leg crossed over the other with casual indifference, his expression suggesting he'd rather be anywhere else. Aurelise resolved to ignore him.

Around them, the magical ballroom filled with Bloomhaven's elite, a swirl of color and movement. Ladies arranged themselves in elegant clusters while gentlemen maintained strategic positions nearby, all leaving a wide ceremonial circle at the center of the room.

With each passing moment, Aurelise's breath grew shallower, her grip on Rosavyn's hand tightening until she feared their fingers might permanently fuse. The familiar flutter of panic beat against her ribcage as her moment of reckoning approached with merciless certainty.

All too soon, a hush fell over the assembly, conversation dying like a receding tide, leaving only expectant silence as the High Lady rose from her pearl throne.

"And now," she began, her voice ringing clear and commanding through the breathless ballroom, "we shall begin the formal presentations of this Season's newly manifested fae."

What followed passed in a blur of disconnected details that Aurelise's anxiety-frozen mind could barely process. She found herself in a beautiful alcove with the other young fae debuting their magic tonight, all in their finest attire, all radiating the particular nervous energy that came with impending public display.

She noticed the strangest things—the way one girl's pearl earring had twisted backward, how a young man's glove had a nearly invisible stain near the thumb, the pattern in the marble that looked almost like a rose if she tilted her head just so. But the actual presentations? Those dissolved into meaningless noise and movement.

Time moved both agonizingly slowly and terrifyingly fast. Each name called felt like an eternity, yet brought her own moment that much closer. Her hands trembled. Her stomach churned. She was certain everyone could hear her heart pounding.

And then, cutting through the fog of her anxiety:

"Lady Aurelise Rowanwood."

The words rang across the ballroom with horrible clarity. Time seemed to crystallize around her, each second sharp and distinct. This was her moment.

Pure terror flooded her veins. Her legs felt as substantial as the clouds they'd crossed earlier, yet somehow they began moving. One step. Another. The walk from the alcove to the ballroom's center stretched before her, the weight of every gaze in the room pressing down upon her shoulders.

You will meet it with the same quiet grace and poise with which you always weather these sorts of overwhelming occasions.

That is not the way I feel inside.

She kept her eyes fixed on the pearl throne, not daring to look at the assembled crowd. When she finally stood before the High Lady and Prince Ryden, she sank into the deepest curtsy she could manage, her gaze locked on the hem of the High Lady's gown.

"Welcome, Lady Aurelise," the High Lady's voice was warm but formal. "Please share with us the gift of your manifested magic."

For one horrible moment, Aurelise's mind went completely blank. Was she meant to face the High Lady or the crowd? No one had explained this part. What had the others done? She hadn't been watching, too lost in her own anxiety to pay attention.

Wait—there had been snow. She remembered seeing the girl's face as delicate snowflakes danced around her. She must have been facing the crowd.

Drawing on every lesson in grace she'd ever received, Aurelise rose from her curtsy and turned to face the ballroom. The sea of faces blurred together into an impressionistic wash of color and expectation.

With trembling fingers, she pulled off her gloves, sliding each one along her wrists with the practiced motion that activated their concealment charm, causing them to vanish into the folds of her gown until she needed them again. Though her magic required no such removal, she'd discovered early in her practice that the barrier of fabric dulled her perception somewhat.

Standing ready before the crowd, she tried to swallow. It was near impossible. Her heart hammered so violently she was certain the entire room could hear it. She lifted her gaze to the dream-sky ceiling, searching until—there. Mariselle's promise made manifest: a perfect pink bow formed from clouds, floating serenely against the sky. And then—

Do you think plants have opinions about us?

R's ridiculous question came unexpectedly to mind, and despite everything, the corner of her mouth twitched toward a smile. She could do this.

Aurelise closed her eyes and drew in a deep breath. Then, with the same certainty she felt when sitting before her pianoforte, she raised her right hand in a graceful sweep.

A deep, resonant note filled the air. Cellos and double basses in perfect harmony, so rich and full it seemed to emerge from the very walls of Dreamland itself. Her left hand rose to join the first, fingers trailing through the air. A cascade of violins joined the foundation, their voices sweet and clear.

As the harmonies settled into place, her anxious thoughts surrendered to the perfect stillness that existed only inside music. This familiar sanctuary, this peaceful void where nothing existed but vibration and emotion—her body relaxed into it, as if returning home after a long exile, and everything else ceased to exist.

With each sweep of her hand, delicate turn of her wrist, or pinch between thumb and forefinger, the music responded. She was both creator and conductor, drawing sound from the ambient magic that surrounded all things, transforming the invisible into something magnificently audible. This was her own composition, something that had lived only in her mind and her private practice until this moment. It bore no resemblance to any piece that might be heard in a concert hall. It was uniquely, entirely hers.

Her fingers fluttered in an intricate pattern, and woodwinds trilled into existence, their playful notes dancing around the steady strings like butterflies around flowers. A sharp gesture of her left hand brought in the bright clarity of trumpets. The music built and layered, each new voice joining the conversation until an entire orchestra sang at her command.

Her hands rose together, lifting the music with them toward a crescendo that had been months in the planning. Even though she knew every note, had heard this same progression a hundred times in practice, the full realization of it sent shivers racing down her spine.

The music crested like a wave breaking against cliffs, soaring and dancing through the impossible space of Dreamland's ballroom. It sang of new beginnings, of hope and fear intertwined, of standing on the brink of transformation. It felt like courage—the kind she dreamed about but would never experience in reality.

Gradually, the tempest of sound calmed, each section of her invisible orchestra taking its leave in turn. The bright flutter of flutes dissolved into silence, followed by the stately horns and the dancing violins. Cellos lingered longer, their voices rich with contemplation, until finally only the deep basses remained for one final, resonant tone.

The music faded into the waiting stillness, and Aurelise's hands settled gently at her sides. Silence filled the ballroom, complete and absolute. She opened her eyes to find the entire assembly frozen, staring at her with expressions she couldn't read. Her chest rose and fell with quick breaths, the exertion of channeling so much magic leaving her almost light-headed.

Was this normal? Were all magical demonstrations met with such stillness? Was there supposed to be applause? She couldn't remember, couldn't think past the pounding of her heart.

She turned back to face the High Lady, clasping her hands together and keeping her gaze carefully directed at the lower portion of the woman's gown. But even from this limited view, she could see something had shifted in the High Lady's perfect posture.

"That was—" The High Lady's voice caught slightly, and she cleared her throat. "That was quite remarkable."

Aurelise's knees nearly buckled with relief. She exhaled a shuddering breath.

"Welcome to society, Lady Aurelise Rowanwood," the High Lady continued, her composure restored. "May your magic continue to grow throughout the Bloom Season."

Aurelise barely heard the formal words through the rush of blood in her ears. She had done it. She had survived. The High Lady approved.

She sank into another deep curtsy, her body moving through the motion by pure muscle memory while her mind reeled with exhausted triumph. When she rose and began the journey back to where her family waited at the ballroom's edge, her legs trembled with each step.

She had done the hardest part. Now she need only survive the rest of the ball without drawing any further attention to herself, which should be simple by comparison. With practiced motions, she recalled her gloves from their magical concealment and pulled them back on. Tomorrow she would write to R. Not about the Opening Ball specifically, of course, but she could certainly mention surviving a dreaded social gathering.

The euphoria of successfully completing her demonstration, combined with the lingering effects of channeling a significant amount of magic, left her floating in a strange, disconnected state. Other names were called, other presentations made, but they washed over her like water over stone, leaving no impression.

It wasn't until she noticed movement on the pearl throne that her attention snapped back to the present. The High Lady was rising, which meant all the presentations must be complete. Relief flooded through her. Now the dancing would begin, and she could fade into the background where she belonged.

"Tonight has demonstrated the extraordinary talents blooming within our realm," the High Lady announced, her voice carrying effortlessly across the vast space. "In celebration of such promise, and acknowledging that His Royal Highness Prince Ryden must soon choose his life companion, I am pleased to announce that this Season, we shall be hosting a Crown Court."

Surprised murmurs rippled through the crowd. Aurelise found herself equally startled. A Crown Court? She'd heard of such things in history lessons, but there hadn't been one in generations.

"I have selected several exceptional young ladies from our most distinguished families to join us as our honored guests at Solstice Hall for the remainder of the Bloom Season," the High Lady continued, "so that Prince

Ryden might have the opportunity to court them properly, and, with fortune's favor, choose his princess from among them."

Aurelise glanced around the ballroom, curiosity temporarily overcoming her exhaustion. Who would be chosen for such an honor? There were so many distinguished families in attendance. Her eyes swept over the crowd, trying to guess which young ladies might catch the High Lady's attention, who might be deemed worthy to stand beside the future High Lord.

"Each lady called forth must approach and receive a fan," the High Lady continued, her voice commanding the room's attention once more, "the symbol of invitation to the Crown Court. These fans represent not merely an honor, but a formal summons to reside at Solstice Hall throughout the Season."

An attendant in royal livery appeared at the High Lady's side, bearing a silver tray upon which rested a collection of folded fans. The High Lady selected one before calling out, "Lady Coravelle Aerwynne."

The girl who'd nearly swooned at the prince's wink earlier pressed her hands to her cheeks, her dark skin positively glowing under the golden light as she let out a delighted squeal audible even from across the ballroom. She hurried forward with barely contained excitement, managing a curtsy before accepting her fan with trembling fingers.

"Lady Olivienne Silverglen."

Aurelise watched as a girl with hair like polished obsidian offered a reserved smile and glided toward the throne with perfect poise. The Silverglen family was known for their rare glenwhisper magic—that gentle enchantment that coaxed vitality from the natural world, making flowers bloom more vibrantly, streams flow with crystalline clarity, and even the air itself feel lighter with unseen potential.

"Lady Willow Blackbriar."

Each name sent a fresh wave of whispers through the crowd. Aurelise watched as the chosen ladies stepped forward, savoring the blissful invisibility that came with no longer being the focus of hundreds of curious eyes.

"Lady Aurelise Rowanwood."

Her heart stuttered.

Her hands went instantly cold.

No.

Chapter Three

PRINCE RYDEN HAD NOT TRULY BELIEVED, UNTIL THE VERY MOMENT the words fell from his mother's lips, that she would actually go through with this madness.

"Please," he had begged her just that morning, abandoning all pretense of his usual cavalier demeanor. "I am asking you, as your son rather than your subject, not to make a public spectacle of my romantic prospects."

"Darling, you are a prince," she had reminded him. "Your romantic prospects were destined for public consumption from the moment of your birth. That is simply the nature of royal existence."

"But a Crown Court—"

"Furthermore," she'd added, her expression softening just slightly, "it is unlikely romance will factor significantly into the proceedings, I'm afraid. We both understand what this is truly about."

Indeed, he understood all too well.

Authority magic—the hereditary gift of the royal bloodline—should have been his birthright in the truest sense. It should have manifested as it had in his mother, as it had in rulers stretching back through generations: a steady, commanding presence that made others naturally inclined to listen, to follow, to trust.

The magic didn't compel obedience—that would be tyranny. Rather, it enhanced the qualities that made someone worthy of being followed. It clarified the voice, strengthened the presence, created an aura of competence that soothed tensions and inspired confidence.

In his mother, the magic was poetry. She could walk into a room torn apart by conflict and, through nothing more than her presence and perfectly chosen words, guide opposing parties toward accord. Her voice carried across vast crowds not through volume but through some ineffable quality that made people want to hear what she had to say.

In Ryden, the magic was chaos.

It coursed through him like a river, sometimes a gentle current, steady and serene, at other times a storm-swollen torrent, surging and crashing with violent force. Without pattern or warning, it would rise, stirred at times by unchecked emotion, yet just as often for no discernible cause. In those moments, his voice crashed over all who heard it, sweeping them along in its force. Not persuaded, not influenced, but *commanded*, their free will stripped away as surely as if he'd placed chains upon their minds.

The mere thought of it made his stomach twist.

This, then, was the true purpose of the Crown Court. Finding a partner whose magic could complement his own, create the stability that would allow him to rule one day without becoming a tyrant who commanded through magical compulsion. Marriage bonds, according to his mother's exhaustive and entirely confidential research—for there were few who knew of his condition—were the only proven method of achieving such permanent stabilization between complementary magics.

His mother reached the end of her announcement, and the crowd erupted in excited whispers. And of course, at this precise moment, Ryden felt his magic stir restslessly within him. He clenched his hands in his lap. Not now. Not with everyone present.

The air around him began to shimmer, so subtle that only someone looking directly at him might notice. But his mother noticed everything. She shifted slightly in her throne, and Ryden felt her own magic unfurl like a protective barrier, sliding between him and the assembled crowd with the ease of someone who'd been managing his surges since he'd first manifested at seventeen.

She leaned toward him, her expression never wavering from its regal warmth. To any observer, it would appear she was sharing some pleasant observation with her son. "Your eyes, dear," she murmured, her voice barely a whisper.

Ryden immediately ducked his head. He knew what she meant—when his magic surged, his ink-blue eyes darkened to something closer to obsidian, an obvious tell to anyone who knew to look for it. The air around him still trembled with barely contained power, and he could feel the words pressing against his throat, demanding release. If he spoke now, if he said anything at all, it might emerge as a command that every soul in this ballroom would be compelled to obey.

He forced himself to breathe slowly, counting each inhalation. Four counts in. Hold for two. Six counts out. The breathing technique his mother had taught him years ago, though it grew less effective with each passing Season as his power strengthened.

This was happening. The Crown Court, the supervised courtship, the inevitable selection of a bride who would serve as his magical anchor for the rest of their lives. He needed to accept it. He needed to find someone suitable, someone whose magic could cage his own. Then these unnatural surges, which should have stabilized within days of his manifestation but somehow still tormented him years later, would finally subside.

Perhaps it wouldn't be entirely unbearable, he consoled himself as his magic began to settle. Some of the chosen ladies might prove interesting companions, at least.

Lady Coravelle Aerwynne would certainly be eager to please—perhaps too eager, given her near-swoon at his earlier wink. Lady Olivienne Silverglen had a reputation for wit that might provide amusing conversation, and her glenwhisper magic could very well prove to be the perfect complement to his authority magic. At least, that was his mother's reason for choosing her for the Crown Court.

Then, of course, there were several unpleasant options, most notably Lady Ellowa Brightcrest. Ryden had to suppress a wince at the thought of her. Both he and his mother knew perfectly well he would never choose her, but her inclusion served other purposes. The generations-old feud between the Rowanwoods and Brightcrests had only recently begun to cool, like embers finally fading after a long blaze. If his mother extended an invitation to a Rowanwood without including a Brightcrest as well, she risked reigniting tensions that were, at long last, giving way to fragile peace.

Thoughts of the Rowanwoods had his mind drifting to Miss—no, she was *Lady* now—Aurelise, and an unexpected shiver raced down his spine. An echo of what he'd felt during her magical demonstration. That music … pure magic given voice, no orchestra required, just her graceful hands conducting power itself into heartbreakingly beautiful sound.

He hadn't been paying attention when she'd first approached for her presentation, too busy maintaining his facade of bored indifference. And then she had been facing away when she began, just another nervous young lady in a sea of silk and expectations.

But from the very first note, she had commanded his attention absolutely.

The memory of it still raised the hairs on his arms. The way the sound had seemed to emerge from the very air surrounding them, how the harmonies had cascaded like water over stone, building and layering until the entire ballroom had become her instrument. He'd forgotten to breathe, forgotten to maintain his practiced slouch, forgotten everything except the music that had seemed to reach inside his chest and squeeze.

When she'd turned back to curtsy, he hadn't recognized her at first. A beat later, recollection stirred—Evryn's younger sister, the one who had performed at a musicale last Season, a little taller now, her features more defined where they had once been softly girlish. He recalled being unexpectedly captivated by her pianoforte performance then, remembered the whispers afterward predicting her magic would manifest as something musical.

But this? This had exceeded every prediction, every expectation.

"Better?" his mother asked quietly, her voice pulling him from his reverie.

Ryden straightened, realizing his surge had fully passed. The trembling in the air had stilled, his eyes presumably returned to their normal shade.

"Quite recovered," he said, injecting his usual careless tone into the words. "If you'll excuse me, Mother, I should circulate among our guests. Find some charming young lady to dance with before I'm condemned to interact solely with your handpicked selection for the remainder of the Season."

He rose from the throne with intentional languor, as though sitting still for so long had been the gravest imposition. He needed movement, needed distraction, needed to escape thoughts of the elaborate charade that awaited him at Solstice Hall in the days ahead.

Finding Evryn would serve. He could congratulate his friend on Dreamland's success, perhaps indulge in some harmless flirtation with whoever happened to cross his path. Anything to avoid genuine emotion. The familiar ache that accompanied that thought settled in his chest. Exhausting, this eternal performance of feeling nothing deeply, caring for nothing truly. But manufactured emotions didn't trigger his magic the way real ones might. Better to play the shameless flirt than risk unleashing a command that stripped away another's will—or worse, an entire gathering's—in a way that might end in tragedy. The weight of past mistakes still haunted him; he would not add to their number.

He spotted Evryn near one of the impossible fountains of cascading butterflies, standing with his younger brother Kazrian just as Mariselle was pulled away by her grandmother to greet someone.

"Evryn!" Ryden called out, falling easily into his public persona as he approached. "The man of the hour! This—" he gestured broadly at their miraculous surroundings, "—is absolutely extraordinary."

Evryn grinned, clasping Ryden's offered hand with the easy familiarity of long friendship. "You know full well it's Mariselle who deserves most of the credit. I merely provided the lumyrite infrastructure."

"Modest as always," Ryden said with a laugh, then turned to the younger man beside Evryn. "Young Master Kazrian, a pleasure," he said, then tried not to feel foolish about the greeting, for though Kazrian was several years his junior—and though Ryden had always been considered tall—the young man now stood at least half a head above him. The youngest Rowanwood brother, it seemed, was now the tallest.

Kazrian executed a perfectly proper bow. "Your Highness."

"I must say," Evryn continued, his eyes dancing with barely suppressed mirth, "last Season when you claimed you might be forced to choose a bride this year, I thought you were being unnecessarily dramatic. Yet here we are. A Crown Court, no less. Your flair for theater remains unmatched."

"Indeed." Ryden's smirk was automatic, as was the teasing jab that followed. He knew exactly how to needle his friend: "Your little sister—"

"No." The word came from both brothers simultaneously, Evryn's jovial expression hardening while Kazrian's formal composure cracked just enough to show genuine alarm.

"Absolutely not," Evryn added for emphasis.

Ryden laughed, the sound rich with implied wickedness he didn't actually feel. "Such touching brotherly concern. I hadn't even finished my sentence."

"We know you well enough," Evryn said dryly. "Or I do, at least."

"If I may, Your Highness," Kazrian interjected, his formal manner at odds with the protective steel in his voice, "while I hold my sister in the highest regard—she is genuinely one of the finest people I know—I feel obligated to point out that she would make a most unsuitable princess."

"Unsuitable?" Ryden arched an eyebrow, genuinely curious now.

"She is …" Kazrian paused, clearly searching for words that were both honest and not unkind. "She possesses a retiring disposition, shy to the point of discomfort. Large gatherings distress her considerably. She seeks nothing more than a quiet existence. The thought of standing at the center of society's attention would be her definition of torture."

"What Kazrian is attempting to say diplomatically," Evryn added, "is that Aurelise is decidedly not the sort of lady who typically catches your interest."

"Is that so?"

"Yes. While we adore her, I imagine you'd find her conversation rather … limited."

Kazrian frowned at his brother "Limited?" he muttered.

Evryn shot Kazrian a frown, sharpened it with a glare, then embellished the performance with a series of pointed eyebrow arches. The effect was unmistakable: a silent lecture compressed into mere seconds, which Ryden interpreted as Evryn's desperate attempt to downplay his sister's intelligence in hopes of diverting Ryden's interest.

"Are you suggesting," Ryden said with deliberate amusement, "that your dear sister is dull?"

"That is absolutely not what I—no. It is simply that she tends to speak only when directly addressed, and even then, her responses rarely extend beyond what politeness demands. I suspect you'd find yourself …"

"Bored?" He gave Evryn a politely confused frown. "Am I understanding you correctly?"

"No, you are deliberately *mis*understanding me," Evryn said with narrowed eyes.

"Am I?"

"Yes. What I mean is that Aurelise wouldn't appreciate your particular brand of humor. She's far too earnest, takes everything quite seriously. You'd scandalize her within minutes."

"So now you're saying she has no sense of humor?"

"Oh stop," Evryn said with fond exasperation, a laugh escaping him now. "I'm simply saying she's not at all to your usual taste."

"Indeed, she is—" Before Kazrian could finish the thought, something behind Ryden caught his attention. Inclining his head, he said, "If you'll excuse me, Your Highness, it seems my mother requires my assistance." With a precise bow, he withdrew into the crowd.

With Kazrian gone, Evryn stepped closer to Ryden, his voice dropping to a more serious register that immediately put Ryden on guard. This was not the tone of friendly banter.

"Ryden," he began, "you are my friend, and I hold you in the highest regard. But I have observed your … attentions toward the fairer sex. Your charm is legendary, as is your tendency to bestow it rather liberally upon any lady who catches your fancy."

The words stung more than they should have. "Evryn—"

"Whoever becomes your wife," Evryn continued quietly but firmly, "will be forced to witness such displays for the rest of her days. To watch her husband flirt with half the ladies at court while she stands beside the throne, pretending not to notice. That woman will not be my sister."

The accusation left a cold hollowness in Ryden's chest. He stepped closer to Evryn, his carefully maintained mask slipping for just a moment. "You think I would—" His voice caught, and he had to swallow before continuing. "You believe that once I am wed, I would be anything but entirely faithful to my wife?"

Something flickered in Evryn's eyes—surprise, perhaps even a touch of guilt—but it only made the wound deeper. "I believe," he said carefully, "that habits formed over many years are … difficult to alter. Even with the best intentions."

The words hung between them like a blade. Did Evryn truly know him so little? Had Ryden played his role so convincingly that even one of his closest friends couldn't see past the performance? Couldn't recognize that the flirtations meant nothing, were merely another mask to keep people at a safe distance? Though could he truly blame his friend for believing the facade, when Evryn was not permitted to know the real reason for the public persona Rydan had so carefully cultivated?

And now that he was considering it, did Ryden himself even know what sort of woman would truly capture his interest? He'd flirted with countless ladies, had stolen his share of kisses in moonlit gardens, had played the role of the scandalous prince with such dedication that sometimes he forgot it was a role at all. But he'd never courted anyone with genuine intent, never allowed himself to know someone deeply enough to determine what—or whom—he truly favored.

Well, there was someone, but things were entirely different with—

"Apologies, my friend. Perhaps you are capable of change," Evryn conceded, interrupting Ryden's thoughts. "Regardless, I must be clear on this point. Aurelise is not available for your … consideration."

The message couldn't have been more explicit if Evryn had drawn a sword.

Ryden forced himself to laugh, falling back into his familiar role. "Never fear, Evryn. Your dull sister—"

"I did not use the word *dull*!"

"—is perfectly safe from my 'legendary charms,'" Ryden continued with a theatrical wave of his hand. "I assure you, I have no interest whatsoever in her."

Again, he found himself wondering what sort of lady *did* capture his genuine interest. Not the giggling debutantes who swooned at his winks. Not the sophisticated ladies who played the game of flirtation as skillfully as he did. Not the ambitious ones who saw him as a crown rather than a person.

An image formed in his mind—not a face, for he had no notion of her appearance. Not a name, for he knew her by only a single initial. The image was more … an idea. Not of how she appeared, but of who she *was.* The unshakable truth at her core, already so familiar to him though they had never even met.

He knew her wit, smart and self-deprecating. He knew her vulnerability, the way she trusted him with her fears and anxieties. He knew her thoughts on matters as mundane as jam versus marmalade, and as profound as whether beauty lies in the thing itself or in the eyes that choose to delight in it. And he knew, too, the contradictions within her: a young woman who blushed and shrank from attention, yet who could be unexpectedly bold in the things she set down on paper.

If anyone embodied everything Ryden longed for, it was her.

Chapter Four

THE DRAWING ROOM CEILING AT JASVIAN AND IRIS'S BLOOMHAVEN residence possessed an unexpectedly fascinating quality when viewed from the floor. Aurelise had never noticed the delicate plasterwork roses that spiraled outward from the central faelight fixture, nor the way afternoon sunlight created shifting patterns through the gauze curtains, painting golden shapes across the white expanse above.

How peculiar, she thought, that she always seemed to find herself confessing her troubles to roses. First the ever-blooming ones back at their country estate who served as her silent confidants, and now these plaster ones frozen in their eternal spiral above. At least the ceiling roses couldn't judge her the way the garden ones seemed to, with their perfect petals and their air of disapproval.

"I wonder if I could simply refuse?" she said, unable to hide the desperation in her voice.

"Oh please do!" Rosavyn replied from somewhere to her left. "How delightfully scandalous."

"Can you imagine the High Lady's reaction?" Mariselle said with a laugh from Aurelise's right.

"She'd probably lock you in a tower," Rosavyn continued. "Just think of the peace and quiet. You'd love it, Lise."

"And the views," Mariselle added. "Towers have the best views."

They'd been lying here for the better part of twenty minutes, ever since Rosavyn had declared that the world looked entirely different from the floor and that contemplating one's troubles from an altered perspective might provide clarity. Aurelise had protested initially—what if the servants saw them?—but Iris had waved away her concerns, insisting the household staff had seen far stranger things. And somehow, Aurelise had found herself sinking onto the plush carpet alongside her sister and sister-in-law.

Iris had declared, with mock-tragic solemnity, that while she dearly wished to join them on the floor, the chances of her ever regaining a vertical position were far too slim to risk it. She had draped herself across the settee instead, one hand resting on the pronounced curve of her belly.

Aurelise shifted slightly, pressing the back of her hand to her mouth to cover a yawn. Despite her exhaustion, she'd been unable to sleep properly after returning home from the Opening Ball the night before. Every time her eyes closed, she'd relived the horrifying moment her name had been called out for the Crown Court.

Time had seemed to stretch and distort, the syllables of 'Lady Aurelise Rowanwood' hanging in the air long after they'd been spoken. A silence had descended, not just in the room but within her, as if her body had forgotten how to function. Her lungs had seized, refusing to draw breath, and the first notes of chaotic, panicked music had begun to rise around her, strings shrieking in protest. Then her mother's hand had found her arm, firm and steadying, and she'd managed to clamp down on the escaping magic as she finally gasped for air.

"Go forward, dear," her mother had murmured, her voice a breath against Aurelise's ear. "Everything will be all right."

Somehow, her legs had carried her forward. Somehow, she hadn't tripped on her gown or stumbled on the stairs. She'd curtsied gracefully, had murmured words of gratitude she couldn't later recall, and had accepted the delicate fan from the High Lady's pale hands as if the moment wasn't fracturing her entire world.

She raised the fan now, studying it yet again. Its pale ivory sticks were worked with delicate cut-outs, curling vines and blossoms fine enough to let the light pass through, while sheer panels of silk shimmered faintly with painted blossoms. Along the slender handle, her name—Lady Aurelise

Rowanwood—was engraved in tiny, damning letters. With a soft sigh, she let both hand and fan fall limply to her side.

"Perhaps if I claimed illness?" she suggested, her voice hollow. "A sudden case of … something terribly contagious but not life-threatening? Just debilitating enough to require complete isolation for, oh, the entire Season?"

"You're a terrible liar," Rosavyn reminded her. "You'd blush the moment anyone questioned you, and the whole scheme would unravel."

"But I'd be confined to Rowanwood House. There would be no one to question me." The more she thought about it, the more brilliant this plan seemed.

"Aurelise," Iris said gently. "I don't think you can reasonably refuse."

Aurelise groaned, pressing a hand over her face. "But I cannot do this. I simply cannot. The very thought of spending the entire Season at Solstice Hall, being scrutinized and evaluated, dancing with and being *courted* by that … that … flirting, winking, incorrigible—"

"You should step on his feet," Rosavyn supplied helpfully. "On purpose, since we all know you'd never do such a thing by accident. You're far too graceful."

"Oh Your Highness!" Mariselle exclaimed in a high-pitched tone that in no way resembled Aurelise's voice. "Your royal feet were improperly positioned in my vicinity!"

Aurelise smacked her with the fan. Mariselle snorted, while Rosavyn dissolved into giggles. From the settee, Iris sighed and muttered, "You two," though she could hardly disguise the amused affection in her voice.

"Stars above," Aurelise moaned, a fresh wave of panic washing through her. "I'm going to step on the prince. I'm going to step on him and cause a diplomatic incident and shame the entire Rowanwood line for generations."

"Don't be ridiculous," Rosavyn said. "I'm the one shaming the entire Rowanwood line with my complete failure to manifest any magic whatsoever. That's far worse than stepping on a prince's toes."

"You will manifest one day," Mariselle said, her tone gentling into something steady and sincere. She reached across Aurelise until she found Rosavyn's hand. "I'm convinced of it."

Rosavyn heaved a breath, and when she spoke, her usual bravado had slipped away. "I'm not." Then she forced a light laugh, the vulnerability vanishing as quickly as it had appeared. "I'm sorry to have to say it, Lise, but

I'm rather grateful for the High Lady's announcement and all this Crown Court gossip. At least today, no one's whispering about the middle Rowanwood daughter's embarrassing lack of magic."

"You would have had nothing to worry about," Mariselle assured her, pulling her arm back. "If there was no Crown Court news today, the gossip birds would no doubt have been shrieking about the fact that my supposed soulbond vanished overnight."

"Oh?" Rosavyn sat up and swiveled sideways. "Did it disappear, then? The mark?"

Aurelise lifted her head from the carpet, craning to see better. Even Iris leaned forward slightly from her position on the settee.

Mariselle extended her right arm, examining her hand and wrist with a puzzled expression. "Well, to anyone looking from a distance, it *appears* to have vanished. That's what we all suspected would happen."

"'The binding mark shall remain until such time as Dreamland stands ready to welcome visitors once more,'" Aurelise recited quietly. They had discussed this numerous times over the past year, wondering precisely when the magical contract that had originally bound Mariselle and Evryn together would consider the terms fulfilled.

"Yes, exactly," Mariselle said. "But look closer."

Aurelise raised her head a little higher, narrowing her eyes as she focused on Mariselle's forearm. There, where a detailed silvery mark had once shimmered, there remained a faint trace, like a delicate scar, still following the same intricate pattern.

"It faded," Mariselle said, turning her wrist to catch the afternoon light. "From that brilliant silver to this. Almost like a memory of itself. Evryn's did the same."

"That's … interesting," Rosavyn said. "I don't believe that's how contract marks are supposed to work. They either exist or they don't."

"Indeed. And didn't we always think it strange that the contract mark took the shape of a soulbond? My grandmother said she and your grandfather never specified that in the contract. Yet this isn't how true soulbonds behave either. Those never fade. So what is this?"

"Strange indeed," Iris murmured.

Mariselle traced the faint marking with one finger. "Whatever it is, I'm glad it's still there. I had grown to like the marking."

"It is rather beautiful," Aurelise said softly, letting her head drop back to the carpet as she resumed her contemplation of the ceiling roses.

Rosavyn flopped back onto the carpet with a dramatic sigh. "Beautiful and mysterious. The gossip birds would have been beside themselves trying to explain it."

"Exactly," Mariselle laughed. "Can you imagine? But thanks to the Crown Court announcement, no one's going to notice our peculiar little mystery. Every gossip bird in Bloomhaven has far more exciting things to screech about."

Aurelise groaned again. "'Exciting' is the furthest thing from the truth. This is *horrifying*. What if, by some catastrophic lapse in royal judgment, he actually *chooses me*? Can you imagine me as a princess? As *High Lady*? The very idea is laughable!"

"You goose," Mariselle said, giving her arm a nudge. "You wouldn't be High Lady. You'd be Crown Consort to the High Lord."

"And I'd have to leave the United Fae Isles! Travel through some sort of … magical portal and live in the the Shaded Lands for most of the year. I would never see any of you!" The panic in her chest swelled like an uncontrolled crescendo as the faint sounds of frantic woodwinds began to flutter around them. "I'd be dreadfully homesick and—"

"Relax," Rosavyn cut in, reaching for Aurelise's free hand and squeezing it. The music faded. "He isn't going to choose you. He'll realize soon enough that you're not interested in him. You'll make it abundantly clear through your complete lack of enthusiasm, and he'll naturally gravitate toward the other ladies who actually want to compete for his attention."

"I imagine the other ladies are absolutely *thrilled*," Iris commented. "They're probably already planning their strategies, deciding which accomplishments to display, practicing their eyelash batting in mirrors—"

"Selecting their most revealing gowns," Mariselle added. "The sorts that make gentlemen walk into pillars and—Oof!" Her words disappeared beneath a muffled splutter as a satin cushion collided with her face

"Don't fluster poor Aurelise more than necessary," Iris said through her laugher.

Mariselle hugged the cushion to her chest. "It isn't so very shocking to know that the prince appreciates a woman with—"

"Stop!" Rosavyn said through her giggles. "You really will make her faint away!"

With another moan, Aurelise dropped her fan and pressed both hands over her burning face. "I cannot believe we're having this conversation. About the prince! Who I'm now supposed to … to … spend time with. In proximity. Where he might … look at me."

"Oh no," Rosavyn gasped dramatically. "He might look at you. With his eyes. The absolute scandal."

"You know what I mean," Aurelise mumbled through her fingers. "I shall spend the entire time blushing and stuttering."

"Actually," Mariselle said, her tone shifting to something slightly more serious, though amusement still colored her words, "I suspect Ryden isn't quite as terrible as he appears. There must be something of substance beneath all that tiresome swagger and incessant flirtation. Surely Evryn wouldn't maintain such a close friendship with someone who was entirely composed of superficial charm and practiced carelessness. At least, one hopes." She sighed contentedly. "Though naturally, he couldn't possibly compare to Evryn, who is absolutely extraordinary when it comes to—"

"I *beg* you not to complete that thought," Rosavyn interrupted with considerable alarm.

"I was merely going to observe his exceptional talent for the management of a household!" Mariselle protested, though her tone suggested otherwise entirely.

"You most certainly were not," Rosavyn said around another laugh. "And poor Aurelise has endured quite enough mortification for one afternoon without adding whatever improper observation you were about to share about—"

The sound of approaching footsteps in the hallway cut through their conversation. Aurelise scrambled to her feet so quickly that the room tilted alarmingly, forcing her to catch herself against the nearest chair. Mariselle rose more gracefully, though she was clearly suppressing laughter at Aurelise's panic. Iris pushed herself up from the settee with visible effort, one hand braced against the arm for support. Only Rosavyn remained on the floor.

The drawing room door opened, revealing Lord Hadrian Blackbriar. He took in the scene—three young ladies standing with varying degrees of composure, and one still sprawled across the carpet—with an expression that suggested nothing about this tableau surprised him in the least.

"Hadrian," Rosavyn greeted with a serene smile, observing him upside down.

"Rosavyn," he replied, his expression showing only the mildest bewilderment mixed with what appeared to be fond resignation—clearly the product of years of exposure to Rosavyn's complete disregard for convention.

He turned to the others with a proper bow. "Ladies. I apologize for the intrusion." His gaze found Iris, concern immediately creasing his features. "Iris, please, sit. I didn't mean to disturb your rest."

"Nonsense," Iris said, though she did lower herself back onto the settee with poorly concealed relief. "You're always welcome, Hadrian."

As she so often did, Aurelise watched them carefully, searching for any hint of discomfort in their interaction. Two Seasons ago, Iris and Hadrian had been engaged before Iris had broken it off, only to become betrothed to Jasvian—Hadrian's closest friend—mere weeks later. The entire situation had seemed impossibly fraught with potential for resentment and hurt feelings. Yet as she observed them now, Aurelise was reminded yet again that she was likely the only person who felt any secondhand awkwardness over the whole thing.

"If you're looking for Jasvian," Iris added, "I'm afraid he's at the tea house. Lady Rivenna required assistance with something."

"Ah. Thank you." Hadrian turned to leave, then paused. "Lady Aurelise, I nearly forgot—congratulations on your selection for the Crown Court. My sister mentioned it this morning."

Aurelise fought to keep her grimace from showing. She'd forgotten that Lady Willow Blackbriar had also been chosen. "How kind of her."

"She's quite nervous about it all, actually. Though excited as well. This entire Crown Court business has rather taken everyone by surprise. No one expected anything quite so dramatic this Season." He smiled kindly. "I'm sure you'll both manage beautifully."

"Thank you," Aurelise managed, the words like ash in her mouth.

After Hadrian's departure, Mariselle collapsed back onto the floor with a laugh. "That poor man. Every time he visits, we're doing something absolutely ridiculous."

"He's used to it by now," Rosavyn said, still not having moved. "I've thoroughly destroyed his capacity for shock."

Aurelise lowered herself back down with considerably less grace than before. "Lady Willow is exactly the sort of accomplished, confident lady who belongs in a Crown Court. Unlike me."

"Stop that," Iris said, her tone firm but not unkind. "You are every bit as accomplished as the others selected, Aurelise. And confidence is often little more than noise. There is a steadiness in you that runs deeper than most perceive, and because of that, you'll survive this. You'll attend the required events, you'll make absolutely no impression whatsoever on Prince Ryden, and by Season's end, he'll have chosen someone appropriate who actually wants to be a princess."

"Exactly," Rosavyn agreed. "We can teach you how to be boring, if you'd like."

"I'm already exceptionally boring."

"That's hardly true. You could be far worse," Rosavyn insisted. "You could talk exclusively about … I don't know … the historical evolution of spoon design."

"The magical properties of lumyrite spoons," Mariselle added.

"The optimal spoon curvature for soup consumption versus dessert enjoyment," Rosavyn continued.

"Oh, Iris!" Mariselle suddenly lifted her head from the carpet. "There's an idea! What about—"

"No," Iris answered flatly. "I am not naming my firstborn child Spoon."

"Oh, but it's so elegant in its simplicity!" Rosavyn chimed in. "And terribly practical. Everyone needs spoons. Jasvian will love it."

"I suppose it's marginally better than Grandmother's suggestion of Teacup Supreme," Aurelise mused.

Mariselle's laughter burst forth in an inelegant snort. "Did she really suggest Teacup Supreme?"

"Yes. Complete with 'Supreme' as a middle name."

"My favorite is still Kazrian's suggestion of Doorknob," Rosavyn said, her whole body shaking with barely suppressed mirth.

"Stop," Iris said through her laughter. "Jasvian has threatened to ban us all from the house if we continue this absurd naming nonsense."

"What about—" Mariselle began.

"No."

"You don't even know what I was going to say!"

"The answer remains no. There will be no *Spoon* in this family."

"And I will not be talking about spoons either," Aurelise said firmly, "though I need *something* boring to talk about. I need to be so utterly forgettable that he'll barely notice I exist."

"Fine." Rosavyn sighed. "We'll come up with some other tedious topics for you, Lise. Weather patterns. Soil composition. The correct method for organizing a linen closet."

"I already talk about weather," Aurelise pointed out. "It's my primary conversational refuge."

"Then you're perfectly prepared," Mariselle declared. "You'll bore Prince Ryden into a state of complete indifference within a week."

Aurelise sighed. "I still don't think I should have been chosen."

"Noted," Rosavyn said. "Your objection has been registered with the committee of sisters who don't have any power to change anything but will enthusiastically commiserate."

They lapsed into companionable silence then, all of them staring up at the ceiling as afternoon light continued its slow progression across the plaster roses. Aurelise tried to find peace in the quiet moment, but underneath the calm, anxiety churned like a restless tide.

The ceiling roses, she decided, offered no more useful wisdom than their living counterparts back home.

Chapter Five

The corridors of Solstice Hall stretched endlessly before Prince Ryden, each faelight casting shadows that felt heavier than usual. He'd been summoned to his mother's private withdrawing room—a space she reserved for matters requiring discretion rather than ceremony—and he trudged forward with mounting resignation. No doubt she wished to discuss her selections for the Crown Court now that this madness was officially happening.

As he approached the double doors, they opened to reveal Lady Rivenna Rowanwood preparing to take her leave. The sight of her wasn't surprising—his mother had long maintained a friendship with the formidable matriarch of the Rowanwood family, speaking of her with the particular fondness reserved for those who'd offered guidance through difficult times. What counsel had his mother sought tonight, he wondered, that required such a private audience?

"Lady Rowanwood," he said, offering a proper bow as she moved toward him.

"Your Highness," she replied. Her curtsy was perfectly correct, yet somehow she still managed to look down at him despite the difference in their heights. As she straightened, her piercing eyes assessed him with an intensity that made him want to fidget.

"May I offer my congratulations on your granddaughter's selection for the Crown Court," he said, falling back on formal pleasantries. "Lady Aurelise's magical demonstration was truly extraordinary."

"How kind of you to say so." Her smile was the sort that didn't quite reach her eyes. She strode forward, then stopped in the doorway before passing him, leaning in just slightly. "Your Highness," she murmured, "I trust you understand that not every flower in a garden is meant to be plucked. Some are far too delicate for careless hands."

"My lady?" he enquired, raising an eyebrow though he understood her meaning perfectly. It seemed the Rowanwoods were of one mind—first Evryn's stern warnings at the Opening Ball, and now the formidable grandmother herself. They had clearly decided their delicate flower needed protection, and he had been unanimously designated as the garden pest.

"Should my granddaughter experience even the slightest distress while under your attention," Lady Rivenna said, her voice carrying the gentle menace of silk concealing steel, "I shall devote my considerable resources to ensuring that your future holds regrets of such magnificent proportions they will eclipse all other memories of your youth."

The words hung between them for a moment as the older woman smiled a frost-bitten smile. Then she was gone, her footsteps fading down the corridor.

Ryden entered his mother's withdrawing room, still processing Lady Rivenna's warning. The space was designed for comfort rather than grandeur, with walls of soft pearl-gray and furniture upholstered in shades of lavender and cream. His mother sat in her favorite chair near the window, a portfolio of some sort lying closed on the low table before her. The moonlight streaming through the glass caught the pale blue of her hair, making it seem almost white.

"Come rest yourself, darling," she said in that voice she reserved solely for him, patting the chair beside her without glancing up from her papers.

Ryden obeyed, sinking into the plush velvet. "Lady Rivenna appears to have her talons particularly sharpened this evening," he observed, hoping his tone conveyed casual amusement rather than the wariness he actually felt.

His mother's lips curved in the faintest smile. "Lady Rivenna's counsel remains consistent with our research. We both believe you need a partner whose magic will provide a grounding influence—earth magic, protective barriers, something with natural stability. The deep magical bond created through marriage should theoretically stabilize your surges."

"She does not seem pleased about her granddaughter's inclusion in the Crown Court."

"Oh, she was fully aware Lady Aurelise would be selected. Grateful that I agreed to it, in fact."

"Agreed?" Ryden straightened, genuinely surprised. "She *requested* her granddaughter be selected?"

"Of course. The Rowanwoods are one of our most distinguished families, yet their position has grown somewhat precarious with their older daughter's continued lack of manifestation. To have their younger daughter debut this Season and not be included in the Crown Court would have invited speculation about the family's standing. Lady Rivenna is far too shrewd to allow such whispers to take root. She does not, however, wish you to actually *choose* Lady Aurelise. She knows her granddaughter's temperament would make her unsuitable for royal life."

Ryden exhaled slowly, remembering Evryn's similar comments. "This seems to be a common sentiment among her family."

"I concur, naturally. We needn't waste time considering her. Music magic could hardly be further from what we're seeking. Far too emotional."

"Her magic was ..." Ryden paused, remembering the way those invisible strings had seemed to reach directly into his chest. Another involuntary shiver ran through him. "Magnificent."

"Oh yes, quite extraordinary. I've never experienced anything quite like it." His mother's brow furrowed slightly. "Though it is curious. The Rowanwoods typically manifest earth-based abilities, particularly those relating to lumyrite. The magic in their bloodline could potentially be the sort of grounding influence we seek for your authority surges. Yet Lady Aurelise's gift appears to have diverged from her family's traditional affinities. An influence from her mother's side, presumably. Nevertheless, given the fact that your surges sometimes correlate with emotional intensity, a magic that so powerfully stirs feeling would be particularly ill-advised."

She waved a hand over the portfolio, and it transformed into something far more sophisticated. A series of translucent panels slid into the air where they hung, bobbing gently, each displaying a moving portrait of one of the Crown Court ladies along with flowing script beneath.

"Now," his mother said as she began swiping elegantly through the panels with her hand, moving and reordering them, "let us review our true prospects."

She paused at Lady Coravelle Aerwynne's panel. The young woman's portrait showed her laughing at something off-frame, her wide eyes sparkling. "Sweet girl, excellent family. They traditionally manifest air-related magic, and hers takes the form of protective barriers of air. Shields, if you will, that deflect and dissipate other magic. Potentially a good match for you, though mere deflection falls short of what we truly need."

Swipe. Lady Olivienne Silverglen materialized, her knowing smile suggesting she was in on a joke no one else understood. "Ah, now here is our premier candidate. Glenwhisper magic is uncommon and often overlooked, but as my research confirmed, one of the ways in which it nurtures life forces within the natural realm is by anchoring plants' roots more firmly in soil—and I believe it might be able to anchor your magic, preventing those troublesome surges."

Ryden made a sound somewhere between acknowledgment and dismissal, shifting slightly as the room seemed to shrink around him.

Swipe. Lady Floravine Nightrose appeared, her serious expression and dark eyes suggesting depths worth exploring. "Her shadeweaving ability could potentially be another form of barrier magic between your surges and the rest of the world. I'm told nothing can pass through the shadows she shapes."

Swipe. Swipe. Swipe.

Each panel brought another face, another list of qualifications, another set of calculations about compatibility and potential magical stability. Ryden felt the walls of the room pressing closer with every assessment, his chest tightening until breathing became conscious effort.

His mother's voice faded to a distant hum as she continued her analysis. This was his life she was methodically arranging like pieces on a game board, his future determined by potential magical compatibility. It was almost as if the ladies in these panels weren't people to her—they were solutions to a problem, variables in an equation that ended with him bound to someone he didn't love for the sake of stability he wasn't even certain would work.

But he had always known it was naive to hope for love. His mother had reminded him as such on numerous occasions. She had not found love in her own arranged match, but had instead discovered genuine love only years later.

"—don't you think?"

Ryden blinked, realizing his mother had asked him something. "Forgive me, I was … considering the options."

She studied him. "You look pale. Are you feeling unwell?"

"No." He forced his shoulders to relax, his hands to unclench. "Simply tired."

"Hmm." She didn't look convinced, but she gestured toward the door. "Go rest, then. We can resume our analysis of the candidates tomorrow."

As he rose to leave, she reached out, her fingers resting lightly on his sleeve. The sudden gentleness in her touch made him pause.

"Ryden," she said, her voice softening. "I love you. You understand that, don't you? This isn't meant as punishment."

Something inside him unwound slightly, the tension in his chest easing just enough to draw a proper breath. "I know."

"I wanted better for you. I wanted you to have …" Her words trailed into silence, her gaze drifting past him to settle somewhere over his shoulder.

"What you found with Ellian?" he asked quietly.

Her eyes returned to his immediately, a flash of something vulnerable quickly masked. "You know we do not speak of that," she said, her voice barely above a whisper.

"You're right. I apologize."

"If circumstances were different—if your magic was stable and we had the luxury of time—nothing would please me more than to see you follow your heart. But the situation demands immediacy."

He gave a terse nod, swallowing the bitter taste of resentment that threatened to rise. "I understand. This isn't your doing." He hoped his words were true. He *wanted* them to be true. Yet in the furthest reaches of his mind, a quiet thought had always lingered—that perhaps his magic's instability was not mere misfortune, but the consequence of what his mother had done. But he loved her, and with no proof to support the thought, it was a suspicion he had never dared to voice.

He rose and inclined his head in a formal bow that concealed his expression. "Good night, Mother."

"Good night, darling. Rest well. Tomorrow we must arrange the formal courtship calendar. Garden parties, riding excursions, evening musicales. We will ensure you have ample opportunity to evaluate compatibility with each Crown Court lady."

And just like that, the walls seemed to contract around Ryden once more, his lungs struggling against the invisible band that had returned to squeeze his chest. With a careful stride that belied the panic rising within him, he departed before his mother could enumerate further delightful torments awaiting him.

The corridors blurred past as he made his way to his private quarters, nodding absently at the guards who opened doors and the servants who bowed in passing. His chambers occupied an entire wing of the palace, a series of connected rooms that had been his refuge since childhood. He bypassed the formal receiving room and headed straight for his study, his magic swinging the door shut behind him.

He crossed the moonlit space to his desk in three long strides and braced his palms against its polished surface as if it might anchor him to reality. His gaze skittered across scattered papers and books, seeing nothing, his vision turned inward to the gathering storm of his thoughts.

He could do this, he told himself yet again. It was the path countless fae elite had walked before him—a marriage of convenience, of strategy, of magical compatibility. He wasn't being asked to do anything extraordinary. Throughout the realm, people bound themselves to partners chosen by family or circumstance every day. He should consider himself fortunate to have any choice at all, to be presented with ten accomplished ladies rather than a single predetermined match. Yet what choice was it truly, when the deciding factor would be the stabilizing effect on his magic rather than any genuine connection?

The panic returned with crushing force. He dragged his fingers through his hair, forcing himself to draw long, measured breaths, the same careful pattern he practiced when fighting to control his magical surges.

Yet for all his practiced techniques, there was only one thing that truly brought him peace these days.

He rounded his desk, dropped into the chair, and reached for the bottommost drawer. A single brush of his fingers across the spelled brass lock was all it took. A faint shimmer of light, a brief hum, and the drawer slid open soundlessly, revealing a hidden stack of letters and a wooden box engraved with delicate roses and twisting thorny stems.

He lifted it carefully, running his thumb along the familiar engravings as he had so many times before. His heart performed that particular skip it always did when he checked for a letter, hope and dread warring in his chest.

He opened the lid.

Empty.

The disappointment that flooded through him was both expected and somehow still crushing. He set the box carefully before him and sank back in his chair.

The box had been a gift from Master Glendale—officially titled Royal Instructor of Magical Theory, but in truth, so much more than that. He had crafted the pair of boxes when Ryden was sixteen, allowing them to exchange letters while Ryden attended the Bloom Season in Bloomhaven and his beloved tutor remained behind in the Shaded Lands. Every complaint about court tedium, every observation about the ridiculousness of social conventions, every moment of loneliness—his tutor had been there, if only in written words.

Then Ryden had forgotten the box at Solstice Hall when they'd returned home. A simple mistake, but by the time he'd realized, it was too late. The following year he'd searched everywhere, but the box appeared to have vanished, and none of the Solstice Hall staff could tell him what had happened to it. That Season had been particularly difficult to endure, with his magic showing signs of manifesting and no confidant to share his mounting fears.

Then, just days after Ryden returned home, Master Glendale had died in his workshop. A magical experiment gone catastrophically wrong. A sudden, senseless tragedy, devastating in a way Ryden hadn't been prepared for; the man was barely any older than Ryden's mother.

And after that … well, other events had unfolded that same terrible week, but Ryden had learned to carefully step around those particular thoughts.

He had kept his mentor's version of the box among his most precious possessions after that, a tangible reminder of someone who had seen him as more than a future High Lord. As more than … a mistake. The box traveled with him everywhere, sometimes left in his trunk, but its presence nearby was a comfort he couldn't quite explain.

Then, one night last Season, he'd heard a familiar hum he couldn't immediately place. It had taken him embarrassingly long to remember that sound, to scramble through his possessions until he found the box vibrating with new magic. Inside had been a letter from someone who thought she was writing to no one.

By then, nearly seven years had softened the edges of his grief. What surged through him wasn't sorrow but startled wonder. Who could possibly have found the box's twin after all this time? Who now held the other half of this forgotten connection?

Despite his curiosity, he'd considered not responding. She was young—seventeen or eighteen from what she'd written about her recent manifestation—while he was twenty-four at the time. But something in her words had reached past every wall he'd built, straight to the core of him where his deepest fears resided, carefully hidden from everyone else.

No one mentions how frightening it can be when magic suddenly flows through you like a river breaking its banks. No one speaks of the paralyzing fear that comes with being unable to control one's newly manifested power.

She had seen him. Without knowing him, without even believing he existed, she'd somehow seen straight to his heart. So he had responded, keeping things mostly light and gently teasing, the same way he did in person, and soon he had forgotten he was corresponding with someone who had scarcely outgrown her girlhood.

Now, he lifted the bundle of letters from the drawer. The papers were softened at the edges, some of the ink slightly smudged from repeated handling. He spread them before him like a map to somewhere better than here, his fingers instinctively finding the ones he returned to most often, their creases deeper than the rest.

Last night I committed the grievous social error of fleeing my mother's midwinter soirée to hide in the kitchens. Cook took pity on my obvious distress and allowed me to assist with the honey soufflé. I managed to get more honey on my sleeves than in the mixture, and later found myself walking alone through the garden (because of course I could not return to the gathering covered in honey), licking the sticky sweetness from my fingers lest I become a walking invitation to every wasp within a mile radius. Imagine me explaining that particular tragedy to my family. 'No, it wasn't the crowd that overwhelmed me, but rather my inability to properly measure honey without wearing it.'

He smiled despite everything, hearing her voice in the words—self-deprecating but clever, finding humor in her own disasters.

Then another reply, one or two letters later:

I KNOW you intended to make me blush with that absolutely improper comment about honey and fingers. You'll be terribly disappointed to learn I remained completely composed while reading it.

Well, perhaps I colored slightly.

(Fine. My lady's maid entered and asked if I had a fever, so I suppose your mission was accomplished after all.)

Oh how Ryden loved knowing that his words could make her blush. The thought of her cheeks flushing pink sent a warm current through him, a sensation equal parts sweetness and exhilaration.

Then he shuffled through the stack until he found the letter that never failed to leave him breathless:

Sometimes I watch my family, so confident in their paths, and wonder how they learned to walk so surely while I'm still stumbling over my own feet. Metaphorically speaking, of course. It's as if we're all performers in the same play, only everyone else received their scripts in advance. I alone seem to be improvising every line, watching others recite with perfect confidence what I'm still struggling to discover.

I keep waiting for the moment I'll find myself in a scene with someone where the dialogue flows naturally, where neither of us needs to search for words because they come as easily as breathing. The way it feels with you in our letters.

The way it feels with you in our letters.

Ryden had read that line so many times, and every time it made his heart contract in a way that was so intense it bordered on pain. He rubbed a hand over his face.

Stars above, he was hopelessly, completely enchanted by a woman he'd never even met. And tomorrow he would have to begin courting other women, smile and charm and pretend interest while his heart belonged to someone known only as L.

He couldn't bear it.

Before he could reconsider, he grabbed a fresh sheet of paper and one of his self-inking quills. This wasn't the time for games or flirtation. This was his last chance to take control of his life before the Crown Court locked him into a path he desperately wanted to avoid.

Dearest L,

Almost a year of letters. Do you realize we've written more words to each other than some people speak in a lifetime of marriage? And yet I still don't know if your eyes are the kind of blue that makes people write poetry or the kind of brown that makes people feel steadied. I don't know if you're tall or short, if you bite your lip when you're concentrating, if you laugh with your whole body or just a quiet shake of your shoulders (my guess is the latter).

But I know you believe that small kindnesses matter more than grand gestures. I know you prefer orange marmalade to strawberry jam, but you'd never correct someone who served you the wrong one. I know you have a quietly devastating wit that emerges when you think no one's paying attention, and that you dream about the sound of rain on a window while safe and warm inside.

I tell myself this should be enough.

But it isn't.

Your letters have become as necessary to me as breathing. I find myself composing responses to you throughout my day, storing up observations and absurdities to share. When something amusing happens, my first thought is how I'll describe it to you. When something difficult occurs, I wait for your words to make sense of it.

I want to know you. I NEED to know you. Not only the carefully curated pieces you share in letters, but all of you. The way you laugh when something truly delights you. The expression you make when you're trying not to cry. The sound of your voice when you're passionate about something.

I know I'm crossing the boundary you drew between us all those months ago when you insisted on maintaining our anonymity. I know I'm asking for something you may not be willing to give. But circumstances in my life are about to change dramatically, and I find myself standing at a crossroads that terrifies me.

Before I take a path I cannot reverse, I need to know: Is there any chance, however small, that you feel for me even a fraction of what I feel for you? Could there ever be something more between us than ink and parchment?

I realize how forward this must seem, but I'm not asking for promises or declarations. I'm only asking if you might consider … more. Meeting, perhaps. Talking in person. Where you can determine if I am worth the risk of reality after the safety of correspondence.

I await your answer with hope I probably don't deserve but can't help harboring.

Desperately yours,

R

Chapter Six

The letter trembled in Aurelise's hands like a living thing, as if R's desperation had infused the very paper with his longing. She'd read it three times now, and each pass only made the ache in her chest expand until she could barely breathe around it.

I want to know you. I NEED to know you.

The words blurred as tears burned behind her eyes. She squeezed her eyes shut, but the tears came anyway, spilling hot and silent. They did nothing to erase the pleading tone of his words, the raw honesty that had stripped away all his usual playful deflection.

How could she possibly explain? How could she tell him that the very thought of meeting him—of transforming their safe, contained correspondence into something real and breathing and overwhelming—terrified her more than any Crown Court could?

A discordant cascade of sound suddenly filled the air around her. Notes in a minor keys tumbling from nowhere, the sound of strings being plucked too hard. She clenched her fists, trying to pull the magic back inside where it belonged, but it only shifted to something worse—a low, mournful progression that sounded like heartbreak given voice.

"Stop," she whispered, pressing a hand to her chest as if she could physically contain the storm brewing within. "Please, just stop."

But the music continued to leak from her in waves. She shoved the letter into the hidden compartment at the base of her dressing table drawer before turning back toward her bed. The coverlet was cool beneath her palms as she sank onto its edge, her nightgown pooling around her.

Before I take a path I cannot reverse...

Cannot reverse? Did he mean … could he possibly be … was he speaking of *marriage*? Her breath caught. No. Surely if he were courting someone with serious intentions, he would have mentioned it in their correspondence. And if his affections were engaged elsewhere, he wouldn't have written to her with such unchecked warmth, such teasing intimacy. No gentleman seriously pursuing another would permit himself such liberties of tone. He would not have written …

Desperately yours.

And she knew—stars above, she knew—that she was desperately his too. That was the entire problem. She cared too much, *felt* too much, was standing on the shore as a tidal wave hurtled toward her, threatening to sweep her away. If they met, if he was as wonderful in person as he was in letters, she would fall completely and catastrophically in love with him, and the tidal wave would crash over her, drowning her in feelings too powerful to survive.

The music around her shifted, violin strings shrieking their protest into the darkness of her bedroom. She pressed her palms against her ears, but it made no difference. The music came from within her, unstoppable as breath.

A knock at her door made her freeze. The music cut off abruptly, leaving a ringing silence in its wake.

"Lise?" Kazrian's voice, barely above a whisper. "Are you all right?"

She turned toward the door, her shoulders sagging with a mixture of relief and guilt. She wiped hastily at her damp cheeks with the sleeve of her nightgown.

"Come in," she called, wincing at how fragile her voice sounded in the silence.

The door opened with its familiar quiet creak, the one that had announced midnight confidences since they were children. Kazrian slipped inside, bleary-eyed and rumpled, as though he'd been pulled from deep sleep.

"I'm sorry," she said immediately. "Did my music wake you? I didn't mean to let it slip—"

"No." He closed the door behind him, then turned to study her in the moonlight streaming through her windows. "I woke before I heard the music. I felt …" He shrugged, that particular gesture that needed no words between them. She knew what he meant. There had always been something indefinable between them, some invisible thread that pulled taut when one of them was in distress.

"I'm sorry," she said again, though she couldn't deny the comfort his presence brought.

"You look terrible," he observed with brotherly frankness, moving to sit on her bed. The mattress dipped under his weight, and she had to resist the urge to collapse against his shoulder.

"Thank you. How comforting."

"You're panicking." It wasn't a question. His eyes tracked over her face with concern. "Is it the Crown Court?"

She hesitated, torn between honesty and privacy. The Crown Court was indeed terrifying, but that fear paled beside the earthquake R's letter had triggered in her chest. Yet she couldn't speak of it to Kazrian. This correspondence was the one thing she had kept carefully secret even from him. Better to focus on the fear she could actually speak aloud.

"How will I survive it?" She pushed up from the bed and began pacing the familiar path between her bed and the window. "I've spent my entire life hiding from attention, and now I am to be at the center of it? It fills me with absolute dread. *Everyone* will be watching!"

"Lise—"

"And I'm supposed to be focused on mastering my magic this Season, not waiting for the prince to realize that I'm the least suitable candidate for princess." Her hands flew to her hair, trying to gather the dark strands over her shoulder, needing something to do with the nervous energy crackling through her. "He will expect me to be charming and accomplished and interesting, and instead he'll find that I'm none of those things. Which I suppose is exactly what I want, but it will be mortifying nonetheless when it happens."

"First of all, you're selling yourself far short. And second—" He broke off mid-sentence as a yawn claimed him. "Second, the sooner he discovers you're supposedly terrible company—which you're not—the sooner he'll direct his attention elsewhere."

"I know, I *know*, but that isn't really—" Her fingers tangled in her hair as she tried to braid it, the usually simple pattern becoming a knotted mess.

"Lise." Kazrian's voice was gentle. "Sit." He patted the space in front of him on the bed. "I'll do it."

The gentle offer broke through her spiral of panic. She sank onto the bed, her back to him, and felt his fingers gently untangle the mess she'd made.

"This isn't …" She swallowed, pressing her eyes shut, and let out a shuddering breath. "This isn't how I envisioned my Season at all. I had a perfectly simple and straightforward plan, and now this Crown Court has upended it completely." Not to mention R's letter had thrown her internal world even further into chaos.

Kazrian sighed, his fingers working through her hair with steady rhythm. He'd always liked knowing how things worked, and braiding hair was no different. When their governess had shown Aurelise how to braid her dolls' hair, Kazrian had sat beside her and insisted upon learning too. "I know you've never been comfortable with surprises or unexpected turns. You need weeks of preparation before anyone dares move your favorite chair an inch to the left. But perhaps there's value in this disruption. Perhaps experiencing something this exciting, even temporarily, might be good for you in ways you can't yet see."

"I don't want exciting," she said, the words breaking on a desperate half-sob. "I want predictable and boring."

"Do you really?"

"Yes! My plan was simple. Survive the Opening Ball, then spend the Season developing my magic and perhaps meeting a quiet, kind gentleman who doesn't mind the fact that I get tongue-tied in public and respects my need for solitude. Then I'd secure an engagement before the Summer Solstice Ball, endure one final magical demonstration before society, and retreat into peaceful obscurity for the remainder of my days."

"That really does sound exceptionally boring."

Aurelise reached back to smack her brother's knee, missing as he yanked it away with a laugh that dissolved into quiet chuckles. "Do you have a ribbon?" he asked.

Without thinking, she raised her hand and made a gentle pulling motion. A pale blue ribbon flew from her dressing table, guided by the faintest whisper of magic. Kazrian caught it, and she felt him tying off the end of the braid.

She pulled the braid over her shoulder, running her fingers along the smooth pattern. "You're still good at that."

He shrugged. "It's easy enough."

They sat in comfortable silence for a moment. The moonlight had shifted, painting silver rectangles across her floor. Beside her bed, a time-bloom shifted through colors as it marked the late hour's passage.

"I know this is a lot," Kazrian said finally. "I know you … *feel* things more deeply than most people, and that can be overwhelming for you. But perhaps consider that your ideal life might exist somewhere between these two extremes—not drowning in the overwhelming emotions you fear, nor withering in the safe but hollow existence we both know wouldn't truly fulfill you. There's a space between terror and tedium where genuine joy might be waiting."

Aurelise remained silent, absorbing his words with a small, sad smile. He meant well, her dear brother, but she couldn't bring herself to tell him that for her, that elusive 'genuine joy' likely resided much closer to the quiet predictability he dismissed as tedium.

"I still have to survive the actual Crown Court," she said wistfully.

"And you will." Kazrian reached over and tugged gently on her braid. "You can do this. You are *Lady* Aurelise Rowanwood, and you've been doing impossible things while terrified your entire life."

She let out a laugh that caught on the remnants of her tears. "I suppose I have."

Kazrian stretched his arms above his head, stifling another yawn behind his hand before asking, "Will you be able to sleep?"

"Maybe." The bone-deep exhaustion that followed panic was already creeping through her limbs. "Probably."

He stood, stretched, and moved toward the door, then paused and looked back at her. "Are you sure?"

She nodded.

"Good." He slipped out as quietly as he'd entered, leaving her alone with moonlight and the ghost of R's desperate words. Speaking with her brother might have helped her feel marginally less apprehensive about the Crown

Court, but it did nothing to ease the turmoil R's letter had left behind. She still had no words for him.

So in the end, she didn't write at all. She slipped beneath her covers, turned her face to the pillow, and tried to ignore the intense ache of guilt at leaving R waiting for an answer she didn't know how to give.

Dear L,

I told myself I would wait at least three days before writing again. A reasonable interval, I thought, to allow you time to process my rather … overwhelming previous letter. Yet here I am, barely twenty-four hours later, unable to keep myself from writing to you again.

I am choosing to believe you haven't responded yet because you're crafting the perfect reply. Perhaps you are on your fifth draft, searching for precisely the right words to gently let me down. Or maybe—and I prefer this theory—you're composing an epic response, a novel-length letter that requires considerable time and thought.

Other possibilities I've considered:

1. *You've been kidnapped by a roving band of theatrical squirrels who demand you write, direct, and stage an original production before they'll release you.*
2. *Your enchanted letter box has developed sentience and is now holding my letters hostage, demanding better working conditions and possibly a small salary.*
3. *A jealous parsnip has intercepted my letter, finally taking revenge for my years of vegetable slander.*

I realize I'm being ridiculous. You're probably just thinking. I know you like to do that.

Hopefully still yours,
R

Dear L,

Something amusing happened today that I immediately wanted to tell you about, and then I remembered—I can. Even if you are not responding, I can still write. That is allowed, isn't it? Please tell me that's allowed.

A staff member cast a charm meant to freshen the draperies in my mother's favorite drawing room and instead made them whisper polite compliments to everyone who walked past. They called me 'Your Most Distinguished Eyebrows,' which I have a sneaking suspicion was the draperies' way of mocking me with excessive courtesy.

I couldn't help wondering what compliment they might whisper to you if you walked past. Probably something truly flattering, as I doubt there exists a single aspect of you the draperies could bring themselves to ridicule.

Still thinking of you,

R

Dear L,

I saw a garden today that made me think of you. Not because it was beautiful—though it was—but because someone had planted roses next to vegetables, and the roses looked personally offended by the proximity to carrots. I could practically hear them gossiping: "Can you believe we're expected to share soil with root vegetables? The absolute indignity!"

I wondered what your ever-blooming roses would think. Would they be horrified? Or would they see it as an opportunity to establish dominance over a new territory?

Missing your thoughts on ridiculous matters,

R

L,

I've realized I don't actually know how to exist without your letters anymore. That's terrifying, isn't it? When did you become necessary to my daily functioning? When did 'I should tell L about this' become my first thought whenever something interesting happens?

Today alone, I've mentally composed five letters to you:

- One about my pegasus staring at his reflection in the water trough in what I can only describe as deep, brooding self-admiration

- Another about the mystery of why sandwiches always taste better when cut diagonally

- A complaint about buttons (why are there so many?)

- A question about whether you think fish get thirsty

- And this one, which is really just me saying I miss you

The last one seems to be the only one that matters.

Waiting (im)patiently,

R

Dear L,

Five days. Has it really only been five days? It feels like months.

I've started three different letters to you today and burned them all. They were all variations of 'please write back' dressed up in different words. This one will probably join them in the fire, but I'm writing it anyway because the alternative is this crushing silence.

Do you know what the worst part is? I can't even be properly angry. I'm the one who broke our agreement. You wanted distance, safety, the protection of anonymity, and I asked for more. Of course you retreated. Of course you're silent.

I only wish I knew if this was goodbye.

Foolishly yours,

R

L,

A full week. The rational part of my mind says I should stop writing. But rationality has never been my strongest quality, as you've probably noticed.

I'm sorry. Truly and deeply sorry for overstepping the careful boundaries we established. I did it because I was thinking of what I wanted rather than what you needed, and that was selfish of me.

If there's any way we might find our way back to what we had before, please tell me. I would do anything. Absolutely anything.

R

L,

Will you ignore me forever?

I need to know. If this is the end—if my confession has severed the connection between us—please tell me. Send back a single word: Goodbye. I'll understand. I'll respect it. I'll stop writing.

But this silence is agony. Every day I check the box, and every day it's empty, and every day I wonder if you've even read these letters or if you've closed the box forever, leaving me to pour my heart into a void.

I'm not asking for what I asked before. I'm not asking for more. I'm asking for an ending, if that's what this is. Even rejected suitors typically receive the courtesy of a refusal.

Please. Just one word. Even if it's farewell.

Still desperately yours despite myself,

R

Please.

Chapter Seven

"Lady Aurelise Rowanwood," the footman announced, and the words seemed to hang in the air like a physical thing, heavy and impossible to retract.

The room turned toward her—a kaleidoscope of silk and suspicious smiles that refused to resolve into individual faces. Aurelise's vision swam, catching fragments: a perfectly arched eyebrow here, lips curved in what might have been welcome or warning there, the glint of curiosity in eyes she couldn't quite focus on. They were all looking at her. Every single Crown Court lady who had arrived before her was looking, evaluating, measuring, and finding her wanting. She was certain of it.

Her heart hammered so violently she could hear nothing else, only that terrible rhythmic pounding that surely everyone else could hear too. The room tilted slightly, or perhaps she did, and she had to lock her knees to keep from swaying.

A delicate trill of embarrassed flutes escaped into the air.

Horror flooded through her like ice water. She coughed loudly, desperately, bringing her gloved hand to her throat as if the musical mishap had been nothing more than an unfortunate clearing of her airways. "Thank you," she managed to the footman, her voice pitched too high, too bright. Another cough. Then another, until she worried she might be overdoing it but couldn't seem to stop.

She stepped past the footman into the room, her legs moving of their own accord toward the nearest refuge—an absolutely enormous arrangement of pale pink peonies that erupted from a vase nearly as tall as she was. The flowers were so abundant, so enthusiastically oversized, that she wondered if she could simply position herself behind them and remain there for the duration of tea. Perhaps if she stood very still, the other ladies might mistake her for a piece of statuary. A decorative element. Anything but a person who needed to speak and smile and pretend she belonged here.

More than a week had passed since the Opening Ball and the High Lady's announcement of the Crown Court. More than a week since R's desperate letter had arrived in the enchanted wooden box. More than a week of silence—hers, not his. The letters had continued to appear daily, his tone shifting from hopeful to confused to hurt to desperately pleading.

Every night, she'd removed them from the box with trembling fingers. Every night, she'd read his increasingly anxious words, his humor growing more strained with each unanswered day. Every night, she'd struggled with the guilt of her silence, knowing it hurt him but unable to find the right words to respond.

She had tried, of course. Multiple times. But the truth was, she still didn't know what to say. With a single letter, R had changed everything about their correspondence. There was no path back to what they'd had before. No way to return to the safe, beautiful distance that had allowed her to be more honest with him than she'd ever been with anyone.

R, thank you for your letter, but I must inform you that I do not feel the same—

No. That was a lie so profound it had made her hand cramp.

R, no, you are not worth the risk of reality after the safety of correspondence—

Cruel and untrue. He was worth every risk; she simply wasn't brave enough to take them.

R, it matters not how I feel because—

Because what? Because she was a coward? Because the thought of loving someone with the same overwhelming intensity with which she experienced every other emotion terrified her more than any amount of public humiliation?

R, I think I may be as desperately yours as you are mine, but—

No. That attempt had been the worst one of all. It had come far too close to the truth she couldn't bear to acknowledge.

She'd crumpled and discarded each attempt, yet she'd packed the wooden box among her things to bring to Solstice Hall, which meant that somewhere deep within, she knew she would answer eventually. Or at least, she missed him too much to leave the box behind.

"Lady Aurelise!" A warm voice cut through her thoughts just as she reached the enormous vase she'd been planning to hide behind. Lady Willow Blackbriar approached with a genuine smile, her light brown hair catching the light like polished chestnut. "How lovely to see you."

"Lady Willow," Aurelise managed, dipping into a small curtsy. "It's good to see a familiar face."

Though the two of them had never formally conversed, Lord Hadrian Blackbriar—Willow's older brother—was one of Jasvian's closest friends, and that connection, however tenuous, felt like a lifeline in a sea of strangers.

"Indeed." Willow took her arm as naturally as if they'd been friends for years. "Come, let's find a comfortable place to sit."

Aurelise allowed herself to be guided to a small seating arrangement near one of the enormous windows, fighting back the sudden and entirely inappropriate urge to suggest that perhaps standing with her face buried in peonies might be a more comfortable arrangement for everyone involved.

Her mind scrambled desperately for conversation topics. She had prepared for this. She had practiced. There was … the weather. And … the weather?

"Is your family well?" Willow asked as they sat.

"They are, thank you." Aurelise forced a steadying breath into her lungs. "And yours?" She internally congratulated herself on the natural progression of the exchange.

"Quite well, though my brother works entirely too hard."

"Oh, I saw your brother just the other day." Aurelise latched onto this thread of conversation like a drowning woman clutching a rope, relieved to have found something concrete to discuss. "Though I confess he almost caught me in a rather unconventional position."

Willow's expression turned quizzical.

"I-I mean," Aurelise stammered, "my sisters and I were … well, we were lying on the carpet, and—" She inhaled sharply, her eyes darting around the room as if it might offer her a more sensible topic. "Isn't the light simply exquisite today? The way it streams through these windows is quite … illuminating, don't you think?"

Willow leaned closer, her expression softening as she placed a gentle hand on Aurelise's arm. Her voice dropped to a confidential murmur. "Are you nervous?"

Aurelise took another quick breath that seemed to race straight to her head rather than her lungs. "Is it that obvious?"

Willow's lips curved into a conspiratorial smile. "Only because I'm nervous myself."

Aurelise forced herself to exhale slowly before leaning forward and whispering, "I cannot believe I'm really here. At Solstice Hall! The fact that I was chosen for this Crown Court business at all still seems like a terrible mistake."

Willow laughed quietly. "I feel rather the same way. My debut was last Season, and I was quite convinced that all of society had forgotten about me already. Apparently not."

"Forgive me," Aurelise said, "but I can't recall the nature of your manifested magic."

Willow's face flickered with a self-deprecating grimace. "It's rather uninspiring, I'm afraid. My family typically manifests abilities related to channeling others' magic. Potentially useful. In my case, however …" She sighed softly. "I can channel others' magic directly into the ground, where it simply … dissipates. Completely disappears."

"Oh, that sounds …" But Aurelise was saved from having to produce a diplomatic response, because a hush fell over the room as the doors opened once more.

A clear, ringing voice announced, "Her Grace, the High Lady of the United Fae Isles."

Silk rustled as every lady in the room rose and sank into a deep curtsy. The High Lady entered, serene, unhurried, her presence filling the space. "My dear young ladies," she greeted warmly. "Welcome to Solstice Hall."

She crossed the room and took her place upon a high-backed armchair upholstered in pale rose silk, a position that allowed her to survey the room with ease. "Please, be seated," she said, gesturing with a graceful sweep of her hand.

The Crown Court ladies shifted in near unison, perching on settees and sofas, smoothing skirts, folding gloved hands in their laps. Aurelise sat beside Willow, and when the High Lady's gaze swept over her—a brief, assessing glance that lasted no more than a heartbeat—she found herself longing desperately for the safety of the enormous vase of peonies.

"I trust your journeys were comfortable?" the High Lady inquired as silver trays laden with teapots and delicate cups materialized on the low tables between them, along with plates and dishes of tiny frosted cakes, crystallized fruits, and other enchanted delicacies.

A chorus of affirmative responses followed the High Lady's question, Aurelise adding her quiet "Yes, Your Grace" to the general consensus.

"Excellent." An attendant moved forward, but the High Lady stopped the woman with a subtle motion of her hand. "Now, before tea is served, permit me a few words. I imagine you all have questions about the Season ahead. The Crown Court is a traditional but rarely employed method of courtship, one that grants the prince the opportunity to know each of you beyond what the usual flurry of social engagements permits. There will be formal events, of course—balls, musical evenings, garden parties—but also smaller gatherings and private audiences with the prince."

At the mention of 'private audiences with the prince,' Aurelise felt a cold prickle of dread travel up her spine. Private audiences meant no crowd to disappear into, no convenient friend to rescue her with timely interruptions.

"I understand that spending the entirety of the Season away from your families may seem daunting," the High Lady continued. "Therefore, I've arranged that each of you may return to your Bloomhaven residences for two days every fortnight, should you wish it."

Aurelise felt her shoulders physically drop with relief, tension draining from her body. Around her, the atmosphere seemed to brighten, the circle of ladies exchanging glances that held new warmth. It seemed she was not the only one grateful for the prospect of occasional sanctuary with her family.

With a graceful inclination of her head, the High Lady motioned the attendant forward. "Now then," she said as the woman began pouring tea, "there are certain practical matters we should discuss. First, your accommodations. You've each been assigned a suite in the guest wing. Your personal maids have been welcomed, of course, but you'll also find you've each been assigned two palace companions."

She gestured gracefully toward the doors, which opened to reveal … nothing. Aurelise blinked, wondering if she'd missed something, until several small, glittering forms darted into the room. Two of them—an iridescent dragonfly and something that resembled a silver hummingbird—hovered in the air beside the High Lady's chair, while a miniature fox with a coat that shimmered like sapphires sat beside the chair's leg, wrapping its fluffy tail primly around its paws like a lady arranging her skirts.

"These magical beings have served the royal household for generations," the High Lady explained. "Each of you will find your assigned companions waiting in your suites. They will guide you through the palace, assist with your daily needs, and ensure you never feel lost.

"And I must emphasize," she added as she accepted a delicate porcelain cup from the attendant, "that these companions are not *pets*. They are to be treated with the same respect and kindness you would show to any in your service."

Murmurs of understanding rippled through the circle of ladies, heads nodding in assent as they exchanged curious glances, clearly wondering what manner of magical companions might await them.

The High Lady lifted her cup in a subtle gesture that encompassed them all. "Now then, shall we become better acquainted? Lady Coravelle, how is your grandmother?"

The conversation continued around Aurelise. Discussions of the upcoming social calendar, the various amenities available to them at Solstice Hall, the protocol for meals and gatherings. She participated when directly addressed but otherwise let the words wash over her. She could feel exhaustion creeping through her bones, that particular weariness that came from extended social performance.

By the time the tea concluded with the High Lady rising from her seat and declaring that they should all take the remainder of the afternoon to rest and settle into their suites, Aurelise's shoulders ached with tension, and a dull throbbing had begun behind her eyes.

She followed a steward through a bewildering series of corridors, trying desperately to commit the route to memory. But the details blurred together,

her mind too occupied with maintaining her composure as faint music threatened to escape her control.

The steward finally paused before a door, opening it with a formal bow. "Your suite, Lady Rowanwood. Your belongings have been arranged, and your lady's maid will arrive later to assist you in preparing for dinner. Should you require anything before then, simply pull the bell-cord by the bedside."

Aurelise stepped inside and nearly gasped aloud. The room was easily three times the size of her bedchamber at Rowanwood House, which itself was generously proportioned. Walls of pale pink provided a backdrop for furnishings of warm wood and gold detailing. A massive four-poster bed dominated one wall, while tall, arched windows offered a view of the palace gardens, currently aglow with late afternoon sunshine.

A sitting area with elegant chaises, upholstered chairs, and a scattering of small tables occupied one corner, while a dressing area with a mirrored vanity and armoire filled another. The plant her grandmother had gifted her to remind her of home—an oversized porcelain teacup that held trailing vines whose leaves shimmered faintly with hints of gold—sat on a table at the center of the seating arrangement.

Curious, Aurelise moved toward a second doorway on the far side of the room, peering through it to discover a separate bathing chamber that drew a soft, involuntary gasp from her lips. Unlike the screened corner tubs common in even the finest fae homes across the Isles, this was an entire room dedicated to bathing luxury.

A gleaming copper tub stood in the center, perched atop a bed of ever-warm stones, which would heat the bathing water to the perfect temperature when the correct enchantment was applied. Around the tub, potted ferns and flowers created a garden-like atmosphere, their subtle perfume mingling with the scents emanating from a glass-fronted cabinet where dozens of crystal bottles sparkled.

"Is there anything else you require, my lady?" The steward's voice startled Aurelise from her reverie, reminding her that he still stood attentively in the doorway.

She turned back to him. "No, thank you."

The moment the door closed, Aurelise crossed the room and collapsed onto the nearest chaise, her legs suddenly unable to support her. Blessed silence enveloped her. Stars, how was she to survive an entire Season of this? It was exhausting.

A faint rustle caught her attention. Her eyes flew open, her gaze darting around the room until it landed on the source—her dressing table, where her personal items had been neatly arranged. Including the enchanted wooden box.

Before she could process this, a flash of pink darted across her field of vision, followed by a shimmer of emerald green.

SHE'S HERE! SHE'S HERE! Oh, look at her, Spark! Isn't she BEAUTIFUL? The high, bell-like voice seemed to speak directly inside Aurelise's mind as a small pink mouse with dragon-like wings of iridescent purple zipped through the air, performing excited loops around her head. *I just knew she would be! The most BEAUTIFUL lady in the entire Crown Court!*

Aurelise flinched backward, pressing herself against the chaise cushions. "I—what—who are—"

Do cease your aerial acrobatics, Thimble. You're going to make the poor girl dizzy. A second voice—dry, resigned, and distinctly masculine sounding—filled Aurelise's head as a tiny emerald-green dragon, no larger than a teacup, swept down to perch on the table in front of her. Small puffs of glittery smoke escaped his nostrils as he regarded her.

Lady Aurelise Rowanwood, I presume. I am Spark, and that whirling pink catastrophe is my cousin, Thimble, who will likely require smelling salts before the hour is out if she does not moderate her enthusiasm. We are your assigned palace companions.

Aurelise's mind caught on the word 'cousin,' then decided not to ask how that was possible. "Oh, hello," she said hesitantly, relaxing slightly. "It's … lovely to meet you?" She hadn't meant for it to sound like a question, but really, how was one expected to respond when introduced to a telepathic flying mouse and a dragon whose deep baritone belonged to someone at least ten times his size?

We're going to be the BEST of friends! Thimble exclaimed, finally settling on the chaise arm, her tiny paws clasped together in delight, wings still fluttering. *And we're going to help you win the prince's heart and become the most beloved princess the United Fae Isles has ever had!*

"Oh," Aurelise managed, "that's very kind of you, but I don't actually—"

We've already begun our preparations, Spark interrupted, his golden eyes narrowing. *I've conducted a thorough assessment of your wardrobe. Serviceable, if uninspiring. We'll need to make strategic adjustments before dinner.*

Dinner! Thimble squeaked, launching herself back into the air. *The first real chance to make an impression! Your hair would look splendid with those sapphire pins arranged in a cascade pattern. The prince simply LOVES sapphires, everyone knows that. And perhaps the rose-gold silk for your first evening?*

Sapphires with rose-gold? Spark huffed. *Perish the thought! The two would clash abominably.*

"Please," Aurelise tried again. "Before you devote too much energy to the endeavor, you should know that I have no desire to win the prince's affections."

Profound mental silence followed this statement. Thimble froze mid-flight before dropping onto the table. Spark blinked his golden eyes, apparently stunned speechless.

I beg your pardon? Thimble's voice was barely a whisper in Aurelise's mind.

Aurelise shifted uncomfortably. "I don't want to be chosen as his princess. I don't even …" She looked around, then lowered her voice, as if the prince himself might somehow be listening in. "I don't even like him."

Thimble's wings drooped visibly, her expressive eyes wide with disbelief. *But … but … he's Prince Ryden! He's handsome and charming and so very lovely! How can you NOT want to be his princess? It would be the most romantic thing in the entire world!*

What my melodramatic cousin is attempting to articulate, Spark cut in, a fresh puff of glittery smoke escaping his nostrils, *is that we've been assigned to you with the express purpose of ensuring your success in this competition. Well, I suppose that was not the High Lady's official directive,* he conceded, *but the implication was perfectly clear—our lady must win.*

"It's not a competition," Aurelise insisted.

Spark's eyes narrowed to golden slits. *Oh, it most certainly is, my lady. It is nothing less than full-scale tactical warfare. Lady Ellowa's companions have already secured information about the prince's favorite desserts and plan to have them 'coincidentally' served whenever she dines with him.*

Oh goodness, Thimble moaned, clutching her tiny paws to her chest. *We're already BEHIND! We need a plan, a strategy, a—*

What we do not need, Spark interrupted, *is panic. Wars are won through superior intelligence and ruthless efficiency, not hysterics.* He turned his penetrating gaze to Aurelise. *If necessary, I am prepared to sabotage Lady Ellowa's wardrobe. One small ember in the right place would be most … effective.*

"No!" Aurelise gasped, genuinely alarmed. "No sabotage! No warfare! No … embers! Please, I just want to survive this Season with as little attention as possible."

Thimble's wings drooped even further. *But …* Her tiny voice wavered with confusion. *Don't you want to fall in LOVE? To find your TRUE HAPPINESS?*

Aurelise's expression softened. "I can assure you, my true happiness does not reside within these palace walls. I'm simply not interested in becoming a princess or a Crown Consort or whatever the title would be."

Precisely why you'd be excellent at it, Spark muttered, then added in a darker tone, *The ones who hunger for power are invariably the ones who abuse it.*

Oh! Thimble suddenly perked up, her wings fluttering back to life. *I understand now! You're playing hard to get! That's BRILLIANT! The prince will be absolutely fascinated by your indifference!* She zoomed upward in renewed excitement. *This is an even better strategy than I'd imagined!*

Aurelise opened her mouth, then closed it again, realizing the futility of further protest. "I think," she said carefully, "that I might need to rest before dinner."

Of course, of course! Thimble chirped. *Beauty sleep is ESSENTIAL! We'll reorganize your bath oils and bubble enchantments. I'm almost certain one of those bottles claims to inspire everlasting devotion—or at least a very enthusiastic infatuation.*

Spark sighed, the glittery smoke forming a small cloud around his head. *If we must. Though I reserve the right to implement more … direct measures should our competition grow too aggressive.*

"No direct measures," Aurelise insisted firmly.

As you wish. Spark inclined his head in a gesture that somehow managed to convey both agreement and the clear intention to ignore her wishes the moment it became expedient to do so. *Rest well, my lady. The battle begins at dinner.*

Aurelise slumped back with a breath of laughter. Too tired to argue, she could only concede that Spark was right—dinner did feel a little bit like going to war.

Thimble launched herself from the table in a blur of pink and purple. Spark spread his wings and followed in a far more dignified manner. *Do try not to get lost among the ferns again,* he muttered, his voice still present inside Aurelise's mind. *I can't spend hours extricating you every time you get yourself trapped inside a sun-eater.*

That happened ONCE!

You must admit you have a remarkable tendency to get lost inside small spaces.

And YOU have a remarkable tendency to eat too many of those silly little custard kisses.

How dare you mock that most magnificent of culinary masterpieces! Your blasphemy shall not stand, Thimble!

Still bickering, the two companions disappeared into the bathing chamber, leaving Aurelise alone once more. The silence felt different now, tinged with the lingering warmth of their bizarre conversation.

Her eyes drifted back to the dressing table, to the wooden box that sat there like a silent accusation. A familiar tightness gathered in her chest, that same anxious knot that had refused to ease all week. She should open it. Should read whatever new letter R might have sent. Should finally, finally respond.

She rose from the chaise and crossed to the dressing table, her fingers hovering over the box's carved surface. After a moment's hesitation, she lifted the lid.

Inside lay a single sheet of paper, folded once. Just one word written in his familiar, bold handwriting:

Please.

The music burst from her before she could contain it—a single violin playing a melancholy melody that filled the room with sweet sorrow. She pressed her hand to her chest, trying to push back the sound, but it only shifted to something more plaintive, more desperate.

How could one word hold so much pain? How could he convey such longing in just six letters?

She squeezed her eyes shut, focusing on transforming the music into something calming, something gentle, something that would soothe her churning emotions. Her hands moved absently through the air, conducting the sound. Two compositions battled for dominance—the sorrowful violin weaving between a gentler countermelody she was trying to coax forth. For several moments, the sounds tangled around each other, notes clashing as neither would yield.

She breathed deeply, her wrists turning in slow, fluid circles. Gradually, the violent strings softened, the jarring notes smoothed, and a tender, lilting melody emerged, not erasing the emotions but transforming them into something bearable.

It wasn't quite enough though. She longed for her pianoforte. She longed to lose herself in the sacred stillness that existed only between musician and instrument. That perfect void where time dissolved, where thought ceased, where nothing existed but vibration and breath and the seamless flow between finger and key, heart and sound.

But there was no pianoforte here. Only the enchanted box and the man waiting for her answer on the other side.

With sudden decision, Aurelise yanked open the dressing table drawers, searching for paper. The steward had mentioned her belongings had been unpacked, and she distinctly remembered tucking a sheaf of—Ah. There. The second drawer revealed her writing supplies, neatly arranged. The stack of paper and beside it, her preferred self-inking quill with its delicate pink feather.

She sat and began to write before courage could desert her again.

Dear R,

Please forgive my silence. I never intended to cause you distress or pain, but I simply did not know how to respond to your letter. In truth, I still don't.

She paused, the pen hovering over the page. The music around her had settled into something softer, a tentative melody seeking resolution.

I miss you. More than I thought possible. I miss your humor, your observations about the world, the way you tease me. I miss feeling understood without having to explain myself. I miss the safety of our correspondence.

She stopped. She couldn't tell him any of that. It was far too honest. She crumpled the letter and began again.

Dear R,

Please forgive my silence. I never intended to cause you distress or pain, but I simply did not know how to respond to your letter. In truth, I still don't. All I know is this: I want to keep writing to you.

Is there any way we might return to what we had before? Because certain events are unfolding in my life, events that require me to be brave, day after day, and I don't know how I am to endure it without the comfort of your words when night finally comes and I can breathe again.

I realize how selfish this is of me. I'm asking you to be what I need, even though I cannot give you what you have asked for. I understand if you do not want to continue as we were. After all, you have a life to live away from these pages, and I have no right to ask that any part of you remain bound to this unnameable thing that has grown between us.

But if you can accept this—if you can continue as we were—please write back.

Still yours, in the only way I know how to be,

L

Chapter Eight

Consciousness returned slowly, pulling Aurelise from dreams she couldn't quite recall, leaving only the impression of ink-stained fingers and words she'd been trying to catch like butterflies. The pillow beneath her cheek was softer than she remembered, and the air held a scent that didn't belong to home.

Memory rose slowly through the fog of sleep, each detail finding its place. Solstice Hall. The Crown Court. Morning light that was somehow brighter, more golden, beyond her closed eyelids.

R.

The thought crystallized before she'd even opened her eyes, and her heart fluttered in its wake. Had he replied? Would there be a letter waiting in the box?

She pressed her face into the silk pillow, willing the sudden rush of feeling to settle. The box had been empty last night when she'd checked after dinner, an event that had been mercifully uncomplicated. While the gathering was small—only the High Lady, the prince, and the ten Crown Court ladies—they'd been seated around a table so vast that conversation across its width proved nearly impossible. This arrangement, which some might have found frustrating, had been Aurelise's salvation. It allowed her to speak only with those seated directly beside her, while the prince remained a safe distance away at the table's opposite end.

Nevertheless, she'd found her gaze straying toward him more than once during the meal. Prince Ryden had devoted his attention primarily to the ladies seated on either side of him. They were opposite ends of the same beautiful spectrum—Lady Coravelle with her warm cinnamon-brown skin and sparkling eyes, and Lady Olivienne, whose dramatic contrast of raven-black hair and alabaster complexion was matched only by the elegant arch of her brow, perpetually suggesting she found everyone else slightly disappointing.

The prince himself reclined in his chair with the air of a man well accustomed to being observed, his posture conveying casual ownership of the space around him. Even while seemingly engaged with the beautiful women vying for his attention, a certain detachment lingered in his expression. Strange, Aurelise mused, for every other time she'd seen him, he'd seemed to bask in the adoration surrounding him.

Later, when dinner was over and Marta had finished helping her into her nightgown, she had practically lunged for the wooden box. The disappointment when she'd lifted the lid to find it empty had been crushing, though she'd immediately chastised herself for feeling it. After a full week of silence on her part—a week of leaving R to wonder and worry—she had no right to expect an immediate response.

But that logic did nothing to quiet the desperate hope now thrumming through her veins.

She sat up, pushing her braid over her shoulder, and padded barefoot across the unfamiliar carpet to her dressing table. The enchanted box sat exactly where she'd left it, innocuous among her brushes and bottles, yet it seemed to pulse with possibility.

She reached for it, then hesitated, her fingers hovering above the carved roses.

There was something she hadn't addressed in her letter last night. Something that lurked at the edges of every exchange they'd shared for months now. The question she could barely acknowledge even in the privacy of her own thoughts.

Where would this end?

Even if R accepted her terms—even if they could somehow recapture the easy rhythm of their correspondence before his confession had changed everything—it couldn't last forever.

One day, perhaps soon, he would write to tell her he was courting someone. Some brilliant, confident lady who could meet him in person without dissolving into panic. Someone who could love him without drowning in the intensity of it. He would find happiness in the real world, with a real person, and their letters would naturally, necessarily fade.

Or perhaps she would find her safe, undemanding gentleman first. Someone who would offer her the quiet life she wanted. Her conscience would demand she cease writing to R then. To continue their correspondence while pledged to another would feel too much like a betrayal, no matter how innocent their words might be.

The thought made her chest constrict painfully. How had she allowed herself to become so dependent on words from a stranger?

She drew in a shaking breath and placed her hand on the box's lid, trying to gather her courage. Perhaps R was wrestling with the same thoughts—that since she could not give him what he desired, this was the moment to end whatever existed between them. She knew the logic of it, knew she had no right to expect him to live half a life in ink when he clearly yearned for more. But that didn't stop her from hoping.

She lifted the lid and—

A folded sheet of paper lay inside.

A sudden, dizzying rush of sensation swept through her, as if the room had tilted beneath her feet. She sank onto the cushioned stool and lifted the letter from the box, unfolding it with shaking fingers.

Dearest L,

You wrote back. You wrote back! And you want to keep writing! Forgive me while I attempt to contain my enthusiasm—and fail entirely.

There. I've thrown my hands up in triumph and shouted YES at the ceiling, possibly frightening a nocturnal gossip bird who witnessed my celebration through the window.

You call yourself selfish for wanting to continue as we were, but darling L, there is nothing I want more than to be what you need. If what you need is a friend who exists only in ink and paper, who makes you laugh when the world feels too heavy, who listens when you need to whisper your fears into the darkness—then that is what I'll be. Gladly. Gratefully. Without reservation.

Certain events are unfolding in your life that require you to be brave? Tell me everything. Or tell me nothing. Tell me only what feels safe to share. I'll take whatever pieces of yourself you're willing to offer.

I must confess, your mention of bravery made me curious. You've always insisted you're not brave, yet here you are, facing something that demands courage daily. That sounds remarkably like bravery to me. But then, we've discussed this before—you refuse to believe me when I point out your various excellences. Should I make a list? I have time.

Actually, let's return to safer ground before I say something that sends you into another week of silence. (Too soon to joke about? Almost certainly. I'm leaving it in anyway because I'm still giddy with relief that you wrote back.)

Here's what I propose: We pretend my mortifyingly desperate letter never happened. We resume our correspondence exactly as it was before I temporarily lost my senses and demanded more than our enchanted boxes could provide. You tell me about your roses (surely they have thoughts on these mysterious events requiring bravery?), I'll mock vegetables and complain about excessive buttons, and we'll both pretend that nothing has changed between us.

Can we do that? Can we be friends who've never met, who know each other's souls but not each other's faces? Can we exist in this strange, suspended space we've created?

Yes. I believe we can. Because the alternative—not having you in my life at all—is unthinkable.

Yours in whatever way you'll have me,

R

P.S. The gossip bird that witnessed my celebration is definitely judging me. It's now sitting on a branch, looking personally offended by my lack of dignity. I've named it Horatio. Horatio thinks I should have more self-respect. Horatio can mind his own business.

The laugh that escaped Aurelise was half-sob. Tears she hadn't realized were threatening spilled over onto her cheeks. She pressed the letter to her chest, not caring if she wrinkled it, needing to hold something tangible that proved she hadn't destroyed their connection forever by remaining silent for too long.

A soft melody began to spin through the air around her. Something light and effervescent. Violin strings played a dancing tune that seemed to skip and twirl around the room, punctuated by the bright chime of bells. The music circled her like an embrace, warm and joyful and absolutely inappropriate for the early morning hour, but she couldn't bring herself to contain it.

With another laugh and a deep breath, she urged the music to quieten, but it was still drifting around her when a soft knock came at her door.

The melody vanished instantly, leaving only the faint echo of joy in its wake. Was it already time for Marta to begin preparing her for the day? Aurelise hastily wiped her cheeks with her sleeve and carefully tucked R's letter into the drawer, feeling as though the heavy dread of the previous day had been replaced by something almost buoyant.

In the clear light of morning, with R's words warming her heart, an idea began to take shape in her mind. Perhaps she didn't have to endure an entire Season of this Crown Court after all.

Chapter Nine

Onyx's wings cut through the cool morning air with steady rhythm, carrying Ryden high above Bloomhaven as the town began its slow awakening beneath them. Sunrise painted the world in shades of rose and amber, transforming the landscape into something ethereal, and Ryden drew in a deep, bracing breath as the air rushed past his face.

He leaned forward slightly, feeling the familiar bunch and release of Onyx's shoulder muscles, the warmth radiating through the creature's glossy black coat despite the cool morning air. This was freedom—just the wind, the sky, and the steady beat of powerful wings.

He turned Onyx toward Solstice Hall, and the pegasus responded instantly. Behind them, another set of wings beat against the morning air. His companion keeping pace, though barely. Ryden smiled to himself. Evryn had never been much of a morning rider. Though, to be fair, neither had he.

As they approached the palace grounds, Ryden felt the familiar tingle of the protective wards, invisible barriers that existed in layers around Solstice Hall. The magic recognized him instantly, a warm pulse of acknowledgment as he passed through.

He tossed a glance over his shoulder and saw Evryn and Cobalt—now falling slightly behind—pass through the barrier a heartbeat later. As an invited guest who'd flown these skies countless times over the years of their friendship, Evryn would experience only a brief shimmer of resistance before the wards recognized and admitted him.

Ryden guided Onyx down toward the landing meadow, a stretch of perfectly maintained grass that sparkled with morning dew. A scattering of palace gnomes scrambled to clear the field, arms waving as they hurried to rescue their tiny wheelbarrows of glimmering dew-crystals from the imminent landing.

Onyx touched down with a soft, rhythmic thud of hooves against the damp grass, the sound muffled and fleeting before he slowed to a graceful halt, wings folding against his sides. Beside him, Evryn's midnight-blue mount landed with equal grace, though his rider swayed slightly in the saddle.

"Getting slow in your advanced age?" Ryden called out as he dismounted. "I seem to recall you claiming you could outfly me blindfolded."

Evryn slid from Cobalt's back with a groan that seemed to come from his very soul. "That was before you sent your deranged messenger pixie to assault me before dawn. The vindictive little creature didn't just wake me—it poked me. In the cheek. Repeatedly."

"It isn't *that* early," Ryden countered, though it was likely even the gossip birds weren't awake yet.

Evryn rubbed his face, then shot Ryden a baleful look. "No one should be conscious at this hour, including you. The sun itself is barely awake. I'm fairly certain that pixie was still half asleep when it jabbed me. It kept yawning between pokes."

Ryden found himself smiling despite the chaos in his chest. Indeed, he had never been fond of early mornings. Their rides typically happened somewhere around midnight, when the palace slept and the world felt suspended between one day and the next. Those dark hours had always felt safer somehow. Less observed, less performed.

But he had woken early this morning and been unable to return to sleep.

After the previous night's endless dinner—smiling and charming and deflecting while his mind churned with thoughts of L's silence—he'd escaped to his chambers and discovered her letter waiting.

Relief and joy had flooded through him like sunlight breaking through storm clouds, like being pulled from drowning when his lungs had already begun to burn. After a week of agony, of checking the box obsessively, of writing increasingly desperate letters into what felt like a void, she'd finally, finally answered. At that moment, Ryden wouldn't have cared if an entire flock of gossip birds had witnessed him cheering at his ceiling.

L had replied. She wanted to keep writing. She needed him, even if only in this limited way.

He'd responded immediately, trying to contain his elation enough to write something coherent, something that wouldn't scare her off again. Then he'd attempted sleep, but his mind wouldn't quiet. Her words kept echoing: *certain events are unfolding in my life, events that require me to be brave, day after day.* What was happening in her life? What was demanding such courage from someone who insisted she possessed none?

Sleep had finally claimed him, but it hadn't lasted. By the time the first birds began their tentative morning songs, he was awake once again. The walls of his chamber had felt too close, the air too thick. He needed movement, needed sky, needed to outrun the tangle of emotions her letter had awakened.

So he'd summoned a messenger pixie—the poor creature had indeed been half asleep, blinking slowly at him as he'd given it instructions—and sent it to wake the one person he might at last dare to confide in about the secret correspondence that had gone on for almost a year.

When the first rush of elation at her reply had faded, a quieter ache had taken its place. She hadn't responded the way he'd desperately hoped she would. She hadn't admitted to feeling what he felt, hadn't agreed to meet, hadn't offered him anything beyond the continuation of their strange, suspended relationship.

And in his reply, he had not lied to her. He *did* want to be whatever she needed, and he would continue to be so for as long as possible. The problem which had crept forward from the corners of his restless mind and grown sharper with every sleepless hour was that this arrangement could not continue forever. It could not even continue past this Season if he was expected to choose one of the Crown Court ladies. The conversation with Evryn at the Opening Ball haunted him—his friend's belief that he might find it difficult to be faithful once wed.

But he fully intended to be. Which meant he could not continue this correspondence with L if he married someone else. Despite what he'd written about being friends, about pretending his confession never happened, the truth pulsed beneath every carefully casual line: he loved her. With a certainty that should have been impossible for someone he'd never met.

He could not maintain that love, couldn't nurture it through letters, while pledged to another. It would be a betrayal of both women.

Which left him in a most wretched predicament: the Season slipping through his fingers while he was expected to choose a bride from among women who stirred nothing in him, while the only one who *did* had made it heartbreakingly clear she did not wish to know him beyond their letters.

"I think I am in love with someone."

The words tumbled free before Ryden could reconsider them. Evryn, who'd been adjusting Cobalt's saddle, froze. "I beg your pardon?"

"I said—"

"No, I heard you. I'm simply trying to process the impossibility of what I heard." Evryn turned to face him fully, his expression caught between amusement and disbelief. "Love? You? So soon? The Crown Court began only yesterday. Don't tell me you've already fallen for one of them."

Around them, the world carried on in perfect indifference. Birds twittered, and two garden pixies swung merrily from one of Onyx's stirrups, chattering in delight as though nothing whatsoever of consequence had just been spoken.

Ryden cleared his throat, tugged slightly at the collar of his riding jacket, and tried to pretend this conversation wasn't already making him infinitely uncomfortable. "It isn't one of them."

Evryn's eyebrows climbed toward his hairline. "Then who—"

"We've been corresponding for nearly a year."

"Corresponding?" Evryn's voice pitched higher with incredulity. "As in … letters?"

"Yes."

"Letters. You. Prince Ryden, who I once witnessed charm three different ladies at the same garden party—in full view of each other, no less—are telling me you've fallen in love through letters?"

Ryden felt heat creep up his neck. "When you say it like that—"

"How else should I say it?" Evryn moved closer, studying Ryden. "You're serious. You're actually serious. You think you're in love with someone you've been writing to?"

"I don't think," Ryden said quietly. "I know."

"Who is she? Where did you meet her?"

Ryden hesitated, mouth parting before the words would come. His hand rose to rub the back of his neck. "I … have never met her. I don't know who she is."

Evryn's eyes widened further. Then he began laughing, a startled, disbelieving bark of sound that broke across the quiet morning. "You don't even know who she is?"

"That is to say," Ryden added, his tone growing defensive, "*I do know her*. In all the ways that truly matter. I know how she thinks, what makes her laugh, what frightens her. I know the … the shape of her *kindness*, the depth of her wit—"

"All right, all right." Evryn held up a hand, but his expression had shifted from disbelief to something more thoughtful. "It is only … Ryden, I've known you for years. I've watched you flirt and charm and scandalize your way through multiple Seasons. I didn't think you were capable of … this."

Ryden shifted his weight and attempted to stand a little straighter. "Of what?"

"Of actual love. Of …" Evryn broke off, making a helpless sort of motion with one hand. This was not the sort of topic the two of them generally discussed. "Of feeling something genuine enough to make you look the way you look right now. Like someone's reached into your chest and rearranged everything."

Ryden turned away, ostensibly to check Onyx's saddle but really to avoid the intensity of his friend's gaze. "Yes, well. It surprised me too."

"I always knew the public persona was at least partially an act," Evryn continued, his voice gentler now. "You hide pieces of yourself from everyone —stars know we all do to some extent. But I thought there was at least some truth to the stories. All those flirtations, those scandals that keep the gossip birds so well-fed …"

"There is some truth," Ryden admitted. "Certainly. But it's mainly—" He gestured vaguely, searching for words. "Surface. Performance. A way to be charming without being real. To be wanted without being known."

"And this woman knows you? The real you?"

"More than anyone else ever has." The admission felt raw, scraped from somewhere deep. She did not know everything, but she knew the things that mattered. She knew that he still struggled with his magic years after manifesting—though he had not told her the exact nature of his ability. She knew his teasing nature, his struggles with loneliness and the weight of expectations.

"Then you must find out who she is." Evryn said this as if it should be obvious.

"She does not want to meet me."

"Ah. That is …" Evryn paused, clearly choosing his words carefully. "That is rather suspicious, don't you think? Are you certain this is actually a young lady you're corresponding with and not some elderly sorcerer having a grand joke at your expense?"

"The thought has occurred to me," Ryden admitted. "It would certainly be embarrassing if that turned out to be the case. But no, I believe she is genuine."

"And you believe she …" Evryn trailed off, his gaze skittering away toward the horizon, as though the rising sun might spare him the discomfort of saying his next words. "Feels for you as you do for her?"

"She is careful with what she reveals, but I believe so, yes. Yet something is holding her back."

A silence settled between them, thick with unspoken thoughts and a shared awkwardness neither seemed willing to acknowledge. Both men folded their arms, suddenly fascinated by the sight of their pegasi nosing through the grass, tails flicking idly as the meadow brightened with morning light.

"Well, my friend," Evryn said eventually, "you are simply going to have to be your charming best and convince her otherwise."

Ryden regarded his friend. "That is entirely unhelpful."

"Perhaps," Evryn said around a yawn so wide it seemed to threaten the structural integrity of his jaw, "if you'd sent a pixie to poke me in the face at a more reasonable hour, I'd have more helpful advice for you." He blinked a few times. "As it is, my brain is still waking up." He placed his hands on his hips then, his expression turning thoughtful. "How did this even begin? How did you find yourself writing to someone you don't actually know?"

Ryden sighed. "A wooden box containing a letter enchantment. The corresponding box was lost years ago and I don't know where it ended up."

Evryn frowned.

"What?" Ryden asked.

"I feel as though I've heard of an enchantment like that before. Or seen a similar box somewhere, though I cannot recall where. Could you show me yours? Perhaps it will stir something in my memory."

An instinctive protectiveness stirred in Ryden's chest. The thought of anyone else handling that box felt somehow wrong, as though it were a sacred relic rather than simply a carved piece of wood and spellwork. The idea of another's hands upon it made something in him recoil.

"Uh … of course," he said aloud, forcing a quiet laugh at his own foolishness. It was only a box, after all—even if it was the sole thread connecting him to L. "Though I'm afraid it will have to wait. My mother has arranged a rather relentless schedule of Crown Court activities for today."

"How dreadful for you," Evryn drawled, lips quirking into a smirk. "Forced to spend your day in the company of ten beautiful ladies, all desperate for your attention. Well, nine, I suppose, given that one of them is my sister, and I prefer not to think about that."

Ryden leveled a pointed gaze at Evryn. "Would *you* find it such a delight when there is only one who holds your heart, and she is not among them?"

"Touché, my friend," Evryn conceded, his expression softening into that particular dreamy-eyed look that appeared whenever his wife was mentioned. "Touché."

Chapter Ten

Aurelise watched the spellthread clock on the mantelpiece with mounting dread, a thread of light endlessly stitching changing numbers along its edge, drawing her inexorably toward her doom. Well, it was not *doom* precisely—merely her impending garden stroll with Prince Ryden—yet her fluttering pulse and quickened breath suggested her body recognized no meaningful distinction between the two.

The Green Drawing Room she was seated in had transformed over the course of the afternoon into a perfect tableau of feminine accomplishment, each lady engaged in some genteel magical pastime that might catch a prince's eye. Some perched on elegant chaises with their charmstitching hoops, needles flashing in the afternoon light as threads of gold, silver, and moonwhite shimmered with quiet enchantments. At the far side of the room, others bent over their bloomcraft arrangements, coaxing flowers to shift their shades and scents until each bouquet sang of quiet perfection. Two or three ladies sat alone quietly playing games of enchanted solitaire—though the sidelong glances they cast at one another hinted that even this was a competition in disguise.

Aurelise, perhaps the only one not endeavoring to impress Prince Ryden, sat in a corner with a book of poetry open in her lap, though she hadn't absorbed a single verse in the past quarter hour. The words blurred together as her attention drifted to the doors through which Willow had just disappeared on Prince Ryden's arm into the gardens. They took the shaded path and disappeared beyond a hedge, Willow the eighth lady of the Crown Court to receive her carefully timed 'private' moment with the prince.

Only two ladies remained now—herself and Lady Ellowa, who appeared thoroughly vexed by the prolonged wait, viciously prodding a delicate blossom into submission within her bloomcraft arrangement. The poor flower trembled visibly with each jab, its blue petals curling inward as if trying to escape her increasingly aggressive attentions.

Aurelise attempted to focus on the poetry book once more, but the chandelier at the center of the drawing room's ceiling drew her attention upward as it began its peculiar performance once again. A thrumming, chattering sound that seemed to emanate from the hundreds of crystals adorning its golden frame. The noise had started soon after they'd all assembled in the room, occasionally growing louder alongside bursts of nervous laughter or animated conversation, and then falling silent again.

"Stars above, not again," Lady Ellowa muttered, releasing the cowering blossom with an exasperated sigh, granting the flower a momentary reprieve from her botanical tyranny. She pressed her fingers to her temples. "How does anyone concentrate with such a racket?"

A nearby steward, who had been discretely arranging a silver tea service by the window, offered an apologetic smile. "A quirk of the Summer Palace, my lady. The chandelier chatters when the room is full. Annoying, certainly, but one grows accustomed to it."

"Accustomed?" Lady Ellowa's voice dripped with skepticism. "To that cacophony?"

The steward's smile never wavered, though Aurelise detected a slight tightening around his eyes. "Her Grace refers to it as the palace's way of joining the conversation."

Several ladies tittered at this, though whether from genuine amusement or the desire to appear charmed by anything connected to the royal family, Aurelise couldn't determine. She returned her gaze to the unread poetry, trying to ignore the way the chandelier's insistent tinkling seemed to scrape against her nerves. She was having precious little success, however.

The jangling sound bore an unsettling resemblance to the chaotic, unruly melodies that often escaped her when her emotions threatened to overwhelm her control. Twice already she'd had to press her palms firmly against her lap, convinced for one heart-stopping moment that the dissonant tones were emanating not from the chandelier but from her own barely-contained magic. But no—the sound remained firmly above their heads.

Nevertheless, Aurelise's fingers twitched involuntarily, the familiar urge to shape and direct music pulling at her. She found her hand moving of its own accord. Just the smallest gesture, hidden by the book in her lap—a gentle sweep of two fingers, as if coaxing a single note from an invisible instrument.

A soft, clear tone emerged, so quiet that she was fairly confident only she could hear it. Then another joined it, harmonizing perfectly. She kept her movements minimal, her eyes fixed on the poetry as if thoroughly absorbed, while her hidden fingers wove a subtle melody.

Above her, the chandelier's chattering began to align with her quiet music, its overzealous tinkling gradually calming until finally it fell into a contented silence, with only the occasional delicate chime as individual crystals swayed in the gentle breeze drifting through the open garden doors.

Interesting, she mused, glancing up as a matching tranquility settled over her, smoothing the jagged edges of her anxiety. Her intent had been to soothe her own nerves, but if she had somehow influenced the chandelier as well, that was even better. For the first time since entering the drawing room, she drew a full, easy breath, her shoulders relaxing and—

"Lady Aurelise?"

Her hand stilled immediately, the melody dissolving as her head snapped up, nerves returning instantly. Prince Ryden stood in the doorway, having returned Willow to the company of the other ladies. The afternoon light streaming through the tall windows did unconscionably flattering things to him—illuminating his dark blue hair and casting shadows that emphasized the line of his jaw.

It was thoroughly irritating, Aurelise decided, that someone so reprehensible should be so absurdly well-formed.

"Y-your Highness," she stammered, quickly moving the poetry book aside before rising and somehow managing to execute a graceful curtsy.

"Shall we?" he said.

Aurelise sensed every eye in the room following her progress to the door, but she kept her gaze fixed straight ahead, her chin lifted despite the heat crawling up her neck. She could do this. She had rehearsed precisely what she would say—while alone, of course. Her enthusiastic little companions certainly would not approve of what she was about to tell the prince.

He offered his arm, and she placed her gloved hand upon it with the lightest possible touch, keeping a strictly proper distance between the two of them. Yet even so, he was near enough that she caught the faint scent lingering about him—something woodsy and … forest fresh. It wasn't what she expected. For all his reputation, she thought he'd smell less like clean, woodland and more like trouble.

They stepped outside and followed a gravel path that wound between hedges and meticulously maintained flowerbeds.

"I trust you're finding your accommodations suitable?" the prince inquired as they walked, and Aurelise couldn't help wondering if this was the ninth time he'd asked this exact same question.

"Yes, thank you," she replied, her voice so quiet she wondered if he could hear her. She cleared her throat as delicately as possible and added, "My suite is lovely."

"Excellent. And your companions? Are they … helpful?"

A memory of that morning flashed through her mind. Thimble and Spark locked in a heated debate about whether she should employ a strategic 'fainting spell' during her walk with the prince.

It's FOOLPROOF! Thimble had insisted, wings fluttering with excitement as she demonstrated by dramatically swooning onto Aurelise's hairbrush. *The prince catches you, carries you dramatically back to the palace—ROMANCE BLOOMS!*

Meanwhile, Spark had looked positively mortified, tiny puffs of glittery smoke escaping his nostrils as he demolished his third custard kiss. *The indignity of it all,* he'd muttered. *Our Lady Aurelise, pretending to succumb to vapors like some melodramatic stage actress!*

The entire scene had unfolded as Marta arranged Aurelise's hair, the maid's reflection in the mirror betraying her struggle against laughter, her shoulders quivering with the effort of maintaining composure even as Thimble detailed exactly which garden location would provide the softest landing spot.

"They are …" Aurelise searched for an appropriate word. "Entertaining."

To her surprise, the prince laughed. A genuine sound that held no trace of the performative charm she'd observed at dinner the previous night.

"That's a diplomatic description. Which of our illustrious magical menagerie have been assigned to your service?"

"Thimble and Spark." She paused, wondering if she needed to describe them, but Prince Ryden spoke before she could continue.

"Ah, *Sparkle*, though he'd attempt to incinerate me for revealing his true name. It's been a source of embarrassment to him his entire life."

Aurelise blinked at the prince. "You know him?"

"I know most of the palace companions. They've been fluttering, scampering, and setting things ablaze around me since before I could walk. They're as much a part of Solstice Hall—and our palace in the Shaded Lands—as the walls themselves. Though considerably more opinionated."

He leaned slightly toward her then, his expression shifting to something warmer and more intimate, as if inviting her to share in a secret. "Did you know Spark and Thimble are cousins? Though it's still unclear to me how a mouse and a dragon manage to be related."

Aurelise found herself leaning fractionally away, creating just enough distance to establish a proper boundary without appearing rude. "I thought it best not to ask," she admitted. "It seemed impolite to pry into their family history."

"Ah, you are far more considerate than I, then. I've been attempting to extract the truth since I was eight years old. They once spent an entire afternoon constructing an elaborate family tree, but I confess the explanation contained so many contradictions and improbable magical accidents that I emerged more confused than when I began."

Aurelise smiled despite herself, a soft laugh escaping her lips before she schooled her features back to polite attentiveness. She cast a curious sidelong glance at him, noting with mild surprise that he appeared genuinely engaged in their exchange, his demeanor more animated than she would have anticipated for what must surely be the ninth near-identical conversation of the afternoon. Perhaps it was simply the relief of approaching the finish line—with only Lady Ellowa remaining after herself—that had infused his manner with this unexpected vitality.

They came to a stop near a spectacular display of roses—deep crimsons mixed with pale pinks and pristine whites, their petals so perfect they might have been painted rather than grown. The familiar scent wrapped around her like an old friend's embrace, and for a moment, her nerves settled.

Then she remembered why she was here.

She drew a steadying breath, gathering what little courage she possessed, and began to turn toward him—only to catch a flicker of movement at the base of the nearest rosebush. Her heart lurched. *No.* Surely not.

But yes—there they were. Thimble, perched boldly on a root, beaming up at her with both tiny thumbs raised in triumph, and Spark beside her, puffing a delicate cloud of glittering smoke that coalesced into a perfectly formed heart.

Horror flooded her. She frantically flicked her fingers in what she hoped passed for a subtle shooing motion, mouthing *Go away!* with desperate intensity.

"My lady?" the prince prompted. "Is something amiss?"

She whirled to face him with alarming speed, positioning herself squarely between him and the incriminating rosebush, her smile so wide and sudden it bordered on alarming. "Nothing at all! The roses are simply … magnificent, aren't they?"

A bemused expression crossed his features. "Indeed they are. The royal garden pixies have outdone themselves this Season."

"Your Highness, I … I feel I must be direct." She fixed her gaze somewhere in the vicinity of his impeccably arranged cravat, finding it far safer territory than his face. "I believe it most improbable that you would select me as your bride, but should you, against all reasonable expectation, find yourself inclined toward such a catastrophic decision, I must insist you reconsider. You most assuredly do not wish to choose me."

There was a beat of silence. "I beg your pardon?" He sounded more intrigued than offended.

"I would be entirely unsuitable," Aurelise said, forging on despite the heat climbing in her cheeks. "I am ridiculously shy, I dislike large gatherings, I have no talent for sparkling conversation, and I frequently retreat into silence when overwhelmed. These are not qualities becoming a princess."

"I see," he said, and she could hear the smile in his voice without needing to look up. "Any other disqualifying attributes I should be aware of?"

Her blush deepened. "I … well, I am the youngest of the Crown Court Ladies. And—"

"I believe Lady Floravine holds that distinction," he said mildly. "You will be nineteen by Season's end, will you not? Whereas Lady Floravine's birthday does not arrive until midwinter."

Aurelise hesitated, momentarily derailed by his unexpected knowledge of such specific details. Her gaze darted up and past his shoulder, and she was momentarily distracted by the sight of a palace attendant standing not too far away. Close enough to ensure propriety was maintained, yet far enough to provide the illusion of privacy. "Nevertheless," she said, refocusing on the prince with renewed determination, "being so young—"

"How does being young disqualify you?" He looked curious.

"Well, it—I am less experienced than most of the others, Your Highness."

His lips curved into an amused smile. "I don't believe *any* of you are experienced in the area of being a High Lord's Crown Consort."

"I … I suppose not." She was floundering now. "But I am likely the only one who might abandon a grand reception and flee into the gardens at the first opportunity. And probably the only one who doesn't even like—"

She stopped abruptly, mortification washing through her. Stars above, she'd nearly said it aloud.

"The only one who doesn't even like … me?" The prince sounded thoroughly amused rather than insulted. "How refreshing."

"No! I mean, of course not, Your Highness. I mean the—" Aurelise stared desperately at a nearby rose bush. "The palace. I don't like Solstice Hall. It's … big." Her voice trailed off lamely.

"Big," he repeated, his tone suggesting he was struggling not to laugh. "A keen observation about royal architecture."

Aurelise wished the earth would take pity on her and swallow her whole. This was worse than any social disaster she'd previously endured, and that was saying quite a lot.

"You can relax, Lady Aurelise," Prince Ryden said, his expression softening into something that looked remarkably like genuine warmth. "I have no intention of choosing you."

"Oh." Relief washed through her, leaving her feeling light-headed from the sudden release of tension. "Truly?"

"Truly."

"Then—" She hesitated, hardly daring to believe this mortifying conversation might end precisely the way she'd hoped. "Might I be permitted to leave at the earliest convenience? Return to Rowanwood House, perhaps?"

A flicker of surprise crossed Prince Ryden's features before he tilted his head fractionally, his expression turning thoughtful. "I could speak with my mother. Arrange something, certainly. However …" He paused, seeming to weigh his words. "There are certain considerations that might make remaining here the wiser course."

Her relief evaporated. "What considerations?"

He glanced around momentarily. "I suppose there's no harm in telling you, since the matter concerns your family directly. You strike me as someone capable of keeping a confidence, and there are no gossip birds within hearing." He made a show of checking the nearby hedges, and Aurelise was relieved to see that Thimble and Spark had disappeared.

"The truth is, my mother selected you for your family's sake, not because she ever considered you a genuine possibility for the role of princess."

The words should have brought pure relief. They *did* bring relief—a loosening of the knot that had lived in Aurelise's chest since the High Lady's announcement. But beneath that relief, something else stirred. A tiny, irrational prick of … offense?

Which made no sense whatsoever. She agreed with the assessment entirely.

"Your grandmother requested it," he continued. "Your family, while undoubtedly still prominent, is in somewhat of a … tenuous position." He appeared to be choosing his words carefully. "To exclude you would have reflected negatively on your family and invited more speculation about … a certain Rowanwood."

Understanding dawned, uneasy and heavy, threading through her like a chill. "Rosavyn," she murmured.

"Indeed. Should you leave the Crown Court early …" Prince Ryden let the implications hang in the air between them.

She understood immediately. Her early departure would be seen as a slight, either from her toward the Crown or from the Crown toward the Rowanwoods. Either interpretation would fuel gossip that would inevitably circle back to Rosavyn's situation, making it even more difficult for her to find a gentleman of suitable standing who might overlook her delayed manifestation in favor of the Rowanwood name and connections.

"But if you truly wish to leave," Prince Ryden added, "I will arrange it. I won't force anyone to remain where they're miserable."

Aurelise drew in a breath. For herself, she would flee this palace without a backward glance. But for Rosavyn …

"No," she said quietly. "Thank you, but … I'll stay."

"Are you certain? You seemed quite determined to escape just moments ago."

"Yes." The word emerged steadier than she felt—an odd mingling of determination and dread tightening her chest. "I'm certain."

He inclined his head slightly, bending to catch her downcast gaze, his lips curving into a half smile. "Do you at least feel a little more at ease now? You may cease worrying about impressing me."

Her brows lifted. "I never worried about impressing you."

Surprise flickered across his features before melting into a grin that was far too pleased for her comfort. "Oho, so you *do* possess a sense of humor! Your brother was trying to convince me you're thoroughly dull."

Aurelise's mouth fell open, her cheeks flooding with heat. "Which brother?"

His lips curved further. "Evryn."

"He would never."

"True," the prince allowed. "He did not use the word *dull*, precisely, but the implication was difficult to miss."

Aurelise narrowed her eyes, tilting her head just slightly, though her blush betrayed her indignation. She studied him for a long moment before replying, her voice level. "He was trying to dissuade your interest in me."

Something in his smile softened. "You are perceptive, Lady Aurelise."

"No, I merely trust that none of my siblings would ever—" She stopped abruptly, remembering with a jolt that she *had* intended to present herself as utterly boring and forgettable. While the prince's assurance that she was not a genuine contender should have freed her from this charade, caution suggested maintaining the strategy she and her sisters had crafted. "Well. Yes. I am. Quite terribly dull, in fact."

Prince Ryden's ink-blue eyes glittered with mirth. "And a lamentable liar, it would seem."

Her mouth fell open again. "Is this your famed charm at work, Your Highness? Insulting ladies to their faces?"

The grin he gave her was pure mischief. Disarmingly handsome and entirely aware of it. "I thought we had agreed I'm not going to choose you," he said lightly. "What need have I to charm you?"

Aurelise drew back slightly, studying him with new consideration. Then, with a soft huff of laughter, half amused, half exasperated, she turned toward the roses, presenting him with her profile as she surveyed the pristine blooms. To her immense relief, there was no sign of her meddlesome companions among the foliage.

"Yes," she said. "In answer to your earlier question, I am feeling more at ease now." She reached out one gloved finger to trace the delicate curve of a blush pink rose, its petals unfurling in perfect symmetry. "You were right," she added quietly. "The royal garden pixies have indeed outdone themselves this Season to coax such beauty to life."

The idea brought to mind Lady Olivienne and her glenwhisper magic—that rare gift that breathed vitality into growing things, awakening in them a brilliance and vigor that ordinary nature couldn't often achieve on its own. Aurelise wondered what spectacular demonstration the woman had presented at the Opening Ball. She had missed it entirely, consumed by anxiety over her own imminent performance.

The memory of that night sent her thoughts drifting to R and their letter exchange leading up to the event. His absurd strategy for surviving conversational lulls.

Emboldened by the thought of his likely amusement, Aurelise looked back over her shoulder and caught Prince Ryden's gaze. Smothering a smile at the utter ridiculousness of the question, she asked, "Do you think plants have opinions about us?"

A startled laugh escaped him, softening his features for a moment before a faint furrow appeared between his brows. "It's funny you should say that, because ..." He trailed off, head tilting as he gave her the strangest look.

Ah, there it was. The expression of polite alarm belonging to someone now wondering whether she had taken complete leave of her senses, precisely as R had predicted. Evidently, the prince fell into the latter category of R's theory: the sort of person who, upon concluding that she was quite mad, would wish to remove himself from her company at the earliest opportunity.

Despite the warmth of embarrassment rising in her cheeks, Aurelise couldn't quite suppress her smile as she turned back to the roses. R's ridiculous advice had proven effective. *I see no flaws in this plan,* he had written. Indeed, he had been entirely correct. She would write tonight and tell him so.

She reached out to cup her palm beneath a particularly perfect bloom, tilting it gently toward her as a quiet laugh caught in the back of her throat. "Elderly chaperones," she murmured, recalling another of R's comments that had always amused her.

Several heartbeats passed in gentle stillness, the faint rustle of leaves and the soft trill of birds filling the pause, before the prince's voice broke it, low and oddly unsteady. "What … did you say?"

"The roses," Aurelise clarified, deciding he likely thought her completely mad by now. She glanced back at him, cheeks still warm, her chin dipping as a shy smile curved her lips. "They disapprove of uncovered ankles, you know. And dancing too close to one's partner."

He stared at her, his gaze growing intent, flicking across her face as though searching for something while the furrow between his brows deepened. The rhythm of his breathing changed—quicker, uneven—and she could have sworn his eyes had darkened. The air itself seemed to tremble, a faint shimmer rippling between them.

"Your Highness?" she asked tentatively. Oh, good stars, what had she done? Had she truly managed to offend him with her silly comments? "Are you … are you all right? Did I—"

He took a hasty step backward, turning his face away. "No, it is—not you. Forgive me, Lady … Lady Aurelise. I've just remembered something. Somewhere … somewhere I must be. Please excuse me."

And without another glance in her direction, he strode away, leaving Aurelise alone among the roses, quite bewildered by what had just transpired.

Chapter Eleven

It was *her*. It was her, it was her, it was her.

The words pounded through Ryden's skull with each rapid stride through Solstice Hall's corridors, matching the frantic rhythm of his heart. She was right here, in the summer palace. She'd been barely a few feet away from him, close enough that he could have reached out and touched her, could have traced the curve of her cheek where that enchanting blush had bloomed. His legs moved with desperate purpose while his mind reeled in absolute chaos.

Lady Aurelise Rowanwood—shy, blushing, declaring herself entirely unsuitable for royal life while quoting his own letters back at him—was L.

His L. His correspondent. The woman who'd held his heart captive for nearly a year through nothing more than ink and paper.

The shock of recognition had struck him as though the world itself had tilted, sending his magic surging through his veins with such violent force that the very air around them had begun to shimmer and warp. He'd had to flee, had to practically run from her, before his magic could spill over and accidentally command her to do something. The possibilities of what he might have said in that moment of overwhelming discovery terrified him.

Tell me you feel what I feel.

Kiss me.

Never leave.

Or something far worse.

Any of those commands, spoken with his magic running wild, would have stripped away her free will entirely. The thought made his stomach turn even as his feet carried him faster through the palace halls.

"Your Highness?" A footman appeared in his path, concern etched across his features. "Is something amiss? You appear—"

"Leave me." The words emerged before he could think. A pure command, his magic threading through them like iron through silk. Power surged outward, sharp and uncontrollable, and the footman was flung backward as though struck by an invisible force. He hit the far wall with a heavy thud and slid to the floor, dazed. Another servant cried out and rushed to his side.

Ryden pressed a hand over his mouth, horror mixing with the wild joy still coursing through his veins. He lurched a step forward, instinct driving him to help, to apologize—but terror stopped him cold. One more word, one wrong breath, and he might unleash something far worse. He had to get away.

This was exactly what he'd feared, exactly why he'd fled from Lady Aurelise in the garden.

Aurelise.

At last, a name. A face. The living reality of the person who had existed only in ink and imagination.

He half stumbled through the door to his private quarters, his magic slamming it shut behind him. The sound echoed through his chambers, but he barely heard it over the roaring in his ears. In a few swift strides he crossed to his study, reaching the large desk. Without pausing to sit, he bent and brushed trembling fingers over the enchanted lock of the bottom drawer. The mechanism yielded at once, the drawer sliding open, and he drew out the familiar stack of letters.

His hands shook as he spread them across the desk's surface, though he hardly needed to read them. He'd memorized every word, every curve of her handwriting. But he needed to see them. Needed to trace the connections, to prove to himself that this impossible thing was real.

Still standing, he pulled one of her earliest letters toward him.

I am perhaps the least brave person in all the United Fae Isles. I am shy to the point of invisibility.

She had stood before him just minutes ago, telling him almost the exact same thing. He reached for another letter, one from several months into their correspondence.

I cannot decide who I am closer to: my twin brother or my older sister.

Twin brother—Kazrian. Older sister—Rosavyn.

And then, from her most recent letter:

Certain events are unfolding in my life, events that require me to be brave, day after day.

The Crown Court. Of course. What else could demand daily bravery from someone who found social gatherings torturous?

Everything aligned perfectly, each piece slipping neatly into place—except for one thing. She'd told him explicitly that her family would not be traveling to Bloomhaven this Season. That single lie stood out like a discordant note in an otherwise perfect symphony.

But of course she'd lied.

Ryden pressed his palms against his eyes, understanding flooding through him. She'd lied for the same reason she'd stopped responding after he'd sent his desperate confession. Because he'd crossed the boundary she'd drawn between them, pushed too hard, asked for more than she was willing to give. Their carefully maintained anonymity was her shield, and he, in his desperation to know her, to make their connection real, had threatened that shield. He'd all but forced her to lie.

He leaned forward, flattening his palms on the desk, his head hanging between his shoulders as he stared down at her letters. Her beautiful, vulnerable words scattered beneath him like a map to her soul. A soul he now knew belonged to a woman named *Lady Aurelise Rowanwood.*

He wanted to go back to her immediately. He wanted to take her face in his hands and tell her he knew who she was. He wanted to thread his fingers through her hair, pull her close, brush his lips over the warmth blooming in her cheeks. He wanted—

But she did not even like him.

Her slip in the garden had been unmistakable. She'd tried to correct herself, but he'd seen the truth beneath her mortified expression. Lady Aurelise Rowanwood did not like His Royal Highness, Prince Ryden. And L, the version of herself that lived in these letters, had made it equally clear she did not want to meet R.

A groan tore from Ryden's throat, raw and frustrated. He turned and slid to the floor, his back against the desk, knees pulled up. His fingers tangled in his hair, tugging hard enough to hurt.

This was wonderful. This was terrible. This was everything he'd wanted and nothing he could have.

His mother had already dismissed Lady Aurelise as unsuitable. Her music magic too emotional, too unstable to balance his own magic. Evryn had warned him off with barely concealed threats. Even Lady Rivenna had all but promised to destroy him if he so much as distressed her granddaughter.

The entire world seemed aligned against him loving her, and she herself stood at the forefront of that opposition.

He sat there for several long minutes, his breathing gradually evening out as the initial shock began to fade. The trembling in the air around him stilled. His magic, still restless but no longer raging, settled.

This was not the end. It couldn't be. He'd been navigating the challenges of court life, had been slipping past his royal footmen and palace sentries to escape Solstice Hall for years. He'd learned long ago that every problem had a solution if one was determined enough to find it.

He pushed himself up from the floor and began to pace, his mind shifting from emotional chaos to strategic calculation. The obstacles were numerous but not insurmountable.

First, her family's opposition. They saw him as the scandalous prince, the shameless flirt who would inevitably break their precious Aurelise's heart. And why wouldn't they? He'd given them every reason to believe the worst of him.

But none of them, not even Evryn, knew him fully. They did not know the man who wrote letters late into the night, who made terrible jokes about vegetables to make a shy girl laugh. They could not know that the mere thought of causing her pain was unimaginable to him. But once they understood this, surely their objections would fade.

His mother's concerns about magical compatibility were more complex but not impossible to address. He would find a way to prove that Aurelise's music was not the unpredictable, destabilizing force his mother believed it to be. Or perhaps he'd find another solution entirely. He had weeks still. Time enough to demonstrate that his choice was the right one.

But the most significant obstacle was Aurelise herself.

She did not like Prince Ryden—the public persona, the performance he gave the world. But she did like R, the man in the letters. He'd seen evidence of her feelings scattered throughout their correspondence. The way she'd admitted to blushing at his words. The way she sometimes teased him in return, with unexpected humor that delighted him. The fact that she *wanted* to keep writing to him, still needed him in her life in some way.

She cared for him. He was almost certain of it. But she was scared—of what, exactly, he was not entirely sure. But she was so convinced she was not brave. So certain she was unsuitable for this life, for him, for anything beyond a quiet existence.

How could he prove to her that a life with him would not be the daunting reality she feared? Royal life had its burdens, to be sure—formal events where every move was watched, tedious councils, public scrutiny, and the weight of decisions affecting many lives. But it also offered real purpose: the chance to protect what mattered and change what didn't. And their true home in the Shaded Lands was nothing like the bustling court she feared. It was a place of quiet beauty with silver forests and pastel colors that shifted across the sky. She would find peace there, he was certain of it.

But first he had to convince her that she was, in fact, brave.

No, he thought as an idea began to emerge. There was no one who could convince her. This was something she had to discover for herself. Her own courage, her own strength, her own worthiness to stand beside anyone she chose.

Including, he hoped with everything inside him, a future High Lord.

Dear R,

All right then. If we are to pretend that nothing has changed between us, I suppose I should begin by addressing the more pressing matter at hand: Horatio the Judgmental Gossip Bird.

I must say, I'm relieved to know that he has taken up residence near your window. Someone needs to keep watch over your dignity, and since you've clearly abandoned that responsibility yourself, the task has fallen to our feathered friend. Please give him my regards and assure him that I, too, find your lack of self-respect deeply concerning.

(Though between us, I laugh-sobbed when your letter arrived. Horatio would have been most unimpressed.)

Now, you'll be insufferably pleased to know that I attempted your suggestion about asking whether plants have opinions about us. I committed fully to the strategy—delivered it with complete seriousness to a gentleman during what was meant to be a perfectly ordinary garden conversation.

Not only did it work, but it was perhaps TOO effective! I completely scared off the gentleman I was talking to, who quite literally fled from my presence!

It was somewhat of a relief to be left alone, I have to admit. Though perhaps also a little … humiliating? Did he really have to depart my presence with such alarming speed? One moment we were discussing roses (elderly chaperones and all), and the next he'd remembered somewhere urgent he needed to be. I've never seen anyone disappear with such haste.

So thank you, R, for that spectacularly successful bit of social advice. I am now quite certain that at least one person in the realm believes I am utterly mad.

Your friend who is apparently very good at frightening people,
L

Dearest L,

I've just had the most undignified fit of laughter at your story. Horatio, naturally, observed the scene with grave disapproval. (I'm beginning to think he may be related to your elderly ever-blooming roses.) I must, however, take issue with your interpretation of events.

This gentleman—whoever he is—either possesses exceptionally poor taste, monumentally poor judgment, or something else entirely unrelated occurred that had nothing whatsoever to do with you or your perfectly reasonable question about plants.

I have an alternative theory that might spare your ego (and mine, since I suggested the strategy). What if he wasn't fleeing from your question at all? What if, at that precise moment, he was stung by a spite gnat?

These are minuscule creatures, barely visible to the naked eye, known for their vindictive nature and poor timing. A spite gnat sting causes an immediate and overwhelming compulsion to flee the area while simultaneously developing an irrational fear of whatever one was looking at when stung. The effects last approximately three hours, during which the victim experiences an inexplicable craving for fermented acorn paste.

So you see, it likely had nothing to do with your brilliant conversational gambit and everything to do with aggressive insects with personality disorders. The gentleman is probably sitting somewhere right now, confused about why he suddenly fled, embarrassed by his behavior, and wondering why he can't stop thinking about fermented acorn paste.

I maintain that my strategy was flawless. The spite gnat was simply jealous of your wit.

Furthermore, the fact that you laugh-sobbed (a term which, I confess, is new to me but conveys a most exquisite degree of emotional chaos) when my letter arrived has made my day. Possibly my entire month. Horatio is once again scandalized. I regret nothing.

Incorrigibly yours,

R

P.S. I've been wondering, L … do you have the courage to play a game with me? I won't say what it is yet. Mystery is half the fun. You may, of course, decline … though I'll take that as an admission that you frighten easily.

Dear R,

A spite gnat? REALLY? That is the most absurd thing you've ever written to me, and that's saying something considering you once devoted an entire letter to the rumored political ambitions of gossip birds.

Though I must admit, the image of that poor gentleman sitting somewhere, inexplicably craving fermented acorn paste, does bring me considerable comfort. Perhaps you're right. Perhaps it wasn't my catastrophically awkward question after all, but rather a vindictive insect with unfortunate timing.

(You absolutely made up spite gnats. But I'm choosing to believe in them anyway because the alternative is too mortifying.)

As for your game … I should tell you no. I'm not the competitive one in my family. That honor belongs to two of my older siblings who turn EVERYTHING into a contest. I prefer to observe from a safe distance where no one expects me to participate, let alone excel.

I'm also terribly suspicious of games proposed by people who have demonstrated a concerning fondness for vegetable-related chaos. What exactly are you planning?

Though I suppose … how frightening can a game conducted entirely through letters actually be? It is not as if you can make me do anything truly mortifying. The worst that could happen is I'd have to write something embarrassing, and I've already done that countless times in our correspondence.

So yes. Fine. I'll play your mysterious game. But only because I refuse to give you the satisfaction of thinking I frighten easily.

(I do frighten easily. But you do not need to know that.)

Cautiously intrigued,

L

Chapter Twelve

The ballroom at Solstice Hall glittered like a galaxy brought to earth. Light spilled across marble floors polished to mirror perfection, laughter sparkled brighter than jewels, and distinguished guests streamed through the grand double doors as heralds announced their names, their voices melding with the hum of dozens of animated conversations.

Prince Ryden registered none of it.

His gaze swept the room in careful arcs, searching the sea of faces with singular purpose. The room might have been entirely empty for all the attention he paid to the assembled nobility of Bloomhaven. Every flash of dark hair, every glimpse of rose silk drew his eye, only to disappoint him moments later when they belonged to someone else.

Tonight marked the first official Crown Court Ball, an occasion of such magnitude that no one of consequence would dare to miss it. There had not been a Crown Court in generations, and curiosity burned bright among the gathered elite. All wished to witness firsthand the young ladies who might one day become their princess, the future Crown Consort to the High Lord.

Every glance, every subtle exchange between him and his potential brides would be dissected and discussed before the night was through. Even the gossip birds were no doubt hiding somewhere amid the towering plants and glittering floral displays, listening with rapt attention and preparing to scatter their embellished reports across Bloomhaven by morning.

He had not seen any of the Crown Court ladies since the previous afternoon. His mother had kept them sequestered for the entire day in what she'd deemed 'essential instruction in matters of state and protocol'—the start of a series of dreadfully dull lectures about trade agreements, diplomatic correspondence, and the proper order of precedence at formal dinners. He suspected it was less about preparing them to be princess and more about testing their patience and composure under tedium.

Which meant he hadn't laid eyes on Lady Aurelise—on L—since the moment in the garden when his world had tilted on its axis.

Ryden tugged absently at his high collar, uncomfortably aware of the restless energy building beneath his skin. That afternoon, he had approached his mother in her private withdrawing room, a request he had never made before poised upon his lips. He'd asked her to maintain vigilant awareness of his magic throughout the evening, to smooth any potential surges before they slipped beyond his control.

Her pale brows had drawn together in concern. "Has something occurred to unsettle your magic?"

"No. Simply …" He'd cleared his throat. "Anticipating a potentially overwhelming evening."

Understanding had dawned across her features, though mercifully she hadn't pressed for details. "I shall keep my senses attuned to any fluctuations. Should I detect the stirrings of a surge, I will do what I can to stabilize it."

Then, before he could leave, he'd swallowed his remaining pride as desperation overcame dignity, and asked if she had the strength to maintain that constant vigilance throughout the entire Season. His words had been an admission of weakness he would normally rather die than reveal. But the memory of the footman's blank stare haunted him. The thought of Lady Aurelise's eyes taking on that same emptiness, of what Ryden might accidentally compel her to do in a moment of uncontrolled magic, was unbearable. He would not risk anything happening to her.

His mother had studied him for a long moment, her gaze keen and searching, before inclining her head. "I will do everything in my power to contain any surges I detect, whenever they may arise."

He had thanked her, but expressed his concerns about this possibly exhausting her.

"This Season will exhaust us both, I suspect," she'd said. "But there will be time enough to rest when we return to the Shaded Lands."

Relief had flooded through him, though it did nothing to calm the anticipation that had been building all day. Because tonight—blessed stars, tonight—he would see his L. He would dance with her, would hold her in his arms, would feel her warmth beneath his hands.

He stood now among the glittering throng, his eyes continuing their search of the ballroom as his magic remained a restless current beneath his skin, controlled but not quite dormant.

Then the crowd shifted, a natural ebb and flow of conversation and movement, and suddenly—there. The bodies parted like a curtain drawn back, and his breath caught in his throat.

Lady Aurelise Rowanwood.

L.

Time seemed to suspend itself as his gaze locked upon her.

She wore a gown not of rose pink, as he had for some inexplicable reason been imagining, but of delicate silver-blue silk, its modest neckline edged with tiny crystals that caught the light when she moved. Her dark hair had been arranged in soft coils atop her head, with strands of tiny blue crystals woven through. Even from this distance, he could see the hesitant curve of her smile as she conversed with Lady Willow Blackbriar, her gaze frequently dropping to the floor in that characteristic shyness she had confessed to him so many times in her letters.

I am shy to the point of invisibility …

I somehow manage to choose topics so utterly tedious that I can practically see my companions' eyes glaze over with boredom …

The memory of her written words now wrapped themselves around the living, breathing woman before him. How wrong she had been. There was nothing tedious about her in the slightest. She was all the more captivating for her quietude, her shy composure a gentler kind of allure than any practiced charm.

She laughed then at something Lady Willow said, the sound carrying across the space between them. Her hand lifted to cover her mouth, as though even her laughter required concealment, and Ryden felt an absurd desire to cross the room and gently pull that hand away, to tell her nothing about her should ever be hidden.

Stars above, he needed to collect himself before approaching her.

Because of course he would approach her. He would dance with her first. Every drawing room in Bloomhaven would buzz with speculation, every gossip bird would wing through the night with urgent whispers, and his mother would most certainly question his judgment once tonight was through. But he would invent some reasonable explanation later. For now, the matter was simple: there was no other first choice but her.

Her eyes sparkled now with renewed mirth at Lady Willow's conversation, and Ryden found himself realizing he did not know their color. He had not paid close enough attention before, when she was merely Evryn's quiet sister, merely a ceremonial addition to the Crown Court. But now he needed to know.

His thoughts were interrupted by a sudden hush falling over the ballroom. The musicians ceased their playing as his mother made her entrance. She moved with grace and that quiet, instinctive command that came from the effortless use of her authority magic. Her pale blue hair cascaded in perfect waves down her back, crowned with a delicate diadem of starlight-enchanted diamonds.

The assembled nobility moved as if responding to invisible signals, the sea of silks and jewels parting in perfect synchronicity to form a path from the entrance to the dais where two thrones awaited. Ryden found himself stepping forward to meet his mother at the foot of the raised platform, his body following years of practiced protocol. Meanwhile, the Crown Court ladies glided through the crowd from various directions, arranging themselves in a perfect line to the left of the dais—ten young women displayed like rare flowers for all of Bloomhaven society to admire and assess.

"Esteemed guests," the High Lady began, her voice carrying to every corner without apparent effort, "it brings me great pleasure to welcome you to Solstice Hall for this first Crown Court Ball. We are honored to host these exceptional young ladies from some of our realm's most distinguished families this Season." She gestured elegantly toward the Crown Court ladies, who curtsied in perfect unison as all eyes turned to them.

Aurelise's cheeks flushed a becoming shade of pink under the weight of that collective gaze, and Ryden felt a subtle tightening low in his chest. She was too beautiful to look away from, standing out among the ten of them like the first blush of dawn breaking through a sky still heavy with stars.

"His Highness will now open the dancing by selecting his first partner for the evening."

The moment felt impossibly significant as Ryden turned to face the ten Crown Court ladies. His palms were damp within his gloves. His pulse had abandoned all sense of decorum. He drew in a steadying breath, and, with deliberate strides that betrayed none of his inner turmoil, he crossed the space directly toward Aurelise.

The surprise on her face was almost comical. Her eyes widened, her lips parting slightly, and that enchanting blush spread across her cheeks like watercolor bleeding across parchment. She looked as though she wanted to glance behind herself to confirm he wasn't actually approaching someone else.

He stopped before her and bowed. Then he straightened, extended his gloved hand toward her, palm upward in invitation, and felt the collective weight of a hundred curious gazes upon them.

"Lady Aurelise, would you do me the honor of this dance?"

His voice came out steadier than he felt, which was no small wonder considering his heart was attempting to beat its way out of his chest.

L. He was about to take L's hand in his.

How many times had he imagined this moment? How many sleepless nights had he spent wondering what it would feel like to touch her, to hold her, to hear her voice at last, shaped around words meant only for him?

For a breathless moment, she simply stared at his offered hand, clearly bewildered by his choice after his assurances in the garden that he had no interest in selecting her as his bride. Then her gaze slid up to meet his—dove-gray, he realized, the soft color of winter mist and gentle rain—before she carefully placed her gloved fingers upon his palm.

Disappointment fluttered briefly at the barrier of silk and kid leather between them. How he longed to feel her skin against his, to discover if it was as soft as he imagined. But this—this tentative touch—was enough for now.

His fingers curled around hers, and his heart made another valiant effort to leap free of his chest. How utterly ridiculous he had become. He, with all his experience among ladies, now found himself trembling like an untried youth at the mere touch of a gloved hand. If anyone had suggested a year ago that Prince Ryden might one day be rendered breathless by such innocent contact, he would have laughed himself hoarse at the absurdity.

Yet here he stood, utterly transformed by her presence, by the knowledge of who she was. He held her gaze, unable to look away, drinking in the sight of her—the delicate curve of her jaw, the unguarded softness of her lips, the confusion in those gray eyes.

She looked down quickly, breaking the connection, and he remembered that he was meant to be dancing with her, not standing there like a besotted fool.

He guided her to the center of the ballroom floor, where they turned to face one another. She kept her gaze carefully lowered, her lips pressed together in what might have been nervousness or determination. When she finally placed her hand upon his shoulder, he felt the slight tremor in her fingers, and it endeared her to him even more.

His hand should have settled at the proper position on her back—the middle. Instead, it found itself lower, his palm curving against the small of her back. He allowed himself the briefest indulgence, the faint slide of gloved fingers as his hand traced upward to its proper place. A mere moment, the smallest of improprieties, and mercifully, she seemed not to notice.

Then the truth of this moment struck him anew: this was *her*. L. Here within the circle of his arms, warm and real and heartbreakingly near. The exquisite reality of her threatened to overwhelm him entirely, and he drew in a steadying breath, forcing his racing thoughts toward some semblance of composure.

The musicians began to play, and he guided her into the first steps of the dance.

L, he longed to whisper, that single letter that had become so precious to him. A sudden curiosity flared—why that particular initial? Was there a second name hidden beneath her formal title? Or had she, in her determination to remain unknown, simply plucked a letter from the air, creating distance even in that small choice?

"Your Highness," she said, her voice so soft he had to lean closer to hear her, a privilege he was in no hurry to forfeit. "I confess I find myself rather confused by your selection."

He managed his usual teasing smile, though it felt strained around the edges. "Does it surprise you so greatly that I might wish to dance with you first?"

A faint crease appeared between her brows. "To be entirely honest, yes. You assured me yesterday that …" She faltered, her gaze flicking over his shoulder as other couples began to take their places on the floor, clearly unwilling for anyone to overhear precisely what he had assured her—though such a risk was laughably small given how softly she spoke. "Well, after our conversation …"

"After our conversation yesterday," he said, keeping his tone pitched just low enough to reassure her of their privacy, "I feel as though we are both … liberated. We may converse honestly, without the tedious pretense of courtship that burdens my interactions with the others."

"I see," she said, though her expression suggested she was not entirely convinced. "Then is this perhaps … a strategic maneuver? A means of increasing interest among the other Crown Court ladies? Because I can assure you, Your Highness, such tactics are entirely unnecessary. They already regard you with utmost admiration."

He laughed, the sound easing the tightness in his chest as he settled more comfortably into their exchange, though every inch of him still tingled with awareness of how close she stood. "No, Lady Aurelise. I merely wished to dance with someone whose company I found agreeable yesterday, despite your determined efforts to convince me of your unsuitability."

"Ah." She fell silent for a moment, her attention seemingly focused on the pattern of their steps. Then, with visible hesitation: "Might I inquire about your rather … abrupt departure yesterday? I hope I did not cause offense with my peculiar questions about opinionated flora."

The reminder of that moment—when her innocent words had revealed her true identity—sent another jolt of awareness through him. "Not at all," he assured her. "In fact, I found your observations quite charming."

Her cheeks flushed anew at that, and she glanced up at him with a flicker of uncertainty still lingering in her gaze. "You seemed almost … unsettled," she persisted. "As if something had disturbed you greatly."

"I recalled an urgent matter requiring my attention," he said, which was, in a sense, true. The surge of magic that had roared through him in that moment had indeed demanded his urgent and immediate retreat. How desperately he wished to tell her everything—that he was R, that he had recognized her, that his heart belonged to her completely. But he suspected she would not respond favorably right now to this revelation. "It was nothing you said, I assure you."

She nodded but offered no reply, her gaze fixing somewhere near his shoulder. Her eyes darted in small, nervous movements as she studied a region of his jacket with unwarranted fascination. Her lips parted slightly, as if preparing for speech, only to press together again in silent resignation. He recognized the struggle instantly. She had described this very predicament in her letters. The paralyzing search for proper conversation, the words that refused to come. He cast his mind swiftly through their correspondence, seeking a subject she might find comfortable enough to discuss.

In that very first letter, she had spoken of her manifestation. She hadn't revealed the exact nature of her magic, but she'd said that the thing she once treasured above all else, her one true solace when the world grew too loud, had become the very thing that overwhelmed her.

Music.

He guided her through a turn, his hand steady at her back as she moved gracefully beneath his touch. "Your demonstration at the Opening Ball was nothing short of magnificent," he said as she faced him once more. "Have you always loved creating music?"

"Oh." That delightful flush in her cheeks deepened, her gaze dropping to where her hand rested in his, as if his praise was too direct a light to face. "I—thank you. Yes, I ..." She hesitated, each word carefully chosen, but as she continued, her voice gained confidence. "The pianoforte has been my companion since childhood. When I play, it is as if ... well, as if I am in another world entirely. Everything else falls away. All the tension inside me releases. The overwhelm of the real world disappears, and I can finally breathe."

"The overwhelm of the real world," he repeated softly, committing this new detail to memory, another precious addition to the collection of things he already knew about her.

She must have misread something in his expression, for she dipped her head and rushed to add, "Oh, I know it sounds foolish. My world ought not to be overwhelming. My life has been nothing but comfort and privilege. A loving family, beautiful homes, every advantage one could possibly want. Such a life should not feel so very difficult to manage."

He paused, regarding her for a moment with quiet contemplation before replying. "The fact that your feelings don't align with your circumstances does not make them any less real. Our emotions follow their own logic, not the logic others might impose upon them."

Her eyes widened as they returned to his, surprise evident in every feature, as if understanding was the last thing she had expected from him.

"What is it that you find so overwhelming?" he asked.

"Oh, well …"

"Only if you wish to share," he added, though his heart ached to know more, to understand the depths that lay beneath her careful reserve, to discover what kept her hidden away from the connection that had flourished between them in their letters.

She drew in a breath, her lips parting as if ready to reveal something important, but then the music drew to a close, and he was forced to release her, stepping back to bow as she curtsied.

The separation felt like physical pain, a severance of something vital. Already he was calculating how many dances must pass, how many other partners he must endure, before he might reasonably claim her hand again without causing unseemly gossip. He yearned not only for her nearness, but for the unspoken words still hanging between them.

"Thank you for the dance, Lady Aurelise," he managed to say.

"Thank you, Your Highness." She slipped away, her silver-blue gown disappearing among the crowd as she retreated to where her family waited at the ballroom's edge.

Her family.

His stomach plummeted like a stone dropped from a great height. Aurelise's face brightened visibly as she reached her sister, clasping Miss Rosavyn's hands in hers while their mother bent close, lips moving in what was surely a torrent of whispered questions. And there, just beyond them—

Ah. Evryn stared across the ballroom, his gaze locking with Ryden's in a look that mingled disbelief and unmistakable warning. And beside him—oh, good stars. Lady Rivenna Rowanwood herself, wearing the expression of a woman calculating precisely how many ways she might ruin him without technically committing treason.

Splendid. Ryden had, of course, entirely neglected to account for that particular consequence when deciding to approach Lady Aurelise before any other Crown Court lady tonight. Naturally her family would be present along with every other distinguished household in Bloomhaven. He would have anticipated this had his mind not been entirely consumed by the earth-shattering revelation of her identity.

He offered Evryn a grin that was equal parts apology and mischief, accompanied by a jaunty wave, before turning smartly away. He could only hope Aurelise would convince her formidable kin that he had already disavowed any interest in her before her grandmother devised a suitably elegant method of ending his existence. He needed more time to convince them all that he was worthy of her.

His mother was watching him now, the tilt of her head conveying a very specific, very pointed expectation. Ryden drew a slow breath, straightened his shoulders, and crossed the floor toward Lady Olivienne for the next dance.

But even as he led the raven-haired beauty onto the floor, his thoughts remained fixed on Aurelise. On L. His mind turned to the idea that had been taking shape in his mind over the past day. A delicious game, a challenge crafted to draw her out from behind the careful walls she had built around herself, and to help her discover the courage she refused to believe she possessed.

She would be horrified, of course. Would most certainly attempt to refuse. But he believed he could convince her, could appeal to that side of her nature that was not quite as demure as she led everyone, including herself, to believe. That quiet spark of mischief that emerged in her letters when she thought no one but he was watching.

He turned Lady Olivienne through a complicated series of steps, his smile automatic while his mind continued weaving plans. The real pleasure of this Season was only just beginning.

Chapter Thirteen

THE DARE LIST

(To be undertaken by Lady L, under no duress whatsoever, except perhaps that of curiosity)

1. *stargaze from a roof*
2. *explore somewhere new and bring back evidence*
3. *flirt with someone*
4. *get rain-soaked on purpose*
5. *keep your eyes up for an entire gathering*
6. *tell someone no*
7. *stand up for someone who cannot stand up for themselves*
8. *take a midnight swim*
9. *smoke driftshade leaf*
10. *be entirely improper*
11. *speak your mind to someone who scares you*
12. *kiss someone*

Completion of each task will result in excessive self-discovery, unanticipated confidence, and my eternal admiration.

Signed,

R — Architect of Questionable Ideas and Occasional Triumphs

P.S. No gossip birds were harmed in the making of this list, though one did call it 'boldly optimistic.'

P.P.S. Before you begin composing a thousand excuses as to why you cannot possibly complete this list (I see you eyeing dare number six), allow me to save you the trouble: it is far too late. You've already agreed, and as such, I am taking you at your word. Yes, I am perfectly aware that these dares range from mildly improper to utterly indefensible. Nevertheless, I have every confidence you will find a way.

P.P.P.S. If, however, any of these prove truly distressing, you are not required to complete them. In truth, you are not required to complete ANY of them. But I suspect, deep down, that there is a very small, very curious part of you that rather wants to.

"No," Aurelise said aloud to the silence of her bed chamber. "Absolutely not."

She paced the length of her suite, R's latest letter crumpled slightly in one hand. The timebloom she'd brought from home sat on her bedside table, its petals shifting from lavender toward silver, indicating that it was close to midnight. She should have been asleep already, but after a day spent resting from the previous night's Crown Court Ball, she was nowhere near tired. Instead, she found herself wearing a path in the plush carpet, her bare feet silent against its softness, her nightgown swishing with each agitated turn.

A dare list. He had sent her a *dare list.*

She stopped, smoothed the paper against her palm, and read it again, though she'd already memorized every outrageous suggestion:

Stargaze from a roof.

Well, that seemed harmless enough, if rather impractical. Why did it have to be from a *roof,* of all places? And how was she to manage such a thing—both physically and without being discovered and sent home in disgrace?

Explore somewhere new and bring back evidence.

Vague, but manageable perhaps.

Flirt with someone.

Her cheeks heated at the mere thought. She could barely manage ordinary conversation without stammering. How was she meant to *flirt*?

Smoke driftshade leaf.

"Absolutely not," she muttered again, her voice rising slightly in indignation. Driftshade leaf was what rakish gentlemen smoked in enchanted gaming parlors where illusionary dice rolled and fortunes unraveled at the turn of a card. Or so she had been told. The very idea of a lady partaking in such an activity was beyond scandalous.

Kiss someone.

The paper trembled in her hands. Kiss someone? *Kiss someone?* Had R taken complete leave of his senses?

"Of course I cannot do these things!" she exclaimed to the empty room. "The sheer impropriety of even suggesting—"

OH MY STARS, WHAT IS HAPPENING? Thimble's voice burst into her mind as the tiny pink mouse zoomed into the air from somewhere behind her. *Lady Aurelise, why are you SHOUTING? Is there danger? Should I alert the palace guards?*

"I—you—when did you come in?" Aurelise stammered, instinctively pressing the letter to her chest.

I've been napping in your slipper, Thimble admitted cheerfully. *It's perfect for curling up in. So cozy!*

Spark's grumpy head appeared over the arm of one of the chairs in the sitting area, his amber eyes narrowed with sleep. *Some of us were trying to get a moment's peace,* he growled, a wisp of smoke curling from his nostrils.

"Oh, you're—also here."

Thimble's sister snores like a hibernating troll, Spark explained dryly. *She couldn't sleep, but was too frightened to navigate the palace's secret corridors alone at night. So naturally, she woke me.* He flicked his tail and added with a knowing glance, *I'd have thought you'd notice us come in, but you seemed rather … preoccupied. Lying atop your bed, eyes fixed on that curious wooden box you were all but snuggling.*

"I was not *snuggling* the—"

What is that? Thimble zipped closer, her tiny eyes bright with curiosity. *Is that a LETTER? At this hour? How deliciously improper!*

"It's nothing," Aurelise said hastily, attempting to fold the paper as she made to move toward her dressing table, but Thimble was already hovering directly in front of her face, wings beating frantically.

It doesn't look like nothing! You're all flushed and pacing and muttering about impropriety! This is the most exciting thing that's happened since Lady Ellowa's gown caught fire at the ball last night!

Which I'd like to point out once again I had ABSOLUTELY nothing to do with, Spark added.

"It's merely a … a bit of correspondence," Aurelise said weakly.

At midnight? Spark's golden eyes narrowed. *From whom? How did it arrive here? I didn't notice any messenger pixies at the door.*

Aurelise sighed. "It arrived via the enchanted wooden box you seem to think I was *snuggling.* And it's from a—a friend."

A friend who has you pacing your chambers and declaring things absolutely not? Thimble squeaked with delight. *This friend sounds FASCINATING! What did they write? Can we see?*

Aurelise clutched the letter to her chest once more. "Certainly not. It's private correspondence."

Private correspondence that has you in such a state? Spark puffed a small cloud of glittery smoke. *Now I'm intrigued despite myself. It wouldn't happen to be from a certain prince who selected you for the first dance of the evening last night, would it?*

"No, of course not!" A letter from the prince himself would have been almost as shocking as the outrageous Dare List R had sent.

Well, Thimble said, settling on Aurelise's shoulder, *if you won't show us, at least tell us what has you so distressed. We are your companions, after all. We're here to help.*

Aurelise sank onto the edge of her bed, the fight going out of her. Perhaps it would help to have someone—or rather, two someones—to discuss this absolute madness with. "It's a list of dares," she admitted quietly.

A list of dares? Spark's mental voice sounded appropriately horrified. *Someone has sent you a list of DARES?*

"Yes."

Can we see it now? Thimble asked, vibrating with barely contained excitement.

With a sigh of resignation, Aurelise smoothed the letter on the bed beside her where both companions could see it. She watched as they read, Thimble's wings fluttering faster with each line while Spark's expression grew increasingly horrified.

KISS SOMEONE? Thimble shrieked in Aurelise's mind, launching herself into an ecstatic aerial loop. *Oh, this is WONDERFUL! This is ROMANTIC! This is—*

This is completely inappropriate, Spark interrupted, breathing out an particularly impressive cloud of glittery smoke. *Smoke driftshade leaf? Take a midnight swim? Be entirely improper? Lady Aurelise, whoever sent this is clearly attempting to compromise your reputation. Should you be discovered undertaking almost any of these activities, you would be removed from the Crown Court immediately. Your family would be scandalized. The gossip birds would feast upon your disgrace for years.*

"I know", Aurelise said miserably. "Which is why I cannot possibly—"

But you COULD do some of them! Thimble interjected, landing beside the letter and pointing at the first item with a tiny paw. *Stargazing! That's perfectly innocent! And exploring somewhere new—that's just adventure! Oh, and speaking your mind—you should absolutely do that one. You're far too quiet all the time.*

"I am appropriately reserved," Aurelise protested.

You're practically mute in company, Spark corrected. *Though that's generally preferable to the inane chatter most people produce. Still, this list is clearly the work of someone trying to lead you astray. Who is this 'R' person?*

Aurelise's fingers twisted nervously in the folds of her nightgown. "A friend. Well, I don't actually know who he is, but—"

HE! Thimble interjected with a mental squeal.

"—but we've been corresponding for some time," Aurelise finished.

Let me understand this correctly, Spark said slowly. *You've been corresponding with a complete stranger who has now sent you a list of increasingly scandalous dares, and you're actually considering completing them?*

"No! I mean … no, of course not. I couldn't possibly …" But even as she spoke, Aurelise found her gaze drawn back to the first item on the list. Stargazing from a roof. It was the least scandalous of all the suggestions. Almost innocent, really. And the night was clear …

You're thinking about it, Thimble accused, delight coloring her mental voice. *You're actually considering it! Oh, we should start with that one! Right now!*

"Now?" Aurelise squeaked. "It's almost midnight!"

Perfect timing for stargazing! Thimble countered. *And I know just the place. The sky garden! On the eastern wing's uppermost level. It's essentially a rooftop terrace, almost hidden and very much out of the way, with magical flowers and glowing fountain stones and the most PERFECT view of the stars!*

Absolutely not, Spark interjected firmly. *We are not assisting our lady in sneaking through the palace in the dead of night to complete questionable dares from mysterious correspondents.*

"No, of course not," Aurelise agreed, but her fingers traced the words on the paper. "I suppose," she said slowly, "stargazing isn't inherently improper. And if this sky garden is as secluded as you say ..."

Perfectly secluded! Thimble assured her.

She glanced at the letter again, at R's teasing postscript about her inevitable excuses. Something in his words—that frustrating, knowing certainty about her character—pricked at her pride. "Very well," she decided suddenly. "Just this once. Just the first dare. If only to prove to R that I'm not quite as predictable as he believes."

ADVENTURE! Thimble squealed, zooming around the room in victorious circles.

Disaster, more likely, Spark muttered, but Aurelise noticed he was already moving toward the door. *If we really are doing this, then you'll need to wear something more substantial than your nightgown.*

Aurelise glanced down at herself, mortification washing through her anew. "Oh! Yes, of course." She hurried to the sitting area and caught up her shawl from the back of one of the chairs. She pulled it close around her shoulders, its fringe brushing her bare ankles as she moved to the door.

Your hair, Spark observed critically. *It looks like you've been wrestling with your pillows.*

Aurelise reached up to find her braid had indeed come largely undone, dark strands falling around her shoulders in disarray. She attempted to smooth it back, but without proper pins or ribbons, there was little to be done.

Leave it! Thimble insisted. *You look romantically disheveled! Like the heroine of a gothic novel!*

"I daresay that is hardly the impression a lady of quality ought to cultivate," Aurelise muttered, pulling the shawl tighter around herself. "Now, how exactly does one sneak through a palace?"

As it turned out, sneaking through a palace with two magical companions who knew every servant's routine, every guard's rotation, and every creaking floorboard to avoid was surprisingly manageable. Thimble flew ahead, scouting for any late-night wanderers, while Spark provided a running commentary on the architectural history of various corridors, apparently finding the whole endeavor beneath his dignity but participating nonetheless.

Behind a heavy tapestry depicting some ancient dance of the fae, they found a narrow doorway and a spiraling stair beyond. The air was cool and faintly dusty, the walls broken here and there by narrow windows that let in slivers of starlight. Aurelise gathered her nightgown in one hand, her other hand still clutching the dare list letter as she wound her way upward.

Finally, Thimble whispered, *Here!* and Aurelise looked up to see a door of weathered wood, its surface inlaid with tiny panes of colored glass. The brass latch was cool beneath her fingers. She pushed it open and stepped out onto—

"Oh," she breathed, wonder temporarily eclipsing her anxiety.

Before her stretched a hidden sanctuary in the sky, intimate and enchanting. Stone paths wound between raised beds where flowers unfurled faintly luminescent petals. The gentle trickle of water drew her attention to a small fountain carved from pale stone that seemed to glow beneath the starlight, and beyond it sat a weathered stone bench near the terrace railing, offering an unobstructed view of both the palace gardens and the night sky.

And the stars … Aurelise tilted her head back, her lips parting in awe. Thousands upon thousands of stars scattered across the velvet darkness, some burning bright and steady, others flickering like distant candles. The constellation of the Silver Swan spread its wings directly above her, while the Archer's Arrow pointed toward the horizon.

She took a few steps forward, still gazing up, overwhelmed by the vastness of it all. Here, finally, was something larger than her anxieties, older than her fears, more eternal than—

A soft sound behind her made her freeze. The creak of a door, a footstep on stone.

She spun around, her heart leaping into her throat, and in her startled panic, her foot caught on the edge of the path. She teetered for one terrible moment between balance and catastrophe before pitching sideways into a flowerbed with a startled cry. The letter flew from her hand as she crashed into a cluster of luminous blooms, their petals bursting into showers of silver sparks upon impact.

"My lady?"

The voice—masculine, familiar, and far too amused—confirmed her worst fears before she even raised her mortified gaze. Prince Ryden stood over her, moonlight silvering his midnight-blue hair and catching on the elegant lines of what appeared to be a riding jacket. She'd seen Evryn in similar gear in the past, returning from what he believed to be his secret late-night pegasus rides.

The prince extended a hand to assist her, but Aurelise was already scrambling to her feet, brushing frantically at the silver pollen that now dusted her nightgown and shawl.

"Your Highness," she stammered, flushing so deeply she feared her face might permanently retain the color. "I didn't—that is—I was merely—" She cast about desperately for a plausible explanation for her presence, her state of undress, and her graceless dive into the sky garden flowerbeds.

"Taking the night air?" he suggested helpfully, his lips curved in that infuriatingly charming smile.

"Well, I …"

The words died in her throat as she watched Prince Ryden bend to retrieve something from among the crushed blossoms. Her heart plummeted as she recognized the somewhat crumpled sheet of paper, now lightly dusted with luminescent pollen.

"I believe you dropped this," he said, his gaze dropping to the paper as he straightened.

"Thank you," she managed, reaching for it with frantic haste.

But he didn't immediately relinquish the letter. Instead, his brow furrowed slightly, his attention caught by what was clearly visible at the top of the page. "The Dare List?" he read aloud, his voice lilting with newfound interest.

Aurelise briefly contemplated throwing herself over the garden railing. Surely death would be kinder than this particular humiliation.

"Forgive me," he said, finally extending the letter toward her. "I couldn't help but notice some of the contents." The corner of his mouth quirked upward as she snatched the paper from his hand. "I must say, you are perhaps the last person I might have guessed to be in possession of something so … spirited."

Her mortification deepened to catastrophic levels. A muffled squeak of woodwinds fluttered briefly around them before she clamped down on the wayward magic with desperate force. "I—well—it isn't what it looks like."

A flicker of confusion passed over his face, his gaze shifting briefly past her in search of the sound's origin, before returning to her, his smile resettling with practiced ease. "Isn't it?"

"Of course not," she said, lifting her chin slightly and meeting his gaze despite the heat in her cheeks. "Such activities would be most unbecoming of a lady. I have no interest in dares."

He lifted a brow, expression openly skeptical. "No interest? Then I must be hallucinating. For it appears to me that you are presently standing atop the summer palace, in the middle of the night, dressed for bed, and attempting —what was it?—ah, yes. To stargaze from a roof."

Her cheeks burned hotter. "You saw that particular item?"

His lips curved fully into that devastating smile. "I must confess I saw the entire list."

If it were possible to perish from mortification, Aurelise would have expired on the spot. Her hands trembled as she folded the letter, her gaze darting about in search of Thimble and Spark. Her coconspirators, it seemed, had vanished most conveniently. How fortunate for them not to be the ones found in so undignified a position.

"I'm quite intrigued by the third item on the list," he continued. "Flirt with someone? How delightfully scandalous, Lady Aurelise."

"That certainly will not be happening," she said firmly, though her voice came out rather breathier than intended.

"Why ever not?" he asked, his tone all innocent mischief. "You could practice with me. I'm exceptionally good at it."

She could only stare, momentarily robbed of speech. Surely he had not just said that aloud.

He tilted his head, the glimmer of mischief never dimming, his lips curving into a smile that was equal parts charm and suggestion. "I could assist you with item number twelve as well."

That, at least, shocked words from her. "I certainly won't—there will be no—I am a lady of good breeding!" The words came out in an embarrassing splutter, accompanied by the faint but decidedly erratic twang of startled harp strings. "I will most certainly not be *kissing* anyone!"

"Hmm. Pity." If he'd heard the music, he chose to ignore it this time. He looked thoughtful now instead, though the wicked gleam remained in his eyes. "I'm curious who gave you this list. Clearly someone who believes you might, under the right circumstances, be willing to kiss someone." He paused, brows lifting slightly, his smile deepening into deliberate speculation. "Or perhaps someone who hopes to be the *recipient* of this kiss?"

She clutched the letter tighter. "I believe I should return to my chambers, Your Highness. If someone were to discover—"

"Oh, no, please stay." The teasing edge vanished from his tone, replaced by something quieter, earnest. His expression softened, all trace of mischief gone. "Forgive me, Lady Aurelise. I did not mean to make you uncomfortable." He inclined his head slightly, the picture of contrition. "Please do not let my impertinence drive you away. The stars are particularly beautiful tonight, and I would be honored if you would remain a little longer to admire them."

She blinked. "With … with you?"

"Yes, with me." He gestured to the stone bench, his smile almost gentle, stripped of its earlier trace of mischief.

"But that would be most improper! We are alone, without a chaperone. If someone were to discover us—"

"We are not alone," he pointed out. "Your delightful companions are here."

Aurelise turned to follow his gaze, and there, at the base of the stone fountain, sat Thimble and Spark, both of them apparently having borne silent witness to the entire exchange.

Though the High Lady had instructed her and the other ladies to treat their companions with the same respect they would give any other member of their household staff, Aurelise doubted the creatures truly fulfilled the traditional role of chaperones tasked with preserving decorum between young people. Still, she didn't wish to offend them.

"Does that … count?" she asked tentatively.

Of course it does! Thimble's enthusiastic voice rang in her mind.

Most certainly not, Spark countered simultaneously.

Prince Ryden laughed, a warm, genuine sound. "I agree with Thimble."

Aurelise started. "You heard them?"

"They can choose who to direct their inner voices toward. Either of us individually, or both." He gestured toward the bench again. "Come. I give you my word, no one will find us here. And I assure you that in spite of my earlier enthusiasm for dares of a scandalous nature, I have not the slightest intention of compromising your virtue. You are safe with me, Lady Aurelise."

She tilted her head slightly, studying him with clear suspicion that softened—just barely—into reluctant amusement. Then, against her better judgment, she found herself following him to the bench. She sat at the farthest possible edge, ensuring a proper amount of space between them, and pulled her shawl more tightly around herself. Despite the mild evening air, the stone was cold through the thin fabric of her nightgown, and she shivered slightly.

Without a word, Prince Ryden leaned forward, brushing his fingers along the paving beneath the bench. A soft shimmer of magic stirred the air, and the stone itself seemed to sigh, revealing a small recess where none had been a moment before. From within, he drew out a neatly folded blanket.

Aurelise blinked. "You keep blankets hidden beneath garden furniture?"

His mouth curved. "Only the most essential of comforts. The evenings grow cooler later in the Season, toward the end of summer." He rose. "If you'll stand a moment?"

Bewildered but compliant, she rose to her feet. He spread the blanket carefully across the bench, letting part of it drape over the backrest, then motioned for her to sit once more. When she did, he lifted the remaining length and settled it lightly around her shoulders. He was close for only a few moments, but his scent enveloped her nonetheless, warm cedar and fresh oakmoss. Strangely steadying when she still expected him to smell more like mischief and poor decisions.

"There. Much better." He resumed his place at the opposite end of the bench, ensuring a proper distance between the two of them.

For a moment, they sat in silence, both gazing upward. Despite her acute awareness of his presence—the way he lounged against the bench with casual elegance—Aurelise found herself relaxing incrementally. The stars demanded attention, and their steady light soothed something restless within her.

"They're different in the Shaded Lands," Prince Ryden said quietly.

She glanced at him, curiosity overcoming shyness. "The stars?"

"Everything, really. But yes, the stars. We're much farther north there, you see. The constellations appear at different angles, and there are some you can only see from there. The Dancing Dragon, for instance, never rises here. While there, one cannot see the Silver Swan."

"Oh." For a moment, her mind went blank, that familiar flutter of panic rising. How did one ever know the right thing to say to keep a conversation going? The silence stretched, but he didn't seem troubled by it, merely waiting with that easy composure of his as he continued staring at the sky.

She forced herself to breathe, to think, to catch hold of a single sensible thread she might follow from what he'd said. "What else is different there?"

"Hmm. It's … peaceful. Compared to the pace of the Bloom Season, it feels as thought everything moves more slowly there. The seasons blend into one another rather than changing abruptly. In high summer, the sun barely sets—just skims along the horizon for hours, painting everything in gold and rose. In winter, the aurora dances across the sky in colors that don't exist anywhere else. And the old enchantments woven through the Shaded Lands keep the air temperate, the storms gentle, the balance ever constant. Nothing harsh or extreme."

"Does it rain there?" she asked, surprising herself by having a question ready without even knowing it was coming. A foolish question, perhaps, but it seemed suddenly important. There was nothing quite like the comfort of being indoors while rain whispered against the windows, soft and steady as a lullaby.

The prince smiled, gaze still turned toward the stars. "It does."

A few quiet moments passed in companionable stillness, and to her surprise, Aurelise found herself relaxing further. This was not nearly as dreadful as she had imagined.

Then the prince turned his head, his gaze settling on her with quiet curiosity. "That music earlier," he said. "It was you, wasn't it?"

Ah. So much for feeling at ease. Heat crept back into her cheeks at once. She looked skyward, as though the constellations might offer rescue. "Yes," she admitted at last. "That was me." A small pause. "It's rather mortifying, really. I am still learning to control it."

"I found it quite remarkable," he countered. "How delightful to have one's life accompanied by music. As if the world itself were keeping time with you."

She glanced at him sidelong, uncertain whether to be flattered or exasperated. "I fail to see what's so *delightful* about one's own emotions announcing themselves to everyone within earshot, Your Highness."

His laugh came softly, warm enough to melt any sting. "I do so enjoy it when you tell me precisely what you think. You ought to do it more often. It's one of your dares, isn't it?"

She blinked, thinking back to the list. "Speak my mind to someone who scares me?" Tilting her head, she considered him for a beat. "Do you suppose I may cross that one off tonight?"

His smile deepened, eyes alight with challenge. "Certainly not. I don't scare you."

"You—" She caught herself before the word 'do' could slip from her tongue, realizing it wasn't true. No, he did not frighten her. Fluster her, confuse her, make her blush until even her thoughts felt pink—yes. But scare her? No.

She pulled her gaze away from his, focusing again on the stars above. "I should go," she said softly. "It's very late."

"Early, technically," he corrected, but he stood when she did, moving to gather up the blanket while she readjusted the shawl around herself.

He stepped aside, allowing her to precede him as they crossed the terrace toward the door. Thimble darted gleefully about her in quick, sparkling circles, while Spark followed at a slower, more dignified glide.

At the threshold, Prince Ryden reached past her to open the door. "Good night, Lady Aurelise," he murmured. Then that roguish smile curved his lips once more. "Do let me know when you're ready to attempt any further dares. I would be *delighted* to assist."

Dear R for Reprehensible,

A dare list? A DARE LIST? I cannot believe your audacity. Kiss someone? Smoke driftshade leaf? Be entirely improper? Have you taken complete leave of your senses?

These are not the suggestions of a friend but rather of someone determined to see me utterly ruined. I can only imagine the satisfied expression on your face as you drafted such outrageous proposals, secure in the knowledge that I would be properly affronted.

Well, congratulations. I am thoroughly scandalized.

And yet …

You'll be intolerably pleased to know that I completed dare number one. Yes, I actually climbed to a rooftop and gazed at the stars. Though 'climbed' suggests far more athleticism than was actually involved. There was a perfectly serviceable staircase.

I would like to say I accomplished this with grace and poise, but that would be entirely false. In fact, I managed to make a complete fool of myself by tumbling backward into a bed of luminous flowers when startled. Yes, the easiest and least embarrassing item on your list, and I still managed to thoroughly humiliate myself. Thank you for that, R.

The stars, however, were magnificent. Thousands upon thousands scattered across the darkness like diamonds on midnight velvet. The Silver Swan was particularly clear tonight.

And while gazing upward, a thought occurred to me. For the first time since our correspondence began, I wondered if we can see the same stars.

You mentioned once that you live beyond the United Fae Isles. How far, exactly? Far enough that our night skies differ? I find myself suddenly curious whether you can see the Silver Swan or if entirely different constellations watch over you.

I still maintain that the majority of your list is absolutely outrageous and entirely unbecoming of a lady. I have half a mind to burn it and pretend I never saw such scandalous suggestions.

But I suppose I should admit … stargazing wasn't entirely terrible.

Still trying to recover my dignity,

L

Dearest L,

You did it! YOU DID IT! Forgive me for shouting in a letter, but I'm simply beside myself with delight. You have no idea how widely I'm smiling right now.

I confess, I half expected you to tear the list into tiny pieces and never write to me again. The fact that you not only kept it but actually completed the very first dare fills me with disproportionate joy. Even if it was, as you pointed out, the least scandalous option available.

As for your embarrassment, you have my sincerest apologies for the incident, though I confess, the idea of you toppling into a bed of luminous flowers does possess a certain charm.

But may I point out something of critical importance? You apparently survived! Your world did not end. Your reputation remains intact. And I suspect, beneath your protests and embarrassment, you feel rather pleased with yourself. There's a particular satisfaction in doing something unexpected, isn't there? In stepping just slightly outside the careful boundaries you've drawn around yourself?

I wonder if this might make it easier for you to attempt a slightly more challenging dare next. Whatever appeals to you. You need not complete them in order, you know. Though I would advise against starting with number twelve. That seems like something to work up to. (Though I remain endlessly curious about who might be fortunate enough to receive such attention from you.)

Exceedingly proud of your bravery (and eagerly awaiting your next dare),

R

P.S. What a strange coincidence—I found myself gazing at the Silver Swan tonight too. It appears the same constellations watch over us both.

Chapter Fourteen

"FURTHERMORE," THE HIGH LADY ANNOUNCED, HER VOICE CARRYING across the Blue Parlor with that effortless command that made even the most casual observation feel like royal decree, "each of you shall host an afternoon tea during your residence at Solstice Hall."

Aurelise felt her teacup nearly slip against her gloved fingers. She hastily steadied it and set it down on its saucer with a delicate chime of porcelain on porcelain, hoping no one had noticed the momentary lapse in composure. Host a tea? An entire event where she would be expected to preside, to converse, to be the center of attention?

She had, of course, been *prepared* for such things. From the time she was old enough to coax a teapot's magic into pouring smoothly, she had assisted her mother in a hundred small ways, arranging flowers, planning menus, overseeing the servants' placement of silver and china, even advising on seating when family friends came to dine.

But as for the parts that required *actual engagement*—greeting guests, ensuring introductions were made, sustaining the gentle current of conversation—those duties had always fallen to Rosavyn. Her sister, though not yet officially out due to her lack of manifestation, possessed a careless confidence that drew people to her with effortless ease. Their mother's anxious glances had never tamed her, and Aurelise had long admired that unshakable confidence from a safer distance. But now she was to orchestrate an entire event on her own?

The Blue Parlor, which had moments before felt perfectly pleasant with its cerulean silk walls and silver-threaded curtains, now seemed to shrink around her. What should have been a pleasant enough afternoon gathering—the Crown Court ladies taking tea with the High Lady while being acquainted with the Season's forthcoming engagements—had transformed into something far more daunting.

"Oh, how delightful!" Lady Coravelle exclaimed from her position on a nearby settee, clasping her hands together with genuine enthusiasm. "I've always adored hosting gatherings!"

Of course she had, Aurelise thought miserably. Lady Coravelle probably emerged from the womb knowing precisely how to flutter about a room making everyone feel attended to and amused.

A gentle pressure against her arm drew her attention. Willow leaned closer, her voice pitched barely above a whisper, though it carried a thread of suppressed amusement. "She's still doing it," she murmured. "If she persists any longer, I think her face might stay that way."

Aurelise followed Willow's gaze across the room. Lady Ellowa Brightcrest sat rigidly upright upon a pale blue settee, her expression arranged into something between disdain and wounded pride. Her mouth was pressed so tightly together that it seemed her lips had forgotten their purpose entirely, and her eyes—cold and crystalline as winter glass—glittered with barely contained fury.

It was the same look Ellowa—Mariselle's dreadful elder sister—had been directing at Aurelise since they'd all gathered in the Blue Parlor that afternoon. Several of the other ladies had cast similar glances her way, though none quite so brimming with hostility as Ellowa's. All because Prince Ryden had chosen Aurelise for the opening dance at the Crown Court ball two nights prior. Apparently, more than a few of the ladies present had taken that particular moment rather personally.

"She seems quite convinced she's the obvious choice for princess," Willow whispered.

Lady Ellowa Brightcrest, the future Crown Consort? The thought sent an involuntary shudder through Aurelise. The realm would suffer under such calculating coldness, every decision filtered through that woman's particular brand of sharp-edged ambition. She almost pitied Prince Ryden at the prospect—though if he actually selected Lady Ellowa, perhaps they deserved one another.

Although, after the previous evening …

No. She pushed the thought away before it could fully form. One unexpectedly genuine conversation beneath the stars did not transform Prince Ryden from an incorrigible flirt into someone worthy of deeper consideration.

She titled her head toward Willow. "Are *you* upset?" Aurelise whispered to Willow. "About the prince choosing me first the other night? It really didn't mean anything, you know."

Willow's laugh was soft and genuine. "Goodness, no. I'm fairly certain I'm only here because my aunt is dear friends with Her Grace. The High Lady likely wished to avoid giving offense." She paused as her gaze flickered briefly toward the High Lady sitting across the room from them. "Not that I'm ungrateful for the honor, of course. But I harbor no illusions about becoming princess. And I was rather hoping … well …" She hesitated, fingers worrying the edge of her teacup as a faint pink colored her cheeks. "There is a gentleman who—before all this began—had shown a certain degree of interest. If the prince makes his decision swiftly, before the Summer Solstice Ball, then perhaps there might still be time this Season for the rest of us to … pursue our own more modest hopes."

Aurelise smiled, warmth unfurling within her. How lovely to know that someone as kind as Willow might have her own quiet hopes waiting beyond all this spectacle. She could almost picture it—a letter exchanged, a glance across a ballroom, the delicate beginning of something real amid all the artifice.

"I hope he proves worthy of you," she murmured softly, sincerity threading through her voice. Then, with a conspiratorial tilt of her head, she added, "I believe my presence here is for similar reasons. My grandmother is close to the High Lady. I suspect there may have been some … influence there. But I am also hoping for something entirely different."

For a brief moment, the thought of R flitted through her mind. But that was not the sort of *different* she meant, she reminded herself firmly.

"One tea per week," the High Lady was saying in answer to a question from one of the other ladies. "You may select from any of the palace's reception spaces—the Rose Veranda, the East Conservatory, Moonlight Terrace, Fountain Court, among others. The palace staff shall be at your complete disposal, and you need only choose your preferred date from the calendar."

With an elegant gesture, she directed their attention to a shimmering panel of light unfurling in the air beside her chair. Lines of silver script formed across its surface, arranging themselves into neat columns of dates, each framed by filigreed borders. Tiny jeweled markers drifted beside the open days, waiting to be claimed.

The effect was immediate. Ten young ladies rose with varying degrees of haste, each attempting to maintain proper decorum while clearly desperate to secure the most advantageous date. Lady Ellowa moved with particular determination.

Aurelise found herself among the last to approach, her natural reluctance to push forward leaving her at the periphery of the elegant scramble. Her fingers moved automatically to refasten the small pearl buttons at her wrists, securing her gloves properly now that the tea-drinking portion of the afternoon appeared to be over.

By the time she could see the calendar clearly, most of the open dates had been claimed. She selected one roughly five weeks hence—safely nestled between her second and third scheduled visits home—and tried not to think too hard about what hosting such an event would actually entail.

"Now then," the High Lady said once they'd all resumed their seats, "perhaps some inspiration would be beneficial."

She waved one hand in a graceful arc, and the small tables that held their tea services began to shift. The delicate porcelain and silver disappeared as though dissolved into mist, and the tables themselves glided across the carpet, melding together like drops of water until they formed a single long surface.

Then, rising from the merged table like flowers blooming in impossibly rapid succession, several miniature scenes materialized. Perfectly detailed vignettes so intricate she could see miniature cakes on tiny dishes and the delicate painted patterns on impossibly small teacups.

"These represent various teas I have hosted over the years," the High Lady explained, gesturing toward the magical display. "Please, examine them at your leisure. You may find ideas worth borrowing."

The ladies clustered around the table, leaning in to study the enchanted memories. Aurelise found herself beside Willow, both of them marveling at a scene depicting an autumn tea where the leaves appeared to be actual gold, each one inscribed with a different poem.

"Look at this one," Willow murmured, pointing to another tableau where everything, even the tea steaming in tiny glass teapots, was blue. Before Aurelise could comment, another lady drew Willow into conversation about the practicalities of a midsummer tea where all the decor appeared to be crafted from ice and frost.

Aurelise nodded along, trying to focus, but the room had grown overwhelmingly full of voices. Ladies exclaimed over various details, debated the merits of different themes, discussed which staff members were best for particular arrangements. The conversations layered upon each other, creating a wall of sound that pressed against her from all sides.

She could make out fragments of polite conversation between Lady Olivienne and the High Lady—questions about all the glittering spectacles that will fill the rest of the Season. The Gleamcatcher's Soirée, the Tournament of Silken Charms, the Festival of Lantern Wishes, and more.

Her chest tightened. The familiar sensation of too much, too fast, too many began creeping up her spine. She needed space, needed quiet, needed—

A delicate trill of anxious piano notes escaped before she could stop it. The sound was soft, likely lost in the general chatter, but she clamped down on her magic immediately, horrified by the lapse. She began backing away from the table, seeking the relative safety of the wall, somewhere she could breathe without feeling surrounded.

She'd nearly reached the edge of the doorway when she sensed movement just behind her. "Are you perhaps in need of rescuing, my lady?"

Aurelise jerked away with a small gasp, her hand flying to her chest. Prince Ryden stood in the doorway, one shoulder propped against the frame with studied casualness, though his eyes held something more intent than his posture suggested.

"Your Highness! No, I—" She remembered herself and hastily dipped into a curtsy. "Good afternoon."

"I heard your music," he said quietly, his voice pitched low enough that only she could hear. "The anxious sound rather gave away your distress."

Horror flooded through her. Had everyone heard? She glanced back at the other ladies, but they remained absorbed in the magical display, apparently oblivious.

The prince's mouth curved in a teasing half smile. "If you'd like, I could spirit you away from all of this. I have the perfect place in mind."

"I cannot simply leave," she hissed. "What would people think?"

"They would think nothing," he said, leaning slightly closer, "because they would not even notice." His lips quirked higher, his eyes dancing across her face with an almost searching curiosity. "Come. I want to show you something."

"I cannot go somewhere with you *alone*," she protested, even as she found herself glancing back at the overwhelming scene behind her. "It would be most improper."

"Lady Aurelise, this palace employs hundreds of staff. There is bustling activity around every corner. We could hardly be considered alone even if we tried. Besides," he added, his expression shifting to something of a challenge, "if you truly consider this improper—and I maintain that it is anything but—then you get to cross something else of your charming little list."

She narrowed her eyes at him. "I have no intention of completing the rest of that list."

Mischief danced in his expression as he tilted his head, pretending to listen to some distant echo. "I hear words ringing faintly in the distance. What are they again? Ah yes—*lamentable liar*."

Her lips parted in indignation, though the corners trembled with the effort of suppressing a smile. "You are incorrigible!"

Apparently delighted by this assessment, he said, "Thank you."

She looked back once more. Willow was deep in conversation with Lady Floravine. The High Lady had moved to speak with Lady Coravelle near the window. No one was paying her the slightest attention. And so, against every proper instinct she possessed, Aurelise slipped through the doorway and followed Prince Ryden.

He led her through the palace with the confidence of someone who had spent a lifetime memorizing its maze of corridors. At first, they passed servants carrying linens, footmen adjusting flower arrangements, and the occasional courtier hurrying to some appointment. But as they ventured deeper into the palace's heart, the hallways grew quieter. The decorations became less ostentatious, the faelights dimmer and spaced farther apart.

"Where exactly," Aurelise ventured as they turned down yet another deserted corridor, "is all this bustling activity you mentioned?"

"Did I say bustling?" He glanced back at her with mock innocence. "I meant to say that the palace has the *potential* for bustling activity. An important distinction."

"That's not—you deliberately misled me!"

"I offered you escape from an overwhelming situation. The specifics of palace population density seemed less relevant than your immediate comfort. And believe me, when you see our destination, you'll forgive my creative phrasing."

She wanted to argue, but they'd stopped before an unremarkable door in a hallway that felt older than the rest of the palace. The wood was darker here, the air holding a quality of longtime stillness. Prince Ryden turned the handle and stepped back, gesturing for her to enter first.

Every proper instinct screamed at her to refuse. Entering a private room, alone with him, without even Thimble or Spark as the pretense of supervision—it was beyond improper. It was the sort of behavior that could ruin a lady's reputation entirely.

But then she glimpsed what lay beyond the doorway, and every objection evaporated.

A pianoforte. Not just any pianoforte, but a beautiful instrument crafted from what could only be elderfae wood, its surface aglow with a soft inner luster, the grain seeming to shift gently in the light like ripples on still water. The sight of it caught her completely, stealing the air from her lungs and the ground from beneath her thoughts. For a moment, there was nothing else—no prince, no impropriety, no world beyond the gleam of polished wood and promise of music and stillness.

"Oh," she breathed, already moving forward as though drawn by invisible threads.

The room embraced her with immediate comfort. It was smaller than most of the palace's grand chambers, more intimate, with mismatched furniture that somehow created perfect harmony. A settee in faded sapphire, wingback chairs in worn burgundy leather, overlapping rugs in soft, earthy tones. Bookshelves against the walls overflowed with sheet music and volumes whose spines suggested years of loving use. Tall arched windows lined one wall, their panes dappled with the shadows of overgrown vines and clusters of pale blossoms. The afternoon light filtered through in a gentle, honeyed glow, as though the world beyond existed only to soften this space.

She moved toward the pianoforte with slow, reverent steps. Not a trace of dust dulled its polished surface. Either the instrument was still cherished and played, or the room had been blessed with a high quality ever-clean enchantment.

"May I?" she asked without looking back at the prince, her fingers already moving to the delicate buttons at her wrists to loosen her gloves.

"Of course. That's why I brought you here."

Aurelise slipped the gloves off almost without thought, draping them neatly over the back of a nearby chair, as she moved closer to the instrument. She sank onto the bench, her fingers trembling slightly as she lifted the lid. The keys gleamed in the filtered light, and she let her hands rest upon them for a moment, not yet playing, simply feeling the potential beneath her fingertips. The familiar calm that came only from this—from the promise of music about to be born—settled over her like a beloved blanket.

She pressed one finger down, then another. The notes rang clear and true, the elderfae wood giving the instrument a resonance that seemed to reach into her very bones.

Then she began to play, instinctively choosing something gentle, a piece she'd learned as a child but which had grown with her over the years, becoming more complex as her skills developed. Around her, the room itself seemed to sigh in contentment.

As her fingers found their rhythm, the world beyond the keys ceased to exist. There was only the music, flowing through her and from her, each note a small release of the tension she carried. The overwhelming tea, Lady Ellowa's sharp looks, the pressure of the Season's remaining events, the terrifying prospect of hosting her own tea—all of it dissolved into the space between one measure and the next.

She moved from the first piece into another, barely conscious of the transition, letting muscle memory and instinct guide her. This was where she belonged, where she could breathe, where the person she was expected to be and the person she actually was could exist in perfect harmony.

When the final notes faded into stillness, she became aware of her surroundings again gradually, like surfacing from deep water. And with that awareness came the startling realization that Prince Ryden was still there, seated in one of the burgundy chairs, watching her with an expression she'd never seen on his face before. Something soft and unguarded, almost vulnerable.

"I apologize," he said quickly, shifting forward in the chair and seeming to shake himself from whatever reverie had claimed him. "I should have left you to your privacy. It's only that when you began playing, I found myself quite … captivated. Would you prefer I go?"

She should say yes. Every rule of propriety demanded it. But there was something in his voice, a quiet sincerity that made her pause. And if she was honest, the thought of being entirely alone in this unfamiliar place, no matter how welcoming, made her slightly nervous.

"I … I suppose you may stay," she said quietly, turning back to the keys. "If you wish."

She began playing again, something lighter this time, maintaining enough awareness to keep from losing herself completely. She lingered over a particular refrain, repeating it a few times as though trying to coax perfection from the melody, then let it melt into another, an unhurried dance of notes that rippled and softened until it resolved into slow, sustained chords. The music unfolded naturally, without plan or structure, her fingers following sound and instinct alike, content simply to feel the smooth glide of the keys beneath her hands.

"This room belonged to my grandmother," Prince Ryden said quietly. His voice was different than she'd heard it before, stripped of its usual teasing quality and replaced by something more introspective. "When she was Crown Consort. She spent hours here during the Bloom Season when the palace filled with guests."

Aurelise shifted her fingers to a new chord, but she tilted her head to show she was listening.

"I would hide here when I was small," he continued. "Behind that settee, actually. There's a toy chest that's still there. I would take out my toy pegasi and stage airborne races. Terrifying obstacle courses through imaginary storms and over mountains of discarded books. My grandmother always pretended not to see me, but she'd change her playing to match the scene. Quick, daring scherzos when the pegasi took flight … soft, lilting waltzes when they soared safely home."

Aurelise's smile bloomed before she could stop it, the image taking root so vividly she could almost see it. A tousle-haired little prince crouched behind the settee, his toy pegasi darting through the air while his grandmother's music provided the appropriate accompaniment. The thought was unexpectedly endearing.

"She was invited to court when she was barely seventeen," he went on, "after manifesting fairly early and catching the attention of my grandfather, crown prince at the time. They married that Season, and she became Crown Consort. She fulfilled every duty asked of her, stood beside my grandfather with perfect grace, but I know she found it all rather overwhelming. The constant scrutiny, the endless social obligations. This room was her refuge. Well, one of her refuges."

Aurelise's fingers slowed on the keys as his words sank in. "She survived all those years, even though she found this life so … challenging?"

"Yes. She hid it well. Only those closest to her knew how much she needed these quiet spaces to restore herself. But she always found her balance again. It wasn't the melancholy existence you might imagine. She simply withdrew when the noise grew too loud, then returned when her spirit had settled once more."

Aurelise nodded slowly. That sounded all too familiar.

Her fingers continued their idle dance across the keys, a gentle melody forming beneath her touch as she pieced together the fragments of royal lineage she'd learned in her lessons. "And then there was your mother," she said softly, almost to herself, "who eventually became High Lady. She married somewhat later than your grandmother, if I recall correctly." Her gaze remained on the shifting patterns her fingers created. "A distinguished family from the southernmost region of the United Fae Isles. And then …" Her eyes flickered briefly toward him. "And then there was you."

The music shifted to something more contemplative, minor chords weaving through the afternoon stillness. Her thoughts drifted to her own family line—her parents who had loved each other so dearly before a tragic accident at the Rowanwood lumyrite mines had claimed her father's life when she was younger.

And that led her thoughts to the prince's own father, who had also passed some years ago. She realized that she couldn't recall the circumstances of his death. The royal family guarded their private matters carefully, and while the realm had mourned their Crown Consort, most had known him only through formal proclamations and rare, brief visits. Unlike the High Lady and her son, he had often remained in the Shaded Lands during the Bloom Seasons, making him something of a distant figure to most of the United Fae Isles. The circumstances surrounding his death remained as mysterious as the man himself had been.

She half turned toward him, her fingers stilling on the keys. "I don't recall what happened to your father," she said hesitantly. "How did he …" The question trailed off as she noticed the subtle shift in Prince Ryden's demeanor. His shoulders tensed, and something in his eyes shuttered, like a window closed against an approaching storm.

"I'm sorry," she said quickly. "I shouldn't have—"

"No," he interrupted, his voice quieter than before. "You can ask." He drew a deep breath, his gaze fixed on some distant point beyond the window. "It was an accident."

The words hung in the air between them. She could feel the weight of all he left unsaid, but propriety—and compassion—kept her from asking what lay beyond that simple truth.

She played a few more measures, letting the notes fill the space where words might have gone. Then, reluctantly, she let her hands fall to her lap. "I should return. If someone discovers us alone in here—"

"No one will discover us, I assure you. This room is safe."

There was something in his tone, a certainty beyond mere confidence, that caught her attention. She gently closed the pianoforte lid and turned fully to face him. "What exactly do you mean by 'safe'?"

A shadow of his usual smile returned. "There are enchantments on the door," he explained. "Only certain people are permitted entry. My grandmother's magic, reinforced by me after her passing. The walls and windows, too, are spelled." He gestured toward the vine-covered glass. "Sound cannot escape. No one would have heard your playing, not even if they pressed their ear to the door."

"A soundproofed room in the middle of a palace," Aurelise murmured, half to herself. "A perfect sanctuary."

"Precisely."

They both rose and moved toward the door. "The room is yours to use at any time," he added. "Thimble and Spark know how to find it."

"Thank you, Your Highness." She curtsied as he opened the door, then quietly added, "I did not realize how much I needed this."

He looked out first, glancing in both directions before turning back to her with a mischievous grin that transformed his face into something boyish and unguarded. "The way is clear, my lady." He gestured for her to precede him into the corridor, then joined her, pulling the door firmly closed behind them. "I'll accompany you back to the Blue Parlor. If my mother has noticed your absence, I'll concoct some suitably noble excuse. You won't be in trouble on my account."

They walked in silence for several moments before a thought occurred to Aurelise. "How will I enter the music room," she asked, "if it's charmed so that only certain people are allowed in?"

He didn't look at her, but she caught the subtle curve of his smile. "Because you, Lady Aurelise, are now one of those people."

Chapter Fifteen

Morning light spilled through Aurelise's chamber windows, transforming the room into a study of golden edges and soft shadows. She sat at her dressing table, fingers drumming softly against its polished surface as she contemplated R's dare list, which lay before her like both an accusation and an invitation.

The music room visit the previous afternoon might have qualified as exploring somewhere new, she supposed, but 'explore' implied a certain independence of discovery—wandering and finding rather than being led. Besides, she'd brought back no evidence of her adventure, unless one counted the melody that still hummed beneath her skin from those precious moments at the pianoforte.

As for counting it toward dare number ten—*be entirely improper*—well. Prince Ryden had been quite correct that nothing truly improper had occurred. Yes, they'd been alone in a private room without proper supervision, and yes, the mere thought of being discovered in such circumstances made her cheeks warm even now. But since nothing untoward had transpired beyond conversation and music, she could hardly claim to have completed that particular challenge.

You're making excuses to attempt more dares, Thimble's voice singsonged in her mind from where the tiny mouse perched on the windowsill, her purple wings catching the morning light. *Admit it! You WANT to be scandalous!*

"I want nothing of the sort," Aurelise protested, though her conviction wavered as she glanced toward the door. Marta had already attended to her morning preparations and delivered a tray of breakfast before departing to see to her own affairs. The corridors beyond her chambers were still quiet, most of the Crown Court ladies choosing to luxuriate in their beds until later in the morning. And no formal gatherings had been arranged until the afternoon.

Which meant …

"I suppose," she said slowly, rising from her seat, "that a brief exploration of the palace would be perfectly acceptable. After all, the High Lady did say we should familiarize ourselves with our surroundings."

Spark lifted his head from where he was curled beside Thimble on the windowsill, basking in the morning sun. *Oh, we're using royal directives to justify mischief now? How delightfully hypocritical.*

"It isn't mischief," Aurelise insisted, moving toward the door. "It's merely … educational reconnaissance."

Educational reconnaissance, Spark repeated flatly. *Is that what we're calling it? Very well. Lead on, my lady, in your pursuit of definitely-not-mischievous education.*

The palace corridors felt different this morning, less labyrinthine and forbidding than they'd felt even just yesterday. Perhaps it was the lingering peace that had settled into her bones after playing that beautiful pianoforte the previous afternoon, or simply the restorative effects of a good night's sleep. There was also the golden sunlight, brightening everything. It streamed through tall windows, painting patterns across marble floors and making the portraits of long-dead nobles seem less disapproving and more merely drowsy.

A housemaid carrying fresh linens offered her a warm smile and a small curtsy as they passed, and Aurelise found herself smiling in return.

"Good morning, Mrs. Fenbridge," she ventured, surprising herself by remembering the woman's name from a brief introduction days earlier.

The maid's face brightened considerably. "Good morning, Lady Rowanwood! Lovely day for a wander, isn't it?"

Aurelise's usual shyness melted slightly under the maid's warm greeting.

"It is indeed," she replied, gesturing to her companions. "And I'm most grateful for my little guides. I would be thoroughly lost without them."

The maid laughed. "Not to worry. You'll know your way blindfolded by Season's end, my lady."

They turned into another corridor and came upon a chaotic scene—four magical companions engaged in what appeared to be a fierce battle over a collection of ribbons. A jewel-toned butterfly, two squirrels and a phoenix. They darted and lunged at each other while two lady's maids stood on opposite sides of the hallway, arms folded and expressions tight with irritation, though neither made any move to intervene.

Aurelise hesitated, wondering if she should help somehow.

Don't bother, Spark muttered. *Those belong to Lady Ellowa and Lady Floravine. Their companions are always at each other's throats.*

It's not really the poor things' fault, Thimble added with uncharacteristic solemnity. *Their ladies are always pitting them against each other, making everything a competition.*

Spark huffed out another cloud of glittery smoke. *I don't blame them for fighting, honestly. When your lady constantly demands to see whose companions will 'win' at every little task …*

"What?" Aurelise whispered, shocked, as they passed the skirmish and turned into a new corridor. She was about to ask more about this disturbing revelation when a flurry of yellow darted toward her.

She stepped hastily sideways as a lemon-yellow mouse with dragon wings zipped past, carrying what appeared to be a stolen scone in its tiny paws.

UNCLE DANDELION! Thimble shrieked with delight, launching herself into the air. *Uncle Dandy, wait!*

The yellow mouse paused mid-flight, hovering with visible reluctance. *Thimble, darling, lovely to see you, can't stop, very busy, important business, you understand.*

You're stealing scones again!

Borrowing! Borrowing with intent to consume! Completely different thing! Uncle Dandelion executed a complicated aerial maneuver to avoid a passing servant. *Give my regards to Sparkle!*

DON'T CALL ME— Spark's roar of indignation was cut short as Uncle Dandy disappeared around a corner, leaving a few crumbs falling to the floor in his wake.

Aurelise found herself laughing, the sound bright and unexpected in the quiet corridor. Perhaps this was it: not the pianoforte's peace nor a good night's rest, nor even the warm golden sunlight, but the fact that this majestic and imposing palace was populated by beings who treated its grandeur with such cheerful irreverence.

She stretched out her palm toward Thimble, who seemed to understand the invitation immediately. The tiny pink mouse landed on her hand with obvious delight, her wings fluttering to a gentle stop. Aurelise brought Thimble close and briefly nuzzled the tiny creature against her cheek.

OH MY STARS! Thimble's mental voice quivered with pure joy. *This is the BEST DAY EVER!*

Spark, gliding in endless graceful circles at her side, huffed a puff of sparkly smoke and twitched his tail with what might have been the slightest hint of jealousy. Aurelise blew him a kiss with her free hand.

"Thank you both," she said. "For making this place less frightening."

Eventually, their wanderings led them toward the kitchens, the air growing warmer and rich with the mingled scents of baking bread, spices, and something that might have been caramelized sugar. Perhaps there she might find her evidence for dare number two. Surely liberating a cream scone or a small tartlet would be less problematic than absconding with an ornamental cushion or decorative figurine from the palace's formal rooms.

As she drew nearer, the murmur of voices and the clatter of metal grew louder, until the full life of the palace kitchen unfolded before her. She paused at the threshold, peering into the organized chaos within.

White-aproned maids bent over long wooden tables, knives flashing as they peeled potatoes and trimmed green beans into neat piles. Two others sat shelling peas into wide earthen bowls, while near the ovens, a broad-shouldered cook slid great rounds of bread onto a cooling rack. The air shimmered faintly with enchantments—spoons stirring on their own, a rolling pin gliding back and forth over a sheet of pastry as though guided by invisible hands.

Aurelise leaned against the doorframe, content simply to observe. This, at least, felt familiar—the kitchens at Rowanwood House operated with similar cheerful industry, though perhaps on a slightly less grand scale.

A scullery boy hurried in from the courtyard, his arms full of freshly cut herbs tied in bundles. At that exact moment, a young maid turned from her station with a bowl brimming with peeled potatoes. Neither saw the other until they collided. The bowl tipped, the herbs flew, and a dozen potatoes thudded and rolled across the flagstones.

"What were you *thinking*?" the maid cried, clutching the rim of her now-empty bowl. "You nearly knocked me over!"

"Well maybe don't stand in the middle of the floor like a statue!" the boy snapped back, herbs still hanging from one arm. "Some of us have work to do!"

"Some of us," she retorted hotly, "are actually doing it properly!"

Voices rose, sharp with embarrassment and temper. The clatter of knives and spoons faltered as nearby maids turned to stare. The cook's head jerked up, her expression darkening as she drew breath to shout.

Aurelise's pulse fluttered. Their anger pressed against her skin, quickening her own heartbeat. She turned swiftly away from the kitchen, pressing her back to the cool wall, desperate not to be noticed—her instinct to retreat from conflict stronger than any intention that had brought her here.

Her fingers began to move of their own accord, tracing delicate patterns in the air beside her. The motion came as naturally as breathing, summoning a soft, wordless sound. A gentle harmony rose like sunlight filtering through leaves. The sound of strings, soft and sweet, wrapped around her like a familiar shawl.

She exhaled, her nerves slowly settling. She was just about to slip away, content to abandon any thought of gathering 'evidence,' when she realized the shouting had stopped. From the kitchen came a burst of laughter. The rhythm of work had resumed—the scrape of knives, the hum of voices, the faint hiss of steam.

Peeking around the corner, she saw the maid and the scullery boy crouched together, gathering the fallen potatoes and scattered herbs, both smiling now at some shared remark.

Well. Perhaps she would linger a moment longer after all. Maybe, if she asked nicely, the boy could be persuaded to part with a bundle of herbs. Or perhaps—

Movement beyond the kitchen window caught her eye, drawing her attention to the herb garden beyond. Her breath caught in her throat.

Prince Ryden stood among the raised beds, though he looked nothing like the polished courtier she'd grown accustomed to seeing. His coat—or was that a riding jacket?—lay discarded on a nearby bench, his shirtsleeves rolled to his elbows in a fashion that would have horrified any proper valet. Sunlight caught the lean lines of his forearms as he and an older man—presumably the herb master—lifted a large wooden planter box.

Their voices carried faintly through the open window, low masculine laughter over some shared observation about the weight of wet soil or the stubbornness of thyme. The prince's expression held none of its usual calculated charm. Instead, he looked … happy. Genuinely, unselfconsciously happy, as though this moment in a kitchen garden, hands dirty and hair slightly mussed by the breeze, was precisely where he wished to be.

Something twisted in Aurelise's chest—a sensation she firmly refused to examine. Her fingers curled against the door frame. She told herself she was merely surprised, that was all. The heat rising in her cheeks was surely from the kitchen's warmth, not from watching the flex of his arms as he shifted the planter or the way the morning light played across his profile when he turned to point at something in the garden bed.

Oh my STARS! Thimble's delighted squeal pierced her thoughts. *You're watching the prince! You're ADMIRING him! Look how pink she's turning, Spark!*

"I am not—" Aurelise hissed, horrified. "I was merely surprised to see—"

Surprised by his masculine forearms? Spark inquired with unusual wickedness. *Surprised by the way he fills out that shirt? How very educational this reconnaissance has become.*

"Surprised," Aurelise insisted, her voice rising slightly in pitch, "to find him laboring in the gardens when he should be—"

"My lady?" a new voice interrupted, making Aurelise start guiltily. "Might I be of assistance?"

She turned to find one of the kitchen staff—a plump, pleasant-faced fae woman with flour dusting her apron—standing before her with a curious expression.

"Oh! I—forgive me," Aurelise stammered, mortification washing through her. "I did not mean to intrude upon your domain."

The woman's eyebrows rose slightly, though her expression remained kind. "No intrusion at all, my lady, though it is rather unusual to find one of the Crown Court ladies in the kitchens. Is there something you require? I can have it sent to your chambers directly."

"No, nothing like that," Aurelise said quickly. "I was merely exploring the palace. At home, you see, I sometimes … that is …" She hesitated, then decided honesty might serve her better than invention. "At Rowanwood House, I sometimes visit the kitchens when social events become overwhelming. To … well, to escape," she admitted. "Our head cook occasionally allows me to assist with small tasks. I find it … soothing."

The woman's expression softened with understanding. "Ah, I see. Well, my lady, while we're delighted by your interest, I'm afraid it wouldn't be entirely proper for you to linger here. If anyone were to discover—"

"Marvella!" a deep voice called from deeper in the kitchen. A moment later, a portly man with an impressive mustache emerged, wiping his hands on his apron. "Who is our visitor? Ah! One of the young ladies from court, I see."

"Yes, cook," the woman—Marvella, apparently—replied with a small curtsy. "Lady Rowanwood was just expressing an interest in our work."

"Oh, yes, I—good morning," Aurelise said, flushing further. "My apologies for the intrusion. I only meant—at home, I sometimes help in our kitchens. Just small things, of course. I realize it's rather … unusual."

The head cook's bushy eyebrows rose almost to his hairline. "Indeed? How extraordinary." He studied Aurelise for a moment, his expression cycling through surprise, curiosity, and what appeared to be carefully concealed amusement. "Well, we can hardly turn away someone with a genuine appreciation for the culinary arts, can we? If you truly wish to observe our work, my lady, perhaps you might care to assist with the dream-tarts for this afternoon's tea service?"

Before she could think better of it, Aurelise found herself following him deeper into the kitchen, her companions trailing behind her with varying degrees of enthusiasm. Thimble darted excitedly from station to station, asking rapid-fire questions about every dish in preparation, while Spark maintained a dignified hover near Aurelise's shoulder, occasionally offering dry commentary on the kitchen's organization.

The head cook, apparently amused by the novelty of having a Crown Court lady in his kitchen, assigned her to help with piping delicate honey-cream swirls onto tiny tarts. He regretted the decision almost immediately.

Within minutes, several of Aurelise's tarts looked less like elegant confections and more like collapsing meringue towers. One swirl resembled a startled snail; another listed alarmingly to the side as though attempting escape. The cook gave a strangled noise and hurried to intercept her piping bag before further casualties occurred.

"My lady," he said with admirable restraint, surveying the sugary devastation, "I do believe the tarts have suffered enough."

Aurelise flushed scarlet, then began to laugh. "You might have warned me you were assigning me the most difficult task in the kitchen."

"On the contrary," he said dryly, already attempting to salvage the survivors, "I thought it one of the safer options."

To prevent further tragedy, she was promptly reassigned to the decidedly less artistic task of whipping up fresh batches of honey-cream. It was safer for everyone involved, though considerably messier.

She left the kitchen an hour later with honey-cream still clinging stubbornly to her fingers, her thoughts torn between composing her next letter to R—she would have to mention the honey—and the memory of a prince in the herb garden, laughing in the sunlight, utterly unaware of her presence.

Dear R,

Dare number two has been conquered, though I use that term quite generously considering the minor disasters that accompanied my efforts. Yes. I have successfully explored somewhere new and brought back evidence.

What, you may ask, was the crowning triumph of my grand exploration? The thrilling destination revealed at the end of my daring adventure? The kitchens. Yes, R, the kitchens. I can practically see you laughing already—trust me to find the most domestic possible interpretation of 'explore somewhere new.'

But, in my defense, this particular kitchen belongs to an intimidatingly grand residence where I'm currently a guest, and navigating its maze of copper pots and intriguing enchanted implements (never mind actually finding my way there in the first place) felt like quite the accomplishment.

The staff regarded me with polite bewilderment. A lady? In their domain? Preposterous! But somehow I managed to convince them to tolerate my presence. Though I suspect my future with decorative piping has been permanently terminated after the mess I made. (See my opening statement about 'minor disasters.')

But it was … lovely, actually. For a short while, I almost felt as though I were back home, safe from all the expectations of polite society. Certainly more at ease than I've been in any of the beautifully appointed drawing rooms and salons where I'm supposed to belong here. I can only imagine the horror on my hosts' faces if they discovered I prefer their kitchen to their meticulously decorated reception rooms.

Oh! And I've discovered the music room. Well, one of what I suspect are multiple music rooms in this absurdly vast place, but this particular one might be the coziest I've ever encountered. I thought nothing could rival my beloved pianoforte at home, but I fear it shall be devastatingly jealous when I confess to the passionate affair I've begun with an absolutely magnificent elderfae instrument here.

So that's three sanctuaries now: the kitchen, the music room, and that rooftop terrace where I became far too intimately acquainted with a flowerbed. Three perfectly acceptable hiding places, none of which feature ever-blooming roses and their perpetual judgment. (Though between you and me, I'm beginning to miss their predictable disapproval.)

There. Two dares completed from your outrageous list. Likely the only two I can manage without causing irreparable damage to my reputation. Though I suppose dare number five wouldn't be entirely impossible … And number seven, while likely challenging to accomplish, does have a certain noble quality to it.

Yours in (very cautious) adventure,

L

P.S. What evidence of this exploration did I bring back, you may wonder? Honey. On my fingers. And since you were not here to assist with the situation as you so scandalously offered after my last honey-related incident, I had to manage the cleanup myself. (And yes, I am absolutely determined that this time it shall be YOU who blushes.)

Dearest L,

Forgive me. I need a moment. Several moments. I've had to read your letter multiple times to confirm my eyes weren't deceiving me, and I'm still not entirely convinced I haven't conjured the whole thing from my fevered imagination.

Did my shy, careful, ever-proper L really just write something so deliciously bold? About honey? And fingers? And a reference to my ever so improper offer to …

Has someone perhaps stolen your letter box? Are you writing under duress? Is this an elaborate prank orchestrated by those judgmental roses of yours?

But no, it has to be you. Only you would consider a kitchen, a music room, and a garden the triumphant spoils of exploration. Only you would befriend the kitchen staff as a strategic social escape route.

I am inordinately proud of you, L. You explored! You ventured into the unfamiliar and discovered that it wasn't quite as terrifying as you feared. Though I notice you've essentially found three new places to hide, which is both progress and perfectly, wonderfully you.

Nevertheless, I am unspeakably glad you have found small corners in which to breathe in this new and 'absurdly vast' setting you find yourself in. And as for your hosts' imagined horror, you might be pleasantly surprised to discover that they understand more than you think.

But L—and this is crucial—a beloved pianoforte? You've been holding out on me! All this time we've been corresponding and you've never once mentioned this apparently significant instrument in your life. I do hope you've at least told this pianoforte about me. Introduced us properly in conversation. "Dearest pianoforte, allow me to tell you about my mysterious correspondent who sends me outrageous dares …"

When you break the news about your torrid affair with the elderfae instrument, please convey my sympathies to your pianoforte. I suspect I understand its forthcoming jealousy all too well.

Thoroughly enchanted by your newfound boldness,

R

P.S. You more than succeeded with that comment. I am blushing. Everywhere.

P.P.S. Are you telling me that if I WERE there, you would you have let me?

Chapter Sixteen

"So," Mariselle said, leaning forward with the particular gleam in her eyes that always preceded an inquiry of the most inappropriate variety, "has Prince Ryden attempted to kiss you yet?"

Aurelise nearly choked on her tea—sugarplum whimsy, her childhood favorite, which the tea house had decided was precisely the blend she needed today—before setting the delicate porcelain cup down on its saucer. "Mariselle!"

"What?" Her sister-in-law's expression was all innocence, though the effect was somewhat undermined by the mischievous curl at the corner of her lips. "It's a perfectly reasonable question, given that he selected you for the opening dance at the Crown Court Ball."

"An entirely reasonable inquiry," Rosavyn agreed, regarding Aurelise with avid curiosity. "One might even say essential to our understanding of current events."

If only they knew how alarmingly close their teasing strayed to the truth. The prince had, after all, offered his assistance with dare number twelve.

The three of them were seated at one of the coveted window tables at The Charmed Leaf Tea House, afternoon sunlight filtering through the vines that framed the glass, casting dancing shadows across their tea service. The scents of exotic teas, warm scones and delicate pastries wrapped around Aurelise like a cherished memory made tangible.

She had specifically requested they come here today. This was her first Season properly out in society, her first opportunity to sit at these elegant tables as a lady in her own right rather than merely Lady Rivenna's granddaughter permitted to lurk in the kitchen or scurry through the garden and the rooms upstairs. Previously, she had only been allowed to visit as a true patron when she was seated demurely beside her mother on quiet afternoons when the tea house was nearly empty.

How ironically fitting that she, despite her new title, should feel like somewhat of an imposter in these elegant surroundings, while Rosavyn—who had yet to make her formal debut—sat beside her as comfortably as though she'd been taking tea at The Charmed Leaf for years.

"It's all the gossip birds have been squawking about since the Crown Court Ball," Rosavyn continued. "He chose *you* to dance with first, after all."

"The gossip birds are full of nonsense," Aurelise said, "as you well know. And I've already explained to you—and Evryn, who seemed for some reason to be particularly upset about it—why he selected me first."

"Oh yes, that remarkably contradictory explanation about him having absolutely no interest in you whatsoever, yet finding you so utterly fascinating that he craves genuine conversation with you instead of the pretense he allegedly maintains with everyone else."

Aurelise sighed. She did not feel comfortable revealing the true reason, which she'd overheard whispered between her mother and grandmother upon her return home. That the prince's choice had been a calculated kindness, meant to further soften the rumors clinging to the Rowanwood name and improve how society regarded her sister.

"You're clearly doing a terrible job of convincing him you're boring, Lise," Rosavyn added.

"Indeed, your grandmother is quite convinced he's plotting to lure you into some shadowed alcove and make off with your virtue before the Season is out," Mariselle added.

"Mariselle!" Aurelise exclaimed yet again, her face burning now, though she could hardly claim to be surprised by her grandmother's opinion. Not after the interrogation she had endured on the matter the previous evening.

She had sought her grandmother's advice about her upcoming tea at

Solstice Hall. After all, who better to help her organize her thoughts and create a practical list of everything that needed to be accomplished than the woman who'd been masterfully running the renowned and cherished Charmed Leaf Tea House for decades? But apparently, that discussion could only begin *after* a full inquest into her interactions with the prince.

"He has not made you feel uncomfortable, I hope?"

Only to the point of near cardiac arrest when I fell into a flowerbed in front of him.

Instead, she'd managed a serene smile and said, "No, Grandmother."

"He hasn't attempted anything … improper?"

Does spending half an hour alone together in the music room count?

"Of course not, Grandmother."

"Good. He is a dreadful specimen—spends his days and nights flirting his way about the United Fae Isles. Stars help us all when he ascends the throne."

Aurelise had nodded dutifully, though her mind was already wandering—to the memory of him beneath the starlight, his voice low and thoughtful as he spoke of the Shaded Lands, and to the sight of him outside the palace kitchens, sleeves rolled up as he helped the herb master lift a heavy planter, sunlight glinting in his hair. That easy, unstudied smile.

"I think perhaps you might be wrong, Grandmother," she had mused.

Lady Rivenna's head had snapped around, her gaze sharp as always. "What was that, young lady?"

Oh, stars, had she said that out loud? "Oh—I simply said—yes, you are right, Grandmother."

"Did he not find the historical evolution of spoon design dull enough?" Rosavyn asked, drawing Aurelise's attention back to the present.

"Oh, I haven't attempted that particular topic yet, but I did ramble about opinionated plants and he quite literally fled in the opposite direction, so I thought my efforts had succeeded. But then he selected me to open the dancing at the ball, and he told me he found my comments charming, so I'm genuinely perplexed about what qualifies as 'dull' these days."

She directed a frown at her teacup as she lifted it. "You needn't concern yourselves, though," she added as she lifted the cup toward her lips. "He's assured me he won't be choosing me. And now that that particular worry is resolved, I find I actually … don't particularly mind his company."

Mariselle gave her a knowing smile. "Did I not suggest he might possesses slightly more depth than his reputation would indicate?"

"Well, whether he possesses hidden qualities or not," Rosavyn said, reaching across the table for Aurelise's hand, "the fact remains that you have survived a full fortnight of this Crown Court with remarkable fortitude. I am exceedingly proud of you, little Lise."

A fortnight. Had it truly been so short a time? In the ten days since she'd completed dare number two on R's list—explore somewhere new and bring back evidence—Aurelise had barely had a moment to contemplate which challenge might be feasible to attempt next. She'd skipped firmly over number three (the mere thought of deliberately flirting with someone still made her stomach perform uncomfortable acrobatics), and before she could properly evaluate the remaining options, she'd been swept into the relentless current of Crown Court obligations.

There had been an afternoon of lawn games where she'd desperately tried to fade into the background while Lady Bernelle demonstrated her superior croquet skills with enthusiasm that bordered on aggression. A musicale the following evening where each Crown Court lady had been expected to perform—Aurelise's magical music had at least spared her the mortification of conversation afterward, as everyone seemed rather stunned into silence. The remainder of the evening had passed in an unusually peaceful manner, with tempers and rivalries apparently subdued. Then came the first of the afternoon teas, hosted by Lady Ellowa with such rigid perfection that Aurelise had been afraid to breathe wrong lest she disturb the militant symmetry of the table settings.

Each evening, she'd collapsed onto her bed once Marta had unpinned her hair, loosened her gown, and bid her a fond goodnight, too weary for anything else. Well, *nearly* too weary. She always found energy enough to write to R.

Their correspondence remained the most cherished part of her day. A delicious warmth unfurled in her chest each time she opened the box and found one of his letters waiting within. When she paused long enough to think about it, she realized her reactions—the fluttering pulse, the breath she forgot to take, the heat that rose to her cheeks—had only grown more intense since their exchange had resumed. It was alarming, really. But fortunately, she'd been far too busy (and far too tired) to dwell on the matter for long.

And suddenly, though it had seemed a lifetime away when she'd arrived at Solstice Hall, her first fortnight was complete. She'd found herself climbing into a carriage with surprisingly mixed feelings, eager to see her family but also realizing she would miss Thimble and Spark—and that beautiful pianoforte she had played twice more since the prince first introduced her to it.

"I do apologize for my tardiness," a familiar voice announced, and Kazrian appeared at their table, carrying the distinct aroma of the kitchen about him—cinnamon and butter and something wonderfully sweet.

"Finally!" Rosavyn exclaimed, straightening as Kazrian slipped into the chair directly beside Aurelise. "We were beginning to think you'd forgotten us entirely."

"Never. I was merely detained in conversation."

"Oh?" Aurelise studied her twin, who had yet to meet her gaze. "With Grandmother?"

"With Lucie," he said, still not looking at her. "Grandmother's set her to enchanting the most dangerously delicious lemon drops in the kitchen. Positively addictive. I swear she's better at that than most fae confectioners, and the magic isn't even hers."

Aurelise nudged him lightly with her elbow, and at last he glanced her way. She lifted both brows in silent inquiry. He narrowed his, a faint flush rising above his collar. They held one another's gaze, and though neither said a word, Aurelise understood all she needed to. Her brother's feelings, it seemed, remained unchanged from what they had been last Season.

They both looked away. Neither of them would speak of this aloud. They both understood the impossibility of a fae gentleman developing feelings for a human girl, no matter how lovely or kind she might be. The social chasm between their worlds remained vast, despite recent progress.

Though as Aurelise glanced around the tea house, she couldn't help but notice the subtle changes that had taken root over the past year or two. There, at a corner table, sat Mrs. Stonemore with her daughter, both possessed of the distinctly rounded ears that marked their human heritage rather than the elegant points of fae. Near the window, Mr. White held a teacup in one hand while reading The Gilded Gazette.

The transformation had begun with Iris, during her apprenticeship at The Charmed Leaf. She'd hosted an event and, to the absolute horror of Bloomhaven's traditional elite, had extended invitations to several human families. The gossip birds had nearly molted from the excitement of carrying such shocking news, but Iris hadn't retreated, and neither had Lady Rivenna. Together, they'd gradually opened the doors wider, welcoming anyone who wished to experience the magic and warmth of the establishment.

But not all of society had embraced this change. Aurelise noticed how other patrons gave the human guests a deliberately wide berth, how conversations quieted when they passed, how some fae ladies clutched their reticules a bit tighter as though proximity to humanity might somehow diminish their consequence. It explained why, despite the official welcome, she saw so few humans among the crowd.

"Oh, Kazrian," she said, suddenly remembering, "I wanted to ask your opinion on something. There is a peculiar chandelier in one of the drawing rooms at Solstice Hall that creates a strange thrumming, chattering sound whenever the room is full, but I discovered something rather curious. I was attempting to calm my own nerves—just a touch of my own magic, barely a whisper of melody—but the magic seemed to influence the chandelier as well. The awful noise ceased entirely."

Kazrian's expression sharpened with the particular focus he reserved for interesting problems. "Fascinating. Your music soothed it?"

"It seemed so. I was wondering if perhaps there might be a way to make the effect permanent? You're so clever with understanding how things work."

"Hmm." He drummed his fingers against the table, already lost in thought. "If we could capture your magic first, preserve it in a form that could—Oh." His eyes lit suddenly, focusing on something beyond Aurelise. "Lord Hadrian. Of course."

"Lord Hadrian?" she asked, twisting slightly in her chair to follow Kazrian's gaze.

"I see him over there! Though …" he paused. "He appears somewhat engaged at present. I might speak with him as he departs—or, if you prefer, we could extend an invitation for him to call tomorrow, before you are due to return to Solstice Hall."

"Oh, yes. We could do that." Aurelise's gaze landed on Lord Hadrian and an unfamiliar woman sitting at a table on the far side of The Charmed Leaf. "Who is that with Lord Hadrian?"

The woman spoke with an easy grace, and Hadrian listened as though the rest of the world had fallen away. There was a softness in his expression, a quiet intensity. It did not take much imagination to see that his regard for her ran deep.

"That is Lady Viola Windweaver," Mariselle informed Aurelise. "This is her first Season in Bloomhaven, though her magic manifested two or three Seasons ago, I believe. Her family lacked the means for such travel until recently. Beyond that, I know little about her, save that her courtship with Lord Hadrian appears to have commenced almost immediately after the Season began."

"He seems quite taken with her," Aurelise observed with a small smile as she turned back to her siblings. "I do hope it proves a good match for them both. And yes, perhaps extend an invitation to him for tomorrow," she added to Kazrian.

She had not previously considered Lord Hadrian in relation to her chandelier dilemma, but now that Kazrian mentioned him, his magic seemed the obvious solution. He possessed the ability to channel another's manifested power into inanimate objects—an art he had already demonstrated when collaborating with her elder brother Jasvian to create a device that could forewarn miners of impending tempests beneath the earth.

"It's curious though," Rosavyn mused. "I don't recall your magic having that particular effect before. Influencing anything beyond yourself, that is."

Aurelise considered this, remembering another incident she hadn't thought significant at the time. "Actually, something similar happened in the palace kitchens. There was general chaos and an argument that was making me anxious. I called upon my music primarily to calm myself, but … I remember now that the entire kitchen seemed to settle. I thought it mere coincidence at the time."

Mariselle reached across the table to squeeze Aurelise's hand, her eyes bright with genuine delight. "Your magic is growing! Developing and strengthening, exactly as it should during one's debut Season. That's why we're all here in Bloomhaven, after all. Concentration of raw magic and all that."

"Though it seems to have done absolutely nothing for me," Rosavyn said dryly. "Multiple Seasons in Bloomhaven and my ability to make plants wither is still my most impressive magical feat."

Mariselle let out an unladylike snort of laughter. "You do not make plants *wither.*"

"Fine, they merely droop mournfully in my presence, as if I've personally offended their leafy sensibilities."

"I doubt you've ever made anything droop mournfully in your life," Mariselle countered with a roll of her eyes. "Quite the contrary. Everything and everyone gravitates toward you like flowers desperate for sunlight."

"As a matter of interest," Kazrian interjected, "I don't believe the concentration of magic in this area aids in actual *manifestation.* More the strengthening of one's magic after—"

Aurelise nudged her knee against his beneath the table and shot him a warning glare. That was hardly a comment that was likely to make Rosavyn feel any better.

"Oh, don't fret on my behalf," Rosavyn said to her, leaning one elbow on the table and resting her chin on her palm (their mother would have fainted straight into her teacup at this point). "When my magic finally decides to cooperate, I'm hoping for the ability to make dance cards spontaneously combust. Think of all the boring waltzes I could avoid!"

"Oh! Or the ability to create sudden bursts of harmless fireworks," Mariselle suggested. "That could certainly help you avoid dancing."

"Hmm, or perhaps I'd like to make gossip birds sneeze uncontrollably whenever they attempt to repeat a scandal."

"No, no. I've got it." It was Mariselle's turn to lean forward now, eyes alight with mischief. "The ability to enchant fans to swoop at any gentleman who dares attempt something improper with a lady, pursuing him relentlessly until he flees the scene in disgrace."

Kazrian leaned back with a sigh and a quiet laugh. "Stars help us all," he said to Aurelise. "Once those two get started, there is simply no hope of returning to sensible conversation."

Aurelise simply watched them over the rim of her teacup, a quiet warmth blooming in her chest. She savored each laugh and wild suggestion, knowing she would miss this easy, familiar chaos when she returned to Solstice Hall tomorrow. And yet, the thought also brought a small smile to her lips, for she could almost hear Thimble's enthusiastic chatter and Spark's long-suffering grumbles waiting to fill the silence in their stead. Different voices, perhaps, but not so different in spirit.

Dear L,

You'll be pleased to know I've been conducting important research on your behalf regarding optimal hiding spots. Behind statuary: ineffective, too exposed. Beneath staircases: dusty and inhabited by spiders with territorial dispositions. My personal recommendation? Befriend someone tediously verbose and stand near them at gatherings—everyone else will actively avoid your vicinity.

Speaking of gatherings, I'm desperately curious to know whether you've made any progress on dare number three? Have you yet found a suitable partner for that particular dare? If proximity were in my favor, I should very willingly offer my assistance—for purely academic purposes, of course.

I must admit, the atmosphere here has shifted rather dramatically. We've had guests for a fortnight—all noise and motion and exhausting social requirements. Now they've left, and the silence feels heavier than it should. One guest in particular seems to have packed all the warmth among her belongings when she departed. Strange how one person can alter the entire feeling of a place, isn't it?

But enough of my philosophical musings. Your letters remain my favorite escape. Each evening I find myself rushing through obligations just to reach the moment when I can read your words.

Eagerly awaiting your next correspondence,

R

Dear R,

Behind statuary is perfectly adequate if one chooses the right statue. The trick is finding one with sufficiently dramatic robes.

This guest who apparently travels with warmth among her belongings—she sounds rather selfish, don't you think? Taking all the atmosphere with her when she leaves? Very inconsiderate.

I find it curious that you have never mentioned her before. I presume you have only recently met her. In which case … this seems an insufficient amount of time to make such an impression. Or perhaps she was just particularly … impressive? I'm merely wondering what sort of person can affect an entire household's ambiance so thoroughly. Does she have other magical qualities besides temperature theft?

Regarding dare three: I accidentally told someone their cufflinks were 'geometrically pleasing' at a small gathering last night (my brother had spent the evening praising the virtues of 'attractive symmetry' in his latest diagrams). The gentleman looked alarmed. I don't believe I can count this toward dare number three.

Yours in mathematical compliments,

L

P.S. How does one pack warmth, exactly? Does she have special baggage? This seems like information I might find useful.

Chapter Seventeen

The rain against the windows created a gentle percussion that seemed to wrap Aurelise's bedchamber in the softest of embraces. She had curled herself into the corner of her favorite chaise, legs tucked beneath her, the pale folds of her nightgown spilling across the cushions. She held a cup of sugarplum whimsy to her lips, sipping the delicate, confection-sweet blend Marta had prepared for her this evening after discovering the small paper-wrapped parcel of tea leaves on Aurelise's bed. Apparently her grandmother had sent a messenger pixie ahead this afternoon to deliver her favorite tea.

The journey from Rowanwood House back to Solstice Hall had been accompanied by a familiar flutter of anxiety, but now, ensconced in the quiet sanctuary of her rooms, the comforting fragrance of pink plum and spun sugar curling through the air and the soft rain tapping gently at the glass, she found herself unexpectedly content.

Well. Aside from R's mention of that mysterious warmth-stealing woman who was absolutely not making her feel confusing feelings she had no business feeling. Fortunately Thimble and Spark, with their endless chatter and spirited disagreements, provided ample distraction from the entirely unimportant subject of what R's next letter might say about this woman Aurelise was most certainly not dwelling on.

Across from her, Spark had claimed the burgundy armchair as his throne, a delicate china dish of custard kisses balanced precariously on the arm. He was currently in the process of devouring his third—or was it fourth?—treat, the sparkly sugar dusting his emerald scales and creating small constellations across the upholstery.

Must you make such a production of eating? Thimble asked from her position on the arm of Aurelise's chaise, her tiny pink paws crossed before her, chin resting upon them as she lay in a languid sprawl. *The sugar is absolutely everywhere.*

I am savoring, Spark replied with immense dignity, though the effect was somewhat undermined by the sugar sparkles adorning his snout. *Custard kisses are the pinnacle of culinary achievement, and I shall not have you diminishing my enjoyment with your pedestrian concerns about tidiness.*

Pedestrian! Thimble lifted her head. *This from the dragon who spent twenty minutes earlier arranging his sleeping cushion to achieve the perfect angle for his afternoon sulk?*

It was not sulking. It was meditative repose.

Aurelise couldn't suppress her smile as she watched them bicker, the familiar rhythm of their squabbling as comforting as the rain itself. "I missed the two of you," she admitted. "Tell me everything that happened while I was away."

Oh! You missed quite the commotion, Thimble began, wings fluttering as she pushed herself upright and sat. *Yesterday afternoon, the garden pixies decided to hold a snail race along the east fountain path, and all the companions gathered to support. It was all very festive until Larkdancer—that's Lady's Coravelle's companion, remember—tripped over a toadstool and accidentally set the finish ribbon on fire.*

Spark gave a long-suffering sigh, a thin curl of smoke escaping his nostrils. *The hydrangeas have only just recovered.*

They were barely singed, Thimble corrected. *And everyone cheered when Blossy's snail won. Well, except Misty, who insisted the humidity had conspired against her snail.*

Indeed, Spark murmured. *An insidious foe, moisture.*

Thimble ignored him. *Nevertheless, it was rather nice for everyone to be together without the ladies for a little while. Several companions said they were immensely relieved to have a moment's peace. Ever since the High Lady announced that each Crown Court lady must host her own tea, they've all been in utter chaos. The poor companions have been running about collecting flower samples and color palettes and debating which cakes are most becoming to serve at three o'clock.*

Most unsatisfactory, Spark declared. *We are, of course, delighted to assist. That is our purpose, after all. But the degree of strain—and responsibility—some of these ladies heap upon their poor companions is quite unconscionable. They've never hosted events before, and yet they are expected to manage every detail while remaining invisible on the day itself. A most inequitable arrangement.*

Oh! But for YOU, our dearest lady, Thimble added quickly, wings fluttering in a blur, *we shall, of course, attempt to do absolutely everything within our limited power! Table linens, flower charms, pastry placement—*

"No, no," Aurelise interrupted, leaning forward to place her teacup on its saucer on the low table beside the trailing vine her grandmother had gifted her. "I wouldn't dream of burdening you with so much of what is clearly my own responsibility."

She drew a steadying breath, willing down the familiar ripple of anxiety that accompanied any mention of her upcoming tea. It didn't quite work. She pulled her braid forward over one shoulder, her fingers absently tugging at its neatness until a few curls escaped—a nervous habit she scarcely noticed.

"I spoke with my grandmother while I was home," she added. "She helped me gather my thoughts and arrange a proper plan for all that needs doing. She also reminded me that every hostess begins somewhere, and that disasters can be charming, provided one smiles through them. I now feel … marginally less panicked. And marginally more capable."

Marginal improvement is still improvement, Spark said solemnly, which made Thimble giggle.

Speaking of improvement, she chirped, Prince *Ryden has been dreadfully mopey these past two days. Quite unlike himself. No dazzling smiles, no teasing remarks, and he even declined a second helping of berry tarts at luncheon.*

Aurelise blinked. "How is that an improvement?"

Well, clearly he missed you DESPERATELY, Thimble said, wings flickering with delight. *We are making SPLENDID progress toward him falling in love with you!*

Aurelise couldn't help her laughter. "If he was moping, it certainly wasn't because of me. More likely because all the attention from the other Crown Court ladies vanished when we all left to visit our families. And besides, I have no wish to be chosen, remember? And he has no intention of choosing me. I've already told you this."

Denial, Spark pronounced solemnly. *A most elegant method of self-deception.*

Aurelise laughed again, softer this time, shaking her head. "You are both being quite ridiculous. Have you even attempted to imagine what life might be like with *me* as the Crown Consort one day? I would be positively—"

A quiet tap at the door interrupted her. She frowned, glancing at the timebloom. It was well past the hour when Marta would have retired to her own quarters. Was it perhaps Willow, coming to discuss something? The thought warmed her. She'd seen Willow earlier that day when Willow's brother Hadrian had called upon Rowanwood House to discuss Kazrian's ideas. They'd managed to transfer some of Aurelise's magic into a crystal bottle, though what Kazrian intended to do with it remained somewhat mysterious.

She rose, padding across the soft carpet on bare feet, already composing a welcome for her friend. Late-night conversations had always been one of her favorite things—slipping into Rosavyn's room, tucking themselves beneath the covers, and talking about everything and nothing until the small hours of morning.

She opened the door with a ready smile—and froze.

Prince Ryden leaned against her doorframe with casual elegance, though his state of dress suggested he'd been interrupted mid-undressing. His jacket was absent, his cravat hung loose around his neck, and his shirt was unbuttoned at the throat in a way that was positively scandalous. His dark blue hair, usually so perfectly arranged, fell in slight disarray across his forehead.

A strangled sound escaped Aurelise's throat as she immediately crossed her arms over her chest in a desperate X, acutely aware that she stood before him in nothing but her nightgown, her hair coming undone from its braid after all her anxious fidgeting.

"Good evening, Lady Aurelise," he said, his lips curving into that particular smile that made her pulse perform acrobatics. "It's raining."

She blinked, her mind struggling to process both his presence and his observation. "I—yes. I'm aware."

"Since you've yet to accept my generous offer of assistance with dare number three, I thought perhaps you might be amenable to help with dare number four."

Dare number four. Get rain-soaked on purpose.

The shock of his presence at her door—at this hour, in this state—rendered her temporarily speechless. When words finally returned, they emerged in a rush. "Did you … did you truly commit the entire list to memory?"

He shrugged, the gesture somehow elegant despite its casualness. "I possess an excellent memory for things that interest me."

She blinked again, still struggling to reconcile his presence with reality. "Your Highness, you cannot—this is—your being here, at my door, at this hour—it is beyond all propriety!"

Though you must admit, Thimble's voice chimed in her mind, *it's absolutely THRILLING! Like something from one of those scandalous novels Lady Olivienne hides beneath her mattress!*

"Technically," Prince Ryden said, "as this is my palace, this chamber belongs to me as well. I'm merely visiting my own property."

"That is not—you cannot simply—that isn't how property ownership functions!"

His grin widened. "Would you care to join me in the rain, Lady Aurelise?"

"Absolutely not!"

"Are you certain? It's remarkably liberating, being thoroughly drenched on purpose. Quite different from those unfortunate incidents involving unexpected downpours and ruined slippers."

"I am not going outside in the rain with you. In my nightclothes. At this hour. It would be—"

"Daring?" he suggested, his eyes twinkling with mischief.

You should absolutely go! Thimble urged, fluttering to Aurelise's shoulder. *When will you have another opportunity like this?*

You should absolutely not go, Spark countered firmly, abandoning his custard kisses to deliver his pronouncement. *You'll catch your death of cold, and then where will we be? Also, the scandal if anyone were to witness—*

Oh, please, Thimble scoffed. *It's the height of summer! The rain is warm, and it would be THOROUGHLY refreshing. Besides, no one's awake at this hour except the night footmen, and they're all playing cards in the servants' hall.*

"I appreciate your companions' spirited debate," the prince commented, looking amused. "Might I add that the rain is indeed quite warm this evening? Perfect for a first attempt at purposeful drenching."

Aurelise worried her lower lip, a habit her mother would have scolded her for. The sensible part of her—which was to say, most of her—insisted this was absolute madness. But there was another part, a tiny rebellious whisper that sounded suspiciously like R's letters, suggesting that perhaps, just perhaps, a small adventure wouldn't be the end of the world.

"I would need to … to cover my nightgown," she said, hardly believing she was even considering this.

"Of course," he agreed readily. "Though I wouldn't bother with slippers. They'll only become waterlogged. Besides," his smile turned almost boyish, "don't you want to feel the grass between your toes?"

She stared at him for a long moment, then made a decision that would have horrified her even a fortnight ago. "Wait here."

She closed the door—not quite in his face, but nearly—and rushed to the end of the bed where her wrapper lay. Still scandalously insubstantial, but it would at least provide some coverage. And besides, he had already witnessed her flailing about in a flowerbed in her nightclothes; the threshold of dignity had surely been crossed long ago.

As she pulled the wrapper on with trembling fingers, she caught sight of herself in her dressing table mirror. Her eyes were bright with something that might have been fear or excitement or very possibly both.

"This is madness," she muttered.

This is adventure! Thimble corrected, already dancing in anticipation.

When she opened the door again, Prince Ryden was still there, looking as though he had every right to be lounging outside a lady's bedchamber at nearly midnight. He offered her his arm with exaggerated formality.

"Your evening constitutional awaits, my lady."

Against every principle of proper behavior she'd been taught, Aurelise placed her hand—*her bare, gloveless hand!*—upon his arm and allowed him to lead her into the corridor.

Solstice Hall lay hushed and dreamlike, soft shadows spilling across marble and gilt. Aurelise, however, noticed precisely nothing of her surroundings. Every scrap of her awareness was consumed by the prince beside her, the warmth of his sleeve beneath her palm, the cool floor beneath her bare feet.

This was complete, unrepentant madness. At any moment, someone would discover them. Her reputation would be not merely tarnished but obliterated. She would have to return to Rowanwood House in unspeakable disgrace.

Her magic responded to her nerves, thin threads of melody trembling into existence around them, high, uncertain notes like harp strings brushed by invisible hands.

A soft laugh came from beside her. "There is no need to panic, Lady Aurelise. I promise, you shall not be discovered, and you shall not melt from the rain."

Thimble darted ahead of them, her iridescent wings catching what little light remained, while Spark followed with obvious reluctance, muttering under his breath about the follies of youth and the inevitability of lung fever.

They passed through the Blue Parlour, its elegant furniture transformed into mysterious shapes in the darkness, then through a smaller sitting room Aurelise had never entered before. Finally, Prince Ryden stopped before a set of glass doors that led to the garden.

He pushed open the doors, and immediately the sound of rain filled the space. Not a violent downpour but a steady, gentle shower that released the green scent of growing things into the night air.

Without hesitation, the prince stepped outside.

Within moments, his white shirt was plastered to his skin, his hair dripping water down his face. He turned back to Aurelise with a grin that was pure mischief, spreading his arms wide as he took a few steps backward, further into the rainy night.

"Come now, Lady Aurelise! What are you waiting for?"

She hung back in the doorway, her fingers clutching the frame. "I'll get wet!"

"Yes, that's rather the entire purpose of the exercise."

"But then I'll be thoroughly soaked!"

"Indeed you will. And what then? Will the world cease spinning? Will society crumble? Or will you perhaps discover that being wet is merely … being wet?"

She shook her head, though she was fighting a smile. "You're impossible."

"I prefer 'encouraging.' Come now. One step. That's all. One step into the rain."

I'm absolutely not going out there, Spark announced, settling himself primly in the doorway. *This is undignified behavior for anyone, but particularly for a lady of quality.*

This is the most exciting thing that's happened in AGES! Thimble squeaked, zipping out into the rain and performing an elaborate loop. *Oh, it feels WONDERFUL! Like tiny kisses from the sky!*

Aurelise took a breath, then another. Then, before she could lose her nerve entirely, she stepped out into the rain.

The first droplets on her skin made her gasp—not from cold but from the strange intimacy of it. Rain had always been something to shelter from, to observe from behind windows. But this—this purposeful stepping into it, choosing to be drenched—felt like breaking a rule she hadn't known existed.

She moved a few paces from the palace wall, her bare feet sinking slightly into wet grass. The sensation made her cringe at first, the squelch between her toes entirely foreign. But as the rain continued to fall, soaking through her wrapper, plastering her braid to her neck, something in her began to unfold.

A laugh bubbled up from somewhere deep in her chest. She tilted her face to the sky, closing her eyes, feeling the droplets trace paths down her cheeks. Without quite meaning to, she spread her arms wide, palms up, catching the rain like gifts.

"You see?" Prince Ryden's voice came from somewhere nearby, warm with satisfaction. "Not so terrible after all."

Spin! Thimble called out, performing her own aerial pirouette. *You must spin! And twirl! This is far too wonderful to stand still!*

"She's right," the prince agreed, and when Aurelise opened her eyes, she found him watching her with an expression that made her stomach perform a peculiar flutter. "Though I'd suggest something even better. Run."

"Run?" She was still laughing, giddy with the strangeness of it all. "I'm not going to run through the rain like some wild creature."

"Why not? There's nothing quite like it. The feel of your blood racing, your lungs burning, the rain streaming past as you move. Pure freedom."

She shook her head, still smiling. "You are thoroughly mad."

His expression shifted then, taking on a quality that sent a different sort of thrill through her. "And if I were to chase you?"

The laughter died in her throat. "You wouldn't—you cannot—surely you would not *actually* pursue me through the gardens!"

He began a slow and purposeful walk toward her, that roguish grin still in place. "Wouldn't I?"

Run, my lady! Thimble shrieked with delight, diving down to tug at Aurelise's thumb with her tiny paws. *This way! Quickly!*

The prince took another deliberate step, and with a squeal that would have mortified her in daylight, Aurelise darted past him and ran into the night.

Her feet flew across wet grass, her nightgown and wrapper plastered to her skin, the soaked fabric tangling about her knees. She ran past the carefully manicured rose bushes, their blooms heavy with rain. Past the ornamental fountains that overflowed with the evening's bounty. Past hedges trimmed into fantastic shapes that looked like creatures in the night.

Behind her, she could hear the prince's laughter, his footfalls, steady and unhurried, as though he could catch her whenever he chose but was enjoying the chase too much to end it. Thimble flew beside her, squeaking encouragement, her tiny form a pink blur against the darkness.

Her lungs began to burn, her legs to shake, but still she ran, powered by something wild and free she hadn't known existed within her. The rain streamed down her face, and she was laughing again, breathless and exhilarated.

Finally, when she could run no more, she stumbled to a stop near the edge of the palace's lake. Her chest heaved as she bent forward, hands on her knees, trying to catch her breath. The lake, Veilmere, stretched before them, its surface dimpled with raindrops. In the center, barely visible through the rain and darkness, sat the small island with its ancient stone archway—the Veil Gate that led to the Shaded Lands.

"Well?" Prince Ryden asked, coming to stand beside her, his breathing quickened, though far less uneven than hers. "Was I correct about the running?"

She straightened, pushing wet strands of hair from her face. "That was … that was actually rather wonderful."

"I do occasionally have good ideas," he said with false modesty, and for some inexplicable reason, Aurelise was suddenly reminded of R and his 'almost always Right About Things.'

The rain was beginning to slow now, softening from a shower to a fine mist. They were both thoroughly drenched, her nightgown and wrapper clinging to her form, his shirt having become nearly transparent.

He looked out across the lake, and something in his expression shifted. "Has it occurred to you, Lady Aurelise, that you could complete two dares tonight?"

She tracked his gaze across the water, understanding dawning. Dare number eight. Take a midnight swim.

"Absolutely not."

A spark of mischief curved his lips. "Why not? You're already soaked through."

"Because … because …" She fumbled for an excuse, but her words died in her throat as he reached for the hem of his shirt. "Stars above! What are you doing?"

He began to peel the sodden garment over his head, and she spun around, pressing her hands over her eyes even though her back was now to him.

"Going for a swim," he said, as though this were perfectly reasonable behavior.

"You cannot simply disrobe in my presence!" The absolute horror. She was fairly certain she might expire from it.

"I'm keeping my trousers on, Lady Aurelise. Have no fear for your virtue."

Oh, but what a VIEW, Thimble sighed appreciatively from her perch atop a nearby branch. *Purely for artistic study, of course.*

"Thimble!" Aurelise hissed, scandalized.

The sound of water splashing told her he was walking into the lake. She peeked over her shoulder and found him wading deeper, the water now at his waist. The moonlight, breaking through the clouds, painted his skin silver, highlighting the lean muscles of his back as he moved through the water.

He dove forward, disappearing beneath the surface for a moment before emerging further out, treading water with easy grace. "The water's perfect. Pleasantly cool."

"I am absolutely not getting in there," she said firmly, though somehow she found her feet carrying her closer to the edge. The rain had stopped completely now, leaving only the gentle sound of droplets falling from the leaves

"Just a few steps and you'll be in the water."

"No."

"Can you not swim, my lady?"

"Of course not! What lady can?"

That unmistakably wicked glimmer returned to his eyes. "Then I daresay I shall simply have to hold you when the water grows too deep."

For a moment, words deserted her entirely. Surely he had not just said that. She shook her head in disbelief. "How do you manage to be so ..."

"Charming? Persuasive? Devilishly handsome despite being thoroughly waterlogged?"

"Incorrigible!" she finally managed.

"That too," he agreed. "I do try to be comprehensive in my attributes." He studied her for a moment, then sighed dramatically. "Very well. I had hoped to avoid this, but you leave me no choice."

He moved his hands through the water in a graceful pattern, and she watched as silver light trailed from his fingers, spreading through the water in rippling circles. A section of the lake began to shimmer faintly, as though the water itself had been transformed into liquid moonlight.

"What did you do?" she asked, suspicion coloring her voice.

"A simple enchantment. One typically used when teaching young boys to swim. The water will support you even when your feet cannot touch bottom. Did your brothers never mention it?"

She chose to ignore the question; it was entirely beside the point. "I'm still not entering the water."

Prince Ryden shook his head with exaggerated disappointment. "How remarkably un-daring of you, Lady Aurelise. And here I thought you were becoming quite the adventuress."

The challenge in his voice pricked at her pride. She looked at the shimmering water, at the prince floating so easily within it, at Thimble hovering excitedly nearby. The rational part of her mind was shrieking about propriety, about scandal, about the absolute madness of swimming with a half-dressed prince in the middle of the night.

But she was already soaked. Already scandalously alone with him. Already so far beyond the bounds of proper behavior that one more transgression could hardly matter.

Before she could lose her nerve, she walked into the water.

The lake was indeed pleasantly cool, and the enchanted section glowed softly around her feet. She waded deeper, her waterlogged clothing floating around her legs. When the water reached her waist, she hesitated.

"Come now, you can certainly go farther than that," Prince Ryden urged, his tone gently teasing now. "You can see where the enchantment ends—the water glows for a reason. You're perfectly safe within it. And if, for some reason, you happen to go below the water's surface, I promise to rescue you."

Well, that was hardly comforting. Still, she drew a steadying breath and waded forward another step. Then another. The water lapped against her ribs, then her shoulders. Her heart thudded wildly.

"That's it," he said quietly. "The magic will hold you up, I promise."

A nervous, breathy laugh escaped her. "I don't think I—Oh."

She blinked. The pressure beneath her feet had vanished, yet she wasn't sinking. The silver light beneath the surface seemed to cradle her. She floated there, simply suspended, weightless, the lake itself holding her aloft. She lifted her arms and trailed them slowly across the surface of the glowing water, each movement leaving a faint ribbon of brighter light in its wake.

"There now," Prince Ryden said softly. "Hardly terrifying, is it?"

"It's …" A laugh broke from her, light and disbelieving. "It's marvelous," she admitted.

"Another dare completed," he murmured, a smile in his voice. "Well done, my lady."

They drifted lazily, circling one another in the softly glowing water. Thimble darted over the surface, scattering droplets like diamonds, while Spark—who had caught up to them now that it was no longer raining—remained dry on the bank, muttering dire warnings about impropriety and scandal.

Something brushed against Aurelise's ankle—a quick, cool flick that made her gasp. "What was that?"

The prince chuckled. "Harmless. The lake's guardians. Little blue-green creatures. They like to investigate visitors."

"Investigate? They feel rather more like tickling."

"They're fond of mischief. The smaller ones in particular."

"That explains why they're swarming you, then, Your Highness."

He laughed, and she couldn't help laughing too. And then, as their laughter faded, she found herself still watching him. The silvery glow of the water illuminated his face, catching along the angles of his cheekbones and jaw, making his dark blue eyes appear brighter, with light dancing in their depths.

His gaze lingered on her in return, and the air between them seemed to still. Heat bloomed beneath her skin. She looked down, unable to hold those eyes for long. Sliding further downward, her gaze caught on something just above his collarbone—a faintly puckered mark, irregular, almost star shaped.

"What is that?" she asked before she could stop herself. "That mark—just there."

He followed her gaze down, and she watched as his expression changed. The humor faded, replaced by something quieter. "Ah. That."

"I'm sorry," she said quickly. "I should not have asked. It's none of my—"

"No," he interrupted. "Think nothing of it. A simple scar, nothing more. The result of an accident, years ago."

Aurelise opened her mouth, then closed it again. She let the silence stand, the only sound the hush of the enchanted water and the soft flutter and splash of Thimble's wings as she skimmed the water's surface nearby.

She knew that for something to leave a mark like that, magic must have been involved. It made her wonder what sort of enchantment could cause such harm—but she also knew better than to ask. She drifted a little farther back, her arms gliding through the water in slow, aimless circles, and then—

His eyes widened suddenly—a flash of alarm—before the world vanished beneath her and she plunged without warning below the surface. Water filled her ears, her nose, and panic seized her chest. She was sinking, she was drowning, she was—

Strong hands caught her beneath her arms, pulling her up. Her head broke the surface and she gasped, sucking in air as she was hauled against something solid and warm, arms swiftly encircling her waist, holding her secure. For a breathless moment, she looked straight in a pair of dark blue eyes mere inches from her own that reflected every bit of the shock thrumming through her.

Then—"You let me sink!" she sputtered, raising a hand to wipe water from her face.

His expression relaxed. He managed a laugh, though it came out unsteady. "I did not. You were the one who moved farther than I advised. I rescued you, just as I promised."

In the next breath, awareness struck. Her body was *pressed against him*, against his very bare, very wet chest, and she could feel every rise and fall of her own. His dark eyes were fixed on her with disarming intensity, droplets of water clinging to his lashes. And his lips—stars above—were parted, devoid of their usual teasing curve—

Then he was moving through the water, and a moment later, her feet touched sand. He released her gently, making sure she was steady before moving back.

His lips lifted, the beginnings of a teasing smile returning, though his voice was rough when it emerged. "Enjoyable?"

She blinked in disbelief. "Terrifying!"

"But you survived."

"Barely!"

"You were perfectly safe," he said, and there was something sincere in his gaze now, all teasing gone. "I would never allow you to come to harm."

The words hung between them, weighted with—

My lady! Thimble's frantic voice broke the moment. *Are you well? That was absolutely TERRIFYING! And dreadfully romantic! Did he save you? He saved you! Just like in Lady Olivienne's novels!*

The spell broken, Prince Ryden's familiar grin returned. "Two dares in one evening. I'm thoroughly impressed by your boldness, my lady."

They began wading toward shore where Thimble waited, wings fluttering anxiously.

"I rather think those will be the last two," Aurelise admitted. "I'm quite convinced I've used up my entire supply of boldness for the foreseeable future."

He laughed again, the sound rich and easy. "Somehow, Lady Aurelise, I doubt that. I have a feeling boldness suits you far too well to be so easily spent."

Dearest L,

'Geometrically pleasing cufflinks.' L, you treasure. That poor gentleman is probably still pondering what you meant. (Though if it was an accident rather than an intentional flirtation, then I believe you're right that it should not be counted toward dare number three.)

Now then, this sudden interest in my warmth-pilfering guest is fascinating. All these carefully casual questions about her impression-making abilities and magical qualities. If I didn't know better, I'd think you were experiencing a touch of … something. Could it possibly be jealousy?

Sweet L, are you perhaps worried that some charming visitor has captured my attention? That while you're off complimenting geometry, I'm here sighing over some enchantress who's stolen the very temperature from my halls?

Rest assured, there is no one who stirs such warmth in me as you. (You should have seen me when you so cleverly turned my improper honey remark back upon me. I was positively burning.)

Though I must say, this new slightly possessive version of you is rather captivating.

Thoroughly amused,

R

Dear R,

Possessive? That's absurd. I'm merely conducting academic research into the phenomenon of atmospheric theft. It's a serious matter that probably deserves formal study.

And I'm certainly not worried about enchantresses capturing anything of yours. You're free to sigh over whomever you please. I'm sure she's lovely, this warmth-burglar of yours. Probably never says awkward things about geometry or hides behind statues.

Actually, now that I consider it, she sounds exhausting. All that temperature manipulation and impression-making? Some of us prefer to leave rooms exactly as warm as we found them, thank you very much. It's called courtesy.

I've decided I don't like her. Not because of any possessive feelings, you understand, but on principle. Anyone who goes about stealing atmospheric conditions is clearly not to be trusted.

Academically yours,

L

My dearest L,

There is nothing left for any enchantress to steal—you already have it all.

R

Chapter Eighteen

HUNDREDS OF SPELL-LIGHT CREATURES DARTED THROUGH THE AIR above the Solstice Hall gardens like enchanted fireflies caught in an invisible wind, their luminous forms painting trails of silver and gold against the deepening twilight. Ladies in shimmering gowns rushed about with delicate nets of silver thread, their laughter rising and falling like music as they attempted to capture the elusive gleams. Gentlemen joined the chase with varying degrees of dignity intact, some maintaining their composure while others abandoned all pretense of sophistication in pursuit of particularly tempting quarry.

Ryden stood at the edge of the gathering, his mother a regal presence beside him, and found his gaze drawn inevitably to one figure among the many. Lady Aurelise moved through the crowd with considerably less competitive fervor than some of the other ladies—Lady Ellowa, for instance, had nearly knocked Ryden's friend Lord Fin Thornhart into a rose bush in her enthusiasm—but her face was alight with genuine pleasure as she laughed and attempted to catch the darting creatures with her net. The sound carried to him on the lilac-scented breeze, and something in his chest tightened at the unfettered joy in it.

A full week had passed since he'd convinced her to venture into the rain with him. Since he'd convinced her to swim in the lake. He could still feel the memory of it branded into his skin—that breath-stealing moment in the water when he'd held her in his arms, her chest heaving, her nightgown clinging to her form, her eyes wide with shock and … something else?

She'd been so close, so breathtakingly, impossibly *close*.

His L, in his arms.

The moment hadn't been planned, hadn't been part of his gentle campaign to help her complete her dares. One moment, cool water had separated them. The next, he was pulling her up and into his arms, her body pressed against his in a way that had made every rational thought flee his mind entirely.

"I was relieved to observe you paying proper attention to the other ladies earlier this evening," his mother said beside him, "rather than seeking out Lady Aurelise first, as you did at the Crown Court Ball." She directed a pointed gaze at him, one brow raised. "And as you did *again*, at several less formal events since then. It was gracious of you to send a clear signal that the Rowanwoods remain in favor despite their recent … difficulties. But I believe you've made your point now. It would have sent entirely the wrong message had you shown such marked preference yet again tonight."

Ryden allowed himself a slight smile, grateful that his mother had accepted his carefully crafted explanation. Even more satisfying was the knowledge that she'd passed this reasoning along to Lady Rivenna, Aurelise's formidable grandmother.

"It would not do to have anyone thinking you've already selected a favorite from among the ladies just yet," his mother continued, her gaze following a particularly energetic chase as Lady Mariselle nearly collided with Lord Bridgemere. "Especially not someone we both know you cannot actually choose as your bride."

I can, Ryden answered silently. *I will.*

His attention was drawn back to Aurelise as she made another attempt at catching one of the gleams, her net sweeping through the air with more enthusiasm than skill. Her startled laugh when she actually managed to capture something—a ribbon-bird, from what he could see—sent an unexpected warmth through him. He watched as the creature dissolved into a translucent charm on her palm, its wings folding into an elegant token. She said something to Lady Willow, who stood beside her, and Willow laughed in response, holding up the three tokens she'd already collected with obvious pride.

The Gleamcatcher's Soirée had always been one of Ryden's favorite events of the Season, a tradition dating back many years. It was one of Solstice Hall's smaller, more intimate gatherings, an evening reserved for the royal family's closest friends and trusted courtiers. The sort of night where conversation drifted easily, laughter carried through the gardens, and the formalities of rank seemed, for a few enchanted hours, to loosen their hold.

The palace enchanters spent weeks preparing the spell-light creatures, each one a masterwork of temporary enchantment. They weren't truly alive, of course, merely flickering wisps of magic given beautiful, fleeting form. Tiny dragons of smoke and starlight wove between the revelers, while ribbon-birds fluttered on gossamer wings that left trails of shimmer in their wake. Silver koi swam through the air as though it were water, and mischievous foxlets darted just out of reach, their forms bursting into sparkles of laughter when finally caught.

The greatest prize, naturally, was the moonflare—the rare moth spun of pure white light. While dozens of lesser gleams drifted through the evening for guests to chase and trade, there was only ever one moonflare conjured each year. Legend claimed that whoever caught it would have one wish granted before the Season's end, though Ryden suspected this story had been invented by some creative matchmaker centuries ago.

He watched Evryn and Mariselle, who had positioned themselves near the fountain. They were both ridiculously competitive as always, turning even this gentle entertainment into a battlefield of wills. Mariselle had tucked her skirts up in a thoroughly improper manner to improve her mobility—a choice that drew a pointed sniff and a lift of Ryden's mother's chin before she discreetly turned away, the faintest hint of amusement tugging at her mouth. Meanwhile, Evryn had removed his jacket entirely, and his shirtsleeves were rolled up. They circled a particularly elusive starlit wyrmling, each trying to prevent the other from claiming it, their good-natured bickering carrying across the garden.

Ryden couldn't help but smile at their antics. After the tedium of the past four days, this was precisely the kind of entertainment he needed.

The private picnics with each lady had been his mother's idea, of course. "Individual attention," she'd called it. "An opportunity for genuine conversation without the pressure of public scrutiny. Longer than a garden stroll, yet far less intimidating than a formal dinner."

What she'd failed to mention was how mind-numbingly repetitive it would become. Three picnics on the first day, then two each on the following three days. He'd always thought himself particularly fond of candied violets and dreamleaf macarons, but by the fourth picnic, he could barely look at them without his stomach turning.

His mother had arranged the schedule with her typical strategic precision. Lady Ellowa had been placed last, a decision that did not surprise him in the least, for both he and his mother tacitly agreed that she was nowhere near a genuine contender. And then she'd positioned Aurelise just before Ellowa, for in her estimation, Aurelise was no more suitable, even if she was far more likable.

Perhaps his mother thought he'd be thoroughly bored and disinterested by the time the picnic with Aurelise arrived, his patience exhausted, his attention wandering. Instead, the delay had only heightened his anticipation, like saving one's most exquisite confection for last.

He'd made certain to request the kitchen replace the standard strawberry jam they'd included in all the other wicker hampers with orange marmalade, remembering a detail from one of L's letters about her preferences. Aurelise had noticed immediately, her eyes widening with pleased surprise. He'd merely nodded along, feigning mild confusion, working desperately to keep his amusement from showing on his face.

And then she'd very nearly undone him entirely when she'd placed the tip of one finger between her lips to catch a drop of marmalade that had escaped her scone. The gesture was so innocently sensual that he'd had to grip the edge of the blanket to keep from reaching out, capturing her delicate hand in his, and discovering for himself exactly how the marmalade would taste on her skin.

"Ryden?"

His mother's voice cut through his increasingly improper thoughts, and he felt warmth creeping up his neck. Thank the stars she couldn't see the direction his mind had wandered.

"Forgive me, Mother. You were saying?"

She inclined her head toward him, her voice softening. "I was inquiring whether you've begun to feel any sort of … magical compatibility with any of the ladies. Perhaps a calming of your magic? A sense of balance or peace in someone's presence?"

"I haven't noticed anything specific," he said carefully, mainly because he hadn't been paying attention. All he'd noticed was the quickening of his pulse, the unsteady rhythm of his breath, and the restless heat that seemed to steal through him whenever Aurelise was near—and an equal and maddening distraction whenever she was not.

"Though I should thank you for keeping my surges under control thus far. I know I don't always ..." He paused, the words feeling stiff and formal even to his own ears. "I don't always express my appreciation adequately, but I know how taxing it is for you, increasingly so as my magic grows stronger. Your efforts don't go unnoticed."

Surprise flickered across his mother's features before she smoothed it away. "I haven't been doing anything," she said quietly, her voice carrying an undertone he couldn't quite identify. "I've remained keenly attuned to the possibility, as you requested before the Crown Court Ball, but I've felt nothing out of the ordinary since then."

The words stirred an uncertainty inside him, though he kept his expression carefully neutral. His mother's eyes lit with sudden hope.

"This could be the influence of one of them," she continued, turning to survey the laughing crowd with renewed interest. "Do you have any idea which one? Have you honestly not noticed feeling settled around any lady in particular?"

Rather than relief or happiness, Ryden had to tamp down a rising wave of anxiety. The only person he wanted was Aurelise, and no, he did not feel *settled* around her because every moment in her presence set his heart alight, his thoughts unraveling beneath the force of a longing so fierce it seemed it might consume him altogether. How was he supposed to endure it if this entire notion of finding someone whose magic might temper his own actually *worked*? If he truly was forced to choose someone else from among the Crown Court ladies?

His mother looked out at the gathering again, quiet for several moments, her expression contemplative in the soft glow of the floating lanterns.

"I've noticed," she said finally, "that the palace at large seems more at peace this Season than usual. I'd assumed that with all the additional activity and excitement, the atmosphere would be far more chaotic. And certainly, we've been busy—exhaustingly so—but there haven't been nearly as many disasters as I anticipated."

She paused, and Ryden could see her mind working, analyzing this unexpected peace.

"Perhaps fate itself is telling us we are on the right path," she continued. "That this was the correct choice, this gathering, this method. By Season's end, you'll have your bride, and your magic will stabilize as it was always meant to."

Ryden drew a careful breath, willing the tightness in his chest to ease as the activity moved closer, the chasing crowds following a cluster of particularly active gleams that seemed to be playing with their pursuers. A group, headed by Evryn and Mariselle, moved toward them, so focused on their quarry that they seemed unaware of their proximity to royalty.

Evryn very nearly crashed directly into Ryden's mother while attempting a particularly athletic leap for an air-koi, his net sweeping dangerously close to the High Lady's head.

"Your Grace!" He landed awkwardly, his face flushing. "My deepest apologies. I didn't see—that is, I was watching—forgive me—"

"No harm done, Lord Rowanwood," the High Lady said with more amusement than censure. "The gleams can be quite distracting."

As Evryn retreated with a smothered grin, Mariselle giggling on his arm, the group shifted, and Ryden's heart leaped as the movement revealed Aurelise standing almost directly before them. She looked as startled as he felt, her net lowering, her eyes widening as she realized how close she'd come to the royal observers.

She dropped into a hasty curtsy, Lady Willow following suit beside her. "Your Grace. Your Highness. Please forgive the intrusion."

"It's quite all right," the High Lady said as Ryden bowed to the two young women, his eyes remaining fixed on Aurelise, a small smile curving his lips.

Aurelise looked as though she might flee—Ryden could see the instinct in the way her weight shifted—but then something made her pause. She straightened her shoulders, and he recognized the gesture. It was the same way she'd steeled herself before stepping into the rain, before wading into the lake. His quiet, careful L gathering her courage.

"Actually, Your Grace," she began hesitantly, "there was something I wished to discuss with you, if I might be so bold."

Bold indeed. Ryden almost laughed out loud, his earlier anxiety easing, delighted at how bold his shy, careful L was becoming. For one reckless heartbeat, he wanted nothing more than to draw her into his arms and kiss her.

"Go on," his mother said, one eyebrow arching upward

"My brother delivered something earlier today," Aurelise said, her voice gaining speed as though she feared her courage might desert her. "He crafted a small crystal drop for the Green Drawing Room chandelier, based on my description of it, and a—well … an idea I had. Relating to my music magic, that is. Just a silly experiment, really, but I wondered if I might be allowed to have it fitted in place of one of the existing pieces. I thought it might …" She faltered, then finished with a simple, "help."

Ryden's gaze darted to his mother, who regarded Aurelise with patient amusement. "Your music is quite lovely, my dear, so if that chandelier were to hum a melody instead of prattling so incessantly, I daresay it would be an improvement."

Aurelise hesitated. "Oh, well, it … that is …"

"Yes, you are welcome to try," the High Lady continued, waving a graceful hand. "I shall have one of the artificers fetch the piece from your chambers tomorrow and see it installed."

Aurelise paused again, her gaze flickering between Ryden and his mother, as though something more pressed at the edge of her tongue. But whatever it was, she swallowed it back. "Thank you, Your Grace." She curtsied once more, Lady Willow following her lead, and together they withdrew into the crowd.

Ryden's eyes followed her as a rush of feeling swelled within him. Longing, frustration, and the unspoken dread that someone else in this glittering crowd would soon be chosen for him, no matter what his heart already knew. He drew a steadying breath, forced his thoughts into order, and turned back to his mother.

"If you'll excuse me, Mother," he said, "I think I shall join the festivities."

"Of course, darling. Do enjoy yourself."

Ryden retrieved one of the enchanted nets, testing its weight experimentally. The silver threads hummed against his palm, already attuned to the frequency of gleam magic. Around him, the gardens were still a battlefield of joy, ladies and gentlemen abandoning dignity in pursuit of the dancing lights.

"Finally decided to participate, Your Broodfulness?" Evryn appeared at his elbow, his own net already showing signs of enthusiastic use. "I was beginning to think you'd spend the entire evening smoldering mysteriously at the edges of the gathering. Very dramatic of you, but hardly sporting."

Ryden's laugh came easily. "Smoldering mysteriously?"

"Yes. Gazing moodily into the middle distance while the rest of us have fun. Dreaming of your mystery lady of letters, were you?"

Ryden tensed, his guard rising at once. He'd had to take care in his recent interactions with Evryn that nothing in his manner betrayed what he now knew—his 'lady of letters' was none other than the sister Evryn had firmly warned him away from. Aloud, he only said, "Perhaps."

Evryn laughed, clapping him on the shoulder. "You truly are smitten with this mystery woman, aren't you? Oh, and that reminds me. You still haven't shown me that enchanted letter box. Perhaps once the festivities wind down, we could adjourn to your study and have a look?"

A sharp chill swept through Ryden. His eyes darted immediately to find Aurelise, terrified she might be within earshot, that she might make the connection between an enchanted letter box and her mysterious correspondent. Relief flooded through him when he spotted her a good distance away, laughing with complete abandonment as she and Lady Willow attempted to corner that single moonflare everyone was so determined to claim.

Stars above, had he ever heard her laugh so unabashedly before? It was captivating, the way joy transformed her face, erasing all traces of the shy, nervous girl who so often let her smiles fall unseen, tucked away behind a downward glance.

"I do hope," Evryn said, his tone carrying a subtle warning, "that it's Lady Willow you're observing with such particular attention."

Ryden forced his gaze away from Aurelise, affecting casual interest in the general crowd. "Merely lost in thought, my friend," he said with a practiced smile. "And as for that box, we'll examine it at some point. Perhaps not tonight. We're all having far too much fun here."

"Well then, I'm off to reclaim my honor from Mariselle," Evryn said, much to Ryden's relief. "She won't be laughing quite so smugly when I catch that moonflare."

The next hour passed in a blur of laughter and light. Ryden joined Evryn, Mariselle, Fin and several of their friends, throwing himself into the chase with enthusiasm, his competitive nature awakening as he pursued the darting creatures through the gardens. He caught three ribbon-birds in quick succession, their wings dissolving into delicate tokens in his palm. A particularly cunning foxlet led him on a merry chase through the rose garden before he finally cornered it near the decorative pond.

But always, always, his awareness tracked back to Aurelise. She seemed to have abandoned her earlier restraint entirely, her chase taking her in wide circles around the fountain alongside Lady Willow, the two of them laughing helplessly whenever their nets caught on one another.

As midnight approached and the gleams began their final dance before the spell would fade, the moonflare finally made another appearance. It descended from wherever it had been hiding, a creature of pure crystallized light. Every head turned, every net raised, as it began a teasing spiral just above their reach.

What followed was chaos of the most entertaining sort. Ladies abandoned all pretense of decorum. Gentlemen crashed into each other in their enthusiasm. Yet it was Ryden, who'd likely had more practice in the art of gleamcatching than anyone else present, who ultimately claimed the elusive prize.

His net swept through the air in a perfect arc, the silver threads singing as they closed around the moonflare. For a moment, the creature's light intensified, filling his vision with brilliant white, and then it dissolved and fell onto his outstretched palm, a small silver token stamped with the delicate impression of a moth.

The gathering erupted in good-natured groans and congratulations. Everyone clapped politely, while Fin coughed something about "unfair royal advantages" that was clearly meant as a jest.

Evryn cursed, not quite under his breath. "I had that thing perfectly positioned—"

"You had nothing," Mariselle interrupted with a laugh, moving to take her husband's arm. "If anyone besides His Highness deserved to catch it, clearly it was me."

"You are aware, darling," Evryn replied, still catching his breath but smiling down at her all the same, "that I had intended to catch it *for you*, before His Lordliness so selfishly claimed it for himself?"

Laughter rippled through the group again, easy and bright beneath the last drifting gleams.

Ryden smiled to himself, slipping the token into the small inner pocket of his waistcoat, unwilling to confess that he'd caught the moonflare with much the same intention. He was merely waiting for the right moment to offer it, discreetly, to the one he'd caught it for.

Later, when the festivities began to thin and the night air cooled, he found himself beside Aurelise once more. She admitted, with that quiet composure of hers, that she had enjoyed the evening. "Though," she added, "so much wild activity leaves me rather in need of stillness, to restore myself, or I shall not survive another day of this pace. I'll likely steal a few moments in the music room once everyone has retired. I know it's late, but …" She gave a small shrug, a shy smile curving her lips. "It's what I would do if I were at home."

He found her there later, just as she'd said, already lost to her music, eyes closed, her fingers tracing slow, graceful patterns across the keys. He said nothing, unwilling to disturb her, and simply set the token atop the piano for her to find. Then, for a few precious minutes, he stood in the doorway, listening as the quiet melody threaded through him with a gentle ache, before he slipped silently away.

Dear L,

You have been curiously quiet these past days.

Did I overwhelm you again?

Still yours (when you are ready),

R

Chapter Nineteen

"I FIND YOUR HAIR RATHER BEAUTIFUL."

The words escaped Aurelise's lips before she could catch them, floating into the night air like one of her wayward melodies. She watched, fascinated, as Prince Ryden's eyes crinkled in surprised delight, moonlight catching in their depths.

"I used to tell myself it vexed me," she continued, her voice carrying a dreamy quality she'd never heard from herself before. "All that midnight blue, drawing everyone's attention. But I cannot seem to locate that feeling anymore. I can find only …"

She shifted slightly. The grass between them was cool and pale, brushing softly against her cheek as she lay turned toward him. Her gloved fingers reached toward those dark strands that looked impossibly soft in the silver light. But at the last moment, some vestige of propriety made her lower her hand, though it took considerable effort.

"It's beautiful," she finished simply.

A slow smile curved Prince Ryden's lips. "I find I rather like you this way."

She laughed, a soft, breathy sound. "Thoroughly addled? My thoughts all …" She turned her gaze toward the branches above and lifted her hand, allowing her fingers to drift lazily through the air. A gentle melody followed her movements, notes that swayed and spun. "Scattered to the winds?"

"No." The prince's voice was low. "I like you utterly honest."

"Ah." She settled back against the grass, feeling the cool blades through the fabric of her dress. "I'm certain *honesty* was precisely your aim when you convinced me to undertake dare number nine."

The reality of her current situation should have horrified her. Here she lay, stretched out on the grass beside the lake at what must be well past midnight, with Prince Ryden similarly reclined barely a few feet away. Between them rested an ornate moonwood pipe, its bowl—spell-tempered to remain cool enough not to burn the grass—still faintly glowing with the last wisps of driftshade leaf, that notorious vanilla-spicy substance she'd sworn she would never, under any circumstances, sample.

Yet somehow, mere hours ago, she'd allowed him to convince her otherwise.

She'd been in the Sun Salon, surrounded by lists and confection samples and an alarming number of decisions for her upcoming tea. Though the event was still ten days hence, the weight of it had been crushing her beneath its expectations. Her music had betrayed her anxiety, high tremulous notes fluttering about like distressed songbirds, despite her improved control these days.

Thimble and Spark had been attempting to help, though their anxiety only added to her own. *Are you absolutely CERTAIN this is the direction you'd like to take your event?* Spark had asked multiple times. *I don't believe any other lady is approaching hers in quite the same fashion.*

That was when Prince Ryden had appeared in the doorway, taking in the scene with those keen ink-blue eyes that missed nothing. "Lady Aurelise, you appear to be under siege by your own preparations."

"Everything must be perfect," she'd said, hearing the edge of panic in her own voice. "Because if not, then—"

"The world shall cease its turning?" He'd strolled into the room with that casual confidence that both irritated and oddly soothed her. "The seas shall boil? The stars shall tumble from the skies?"

"No, because I—I am attempting something that is somewhat … *daring*, and I fear that if every other element is not perfect, then this single *daring* element will not be well received."

He had looked utterly intrigued at her mention of a 'daring' element—something she had not breathed a word of to anyone else. Leaning against the back of an armchair, he had tilted his head in that infuriatingly attentive way of his.

"Daring?" he'd echoed. "Do tell me more."

But at that, her music had risen in a flurry of anxious notes, and her composure had splintered. She'd pressed her hands to her face, trying to steady her breath, whispering silent reassurances that she could manage this. It was only a small event. It was surely not as overwhelming as it seemed.

Surely not as overwhelming as R declaring, in his last letter, that she had already stolen everything there was of him to steal—a confession she still had not found the courage to answer.

Perhaps the prince realized how close she was to unraveling, because he'd straightened from the chair and taken a careful step closer. "This calls for desperate measures. I know precisely what you require."

She'd lowered her hands, taken a deep breath, and regarded him with deep suspicion. "If you're about to suggest another midnight adventure—"

"Of course." That wicked grin had appeared, the one that inevitably preceded trouble. "With the express intent of sampling a small remedy for overwrought nerves. And," he'd added, eyes glinting with amusement, "it will conveniently allow you to cross another item from that list of yours."

Now, lying beside him under the stars, Aurelise had to admit his 'remedy' had been remarkably effective. The crushing weight of anxiety had dissolved into something soft and manageable, like clouds she could shape with her fingers.

At least for this particular dare she'd maintained enough presence of mind to dress properly. After Marta had retired for the evening, Aurelise had donned a walking dress of deep burgundy silk, complete with gloves and sturdy slippers. Not that proper attire would save her reputation if they were discovered. A lady alone with a gentleman, unchaperoned, partaking of drift-shade leaf? The scandal would destroy her family's standing entirely. She would become the cautionary tale mothers whispered to their daughters.

Yet somehow, with the gentle haze wrapped around her thoughts like silk, she could not summon the appropriate alarm.

The night sang around them—whisperwings weaving their rhythmic chorus through the dark, the lake murmuring softly against the shore, a few garden pixies giggling in the branches above. Even the air felt different, charged with possibilities she normally would not allow herself to consider.

"What else could I possibly have been after," Prince Ryden asked, "beyond the simple satisfaction of watching you complete another dare?"

"I suspect," she said, rolling onto her side again to face him properly, "that your true intention was to render me thoroughly insensible, whereupon you would take advantage of my compromised state like the notorious scoundrel everyone knows you to be."

He laughed, a startled sound that seemed to surprise him as much as her. "Scoundrel, am I?"

"Mmm." She nodded sagely, though the effect was somewhat ruined by her inability to stop smiling. "Everyone speaks of it. Your reputation quite precedes you."

The playfulness vanished from his expression as he pushed himself up on one elbow, looking down at her with sudden intensity. "I hope you know I would never do such a thing. I would never take advantage of you, not in any state."

For a few quiet moments, she merely stared up at him, sensing the weight of his sincerity. When she spoke, her words were soft: "Your reputation suggests otherwise."

"My reputation," he said simply, "is largely fabrication."

Some of the haze cleared from her mind. "Truly?"

"Well." That familiar grin tugged at his lips again. "Not entirely fabrication, I'll grant you. There exists more than a little truth within the stories." The smile gentled, became something more vulnerable. "But I would never do anything you did not wish me to do."

The implication hung between them, unspoken but clear in the way he held her gaze, and a strange, breath-stealing warmth unfurled low within her. He *would* do something … if she wished it.

But she did not wish anything of the sort. Certainly not. It was merely the driftshade muddling her thoughts, making her notice how the moonlight played across his features, how his shirt had come slightly undone at the top, revealing a triangle of skin that she very definitely needed to look away from now.

She rolled onto her back again, needing distance from that intense gaze. He followed suit, stretching out beside her once more.

"Tell me something I don't know about you," he said softly. "Something most people do not know."

"Hmm." Her gaze drifted upward, tracing the dark lacework of branches overhead. The silence between them was easy—warm, unhurried. "My siblings call me Lise," she offered eventually.

Several moments of quiet followed. Then: "Lise." He spoke the name like a secret, the sound barely more than a breath. Then he laughed, quiet and wondering, and when she turned to look at him, he was shaking his head as though he'd just discovered something miraculous.

"What?" she asked.

He met her eyes, and the tenderness in that single glance caused her breath to falter. "Nothing," he answered, though his smile held secrets she couldn't decipher. "It suits you perfectly. I like it. *Lady Lise.*"

The way he said it, like he was tasting something sweet, sent heat flooding through her. "Your turn," she said quickly, though she did not look away. "Tell me something about yourself that remains hidden from society."

He was quiet a long time, and when he finally spoke, his voice had gone distant. "My father never loved me."

The words fell between them like stones into still water. Aurelise's lips parted on a soft exhale. "What?" She rolled onto her stomach, propping herself up on her elbows, her gaze intent on him.

"He was not a good man." Ryden stared up at the canopy of leaves above them, his profile sharp in the moonlight. "He treated my mother abhorrently. His treatment of me was hardly better. He gave me this, actually." Without looking at her, he pulled aside the loose collar of his shirt, pointing to the vaguely star-shaped marking just above his collarbone. The scar she'd asked about the night they had swum in the lake.

Without conscious thought, her hand moved toward him. Through the fog in her mind, some part of her shrieked in alarm—what was she doing, touching him like this?—but the voice seemed very far away. He went utterly still beneath her touch, his breathing shallow, while her gloved finger traced the edges of the scar.

"You told me it was the result of an accident," she murmured.

"In a way," he said, his voice little more than a breath, "it was."

She became acutely aware of their proximity then. The now familiar scent of fresh rain on cedar trees, of how she was almost leaning over him, how if she simply lowered her head …

No.

She pushed herself upright abruptly, her hand flying to her hair which had become somewhat disheveled and likely had bits of grass in it. "That was … considerably more serious than my own revelation."

"Would you prefer something lighter?" His voice had gone rough in a way that sent shivers down her spine.

"Only if you wish to share it."

"Very well." He sat up as well, though they were somehow far closer now than when they'd first positioned themselves on the grass. "My favorite event of the Season—that's appropriately frivolous, isn't it?"

"Perfectly so." She drew her knees up, wrapping her arms around them in a gesture that would have horrified the majority of her family and made Rosavyn grin with delight. "Let me guess—the Gleamcatcher's Soirée? You did win the moonflare, after all."

"And gifted it to you," he said quietly, his gaze steady and unguarded.

A faint tremor stirred in her chest as their gazes held. She had found his gift the night of the Soirée, a small silver token resting atop the pianoforte. It had unsettled her then, though she'd pretended it hadn't, insisting to herself that it meant nothing. But now, under the stars, with that quiet intensity in his eyes, *nothing* no longer felt like the truth.

She swallowed and looked away. "So … the Gleamcatcher's Soirée, then?"

"Yes, though there is perhaps another event I enjoy equally. The Festival of Lantern Wishes."

"I don't believe I've heard of that one."

"It's one of our smaller gatherings, usually held close to the Summer Solstice Ball." His eyes took on a distant quality, seeing something beyond the present moment. "Guests inscribe wishes on enchanted parchment, then fold them into lanterns. When released, they rise into the night sky. The wishes that align with the constellations—that is to say, that find their matching stars—are said to come true."

She smiled. "It sounds beautiful."

"It is." He turned to look at her again, and something in his expression made her heart skip yet again. "You'll see it for yourself this Season."

For a long, quiet moment, the space between them seemed to deepen, filled with a warmth that swelled and grew until it was almost too much to bear. It felt big, too big, as though it might spill over and remake everything she thought she understood.

I have no intention of choosing you.

What need have I to charm you?

We may converse honestly, without the tedious pretense of courtship.

And yet … the way he looked at her now suggested something entirely different. She drew a steadying breath and looked away before the feeling could completely overtake her.

"I'm feeling wonderfully drowsy," she said, needing to break the moment. "I should return to my chambers before I accidentally fall asleep beneath the stars."

"Rest easy," he said, that teasing tone creeping back into his voice again. "I would carry you back to your bed, should that occur."

She shook her head, though she found she was not nearly as scandalized as she ought to be. "If your aim is to shock me with impropriety, I'll have you know I'm developing quite an immunity to your scandalous suggestions."

"Then I shall simply have to become increasingly creative in my impropriety."

She laughed at that. "You are incorrigible."

"I do try to be consistent in my character." A faint smile tugged at his mouth before he tilted his head, a touch of hesitation softening the easy charm in his manner. "May I ask one more thing before I escort you back?"

"That depends entirely upon what you're asking."

"Would you …" He drew a careful breath. "Would you play for me? Not the pianoforte—though I count myself fortunate for every time you've permitted me to remain in the music room with you and listen. What I mean is … your own music."

The request was so unexpected, so earnest, that she could only stare at him. He'd heard her music before, of course—it had escaped often in his presence, and he'd been present at the musicale early on in her stay at Solstice Hall, when all the Crown Court ladies had been expected to perform. But this was different. He was asking her to deliberately share this part of herself that she treasured most deeply with him and only him.

"Please?" His eyes captured hers, the blue of them seeming darker, depthless. And it was surely only the haze of the driftshade, the enchantment of the night, but she felt herself sinking, helplessly, into their depths.

"Very well," she whispered, though she couldn't seem to look away, nor remember how to move her hands.

He reached for her then, his touch slow, deliberate. His gaze never wavered from hers as his fingers found her wrist. "You removed your gloves at the Opening Ball," he murmured, his voice low, the words curling through the night like a secret. "And again at the musicale. Do you always do that?"

But he was already easing at the tiny buttons along her wrist, one after another, his movements unhurried, almost reverent.

She swallowed. "Yes," she managed, though the word came out unsteady as he gently grasped the fingertips of her glove. "It … it allows me to …" A shuddering breath escaped her as the glove began to slide down over her hand. "To better feel the magic around me," she finished on a breath.

The fabric slipped free beneath his hands, satin whispering against her skin, leaving his palm warm against the bare skin of her forearm. His fingers traced a slow, lingering path downward, following the curve of her arm until his hand found hers.

Then he reached for her other hand, fingers moving to the buttons there, undoing them with deliberately aching slowness. And surely this was the driftshade's influence, because she would *never, ever*, under any normal circumstances, allow a gentleman to undress any part of her, no matter how small. Yet she could not look away from his face, from the intensity in his eyes as he revealed her bare skin inch by careful inch.

By the time the second glove lay on the grass beside the first, she could barely breathe.

"There," Prince Ryden murmured, his voice rough as his thumb brushed across her bare palm before releasing her. "Now you are ready."

Ready? She was the very opposite of ready. She'd quite forgotten what she was even meant to be doing. *Music*, she reminded herself with another shuddering breath, her skin still tingling beneath the memory of his touch.

"Can I—that is—would you mind if—" She took another steadying breath, forcing herself to look away from him. "I find it easier if I close my eyes."

"Of course," he said.

She let her eyelids fall shut and drew several deep, steady breaths, willing her pulse to slow. The driftshade was still there—soft and heady—curling through her veins, loosening her restraint, quieting every careful thought. She let her mind wander toward the melodies and harmonies that were ever-present beneath her skin suspended, invisible, in the air around her, waiting to be caught and shaped into something beautiful.

She breathed again.

Slow … deep …

In … out …

Then she lifted one hand and swept it through the air in a languid arc before her. Music unfurled like silk ribbons in the dark—low, velvety cello notes weaving with the crystalline shimmer of harp and viola. A meandering melody that wound and looped around them both, encircling them in a cocoon of sound. Her hands moved in slow, graceful patterns, tracing arcs and spirals through the air as the music swelled, gathered upon itself, and rose toward a shimmering crescendo before softening once more. Gradually, the sound gentled, each note folding into the next until it faded to near stillness, like the final sigh of a dream.

When the final note drifted into silence, Aurelise opened her eyes to find him watching her with an expression that made her chest tighten painfully. Did it touch him the way it did her? That sensation of being threaded through with something that was like warmth and color and light, and yet somehow none of those things.

"Has anyone told you before how utterly extraordinary you are?" Prince Ryden murmured.

She blinked, slowly. The driftshade still lingered in her veins, and the memory of the music still hummed around her, and what she wanted to say was, *Not while looking at me like that.* But she forced another breath into her lungs and lowered her eyes. She might have been feeling light and unguarded, but she possessed just enough sense to know she ought to return to her rooms before she said or did something she would most assuredly regret.

I would never do anything you did not wish me to do.

"I believe it is time to return to my chambers now," she said a little too loudly, as though attempting to drown out her own thoughts.

"Yes, of course." The prince stood and offered her his hand, but before she could reach for it, she remembered her hands were bare.

"Oh. My gloves." She reached for them, trying her utmost to sound casual, though she very much suspected she would never look at another pair of gloves in quite the same way again.

She slid them on, fastening the tiny buttons with careful fingers before placing her hand in his and allowing him to pull her to her feet. The world tilted slightly, and she steadied herself against his arm with a small laugh. "Oh. Perhaps the ground isn't quite as stable as I recalled."

"The ground is perfectly stable," he said, unmistakable amusement coloring his tone. "You, however, are delightfully unsteady."

He kept hold of her arm, and she made no effort to draw away.

As they made their way back through the moonlit gardens, the charged tension between them gradually softened into something warmer, easier, perhaps aided by the fact that she seemed incapable of walking in a straight line. She tripped over roots that weren't there, lost her balance on even ground, and giggled at his teasing insistence that Lady Aurelise, paragon of grace, could not possibly be capable of such clumsiness unless the universe itself was conspiring against her.

It was, frankly, a wonder they reached her suite at all without waking half the palace. There had been the small table that appeared out of nowhere and caught her hip, and the towering flower arrangement she somehow managed to topple—though she could have sworn it had been nowhere near her path. Prince Ryden, of course, found every mishap thoroughly entertaining, especially the part where they were forced to hide behind a marble statue while several footmen came to investigate the mysterious crash.

By the time they arrived at her door, she was deliciously drowsy and pleasantly content, already imagining the bliss of sinking into her bed and not stirring until noon. Though perhaps—just perhaps—she might first find the courage to reply to R. After all, she could now claim to have completed a dare he surely believed she would never attempt.

She stepped inside and turned to bid the prince goodnight. He was already leaning against the frame with that casual grace that seemed as natural to him as breathing. "I still can't quite believe you actually allowed me to talk you into this," he said.

"Nor I," she agreed with a small smile. "I'll likely be horrified when I wake in the morning and remember."

"I hope not. I thought it rather fun. We may have to attempt it again."

She laughed, then quickly pressed a hand over her mouth when the sound rang far too loudly in the quiet space. "Definitely not. Though I suppose if I'm ever to complete dare number three, I may require a similar degree of … assistance."

"Oh?" The prince's brows rose in exaggerated interest. "Are you saying you have plans now to complete that particular challenge? You seem to have been firmly against it since the beginning."

She tipped her head and gave him a shy smile that was laced with something … daring. "Why, I've been saving it for you, of course."

Something flared in his eyes. He leaned closer, hand rising to ghost along her jaw before tucking a wayward strand of hair behind her ear. Then he bent nearer still, his lips grazing past her ear as he whispered, "I believe you may now cross that one off your list as well, Lady Lise."

Dearest Remarkable Ridiculous Ravishing R,

At last, I have found a way to shock you rather than the reverse.

Dare number nine. Smoke driftshade leaf. I daresay you thought I wouldn't do it. But I have triumphed. I have

In addition, I should warn

It is highly probable my mind is still drifting while writing this.

And highly probable that I shall regret this tomorrow when I

But I keep telling myself that I should try. At least try. To explain. Because am I not supposed to be bolder now? Is that not what you've been trying to show me with this darned list of yours? That I can

Did you overwhelm me again? Yes. You absolutely did. Your words have a terrible way of slipping past all my carefully constructed barriers. As if they know exactly where the cracks are.

I should be furious with you for that 'you already have it all' declaration. It was unfair, you know. Spectacularly, breathtakingly unfair. You broke the rules. You were supposed to pretend that nothing has changed between us. That you are not desperately mine.

You were supposed to pretend you are not fully aware that I am

That I am also

Have you ever wondered what it's like to feel everything too much? Every emotion amplified until it's almost unbearable? The smallest joy becomes ecstasy. The mildest disappointment becomes

I have spent my life learning to contain it all. Building walls. Creating distance. Finding safety in solitude and

Music.

I am not certain whether I have spoken to you of the music. I think not, for I still cling rather tightly to the safety of this anonymity, and I've been wary of sharing anything that might give away

But the music helps.

It is not that I do not want to feel. It is that I feel too intensely. I am a cup filled beyond its capacity, perpetually spilling over.

And LOVE? Love terrifies me more than anything. Because if ordinary emotions already consume me, then love would

I do not want to drown in it, R.

I do not want to drown.

I do not want to drown.

And your words. Your terrible, wonderful words. They keep finding me, no matter how I hide. 'You already have it all,' you said. As if you've surrendered something precious into my keeping without my consent. As if I'm supposed to know what to do with this … this …

It feels like

SO MUCH.

TOO MUCH.

I believe I should climb into bed before my quill wanders its way right off the edge of this

My dearest L,

I find myself oddly speechless after reading your letter—an unusual state for me, as you well know. Your driftshade-induced honesty has given me a glimpse of something I've long suspected but never fully understood until now.

First, I must congratulate you on your triumphant completion of dare number nine. I confess to a not-so-small smile at the thought of you, my cautious L, engaging in something so delightfully improper. Though I suspect by the time you read this letter, you may be cursing both me and my 'darned list.'

Please do not regret what you've shared. I understand the morning light often makes us wish we could reclaim our nighttime confessions, but I beg you—do not take these words back. They are precious to me beyond measure.

I cannot claim to understand what it means to feel everything so intensely. To experience the world as you do, where every emotion threatens to overflow its boundaries. I can only try to imagine what that must be like, to live with such depth of feeling that you must build walls to contain it.

And now I understand why my words sometimes require days of silence afterward. Why you need time and space to process what passes between us. Each letter is not merely words on paper for you, but waves that crash against those carefully constructed barriers.

But listen to me, L. Listen carefully.

I swear to you that I would never let you drown.

If you fear the overwhelming tide of feeling, then let me be your anchor. Let me be the steady rock against which those waves break. I promise you—with everything I am—that I would hold you firm through any storm of emotion. You will not be swept away.

You fear that love would consume you? It need not. Not if you have someone to help you carry it. Not if you have someone who understands that sometimes you need retreat, sometimes you need silence, sometimes you need space to breathe when it all becomes too much.

I know these are only words, and perhaps you cannot bring yourself to trust them. You know me as teasing, light-hearted, rarely serious. It may be difficult to reconcile that with someone who claims to be solid and steadfast —an anchor in turbulent waters.

But L, I am still here. After nearly a year of letters, I am still here. I have watched the seasons change through our correspondence, have shared countless thoughts with you, have found myself transformed by your words. And if there is one thing you can trust, it is this:

I love you.

I have kept myself from writing those words for so long because I knew they would frighten you, but I want to leave you with no doubt:

I LOVE YOU.

(You are terrified right now, reading those three little words. Your hands are shaking. Perhaps you're finding it hard to breathe. For this, I apologize. My words are overwhelming you all over again, but I will not take them back. You need to know them.)

If you could bring yourself to take this risk—to let this feeling in—I believe you would discover something wonderful: that when the wave washes over you, you remain. Different, perhaps. Changed, certainly. But not washed away. Not drowned. Not consumed.

And I would still be there, holding fast to you.

When you are ready—and only when you are ready—I am here. I have patience enough for both of us. I have always suspected that anything truly worth having with you would require time and care and gentle persistence.

Take your time, my L. Process this in whatever way you need.

I will be waiting, as always, for your next letter.

Yours, steadfastly,

R

Chapter Twenty

No. She did not need to *process* anything. She needed to move *beyond* it.

Beyond the tender confession that had arrived in R's latest letter, beyond those three devastating words that had burrowed beneath her skin like seeds threatening to bloom. Beyond the person whose beautiful words were slowly, inexorably drawing her heart from its carefully maintained fortress. And most certainly beyond the charmingly flirtatious prince whose very presence seemed to unravel every thread of sense she possessed.

She needed to move beyond *both* of them. Before they destroyed her.

Aurelise pressed her fingers to her temples, trying to massage away the persistent ache that had taken residence there since the previous evening. The driftshade had long since faded from her system, leaving her with crystalline clarity about precisely how inappropriate her behavior had been. Not only the previous night, but the entire time she'd been here at Solstice Hall.

Running through rain-soaked gardens. Taking illicit midnight swims. *Smoking*, for goodness' sake. And then an attempt at *flirting*? Stars above, when assembled in such damning succession, it painted a portrait of impropriety that would have sent the Aurelise of several weeks ago into a dead faint.

She needed to put an end to this immediately.

Which was precisely how, on this uncomfortably warm afternoon, Aurelise found herself strolling through the palace gardens alongside Prince Ryden, trying desperately to maintain an appropriate distance while the sun beat down mercilessly from a cloudless sky.

Fortunately, a retinue of palace pixies had followed them from the terrace, holding between them a swath of shimmering mistcloth. It drifted above her and the prince like a weightless canopy, scattering the sunlight into golden haze. She was grateful, of course—the day was far too warm for comfort—but it made her acutely aware of every word she spoke, as though even the pixies might be listening.

She'd requested this audience through proper channels that morning (after much anxious pacing about her suite), and when Prince Ryden had suggested a garden walk, she'd readily agreed. It would be properly chaperoned—an attendant walked a respectable distance behind them, her presence a constant reminder of propriety. And the timing was perfect: as soon as this conversation concluded, she would depart with the other Crown Court ladies for their fortnightly visit home. If things went poorly, at least escape was readily available.

"You seem uncommonly serious today," Prince Ryden observed as Thimble darted beside them, performing a series of gleeful aerial pirouettes, her wings catching the sunlight in bursts of violet and rose. Spark glided a few paces ahead. "Should I be concerned?"

"Not at all," Aurelise replied, keeping her tone carefully neutral. "I merely wished to discuss certain matters before my departure."

"Certain matters," he repeated, that familiar amusement threading through his voice. "How delightfully mysterious."

They turned down a path lined with blossom arches, where the air grew heavy with warmth and perfume. The heady scent of sun-drenched honeysilk roses mingled with something sharper—mint, perhaps. The soft trill of hidden songbirds threaded through the air, accompanied by the small, indignant shouts of two garden gnomes locked in a heated debate at the base of a nearby hedge.

As they emerged from the path and walked toward a large ornate fountain, Aurelise tried to recall the careful phrasing she'd practiced in her room that morning. Nearby, Spark alighted on the rim of a large earthen pot in which a lemon tree grew. The sunlight gleamed across his emerald form as his voice brushed through her mind: *Lemons*, he declared with grave solemnity. *Deceptively dangerous. Their scent is addictive.* He inhaled again. *Almost as good as custard.*

Neither he nor Thimble had been supportive of her plan to ask the prince to resume a more proper distance. Naturally, they had objected, Thimble first and Spark with rumbling indignation soon after. But Aurelise had stood her ground. This was how it must be, she reminded them. Did they not recall her telling them, the very day she arrived here, that she had no wish to be princess?

Thimble's tiny eyes had shimmered with unshed tears when she whispered that Aurelise would make such a lovely one. Even Spark, whose usual emotional range ran from mild irritation to faint disapproval, had sounded gruffly unsteady when he muttered something about being unable to imagine anyone else as Crown Consort to the High Lord.

The guilt of disappointing them had wrapped tightly around her ribs, squeezing until it was almost difficult to breathe, and making her think yet again of the words she'd unintentionally spilled onto paper addressed to R the night before.

Every emotion amplified until it's almost unbearable …

But she'd managed to smile and tell her lovable companions that they must recover from their heartbreak and perhaps redirect their enthusiasm toward one of the other ladies. Not Willow, who, if Aurelise had interpreted matters correctly, already harbored a fondness for another gentleman. So perhaps Lady Coravelle. In Aurelise's few interactions with her, she had seemed perfectly kind, and far more suited to the role. Thimble and Spark had exchanged a look so brimming with unspoken mischief that Aurelise had immediately narrowed her eyes. "No sabotage," she'd warned.

They had then insisted on accompanying her this afternoon as a mark of solidarity, though Aurelise suspected their true intentions leaned more toward interference than assistance.

"Shall we stop here?" Prince Ryden suggested as they reached the fountain—a magnificent creation of white marble depicting water sprites at play, their frozen forms sending streams arcing through the air. The sound of splashing water provided a soothing backdrop, though it did little to calm Aurelise's racing heart. "The spray provides some relief from this heat," the prince added.

Indeed, the fine mist that drifted from the fountain was pleasantly cool against her flushed skin. She turned to face him properly, squaring her shoulders. Their chaperone had found a bench in the shade several yards away, her attention politely averted, though the pixies still fluttered overhead with the mistcloth.

"Your Highness," Aurelise began formally, "I believe recent events have led to a certain … informality between us that is neither appropriate nor advisable."

The prince's expression shifted to one of polite attention, though she didn't miss the way his lips twitched. "Indeed? Do elaborate."

"The dare list," she said in a low tone. "Which, I might add, was never meant to involve you in the first place. All these inappropriate adventures, these … clandestine meetings. They must cease immediately."

"Must they?" He tilted his head, studying her with those deep blue eyes. "And here I thought we were making excellent progress."

"That is precisely the problem. You should be making progress with the other ladies of the court. Ladies who actually wish to be chosen. Ladies who could fulfill the role of Crown Consort."

"Ah." He nodded sagely. "Ladies who wish to fulfill a role. How romantic."

"If it is romance you seek, I'm certain any one of them would be happy to—" She paused, noticing the way his gaze kept drifting toward the lemon tree where Spark—and now Thimble—sat. "Your Highness, are you listening to me?"

"Every word," he assured her, though she caught the telltale flicker of amusement that suggested another conversation entirely was happening beyond her perception.

He's terribly handsome in this light, came Thimble's dreamy mental voice in Aurelise's mind.

Prince Ryden coughed, poorly disguising a laugh.

Oh, forgive me, Your Highness! Thimble squeaked. *That one was supposed to be directed only at Lady Aurelise!*

"Are you silently conspiring with my companions while I am endeavoring to converse with you?" Aurelise asked, trying to sound disapproving.

The prince's smile curved higher. "I am doing nothing. They are the ones who seem to have important things to tell me. Such as how pretty you look with the sunlight catching your hair and turning it to gold—as though I might have failed to notice."

Aurelise's mouth opened, then closed again. Heat rushed to her cheeks, and for a moment, her carefully rehearsed words scattered. "I—that is—" She drew a sharp breath, her gaze darting toward the attendant before returning to Prince Ryden. "You see? This is precisely what I mean. You cannot go about saying things like that to me when we both know you have no interest in me."

"No interest?" His voice softened, the teasing edge tempered by something … else. He took a single, measured step closer. "Lady Lise, I think we both know that could not be further from the truth."

She suppressed a groan. She should never have shared that name with him. On his lips, it sounded far too … intimate. Darned driftshade leaf.

"I—that is—" She took a purposeful step backward. "Your Highness, I believe it would be wiser if we … maintained a certain distance."

"Of course," he answered, though the glint in his eyes and the slow curve of his mouth suggested no such intention. "You wish for the two of us to be perfectly proper in every way."

"Yes."

He tugged one of his gloves off. "Because being perfectly proper makes you happy."

She frowned, her eyes on his bare hand now. "I don't see how *happiness* has anything to do with it. And what are you—"

"Hmm." He removed his other glove, studying the water as though it might contain answers. Then he leaned sideways in that elegantly lazy way of his and trailed one hand through the water.

"Your Highness, what are you—"

He flicked a few droplets in her direction. They landed on her arm.

She stared, aghast. "Did you just—"

"You appeared overheated by the weight of your good sense," he said mildly.

"Your Highness!" She was half scandalized, half—something else entirely. "You did not just do that."

He sent another playful scatter of droplets her way, this time landing squarely on her glove.

"You did," she breathed, incredulous.

He only smiled, entirely unrepentant. "You looked as though you needed cooling off."

Without thinking—certainly without considering the consequences—Aurelise bent swiftly, cupped her gloved hand in the fountain, and flung water directly at his face.

The surprise in his expression as water dripped from his perfect blue hair was perhaps the most satisfying thing she'd seen all week. "My lady—"

She pressed her other hand to her mouth, trying to smother a laugh. "I … I am merely returning the favor," she managed to say around a snort of suppressed laughter.

"Oh? In that case—" He sent another splash, straight at her face this time.

She gasped, tensing, then started laughed, the sound bursting out of her before she could restrain it. From the corner of her eye, she saw the attendant stand, heard her make a helpless sound of protest, but it was quickly drowned out as all decorum vanished entirely.

Prince Ryden had already retaliated with a considerably larger splash that caught Aurelise full in the chest, soaking through the front of her dress.

"Oh, you absolute—" She didn't finish the sentence, too busy launching her own counterattack. The two of them began circling the fountain like duelists, each seeking the advantage, sending increasingly dramatic sprays of water at each other while the attendant fluttered helplessly nearby and the palace pixies giggled, having given up entirely on holding the mistcloth aloft.

Go for his hair! Spark cheered from his perch on the lemon tree pot. *Destroy it completely!*

His cravat! Thimble shrieked.

Prince Ryden hopped over the basin's edge in one swift motion and stepped straight into the shallow basin. "Surrender!" he called out, using a burst of magic to send a truly impressive wave in her direction. "You're outmatched!"

"Never!" Aurelise darted around the fountain's circumference, still launching attacks from the edge while determinedly avoiding the water itself. "I've survived years of tedious etiquette lessons—I have remarkable endurance!"

"But I have the tactical advantage!" He waded closer, water streaming from his now thoroughly ruined clothing. "Come and face me properly!"

"I'm perfectly capable of defeating you from—" She leaned forward for another attack just as he lunged toward the edge. His fingers caught her wrist, and her balance—already precarious from her enthusiastic water-flinging—completely failed her.

She toppled forward with a shriek, directly into the fountain and directly on top of the prince, who tried to catch her but only succeeded in cushioning her fall as they both went under.

For the briefest instant, panic flared—born more of shock than true fear, for she knew perfectly well the water was shallow—and in that suspended moment, the memory of his words broke through her thoughts. Or were they R's words?

I swear to you that I would never let you drown.

And then they surfaced, sputtering and laughing, absolutely drenched. Aurelise's careful hairstyle had completely collapsed, wet strands plastered to her face. The prince's hair hung in dripping disarray, his fine clothes clinging to him in a manner that was decidedly improper to notice.

"In case you had any doubt," he said, "as to whether some of your recent activities count as 'entirely improper,' I believe a water fight in a palace fountain sufficiently covers dare number ten."

A breathless laugh escaped her. "Yes, I believe I've quite thoroughly accomplished that particular dare by now."

Their laughter gradually faded as she became intensely aware of their position—her hands braced against his chest for balance, his arm around her waist from when he'd tried to catch her, water dripping from them both.

"Tell me," he said quietly, his voice low enough that only she could hear over the fountain's spray. "Do you truly want me to keep my distance? Or is that merely what the proper, perfectly composed version of Lady Aurelise Rowanwood believes she *should* want?"

The question hung between them. She could feel her heart racing beneath her soaked bodice, could sense a tide of feeling gathering inside her, rising higher with every breath until it threatened to spill over.

"I … I …"

"*What* in the name of all the stars is happening here?"

Aurelise jerked back at the sound of that voice, mortification crashing through her in a cold wave. But her drenched skirts tangled about her legs, and she went down again, colliding with the prince in another graceless splash. His arm curved around her again, and he helped her upright, both of them dripping and breathless.

The High Lady stood at the garden path's bend, flanked by two ladies-in-waiting who looked perilously close to dissolving into laughter. The High Lady herself looked as though she was witnessing something that defied all natural laws.

"Mother," Prince Ryden said with remarkable composure for someone standing knee-deep in a fountain. "We were merely cooling off. It's an uncommonly warm afternoon."

"Cooling off," the High Lady repeated flatly, her gaze taking in their thoroughly soaked state, the water spreading in puddles around the fountain's base, and the attendant who'd been tasked with chaperoning them, who looked ready to faint from mortification.

"Your Grace," Aurelise stammered, attempting a curtsy. "I apologize for—this was entirely—that is to say—"

"The fault is entirely mine," Prince Ryden interjected smoothly, offering Aurelise his hand and helping her from the fountain with far more grace than anyone caught behaving like a mischievous schoolboy ought to possess. "I'm afraid I started it."

The High Lady's expression remained unreadable, though Aurelise caught the tiniest twitch at the corner of her mouth—there and gone so quickly she might have imagined it.

"Lady Aurelise," she said crisply, "the carriages depart shortly to convey the Crown Court ladies to their homes. I suggest you make yourself presentable for travel. Your current state would likely cause your family some concern."

"Yes, Your Grace. Immediately, Your Grace." Aurelise dropped another curtsy, sending more water spattering, then began to flee.

"And Ryden," the High Lady added, "you have a visitor. From the Shaded Lands."

Aurelise hurried away beneath the blossom arches, but not before glancing back and seeing Prince Ryden's demeanor shift entirely, the playful, mischievous young man gone, and a sudden unfamiliar vulnerability taking its place.

Chapter Twenty-One

Just over a week later, Aurelise sat at the pianoforte in Solstice Hall's forgotten music room, her fingers moving across the keys. Tomorrow's tea loomed before her like an approaching storm, and she was employing every method at her disposal to keep the threatening tide of panic from washing over her entirely.

She focused intently on counting the beats as she played. Not on the dwindling hours until her tea (fewer than twenty-four). Not on the number of dares she'd attempted since her most recent visit home (a resounding zero). Not on the number of nights that had passed since R's letter arrived with those three words that still echoed through her every waking moment (nine). Not on the number of days a certain prince had been gone from Solstice Hall (eight). And certainly not on how many times her thoughts had drifted to said prince since she'd taken refuge at this instrument a mere half hour ago (at least a dozen).

She inhaled deeply, savoring the scent of sugarplum whimsy tea. She wasn't entirely certain how the kitchen staff had learned it was her favorite—though she strongly suspected Thimble or Spark's meddling—but not long after she'd retreated to her suite that afternoon, there'd come a gentle knock at the door.

Outside stood the same maid who had caught her muttering and pacing about the Sun Salon an hour earlier, now balancing a tray with a delicate teacup and a plate of miniature tarts. The girl had stammered, cheeks pink. "Forgive the intrusion, my lady, but we thought—well—it seemed you might be in need of this. Cook insisted upon the dream-tarts when he heard it was for you. I … I do hope I'm not overstepping."

Aurelise had very nearly hugged the girl—and then promptly started crying the moment the door had closed behind her.

Now the teacup sat on the low table between the music room's mismatching chairs, almost finished, its soft, sweet scent reminding her of home.

"Lady Lise."

A gasp caught in her throat, her hands faltering instantly, a discordant jumble of notes filling the air as she turned swiftly on the bench.

And there he was—Prince Ryden, with that crooked smile of his, his blue hair just slightly disheveled as though he'd run his fingers through it. Something twisted in her chest, a beautiful, consuming ache that stole every breath she might have drawn. It seemed that time and distance had done absolutely nothing to dull the alarming effect he had on her.

"Stars above!" she breathed, pressing a hand to her chest. "You startled me."

He closed the door—which she certainly had not heard him open—and moved closer, choosing the chair nearest the pianoforte. He sat with his usual casual elegance, though this time he remained perched forward on its edge rather than reclining as he had on previous occasions when they'd been alone in this room. There was a certain tension in the way he held himself, something coiled and restless that would have been easy to miss had she not been studying him so closely now.

She turned fully on the bench to face him properly. "You've returned."

"Yes."

When the Crown Court ladies had all returned from their home visits, they'd found Prince Ryden conspicuously absent. "Dealing with important matters in the Shaded Lands," the High Lady had informed them, adding that he would likely return within a few days, perhaps a week at most. She'd then suggested this was an excellent opportunity for those who hadn't yet hosted their teas to focus entirely on their planning.

"Did you have a pleasant visit with your family?" he asked.

"Oh. Yes, quite pleasant, thank you." She refrained from mentioning that she'd endured another thorough interrogation from her grandmother—somehow even worse than the first—and that for reasons she could not fathom, her grandmother seemed far less inclined this time to believe her assurances that the prince was behaving with perfect propriety.

"And you, Your Highness?" she asked. "Was your trip … successful?"

"Yes." His lips curved into that familiar, flirtatious smile she'd come to know far too well. "Did you miss me?"

"No," she answered immediately.

His smile deepened into something positively wicked. "Shall we play a game, Lady Lise? I'm thinking of two words. They both begin with L."

She narrowed her eyes at him, though her heart continued its traitorous flutter and she couldn't seem to tear her gaze from his face.

"Lamentable liar," he whispered.

She turned swiftly back to the pianoforte. "It has been pleasantly uneventful here without you," she said, resting her fingers on the keys. "No midnight escapades. No attempted dares. I find I am thoroughly rested."

She was not well rested in the slightest. Thoughts of him and of R and of this wretched tea that simply needed to be over had consumed her every night, making sleep nearly impossible.

"I should certainly hope there were no midnight escapades in my absence," Prince Ryden said. "If you were attempting to finish that dare list with someone else, I would be thoroughly jealous."

A flare of something deliciously warm unfurled low in her belly, spreading through her limbs like honeyed wine, leaving her feeling light-headed and wonderfully unsteady. Her fingers trembled against the keys where she still had not resumed playing. She flexed them, trying to still the tremor.

I will not be overwhelmed by this, she firmly instructed herself.

I will not be overwhelmed by this.

"Are you all right?" he asked quietly from behind her. "I understand your tea is tomorrow. Are you feeling prepared or dreading it entirely?"

Why did he have to be so genuinely kind beneath all that disarming charm? It really wasn't fair.

"I am … attempting not to think about it," she admitted. "So perhaps discussing it is unwise." She looked over her shoulder at him. "Might we speak of your trip instead—if that is permitted, of course?"

"Of course we may speak of it," he said, shifting slightly in his chair. "In fact, I had intended to tell you regardless." He paused, and something flickered across his face—a momentary uncertainty that seemed foreign on someone usually so assured. "I was visiting some … distant family."

He drew in a breath, as though preparing himself for something significant. "On the afternoon you and the other ladies departed, someone arrived at Solstice Hall. My uncle. From the Shaded Lands."

"Your uncle?" Aurelise turned turn face him once more, surprise coloring her voice. "I was not aware you had—" She caught herself, realizing how presumptuous that sounded. She knew almost nothing of his family beyond the High Lady herself. This uncle must be from his late father's side, she reasoned, though something about the prince's expression suggested the matter was more complex than that.

A small, almost rueful smile touched his lips. "Not many are aware." He leaned forward slightly, his elbows resting on his knees, hands clasped loosely together. "My uncle came bearing welcome news. One of my cousins had found a match. The wedding was to take place this past week."

The warmth that entered his voice as he spoke of it caught Aurelise off guard. This prince who had always seemed to exist solely in relation to his mother, to the court, to his royal duties—yet here he was speaking of cousins and an uncle and a wedding with such genuine affection. The expression on his face was one she'd never seen before, soft with familial love in a way that reminded her painfully of how she felt about her own family.

"They did not wish to impose upon my mother and myself during the Bloom Season, knowing our responsibilities here. But as I am rather fond of this particular cousin, my uncle thought to inform me personally. I had intended to stay only a few days, but it stretched into a week. Despite the fact that"—his gaze found hers then, steady and intent—"there were certain things at Solstice Hall I found myself missing rather desperately."

The flutter returned to her chest, an ache that made breathing feel oddly difficult. A part of her knew he spoke of *her*, yet she clung stubbornly to denial.

"The High Lady did not wish to accompany you?" she asked carefully. "Not even for a day or two? Surely for a family wedding …"

The pause that followed was heavy with unspoken meaning. Prince Ryden's jaw tightened almost imperceptibly before he answered. "I know my mother would have wished to attend, but she cannot publicly acknowledge any connection to that particular branch of the family."

Aurelise felt her brow furrow. "I'm not sure I understand."

Prince Ryden rose from his chair then, moving with sudden purpose toward the far corner of the room. There, partially hidden behind a settee, sat the wooden toy chest he had pointed out to her the first time he'd brought her here. Aurelise had noticed it during her solitary practice sessions, had felt curiosity pluck at her each time she looked at it, but she'd never presumed to open it.

She watched as he knelt beside it, lifting the lid with careful reverence. His hands moved through its contents with the care of someone revisiting precious memories. When he straightened and returned to her, he carried a small, enchanted frame that gleamed softly in the afternoon light.

He resumed his seat and extended the frame toward her. "This," he said quietly, "was Master Ellian Glendale. The Royal Instructor of Magical Theory. My tutor."

Aurelise accepted the oval frame, looking down at the moving portrait within. The man captured there was distinguished, with intelligent eyes that crinkled at the corners as he smiled. He had dark skin, rich and warm in tone, an angular jaw that spoke of determination, and—

Everything went peculiarly still.

Her gaze lifted slowly from the portrait to Prince Ryden's face, then back again. The resemblance was … undeniable. The shape of the nose, the slant of the brows, something about the expressiveness of the mouth—all of it echoed between the portrait and the prince sitting before her.

"Yes," Prince Ryden said softly, watching her with an expression that suggested he'd expected precisely this reaction. Perhaps even wanted it. "Your supposition is correct."

"This man," Aurelise whispered, her voice barely audible as she stared at the portrait, "is your … father?"

"Yes. The man who held the title of Crown Consort was not. He was … not a good man, as I've mentioned before. There was never any affection between him and my mother."

He paused, his gaze dropping to his clasped hands. "I was twelve when I accidentally discovered the truth about my mother's relationship with Ellian. It had been … ongoing for many years. Once I knew to look for it, the truth of my own parentage became rather obvious." A bitter smile touched his lips. "It took me somewhat longer to realize that nearly everyone else in our palace there already knew—or guessed, at least. As you've noticed, the resemblance is rather striking."

"Everyone knew?" Aurelise breathed.

"Everyone except the Crown Consort himself. Or at least … I believe he knew but chose to live in denial."

Aurelise's fingers tightened slightly on the frame. "Were you angry with your mother?"

"At first, yes. A little. I understood that a wife was expected to keep her vows. And I did not wish to think of myself as … illegitimate. But the anger faded quickly. I had never harbored any affection for the Crown Consort, and he had treated my mother abominably behind closed doors. Ellian, meanwhile, had always been everything a father should be to me. Kind, patient, endlessly encouraging. It did not take long for me to make peace with the truth."

Silence stretched between them for a moment before Aurelise ventured, "What happened to him? To Master Glendale?"

The prince's expression shuttered. "There was an accident. In his workshop. It was ruled a tragedy. An unfortunate mishap."

"Oh," Aurelise breathed, her heart constricting. "I'm so terribly sorry."

"Thank you. It was years ago now. The grief has mellowed. Though I believe my mother still mourns him far more deeply than I. They truly loved one another."

Several moments passed in contemplative quiet, the only sound the distant trill of birds beyond the windows. Finally, Aurelise found her voice again. "Why are you telling me this?"

The question hung in the air between them like a held breath.

"Because," he said softly, his eyes finding hers with an intensity that made her pulse quicken, "I want you to know." He paused. Then: "I want you to know *me*."

She felt it then—that sensation of something vast and overwhelming approaching, like a wave gathering strength far out at sea. Her breath grew shallow as she met his gaze, unable to look away despite every instinct screaming at her to flee. The feeling rose higher, threatening to crash over her, to pull her under into depths from which she might never surface—

No. She couldn't. She would not allow it.

She turned abruptly back to the pianoforte, her movement so sudden that the portrait frame nearly slipped from her lap. Her fingers gripped it tighter as she drew in a steadying breath.

But then she paused, glancing back over her shoulder. He had just entrusted her with something of great consequence. She could not let him think she was rejecting him for it, that she thought less of him for being illegitimate. It wasn't *him* she was turning from—it was the terrifying depth of feeling he stirred within her.

"Thank you," she said quietly, meeting his eyes. "For telling me. That cannot have been easy to share."

A small, genuine smile curved his lips. "Surprisingly, it was not as difficult as I anticipated. I find myself wanting to tell you things. Many things."

Heat rushed to her cheeks, and she quickly faced forward again. "Would you—that is—might I play something for you?"

"I would like that." His voice carried that familiar thread of mischief now. "But only if you'll permit me to play alongside you."

Surprise made her turn again, though only slightly, as he was now standing beside the pianoforte. "You play?" she asked.

"I do, though not nearly as well as you. My grandmother taught me. Or should I say … *attempted* to teach me."

"But—in all the times we've been in here together, you've never once mentioned this."

He smiled down at her, amusement flickering in his eyes. "You did not ask."

She hesitated, her pulse fluttering. Why did she keep finding it so difficult to look away from those very blue eyes? "I … I suppose that is true."

"So then," he said lightly, "may I sit beside you?"

He seemed to be asking for more than that. The air shifted, subtle, invisible, but she felt it all the same. That same tremor beneath her skin she kept sensing around him, as though something vast were drawing nearer. It pressed against her ribs, stole her breath, filled her chest with that dangerous mixture of dread and delight.

She should say no. Now would be an excellent time to prove that dare number six was hardly insurmountable. And yet … she did not want to.

"Yes," she heard herself say softly. "You may."

He moved to sit beside her on the bench, positioning himself to her left where the bass accompaniment would naturally fall. The bench, which had seemed perfectly adequate when she sat alone, now felt impossibly small. His thigh pressed against hers through the layers of her dress, and she could feel the warmth radiating from him, smell the warm steadiness of cedar and the freshness of a rain-drenched forest.

"Well then," she managed, her voice only slightly breathless. "Shall we attempt something simple? Perhaps a traditional solstice duet?"

"Lead the way, my lady."

She began with a familiar piece, one she'd learned years ago, her fingers finding the notes easily despite her heightened awareness of him beside her. The melody flowed forth, sweet and uncomplicated, perfect for a duet.

Prince Ryden studied her hands for a moment, then attempted to join in with what should have been a complementary bass line. What emerged instead was a series of notes that bore only the vaguest relationship to the proper key.

Aurelise bit her lip, trying desperately not to laugh as he fumbled through another measure, his timing completely at odds with hers. "That is …"

"Magnificent?" he suggested.

"Atrocious," she corrected, finally allowing a giggle to escape as her hands stilled on the keys. "Truly, spectacularly terrible. Your poor grandmother must have possessed remarkable patience."

"She did frequently invoke the stars for strength," he admitted. "Shall I try again?"

"Please do. Though perhaps this time you might consider playing in the same key as I am?"

"Such rigid expectations," he murmured, but he positioned his hands again, this time managing something that at least *resembled* the proper accompaniment for several measures before dissolving into chaos once more.

"You're doing that on purpose," she accused, though she was laughing properly now.

"I assure you, I am not nearly skilled enough to be deliberately this bad." His fingers brushed against hers as they both moved toward the same octave, and she felt the contact like a spark. "Though I admit, there are certain … advantages to my lack of talent."

He did it again—let his hand drift just close enough that their fingers tangled briefly before pulling away. Her breath caught, and she missed a note.

"You're distracting me," she said, heat flooding her cheeks.

"Am I?" His voice had dropped lower, taken on that particular quality that made her stomach flutter. "How unfortunate. Please, continue. Pretend I'm not here."

She tried to focus, but he'd shifted closer somehow, his shoulder now pressing against hers. Every breath she took brought that intoxicating scent, every movement created friction that sent little shivers along her skin.

His attempts at accompaniment grew increasingly sporadic until finally, his hands stilled entirely on the keys. She felt him turn toward her, his body angling so that he was no longer facing the instrument but facing her instead.

"You know," he said softly, "you always seem to disappear when you play. As though you've slipped into another world entirely."

Her fingers continued their movement, though the tempo had slowed considerably. "It's true," she admitted, though there was little chance of such a thing happening now, with him sitting so near. "That's why I love it so much. When I play, I feel … transported. Nothing can reach me when I'm truly lost in the music. No worries, no fears, no overwhelming feelings. Just me and the instrument and perfect, blissful focus."

She closed her eyes, fingers tracing the familiar path of the keys. The rhythm of it soothed her, the effortless slide and rise of each note, the whisper of touch and response. For a moment, she could feel the promise of that tranquil focus hovering close, as though she might actually be able to grasp it if she kept her eyes closed long enough—even with him sitting so near.

"You cannot say something like that," he murmured, "and not expect me to take it as a challenge."

Her eyes flew open, that glimpse of perfect focus flittering away in an instant. "What do you—"

His fingertips touched the back of her hand, the lightest possible contact, barely there at all. Just a whisper of skin against skin as he traced the delicate bones beneath. Her playing faltered for a moment before she forced herself to continue.

"Keep playing," he murmured, and there was something dark and delicious in his tone that made her shiver. "Show me this perfect focus of yours."

His fingers began a slow journey upward, tracing the inside of her wrist where her pulse hammered frantically. She tried to maintain the melody, but the notes were becoming uncertain, the rhythm uneven. His touch moved higher, following the line of her forearm, finding sensitive places she hadn't known existed.

I should stop this, she thought hazily. *I should tell him to cease immediately.*

But she did not. Could not. Because despite her terror, despite the knowledge that this would consume her in the worst possible way, a part of her wanted to know what would happen if she let herself *feel everything.*

His fingers reached her elbow, then traveled upward still, ghosting over the fabric of her sleeve. When they found the bare skin where her shoulder curved toward her neck, she inhaled sharply and bit her lip, her hands stumbling over the keys.

"Still focused?" he asked, and she could hear the smile in his voice as he leaned closer.

She tried to recover the melody, her fingers moving by pure muscle memory, but the music had become something else entirely—slower, dreamier, notes bleeding into each other without structure or thought.

His fingertips grazed over her collarbone, then began tracing up the column of her neck. Goosebumps erupted in the wake of his touch. Her eyes fluttered closed, her breathing shallow and uneven.

"Still transported?" His lips were so close to her ear that she felt the words as much as heard them. "Still unreachable?"

Her playing had slowed to almost nothing now, just occasional notes that rang out in the hushed room. His fingers traced the shell of her ear, then moved to tuck a strand of hair that must have escaped her careful arrangement. The gesture should have been innocent, but the way he did it—slowly, deliberately, his fingers gliding down over her skin and then around the back of her neck to thread into the soft coils of hair gathered at her nape—made it feel impossibly intimate.

Then his lips brushed against her neck, just below her ear, and she stopped playing entirely. Her hands trembled above the keys as delicious shivers cascaded through her body. A tidal wave of exquisite intensity that she could not bring herself to pull away from.

She was leaning into him now, almost cradled against his chest, his arm curved securely around her, fingers tangled in her hair, while his other hand found hers upon the keys, enclosing it in a warm, unyielding hold. His head shifted, mouth above her ear, and she felt him sigh into her hair. "I want," he whispered on a shuddering breath, "to choose you."

And in an instant, the spell shattered. Feeling flooded her, too much, too fast, splintering through her chest until she could hardly breathe. She rushed to free herself from his hold, pushing herself backward off the bench, hands finding the edge of the pianoforte as she steadied herself.

"Aurelise—"

"No—I—I cannot—" She struggled for breath, refusing to look at him, both hands rising to press against her flushed cheeks.

"Please," he said, something desperate in his tone. "I'm sorry if I—"

His words cut off abruptly, and there was … something. A shift. A change in the atmosphere. The very air around them seemed to ripple and bend, as though reality itself had become uncertain.

Aurelise lowered her hands, finally finding the courage to meet Prince Ryden's gaze, and what she saw there made her breath catch. Like her, he was still flushed, breathless, but his eyes held something else entirely. A wild, desperate fear she did not understand. His blue eyes were darkening, deepening into something that seemed to swallow light, and the air around him shimmered like heat waves rising from sun-baked stone.

"You need to go," he said, and his voice cracked with barely controlled panic. "Now. Please."

Despite her own thundering heart and the overwhelming sensations still coursing through her, Aurelise recognized true distress when she saw it. "What's wrong?" she asked, taking an instinctive step toward him rather than away.

But he was already shaking his head frantically, backing away from her. "Please go, please go, before I—" His hands flew to his mouth, pressing hard against his lips as though desperate to contain something that threatened to escape. The gesture was so vulnerable, so frightened, that it pierced straight through her own turmoil.

Music began to spill from her without conscious thought, notes cascading into the air in shimmering ribbons of sound. The air grew hotter, heavier, pressing against her skin with an almost physical weight. He was trembling now, his whole body shaking as he continued to retreat. It was pure instinct that drove her forward, ignoring his desperate protests, ignoring the strange heat that made her skin prickle.

"No, don't—" he gasped, but she was already there, wrapping her arms around his trembling form and pulling him tight against her.

She squeezed her eyes shut and let the music pour out of her completely. It filled the room like water filling a vessel, surrounding them both in long, sweeping currents of sound—a low, resonant hum, like cello strings vibrating beneath a bow drawn slowly back and forth. Each tone thrummed through the air, deep and steady, grounding, the kind of sound one *felt* as much as heard.

She breathed slowly, deliberately, and gradually she felt him begin to match her rhythm. His chest rose and fell against hers, the frantic pace slowing to something more measured. His arms came up around her, and she felt him press his face against her hair, drawing deep, slow breaths as the strange heat finally began to dissipate, leaving behind only the warmth of their embrace.

The music gradually faded to whispers, then to silence. They stood there, wrapped around each other in the quiet afternoon light, the rest of the world forgotten.

"What," she asked shakily against his shoulder, "just happened?"

He did not pull away, did not release his desperate hold on her. When he spoke, his voice was rough, exhausted. "My … authority magic. It surges sometimes. Out of control. Without warning." She felt him swallow hard. "It is not supposed to do that. I've often wondered if it's some form of divine punishment for the circumstances of my birth, or if my magic would have been chaos regardless."

Part of her wanted to draw back so she could look at him, but there was something so blissfully *right* about being wrapped in his embrace—despite the whirlwind of sensation still coursing through her and the chaos that had just unfolded in this room.

"I've been terrified of it for so long," he continued, the words pouring out like a confession. "It has caused terrible tragedy. I told you Ellian's death was an accident. I told you my father's—the Crown Consort's—death was the same. Neither was true."

Aurelise went very still in his arms.

"Ellian's death was orchestrated to appear accidental, but I discovered the truth. It was my father who arranged it. He finally faced the fact that my mother loved another, that I was living proof of his inadequacy—and he could not bear it."

His voice dropped to barely a whisper. "I confronted him. We were in the skies, on pegasi, and he was taunting me, saying …" He trailed off, exhaling against her hair. "Terrible things. We began fighting. There was magic streaking back and forth. He … struck me. My authority magic had been on the verge of manifesting that entire Season, and in that moment, as we were yelling at one another, it erupted from me without warning. And when I yelled at him to get away from me … my magic carried out the command."

She felt him shudder against her.

"It flung both him and his pegasus from the sky." The prince's voice broke entirely, shuddering as he added, "And I have been trying to control it ever since."

They remained like that, suspended in silence, time slipping away as Aurelise tried to take in the weight of what Prince Ryden revealed. Finally, he drew back enough to look down at her, his eyes rimmed with exhaustion and something like wonder. "You calmed it. How did you do that?"

"I think," she said unsteadily, peering up into his eyes, "my magic can do for others what it does for me. Bring peace. Calm. Serenity. It stopped that chandelier in the Green Drawing Room from chattering. Not a pleasant melody as your mother was imagining, but complete stillness. And it brought calm to the chaos in the kitchens. It seemed to positively influence everyone's mood after my performance at the musicale we had here earlier on in the Season. And now … this."

"It's you," he breathed, and his voice was thick with emotion, with a kind of desperate relief. "Stars above, it has been you all this time."

She shook her head slightly, confusion pulling at her brow. "What has been me?"

His hands came up to frame her face, thumbs brushing over her cheekbones with infinite tenderness. "I need to tell you something. The truth about the Crown Court. About why my mother truly brought you all here."

A ripple of unease coiled low within her, though it tangled helplessly with the shiver that chased through her at the brush of his thumbs.

"The real purpose was for me to find someone whose magic might stabilize my own. It's a theory my mother discovered in several old texts, one your grandmother happened upon as well. The deep magical bonds formed in marriage can sometimes create a permanent stabilizing effect between different magics." His eyes searched hers, bright with something she couldn't quite name. "My mother dismissed your magic early on, believing that anything that tugged too strongly on one's emotions would be volatile rather than stabilizing. But she was wrong." He shook his head. "Your magic is entirely the opposite."

Understanding began to dawn, terrible and wonderful all at once.

"It's you," he breathed again. "Since the day this ridiculous Crown Court began, I've been longing to choose you, terrified that I would be forced to select someone else for the sake of—"

"Wait, you—" Her voice came out strangled. "You've been longing to choose me? Since the Crown Court began? You did not even know me! You told me you had no intention of choosing me!"

"I—" Something flickered across his features. An uncertainty and vulnerability she so rarely saw there. "There is something else I must—"

"No, no, no," she whispered.

He wanted to choose her. *Choose her.*

Princess. Crown Consort. *Love.*

In an instant, she was sitting in front of that pianoforte again, curled against him, her heart full to bursting—and the tidal wave she'd always feared finally crashed down upon her, and she was drowning, drowning, drowning in the terrifying immensity of it all.

"I cannot …" she mumbled, disentangling herself from his grasp and stumbling backwards.

"Wait, please just—"

But she was already turning, already running, already tugging the door open and fleeing from a future that threatened to swallow her whole.

Chapter Twenty-Two

The enchanted carriage slid to a halt outside The Charmed Leaf Tea House, and Aurelise pressed her palms against her temples, trying to quiet the chaos in her mind. Every emotion she'd spent years learning to contain was now crashing against her carefully constructed barriers like waves against a crumbling seawall. It was too much—this breathless, terrible, wonderful rush that swelled inside her until it ached, as though her heart could not possibly hold so much feeling without splintering under the weight of it.

She needed Kazrian. She needed someone who would understand this drowning sensation without judgment, who knew her well enough to recognize when she teetered on the edge of being utterly consumed.

Oh, Lady Aurelise, we're here! We're here! Thimble's telepathic voice bubbled with nervous energy as she perched on Aurelise's shoulder, her tiny paws tangling in loose strands of hair. *Everything will be all right, I promise!*

When Aurelise had burst into her chambers after escaping the music room, Thimble had taken one look at her face and immediately demanded to know what was wrong. Aurelise had tried—through tears and uneven breaths—to explain. It hadn't been an easy tale to make sense of: something along the lines of "The prince is entirely too wonderful, and I may be hopelessly in love with him, which is precisely why I must flee both my feelings and this palace at once."

To their credit, her companions had grasped the general sentiment with remarkable speed and leaped into action—after Thimble's brief, squealing interlude of, *You LOVE him! I KNEW it! I told you from the very first day how wonderful he is!*

Then the tiny pink mouse had created a distraction with the palace guards while Spark had somehow procured use of one of the lesser enchanted carriages—Aurelise did not dare ask how—and the two of them had smuggled her out through the servants' entrance.

They'd gone to Rowanwood House first, of course. It had been Thimble's idea to scout ahead while Aurelise waited in the carriage, her tiny form and Spark's diminutive size allowing them to slip through the house unnoticed. They'd returned with disappointing news—Kazrian wasn't there, though Thimble had overheard one of the footmen mentioning he might be at the tea house.

Now, Aurelise climbed from the carriage, her voice still a little wobbly as she said, "Thank you for your help, dear ones. Will you … will you wait for me? I presume I shall need to return to Solstice Hall after I've spoken to my brother."

Of course! Thimble squeaked.

As if we would abandon you, Spark huffed.

The carriage door swung itself shut, and Aurelise stared at the familiar ivy-covered walls of her grandmother's establishment. She could hear the gentle hum of conversation from within. The front entrance was out of the question—walking through the main tea room in her current state would set every gossip bird in Bloomhaven squawking before sunset. So the back entrance it would be.

Aurelise gathered her skirts and hurried along the path around the side of the tea house. She rounded the corner toward the kitchen door, moving too quickly to properly watch where she was going, and nearly collided with someone emerging from within. Strong hands caught her shoulders, steadying her, and she looked up to find—

"Kazrian!"

Her twin's storm-gray eyes widened with surprise, then immediately narrowed with concern. There was something off about his expression—a tightness around his mouth, a brightness to his eyes that suggested he'd been wrestling with his own troubles.

They stared at each other for a suspended moment, and then, in perfect unison, both said, "What happened?"

Despite the emotional storm still raging in her chest, Aurelise nearly laughed at the absurdity of it.

Kazrian recovered first, shaking his head. "Nothing. Nothing at all. I'm perfectly well. But you—Lise, what's wrong? Aren't you meant to be at Solstice Hall?"

"I—yes. But I …" She pressed her shaking lips together, trying to hold back the flood of emotion. She took a breath, opened her mouth, and words spilled out. "But I think I have fallen in love, and not merely with one person, but two, and it's really quite awful!"

Kazrian's eyebrows shot upward, confusion written plainly across his features. Then he started laughing. "You … what?"

"Do not *laugh*!" she scolded. Then she threw her arms around him and buried her face against his shoulder. He returned the embrace, holding her tight as she struggled to contain her sobs.

"Might we speak somewhere private?" she managed, voice muffled against his coat. "Somewhere we won't be observed?"

"The gardens?" he suggested. "The back portion should suffice. There's no one about except the garden gnomes and pixies, perhaps a sprite or two."

"Hopefully no gossip birds," Aurelise added with a watery laugh, pulling back to wipe at her eyes.

Together they walked through the kitchen gardens, past neat rows of herbs and flowers. They passed the fountain and the outdoor seating area and finally settled behind a particularly large glimmerbark tree whose trunk would shield them from any curious eyes in the kitchen.

They sank onto the grass, backs against the rough bark, and for a moment Aurelise simply breathed. The afternoon sun filtered through the leaves above, dappling them with golden light. A bee droned lazily past, while the fountain tinkled pleasantly. The peaceful setting helped, though that tide of emotion still surged within her chest, threatening to pull her under at any moment.

"So," Kazrian said carefully, "two people? I do hope one of them isn't our charming prince who enjoys flirting his way through every Season."

Aurelise covered her face with both hands.

"Truly?" Kazrian's voice rose in shock. "I was not being serious! Do you mean to tell me you have genuinely fallen in love with Prince Ryden?"

"I'm endeavoring very hard not to," she groaned, lowering her hands to peer at him miserably. Then, because there seemed little point in maintaining secrets after going to the effort of sneaking out of a palace in order to confide in him, she told him everything.

She spoke of R first—"I've been corresponding with a gentleman I've never met in secret for nearly a year now"—and had to pause when Kazrian spluttered, "What?!" She told him of the letters, of how she'd shared essentially everything except her identity with R, and how he had done the same in return. How it felt as though she knew him better than almost anyone else in her life.

She told him of the dare list, of how Prince Ryden had somehow found his way into nearly every challenge she'd attempted. How he'd teased and encouraged her, how one absurd escapade had led to another until she'd quite lost control of her own heart. She'd flirted—badly—swum in a lake at midnight, climbed to a rooftop to stargaze, run through rain-drenched gardens, and been outrageously, scandalously improper at least half a dozen times.

"Oh, and there was the driftshade smoking," she added as an afterthought. "I'd nearly forgotten about that."

"The—you *smoked driftshade leaf?*"

By the time she concluded her account—ending off with the fact that she was now ignoring R's written confession of love and had fled from a prince who had all but declared the very same thing with his 'I want to choose you'—Kazrian was staring at her as though she'd suddenly become an entirely different person.

"I genuinely don't believe I know you at all," he said slowly. "When did you become so … *bold?* I'm beginning to think I knew nothing of what I spoke when I told Prince Ryden at the Season's start that my sister desired nothing more than a quiet, unremarkable existence."

Aurelise straightened indignantly. "You also told him I was dull? Both you and Evryn? I am not dull!"

"Firstly, neither of us employed the word 'dull.' And secondly, yes, I am now shockingly aware of precisely how *not* dull you are."

A few moments of quiet fell between them. Aurelise sighed, tipping her head back against the tree trunk and covering her face once more. Through her fingers, she found herself describing all the reasons her mysterious correspondent was so wonderful—his wit, his patience, his ability to see straight through to her heart with mere words on paper. Then all the reasons the prince was equally wonderful and nothing like society's perception of him as a shallow flirt. He was kind and genuine, protective and vulnerable, with depths she'd never expected to discover.

"And it's all so terrible," she concluded miserably as she lowered her hands, "because I never wished to love anyone, let alone *two* people."

"But … why?"

She heaved another breath, struggling to find the words to explain. "Because it's … so vast. So overwhelming. It will consume me entirely."

"And that's necessarily terrible?"

"Yes! It's … it *hurts*! It hurts, Kazrian, because there is just so much of it, and it leaves me feeling as though I can barely breathe. As though I'm drowning. Drowning in *him*—whichever one I might choose."

Kazrian was quiet for a long moment, then sighed, tipping his own head back to gaze up through the canopy of leaves. "Perhaps drowning in someone is not the terrible fate you imagine. Perhaps that is precisely how it's meant to feel when you fall in love." His voice had gone soft, distant. "If she would permit it, I would gladly drown in her."

Aurelise blinked, turning to stare at her brother. He looked back at her, momentarily astonished, as though he couldn't quite believe he'd spoken those words aloud. Then she collapsed into laughter, pressing a hand over her mouth while Kazrian groaned and covered his face with both hands.

"Goodness, Kazrian," she gasped between giggles. "Who knew you possessed such romantic sensibilities?"

"If you breathe a word of this to anyone—"

"I won't," she assured him quickly.

And she wouldn't. She knew it wasn't embarrassment over admitting the depth of his feelings that concerned him. It was precisely *whom* Kazrian seemed to hope he might drown himself in, and the fact that she was decidedly *not* someone he should be harboring such feelings for.

After another stretch of quiet, Kazrian spoke again. "What of him?"

"Him? Which him?"

"Well … either of them, I suppose. Though particularly this fellow who appears to have been entirely besotted with you for almost a full year at this point. Have you considered that if he truly loves you, you'll leave him utterly broken by rejecting him? By retreating to your safe, unremarkable corner of the world?"

Oh no. That dreadful thought hadn't even occurred to her. R had always seemed so … resilient. But all she could see now were those words that had sent her into another spiraling panic:

There is nothing left for any enchantress to steal—you already have it all.

She had his heart, his hopes, his devotion. And if she said no to him a second time, she suspected there would be no going back to what they had before. This would be it. She would lose him, and he would be crushed.

As if her own tumult of feeling weren't enough, she was suddenly burdened with the imagined ache of someone else's heartbreak, a wave of secondhand sorrow she could neither soothe nor escape.

"I'm not attempting to make you feel worse," Kazrian said quickly, apparently reading her distress. "I'm only trying to remind you that there is another person in this equation. Well—two, which does make the arithmetic rather untidy. But for simplicity's sake, let us consider just one. Suppose he—either of them; both of them—truly is all that you've said. Caring, patient, witty, wonderful. Do you honestly believe such a man would stand by and let you drown?"

The words rose unbidden in her mind, R's careful script seeming to shimmer before her eyes:

I swear to you that I would never let you drown.

Let me be your anchor.

You will not be swept away.

And the prince, whom she had not spelled out her exact fears to, but who had guessed the essence of them nonetheless:

You were perfectly safe. I would never allow you to come to harm.

"No," Kazrian continued. "Of course he would not permit such a thing. You're frightened, Lise. I understand that. I know you experience everything with far greater intensity than most. But you need only do what you've always done. Retreat when necessary. Take time to restore yourself through your music. Then face your feelings again when you are ready. If this gentleman—we're still pretending there's only one—truly loves you, he will understand. He'll grant you whatever time and space you require."

And she nearly began crying again, because hadn't R written almost exactly that?

I have patience enough for both of us.

Take your time.

But if she did decide to take this leap … if she decided it was worth the risk of seeing whether she could survive the wave crashing over her … whom would she choose?

The world carried on quietly around them while Aurelise attempted to sort through the tangle of her thoughts. R versus the prince. The prince had awakened feelings in her she'd never experienced—had desperately *hoped* never to experience, though now that she'd felt a hint of them and survived the encounter, perhaps she could survive more?

He was the one who had shared every reckless dare with her, the one beside whom she'd truly *lived*—not merely existed. With him, the world had felt vivid and immediate, not a thing to be observed from a safe and careful distance, but something to be touched, breathed, and wholly experienced.

But surely R knew her better? He was the one who'd penned the dare list in the first place. The one who knew precisely how to challenge her. He knew her heart, her soul, her deepest fears. He was the one to whom she'd confessed how intensely she felt everything, and he was the one who'd promised to hold fast to her through any storm of emotion.

And there was the fact that she simply could not be a princess. The very notion remained absurd. Perhaps not quite as absurd as it had seemed at the Season's start. Solstice Hall, she had to admit, was rather lovely. Thimble and Spark were the most delightful of companions. The kitchens had proven an excellent hiding place, the sky garden terrace a sanctuary, and the music room a haven all her own. And there was that beautiful pianoforte …

But still. That could not possibly be her life.

What *could* be her life, however, if she took that single brave step …

I am still here.

I have patience enough for both of us.

And I would still be there, holding fast to you.

There is nothing left for any enchantress to steal—you already have it all.

From somewhere nearby, a voice called out softly, breaking through Aurelise's thoughts. "Kazrian?"

Kazrian tensed immediately beside Aurelise. They both looked up as the owner of the familiar voice stepped into view around the glimmerbark's broad trunk.

"Lucie!" Aurelise exclaimed, perhaps a little too loudly. She rose swiftly to her feet and moved forward, hoping to draw attention away from Kazrian, whom she sensed was uncomfortable in Lucie's presence. "How are you? I don't believe I've seen you yet this Season. Everything was a bit of a whirlwind at the start."

"Aurelise." The girl smiled, her warm hazel eyes crinkling, then hesitated. "That is, Lady Aurelise. I—"

"Oh, please, none of that 'lady' formality," Aurelise insisted, feeling suddenly awkward. She couldn't bear the thought of being *Lady* Aurelise to the girl with whom she'd shared so many afternoons of laughter in these very gardens over the past several Seasons.

Lucie hesitated another moment before nodding, and Aurelise noticed how she very deliberately did *not* look in Kazrian's direction. He had also risen by now, and moved to stand beside Aurelise.

"Your grandmother sent me to find you," Lucie said, still not looking at Kazrian.

Aurelise's stomach dropped. "Grandmother knows we're out here?"

"I don't believe she's aware of *your* presence, my—Aurelise." There was a clear pause as she caught herself before the formal address. "She simply requested I locate Kazrian, assuming he remained somewhere within the tea house, and I—well, I had observed him depart after—" Her cheeks colored slightly. "And then I saw him encounter you and proceed in this direction."

"Is all well?" Kazrian asked, his voice stiffer and more formal now.

"Yes." A warm smile broke out across Lucie's face. "Your grandmother just received word—Lady Iris has had her baby."

R,

Are you still standing at a crossroads?

That cryptic comment … It left me both frustrated and terrified, not knowing precisely what you meant by it, fearful of change and fearful of losing you, yet unable to give you what you asked for.

But now I want to.

I want to know you, see you, touch you. I want to be known.

I want to risk being drowned and find that you are still standing with me, holding fast to me, after the wave crashes over us.

Please tell me I am not too late.

Please tell me you are still … mine.

L

L,

I am always, and will only ever be, yours.

R

Chapter Twenty-Three

One advantage of fleeing across Bloomhaven in a stolen (borrowed without permission) palace carriage to untangle one's desperately complicated feelings about not one but two gentlemen—and then receiving the delightful news of becoming an aunt—was that it had left Aurelise precious little time to properly panic about hosting her first tea.

Now, however, the hour had arrived, and with it came a swell of anxiety.

The previous evening had passed in something of a blur. She'd returned to Solstice Hall with just enough time for Marta to dress her before the dinner gong sounded, barely managing to maintain her composure through the meal while her thoughts churned like storm-tossed seas (and while she actively avoided Prince Ryden's gaze).

Afterward, she'd retreated to her chambers and collapsed into bed, thoroughly depleted by the day's emotional tempest. Then, before sleep could claim her, she'd risen and found paper and quill, drawn to her enchanted letter box by an urgency she could no longer ignore. She had made a decision, and nine nights of silence was cruelty enough. She did not want to keep R waiting any longer.

Then she had collapsed a second time and allowed exhaustion to claim her.

His reply, which she'd found in the box when she'd woken that morning, had sent a rush of feeling—exhilarating and utterly terrifying—flooding through her.

I am always, and will only ever be, yours.

Her heart had swelled so fiercely it ached, as though it had outgrown the fragile confines of her chest. He was still hers. She would meet him. She would discover who he was. She would *know* him.

But first, this tea. Then, at last, she could untangle everything with R.

Now, standing in the Starlace Garden with afternoon light filtering through the flowering arbor above, Aurelise drew a steadying breath and let a gentle cello melody unspool from her fingertips—low, resonant notes that thrummed through the air and helped anchor her racing heart. Before her lay the fruits of her morning's frantic preparations: tables dressed in cream linens embroidered with tiny silver stars, delicate Moonbloom china arranged just so, and tiered dishes of lemon-glazed teacakes, sugared berry scones, honeyed biscuits, petite fruit tarts crowned with candied petals, and of course, Spark's beloved custard kisses.

But it was the peculiar additions to the usual arrangement that made her stomach flutter with nervous anticipation. Alongside the standard elegant chairs, she'd arranged something altogether more whimsical: dozens of miniature furnishings raised on pedestals that brought them level with the regular tables. There were tiny velvet cushions no bigger than her palm, delicate perches fashioned from twisted willow branches, minuscule chaises that might accommodate a mouse, and even a collection of thimble-sized chairs upholstered in silk. Each bore a carefully lettered name card in her finest script.

The inspiration had struck her during her first visit home, born from memories of Iris's groundbreaking tea at The Charmed Leaf—the one where she'd dared to invite humans alongside fae nobility, setting Bloomhaven's gossips aflutter for weeks. But more than that, it had come from watching how some of the Crown Court ladies treated their magical companions. Not cruelly, perhaps, but with a casual dismissiveness that made Aurelise's heart ache. These dear creatures who offered such faithful service, such genuine affection, deserved better than to be treated as mere accessories.

Several palace attendants moved quietly about the garden, making final adjustments. A flick of a finger coaxed a napkin's fold into perfect symmetry; a whispered word set the silver to gleaming beneath the sun. One attendant adjusted a teapot that had begun to steam a touch too eagerly, the vapor obediently curling back into the spout. Aurelise inclined her head in thanks as they withdrew to the perimeter of the gathering. One bent to murmur a few low words to the steward, who stood with hands clasped behind his back, discreetly overseeing the proceedings.

They're arriving! Thimble's telepathic squeak rang through her mind from her hiding spot among a nearby rose bush. *Oh, Lady Aurelise, everything looks so beautiful! The tiny furniture! The little name cards! I could cry!*

Aurelise smoothed her hands down her blush-pink silk gown—chosen specifically because Thimble had declared it 'the most romantically beautiful dress in all existence'—and moved to greet the first of her guests.

The Crown Court ladies arrived in small clusters, their reactions to the unusual seating arrangements varying wildly. Lady Olivienne paused mid-step, her sharp eyes taking in the miniature arrangements before a genuine smile curved her lips. Lady Bernelle looked utterly bewildered, whispering frantically to Lady Ellowa, who responded with an indelicate snort. But it was Willow's delighted laugh that gave Aurelise courage—she appeared to immediately understand and appreciate the gesture.

More courtiers filtered in, the garden filling with the rustle of silk and the music of conversation. Aurelise's conducted melodies wove through the air, soft as butterfly wings, creating an atmosphere of gentle enchantment.

Then the temperature seemed to shift, the very air growing somehow more significant, and Aurelise knew without looking that the High Lady had arrived. She turned to offer her deepest curtsy, and her treacherous gaze immediately found Prince Ryden beside his mother.

He wore midnight blue today, the color making his eyes seem impossibly bright, and that familiar smirk played at the corners of his mouth—the one that suggested he knew secrets the rest of the world could only guess at. When their eyes met (curse her weakness for looking), his expression shifted to something more vulnerable. There was a question there, and she could not help but think of all that had transpired in the music room the previous afternoon before she had fled. The memory of his fingers tracing her skin, his lips whispering against her neck, her own arms tightly embracing him as her music enveloped them both—it set her cheeks aflame.

She forced herself to look away, focusing on the High Lady's serene countenance instead. "Your Grace, Your Highness," she managed, her voice only slightly breathless.

The High Lady inclined her head graciously, those shrewd eyes taking in every detail of the garden arrangements, though her expression revealed nothing of her thoughts. Prince Ryden bowed, and Aurelise absolutely did not notice how elegantly he moved, or how the afternoon light caught in his hair. She wondered if he'd told his mother of their monumental discovery the previous afternoon. That Aurelise's magic had stilled his own. That he was hoping she would—

No. She had a tea to host.

Drawing herself up, Aurelise moved to stand before the assembled company as the last of her guests were seated. Dare number five whispered through her mind: *Keep your eyes up for an entire gathering.* Surely she could manage that much. This was not an entire ballroom full of people. It was merely a small gathering. The Crown Court ladies, a few additional courtiers, the High Lady, and the prince. If she could sneak through the palace at night, swim in a lake when she had never previously done more than dip her feet into the shallows, if she could commandeer one of the High Lady's carriages, flee the palace without permission, and return with her world miraculously still intact, then she could surely manage a simple tea.

She lifted her chin, found Willow's encouraging smile among the group, and began.

"My lords and ladies," she said, and if her voice trembled slightly on the first words, it grew stronger with each syllable. "I am deeply honored to welcome you all to this afternoon's tea." A pause, a breath, then onward. "When I arrived at Solstice Hall, I confess I felt rather like a small boat set adrift upon a vast and glorious sea. Everything here sparkles with such magnificence, such … such overwhelming grandeur."

A few knowing smiles appeared among the ladies. They understood that feeling.

"But I have discovered," Aurelise continued, her music swelling gently beneath her words, "that it is often the smallest wonders that make a place truly bloom. The unexpected kindness of a new friend." She smiled at Willow. "The perfect cup of tea appearing just when one needs it most. And perhaps most especially …" She glanced toward the roses. "The devoted companionship of those who ask nothing more than to serve and to care for us with their whole hearts." She raised her hand in a graceful gesture. "Ladies and gentlemen, I would like to welcome our most honored guests."

At her signal, the garden erupted in a flurry of movement. From behind bushes and flowers, and from the branches of trees, came a parade of magical creatures. Thimble led the charge, her tiny pink form zipping through the air with wings glittering. Spark followed with considerably less enthusiasm but perfect dignity, emerald scales catching the light. Iridescent moths, foxes, pocket phoenixes, miniature dragons in every jewel tone—dozens of magical companions converged upon the tea party.

The air filled with delighted gasps and surprised laughter as each creature found their designated place. Thimble dove for her velvet cushion with a squeak of joy, while Spark settled onto his perch with an air of dignified composure (though Aurelise caught him eyeing the plate of custard kisses she'd strategically placed within his reach).

"These dear creatures," Aurelise said, "have made each of us feel welcome in this grand place. They have guided us, shared our laughter, and kept our secrets." Her voice grew softer, more sincere. "It seemed only fitting that they should be honored as the treasures they truly are."

Most of the ladies were smiling now, some even cooing over their companions as they settled into their miniature seats. Aurelise did catch Lady Ellowa rolling her eyes, muttering something about 'unnecessary sentimentality,' but even she seemed pleased when her silver cat curled itself up on a miniature chaise.

Aurelise risked a glance at the High Lady, desperate for some sign of approval or censure. But the woman's expression remained as serenely unreadable as always—the same perfect mask of polite interest she'd worn at every tea thus far. It was Prince Ryden's expression that caught her off-guard: he was watching her with something that looked almost like … pride? The warmth in his gaze made her stomach perform an alarming flip, and she hastily returned to her table before she could do something foolish like smile back at him.

The tea progressed beautifully. Conversation flowed as freely as the enchanted teapots that never seemed to empty, and Aurelise let her music weave softly through the gathering, a tranquil undercurrent that bound the afternoon together in gentle harmony. The companions were having a marvelous time; she spotted at least three of them sneaking extra cakes, and

Thimble had somehow organized what appeared to be a very serious discussion between several of the mouse-dragons about the proper way to hold a tiny teacup. Spark, meanwhile, had stationed himself as guardian of the custard kisses, breathing small puffs of glittery smoke at any creature who dared approach his hoard.

"He's utterly devoted to those things," Lady Willow observed with a laugh, settling beside Aurelise. "One would think they were made of solid gold rather than custard and sugar."

"I requested extra specifically for him," Aurelise confided. "Though I'm beginning to think I should have asked for twice as many."

Willow smiled, but there was something distant in her expression, her gaze unfocused as she stared past the festivities.

"Is everything well?" Aurelise asked gently.

Willow startled slightly, then sighed. "Oh, yes. That is—no, not entirely. I'm rather worried about my brother, if I'm being honest."

"Lord Hadrian?" Aurelise's concern sharpened.

"He offered for the lady he has been courting," Willow said quietly. "She refused him. And naturally, those dreadful gossip birds caught wind of it almost at once. By now, I daresay all of Bloomhaven knows."

Pain bloomed in Aurelise's chest. This sounded heartbreakingly similar to what Lord Hadrian had endured two Seasons ago with Iris—another public refusal, another round of humiliation. The poor man.

"Oh, Willow," she breathed. "How devastating for him."

"Indeed. I had such hopes for them." Willow's fingers worried at the edge of her napkin. "But it seems the lady in question has rather loftier ambitions. Apparently, a Blackbriar isn't distinguished enough for her tastes."

"But your family is one of the most respected in Bloomhaven!" Aurelise couldn't keep the shock from her voice. "Your brother is—he's wonderful! He's kind and accomplished and—Well, that is to say, it sounds as though he's well rid of her. Anyone who cannot see his worth clearly does not deserve him. There's someone far better waiting for him, I'm certain of it."

Willow's smile was wan but grateful. "I do hope you're right."

Aurelise wanted to say more, to offer some greater comfort, but movement in her peripheral vision caught her attention. She'd been doing so well at avoiding Prince Ryden's gaze, but her traitorous eyes seemed drawn to him like flowers to sunlight. Sure enough, when she glanced his way, he was already watching her. The corner of his mouth quirked up in that private half-smile that made her insides melt like warm honey.

She tore her gaze away, but the damage was done. Her cheeks burned, and she could feel his attention like a physical touch even when she wasn't looking at him.

The tea was beginning to wind down, conversations growing softer, when Thimble suddenly zipped over to land on Aurelise's shoulder. The little mouse nuzzled against her cheek with such affection that Aurelise's heart squeezed.

Thank you, thank you, thank you! Thimble squeaked in her mind. *This was the most wonderful thing anyone's done in ages! You made us all feel so special and valued and loved and—oh, I could cry!*

Aurelise reached up to gently stroke Thimble's soft fur. "You'll have me crying next," she said with a soft laugh. "And that would be dreadfully improper at my own tea."

Well, my lady, you have acquired an impressive talent for conducting the most improper of deeds with perfect grace, Thimble observed, whiskers twitching. *I'm sure no one would even notice.*

Aurelise chuckled at that. Then, keeping her voice so low that only the mouse could hear, she whispered, "Thimble, dear one, I need you to take a message to Prince Ryden."

The mouse practically vibrated with excitement. *Of course! Anything! Are you going to confess your feelings? Please say you're going to confess your feelings!*

"We need to speak privately. Tonight, after dinner."

Ooh, where shall I suggest? The music room? The sky garden? Beside the lake?

"The sky garden," Aurelise said quickly. The music room held too many dangerous temptations—she could not trust herself there, not with the memory of his hands in her hair and his lips against her neck—and the risk of discovery was greater if she had to walk all the way to the lake.

The sky garden! Thimble sighed dreamily. *Where it all began! How romantic! Things are coming full circle! This is like something out of a story! You're going to tell him you love him where you first—*

Aurelise gently cupped the excited mouse in her palm, unable to bear correcting those delighted assumptions. She could not bring herself to explain that tonight, she would be ending this … whatever it was that existed between herself and the prince.

Instead, she simply whispered, "Thank you, dear one," and watched as Thimble zoomed off toward the prince, pink wings glittering in the afternoon light.

Tonight, she would set things right. Tonight, she would make sure Prince Ryden understood there could be nothing between the two of them. Even if the very thought made her heart feel as though it were cracking like glass.

Chapter Twenty-Four

The sky garden lay hushed beneath a wash of moonlight, but Aurelise could not seem to match its calm. She paced between the flowering arches again and again, her heart thudding in counterpoint to the soft rustle of the night breeze through the vines.

A tangle of emotions writhed through her chest. Giddiness from her earlier triumph at tea, where even the High Lady had graced her with an approving nod before departing. The memory of it still sparkled through her veins like champagne bubbles, that heady sense of achievement at having not merely survived but genuinely succeeded at something so far outside her usual sphere.

And beneath that effervescence lurked a thrilling anticipation that made her fingers itch for quill and parchment. Tonight, she would write to R again. She would tell him who she was, ask where he suggested they might meet, how they should proceed from this momentous revelation forward into whatever future awaited them.

But threading through both joy and anticipation came a horrible, leaden dread that sat like a stone in her stomach. Because tonight—stars help her—tonight she must tell Prince Ryden that whatever existed between them must end. The very thought sent an aching pain lancing through her chest, as though someone had reached inside and squeezed her heart with merciless fingers.

She had asked Thimble and Spark for privacy after they'd helped her slip out here unseen, and something in her expression must have conveyed the gravity of her request, for they'd actually taken her seriously. Thimble had squeaked something about checking on the kitchen mice, while Spark had muttered about needing to inspect the quality of the evening's custard kisses, and both had vanished with unusual haste.

Now she was alone with nothing but the rooftop terrace's nocturnal symphony—the gentle splash of water from the fountain, the rustle of leaves in the evening breeze, the distant trill of night birds.

She paused at the balustrade, gripping the cool stone as she gazed out over the palace grounds. The stars shimmered like scattered frost across the skies, their light falling over her skin in a whisper of silver. She drew it in with a slow breath, tasting night and starlight and something quieter still—peace.

A thought drifted through her mind, unbidden: *This could all be yours. You could stand here every night.*

The soft sound of footsteps on stone sent a bolt of panic shooting through her. She turned, and there he was—Prince Ryden, stopping a few paces away, that slow, lazy smile already curving his lips in a way that made her insides melt.

"Have I mentioned," he said, his voice carrying that particular quality of intimate amusement that never failed to undo her, "how I love you in pink?"

Aurelise glanced down at herself, heat rushing to her cheeks. Thimble had helped her back into the rose-hued silk tonight after Marta had left, somehow managing the ties at the back with her small paws. Aurelise had certainly not been about to face this conversation in her nightgown.

"I—that is—such observations are hardly—" Flustered, she raised a hand to her hair, tucking a stray strand back into its arrangement, though she suspected the gesture only drew attention to how her fingers trembled.

"And I adore how easily you blush. I suspected as much from the very beginning."

"You … what?" That was really a rather strange thing to say. But Aurelise shook her head, not wanting to be pulled into his orbit, not when she had such difficult words to speak. "Your Highness, I need to tell you—"

"First," he interrupted smoothly, "allow me to congratulate you on not merely surviving but truly conquering your tea this afternoon. That inspired touch of honoring the companions?" His expression shifted to something softer, more genuine. "I loved it."

She could not think of what to say, especially when he was looking at her with such open admiration, but she managed to stammer out her thanks. Then, drawing a fortifying breath, she launched into the speech she'd been preparing since the moment she'd asked Thimble to arrange this meeting.

"I believe," she began, proud when her voice emerged steady, "that I have discovered a solution for your magical difficulties. One that does not require you to bind yourself to someone merely because her magic appears to stabilize your own."

That mischievous curl returned to his lips. "If you are imagining it would be some terrible hardship to bind myself to you for the remainder of my—"

"Please." The word came out sharper than intended. "Do not jest. I am trying to say something important."

His expression sobered—almost convincingly. "Forgive me."

She nodded, gathering her thoughts again. "I spoke with my brother Kazrian yesterday—when I, well, briefly departed Solstice Hall—"

"Absconded with palace property," the prince supplied. "I confess to being thoroughly entertained when a palace companion told me what she'd witnessed. The Lady Aurelise of five or six weeks past would never have dared such audacity."

Aurelise frowned at the interruption, though the expression lacked true censure. "As I was saying, I discussed with Kazrian—without revealing the specific details of your situation, naturally—the possibility of crafting a sort of … enchanted cuff. For someone struggling to control wayward magic." She twisted her fingers together, watching his face carefully. "If he could infuse my magic into such a device, the way he did for the chandelier crystal, it might serve to calm your volatile magic. He believes it entirely feasible. You could use your authority magic without fear of it unraveling beyond your restraint. There would be no pressure to choose a bride based on magical compatibility."

Something shifted in his expression—surprise mingling with an emotion she could not name. "I … that is … I was not aware something like that might even be possible. Do you think … could your brother actually achieve that?"

There was something unexpectedly endearing about his uncertainty—a rare glimpse of the prince unguarded, momentarily unsure of himself. "I don't see why not," Aurelise said with a small smile. "He is very good with things like that. He always has been."

Prince Ryden nodded slowly. "Thank you."

"Of course." She dipped her head, then forced herself to continue with the harder part. "And now I must impress upon you the fact that … that things cannot continue between us as they have been."

"Ah." He tilted his head, studying her with eyes dark like a midnight sky. "Yes, I knew this was coming. I must confess, I found myself irrationally jealous."

"Jealous?" She blinked at him, frowning.

"Yes. Of myself."

"That … that makes no sense, Your Highness."

"I know. Because I still have not told you—"

"I cannot be your princess." The words tumbled free in a rush, but she needed to say them before he could distract her again.

Instead of being upset, that slow smile returned, spreading across Prince Ryden's features like sunrise. "My princess," he said softly. "I confess, I very much like the sound of that."

Frustration flared through her, and she drew herself taller. "You are deliberately ignoring the rather crucial words 'cannot be.'" Another breath, another attempt at steadiness. "I should like to request permission to leave Solstice Hall. To withdraw from the Crown Court entirely. I believe I've remained long enough that my departure would not reflect poorly upon my family, and with—"

"Lady Aurelise."

"The timing is actually quite fortuitous," she forged ahead, ignoring his interruption, her words coming faster now, "given my brother's new child. I wish to be closer to my family at this time. We could announce that—"

"Aurelise." He took a step toward her, closing some of that careful distance she'd maintained.

"That my family—"

"I love you."

The words struck through her like a bell's toll, reverberating until there was nothing left in her but silence. For a heartbeat, she was utterly still—breath, thought, and reason suspended—before the enormity of it all came crashing back, sharp and bright and terrifying.

"No." The word emerged as barely a whisper. "You cannot say such things. It isn't—"

"And I know you love me."

"I—that is—you cannot simply presume—"

"It is not presumption." His voice had gone quiet, certain, gentle in a way that threatened to undo every defense she'd carefully constructed.

"Nothing has changed since the Crown Court began!" The words burst from her, desperate and slightly frantic. "I remain entirely unsuitable for this role, this … this life. You require someone dazzling and unafraid, someone who does not hide in kitchens and flee from ballrooms. I would make the most dreadful princess imaginable."

"That is categorically untrue."

Her music began to trill around them, agitated notes spiraling through the air. "It is! You believe you know me because you've convinced me to attempt various improper adventures with you these past weeks, but you don't. You—"

"If you would allow me a moment to—"

"No!"

"Lise—"

"You do not know me at all!"

Suddenly he was directly before her, hands pulling her against his chest, arms wrapping around her with firm, steady certainty. "I do know you!" he declared, his tone almost fierce.

The suddenness of it stole her breath. She went utterly still—frozen, wordless, scarcely certain she was even breathing. But there was something in his unyielding hold, in the steady warmth of him, that slowly unraveled her resistance. Almost without meaning to, she found herself yielding, softening against him.

"I do know you," he repeated, quieter now. One hand came up to cup the back of her head, drawing her closer to him, and his lips pressed against her hair, his breath stirring the carefully arranged strands.

She could not prevent her eyes from sliding shut, could not stop the shuddery exhale that escaped her. Moments passed as they stood wrapped in each other, and she found her breaths slowing, calming.

"I know," he murmured against her hair, "that your eyes are not the kind of blue that makes people write poetry, nor are they the kind brown that makes people feel steadied. They are the kind of gray that soothes and quiets. You are neither tall nor short but exactly the right height to fit perfectly against me, and you *do* bite your lip when you're concentrating. And when I guessed that you laugh with a quiet shake of your shoulders rather than your whole body, I was entirely correct."

She pulled back to look at him, confusion mingling with the warmth spreading through her chest. Those words … they were so achingly, beautifully familiar. She'd heard them before. No—not heard. Read. She'd *read them before.* Too many times to count.

The realization struck her like ice water poured over her head, shocking and absolute. She shoved away from him, her eyes raking over his features, wild with disbelief. A crashing crescendo of discordant music erupted around them.

R. He was R. Prince Ryden was R.

No. This was … this could not …

"And when I wrote you that dare list," he continued, his gaze holding hers with a quiet intensity, "it was because I saw the bravery in you long before you did. I knew you needed something to draw you from behind those careful walls, to remind you that fear and wonder often walk hand in hand. Every challenge was meant to show you what I already knew—that you are far stronger than you believe."

But she was shaking her head, stumbling away from him, overwhelmed by the enormity of this revelation. He reached for her, trying to grasp her hand, but she'd already stepped beyond his reach.

He couldn't be R. He couldn't be R. And yet … of *course* he was. Of course they were the same person! How had she not recognized it before? She felt suddenly, overwhelmingly foolish. They had the same teasing, affectionately provocative personality. The same kind, genuine heart.

Ryden. R. She pressed her fingertips to her temples, squeezing her eyes shut as she struggled for breath. Of course the prince remembered every dare on the list—he'd written the darned thing!

And he must have known that she was L since … oh, stars above, since the day she'd first arrived at Solstice Hall! She remembered standing among the roses, thoughtlessly repeating his own comments back to him, completely naive as to his true identity, and he'd … something had happened. He'd recognized her, and then his magic had surged beyond his control. She remembered now—the darkness in his eyes, that strange shimmer in the air.

Her thoughts tumbled, tripping over one another, landing on snatches of letters, phrases, half remembered words.

I found myself gazing at the Silver Swan tonight too.

One guest in particular seems to have packed all the warmth among her belongings when she departed.

That supposedly charming 'warmth-burglar' she'd been so jealous of—he'd been writing of *her.*

"How?" The word escaped her as barely more than a gasp. "How … how did this happen?"

The prince … Ryden … *R* … was watching her with careful wariness. "Ellian created the enchanted letter boxes. The one I possess now was originally his. The one I'd initially used, years ago, was lost. I had no notion of where it had ended up. Until the night you sent your first letter, neither box had been used in years."

Aurelise found herself pacing back and forth across the terrace, breathless, flushed, her thoughts spiraling faster than her feet could move. It was as though her mind were determined to retrace everything—every letter, every dare, every glance and stolen breath in the prince's presence—reassembling it all into an entirely new picture.

"That … that night you discovered me here—on this very terrace—with the dare list. That was deliberate. Planned. You … you wanted to involve yourself with the dares."

"Well … yes." He had the grace to look slightly abashed. "The dares were meant to help you find your own courage, but also to give you the chance to know *me*, as I truly am. Not the prince everyone else believes they know."

"And you made it appear … accidental. You deceived me."

"I … withheld the truth.

"How could you?" Her voice rose, cracking slightly on the words.

"You did not like me!" The words burst from him with surprising desperation. "Not at all! You were entirely set against me the prince, and you had refused to meet me the correspondent. I had to convince you gradually, as both versions of myself, or you would have fled immediately."

She continued pacing, shaking her head, music crashing chaotically around her as she attempted to process this sky-shattering revelation. She'd believed she'd made the right choice—the safer one—because the alternative was simply inconceivable. Aurelise Rowanwood could not be a *princess.* Could not be *Crown Consort.*

But now both choices had collapsed into one. R was not dwelling in some distant, mysterious land, waiting to travel here to meet her. He was already *here.* He had danced with her, held her, laughed with her, threaded his fingers through her hair and pressed his lips to her neck and—

"No, no, no," she breathed again, palms pressed against her burning cheeks, because this was all too much. This time, it truly would pull her under and drown her entirely.

"Aurelise—"

But she was already turning and hurrying for the terrace door, fleeing, this time, from both of them.

Chapter Twenty-Five

Ryden paced the length of the sky garden terrace, his footsteps echoing against the stone with a hollow persistence that seemed to mock his restraint. Every instinct screamed at him to follow her, to explain his motivations properly, to make her understand that this revelation—badly delivered though it had been—changed nothing of what lay between them.

He kept replaying every word, every gesture, every shift in her expression as understanding had crashed over her like a wave. The way her voice had cracked on "How could you?" The betrayal written across her features. The sound of her footsteps fleeing across the terrace stones.

He should not have revealed it like that. The thought circled through his mind again and again. He knew her—stars above, he knew her better than he knew almost anyone. He knew that she processed difficult emotions best in solitude, that she needed the safety of distance to examine her feelings without the pressure of immediate response. He should have written it in a letter, should have given her the courtesy of privacy for her initial reaction. Then she might have been less overwhelmed while her world reorganized itself around this new, impossible truth.

But no. He'd been swept up in the moment, in the soft rose silk of her gown, in the intoxicating feel of her in his arms. And the addictive taste of the words 'my princess' on his lips—stars above, what he wouldn't give to be able to whisper those words into her hair, night after night, for the rest of his—

Fool.

This was precisely the problem. He was so caught up in imagining the rest of their life together, while she was still trying to process the fact that he was the same man she'd been pouring her heart out to on paper for the past year.

Well. It was done now.

Ryden dropped onto the stone bench with a sigh that seemed to come from the very depths of his being, his elbows on his knees, his head falling into his hands. Either way, she would require time. Time to process what he'd revealed. Time to reconcile the two versions of him that had, until tonight, existed as separate entities in her mind. Time to decide if she could forgive the deception, even if it had been born of desperation rather than malice.

His thoughts drifted to her earlier words about her brother—Kazrian could craft something to keep his magical surges in check. The possibility stirred a complex mixture of gratitude and melancholy in his chest.

If it worked, it meant freedom from the constant threat of uncontrolled power. No more careful distance maintained from others for fear of what his magic might do if provoked. It was a gift beyond measure.

And yet …

Some shamefully selfish part of him had found comfort in the knowledge that Aurelise's music could soothe his magic. That she alone could bring peace to the chaos that threatened to consume him. It had felt like proof of something larger, something destined—as though the very universe had crafted them to be two halves of a whole.

But that was a dangerous thought, was it not? He did not want her to feel obligated to choose him simply because his magic responded to hers. Did not want her to wonder, years hence, if she'd been forced into a marriage by circumstance rather than choice. If Kazrian's solution worked, at least that particular burden would be lifted from her shoulders. She could choose freely, without the weight of his magical instability influencing her decision.

"L," he murmured aloud. Then, softer, "Lise." And finally, with a tenderness that would have mortified him had anyone been present to witness it, "Aurelise." A thoroughly besotted smile spread across his face, despite everything.

The confrontation on the terrace had been disastrous, certainly. She'd fled from him as though he were something to be escaped, her music spiraling into chaos around her. But beneath the sting of that rejection lay a profound relief that the truth was finally in the open. No more careful performances, no more measured words designed to reveal just enough while concealing the full truth.

She knew now. She knew everything.

And though the uncertainty of her response was eating at him like acid—would she refuse him entirely? Would she return home and never speak to him again?—he could not suppress the hope that fluttered in his chest like a caged bird. Perhaps, if fortune smiled upon him, she would grant him one more chance. Perhaps he could write to her properly, as both himself and R united in one voice, and find the words to make her understand that they had always been the same person. That every word he'd written had been true, every confession genuine, every declaration of love absolutely real.

Perhaps—

The sound of wingbeats cutting through the night air broke through his reverie. Ryden straightened, looking up to see a midnight-blue pegasus swooping toward the sky garden, silver sparks trailing from its wings.

Cobalt, he realized. Cobalt and Evryn.

The pegasus swooped low over the terrace, and Evryn dropped from the saddle. His boots hit the stone with a solid thud, and he tore off his riding cap, throwing it to the ground as Cobalt glided away into the night.

Ryden rose slowly from the bench, his muscles tensing instinctively.

"Tell me the truth." Evryn's voice was deadly quiet, all trace of his usual humor absent. His face was hard as granite in the moonlight, his hands clenched at his sides. "Tell me you did not know it was her."

A chill shot through Ryden, swift and absolute. Somehow, Evryn had found out.

"Tell me," Evryn continued, taking a step closer, "that you did not look me in the eye and lie when you spoke of this mystery woman whose identity you supposedly did not know."

Ryden drew in a careful breath, forcing himself to meet his friend's furious gaze. "I did not lie."

"Really?" Disbelief dripped from the word. "You did not know you were writing to my *sister*? That you—"

"I did not know!" The words burst from Ryden with more force than he'd intended. "I know *now*, yes, and have known for some weeks, but when we spoke that morning—when I confessed to you about the letters—I had no notion that the woman I was writing to and Lady Aurelise were one and the same."

Evryn released a cry of pure frustration, his hands flying to his hair, tugging at the dark strands as he lurched away. His voice, when it came again, was thick with self-recrimination. "How could I have let this happen?"

"You?" Ryden frowned, confusion momentarily overriding his defensive posture.

"Yes, me!" Evryn spun back to face him, and there was something almost wild in his expression. "I suddenly remembered where I'd encountered such an enchanted letter box before. We were merely perusing an oddities shop in Bloomhaven—Aurelise and I—and she discovered a curious wooden box that promised correspondence with an unknown recipient. And I, in my infinite wisdom—" his voice turned bitter with self-mockery, "—believed the shop owner's assurance that it was nothing more than a simple trick of magic and purchased it for her. And now here we are."

He spread his hands wide, the gesture encompassing the terrace, the palace, the entire mess of a situation they now found themselves in.

"All she has ever wanted was a simple, quiet existence. A peaceful life away from the busyness of society and court and—" he gestured sharply at Ryden "—and men like you. And instead she's wound up trapped at Solstice Hall, while you've been toying with her affections, leading her into stars know what manner of impropriety and—"

"Trapped? *Toying* with her?" The words ignited something hot and dangerous in Ryden's chest. Yes, he'd convinced Aurelise to embrace a few improprieties—midnight swims and rooftop stargazing and that memorable evening with the driftshade—but he knew precisely what Evryn was implying, and it went beyond innocent mischief. "Is that truly what you believe? That I have been amusing myself at your sister's expense? Are you still so determined to think so little of me?"

"Yes!" Evryn stalked forward, his jaw tight with fury. "Because all evidence suggests—"

"Even after I told you that was little more than a public persona? A performance?"

"That was before I discovered it was my *sister* on the other end of your correspondence!"

Evryn closed the distance between them in two quick strides, his hands fisting in the front of Ryden's jacket, yanking him forward until they were nearly nose to nose. His voice dropped to something low and dangerous.

"Tell me the truth. If you have been anything but a perfect gentleman with her—if you have taken even the smallest liberty that—"

"I will tell you the truth!"

Ryden gripped Evryn's wrists and shoved him away, his own voice strained with the weight of everything he'd been holding back. The words came pouring out, raw and desperate and absolutely honest.

"I love her. Completely and endlessly, with everything in me. She has captivated me entirely—first through her words, her thoughts, and now in person, where she has exceeded every impossible dream I had of her. For almost the entirety of our correspondence, there has been no one else for me but her. No other lady has turned my head or touched my heart since her letters began arriving in that wooden box."

He saw Evryn's expression shift, some of the murderous intent fading into uncertainty, but Ryden pressed on, needing him to understand.

"You may believe me entirely unworthy of her, and in that, I—" He broke off with a bitter laugh, shaking his head. "I would not disagree. She is far too good for me, too pure and smart and extraordinary for someone who has spent years playing at being someone he is not. But if she will have me—if she can step beyond her fear of what she believes royal life will be like, and if she can forgive the fact that I did not immediately reveal who I was upon first recognizing her—then I will spend the remainder of my days and nights devoted to ensuring she never regrets choosing me."

Silence fell between them, heavy and complete save for the sound of their breathing gradually slowing from its heated pace. Somewhere in the garden below, night creatures chirped their endless songs. The fountain continued its gentle splash, indifferent to the drama playing out beside it. The moon continued its path across the sky, painting everything in shades of silver and shadow.

Evryn stood very still, his expression cycling through several emotions Ryden could not quite identify. The fury had faded, replaced by something more complex. Resignation, perhaps. When he finally spoke, his voice carried a different quality.

"Well." He cleared his throat, looking suddenly uncomfortable. "It seems I may have been … somewhat excessive in my response upon discovering precisely who your mysterious correspondent was."

"Understandable," Ryden responded tightly. "She is your sister. You clearly care for her. I don't fault you for feeling protective."

"And I apologize for …" Evryn rubbed the back of his neck. "Assuming the worst of you."

"Again," Ryden said, softer this time, "understandable."

Silence settled between them, not uncomfortable so much as uncertain. Both men turned their gazes toward the moonlit gardens, as though the silvered calm below might offer a way to navigate the unease between them.

"I suppose," Evryn said slowly, "if this all works out as you hope, you and I will be brothers."

Ryden blinked, a tug pulling sharp and low in his chest. Brothers. The word landed in an unexpected way, spreading into warmth, longing, the ache of old loneliness easing. He had always loved and envied Ellian's family. The loud, chaotic jumble of siblings and cousins and aunts and uncles. But though they were Ryden's family too, they remained distanced by the fact that his link to Ellian was not one that could ever be claimed publicly.

The thought of gaining not just a wife but an entire new family who would tease and argue and support each other through everything life might bring … Well, it had not even occurred to Ryden.

"I think," he said quietly, his voice rough with emotion he did not try to hide, "I would rather like that."

Chapter Twenty-Six

The music room lay shrouded in darkness, save for the faint shimmer of moonlight that crept through the tall windows. Aurelise had tucked herself into the narrow space behind the settee where Prince Ryden's childhood toy chest sat, her knees drawn up to her chest. He might search for her here—he knew this had become her favorite sanctuary within Solstice Hall, after all—but from this particular angle, she remained invisible from the doorway. If he glanced inside and saw nothing, perhaps he would continue his search elsewhere.

She needed time. Time to think, to breathe, to make sense of the impossible truth that had just shattered her understanding of everything.

R and Ryden. The same person.

It felt as though the world had tipped on its axis, leaving her to view everything from a strange new angle. At first, the revelation had been too vast to comprehend, too impossible to hold all at once. She had tried, quite literally, to run from it. But as she sat there in the stillness of the music room, her heartbeat gradually steadying, another feeling began to surface, quiet, startling, and entirely unexpected. Relief.

A small, incredulous laugh escaped her lips, quickly muffled behind her hand. How had she not seen it? They possessed the same teasing wit, the same ability to coax her from her careful reserve with gentle provocations.

They both saw through her protests to the truth beneath, both challenged her to be braver than she believed possible. The man who'd written 'take a midnight swim' was the same one who had chased her all the way to the lake and persuaded her to step into it. The correspondent who'd penned 'be entirely improper' had stood beside her through every scandalous moment.

No wonder she had fallen in love with both of them.

The thought sent a flutter of something dangerously close to joy through her chest. She would not have to choose. Would not have to break anyone's heart by selecting one over the other. She could have them both—the man who knew her soul through ink and paper, and the one who'd drawn her so thoroughly from her shell that at times she barely recognized the brave creature she'd become.

Except …

She tipped her head back against the settee, eyes sliding shut as a quiet groan escaped her. Saying yes to them—*him*—meant marrying a prince. Taking on a role she'd insisted from the very moment of the Crown Court announcement that she could never, would never, absolutely *could not possibly* fulfill.

Though, a traitorous voice whispered in her mind, she would have sworn with equal vehemence that she could never swim in a lake, or smoke drift-shade leaf, or stand up on behalf of those who were not in a position to stand up for themselves. Yet she'd done all those things and more.

Perhaps she had been just the tiniest bit mistaken about the princess matter as well?

A smile curved her lips despite everything. Ryden had known exactly what he was doing with that dare list. Each challenge carefully calibrated to push her boundaries while keeping her safe, building her confidence one small rebellion at a time.

And this room—stars above, this room. When he'd brought her here, speaking of his grandmother who'd been quiet and shy, who'd needed sanctuary from the overwhelming demands of court life, he had not been making casual conversation. He had been showing her that there would always be a place for her here. A refuge when the world became too much.

The realization made her heart ache with a tender sort of pain. He'd been preparing a space for her in his life before she'd even known who he truly was.

But that pain—that aching flood of feeling—was still the most terrifying part of all of this. She was not yet convinced that she would actually survive it if she let go entirely and stepped over the edge and into the unknown.

The sound of the door opening shattered her reverie. The faelights flared and brightened, filling the room with a warm glow. Footsteps—no, two sets of footsteps—entered the room. Aurelise pressed herself deeper into her hiding spot, barely daring to breathe.

"We can speak freely here," came a voice that made Aurelise's blood turn to ice. The High Lady herself, her tone carrying its usual regal authority. "The room is enchanted to prevent any sound from entering or leaving. We shall not be overheard. Had I known of your visit in advance, we might have used my private withdrawing room, but it is currently undergoing a rather thorough overnight cleansing spell."

"I suppose this will suffice," came another familiar voice that sent a different sort of chill through Aurelise's veins. *Her grandmother.* What was she doing at Solstice Hall at this hour? "I've been in this room before, as it so happens. Many years past. With your mother."

The soft rustle of silk indicated they were settling themselves somewhere within the room. Aurelise held herself perfectly still, terrified that even the slightest movement might betray her presence.

"Was this unexpected visit truly necessary?" The High Lady's voice carried a note of barely concealed irritation. "You realize we might have spoken tomorrow evening at the Festival of Lantern Wishes? I believe an invitation was dispatched to Rowanwood House."

"No." Her grandmother's tone left no room for argument. "I must remove my granddaughter from this situation without further delay. The improprieties that have transpired here—I cannot allow them to proceed even a moment longer."

Aurelise's heart hammered against her ribs. This concerned *her*. And the prince. But what improprieties did her grandmother know of? And more importantly, *how* could she possibly know?

"In addition," Lady Rivenna continued, "the tea leaves have revealed glimpses of something I simply cannot permit to unfold."

"Cannot permit?" A thread of amusement wove through the High Lady's response. "You attempt now to interfere with fate itself?"

"Your Grace, you know I have been happily interfering since The Charmed Leaf's creation."

The High Lady sighed. "Yes, I suppose I am well aware of this." Several moments of weighted silence passed, during which Aurelise wondered if they could hear her thundering heartbeat.

"So," Lady Rivenna continued eventually. "As I said, I would like to remove—"

"He loves her."

Aurelise went utterly still. She wasn't certain she was even drawing breath.

"Love?" Her grandmother's voice dripped skepticism. "With all due respect, Your Grace, I do not believe your son is capable of—"

"And that," the High Lady interrupted, steel threading through her tone, "is precisely where you are mistaken. You believe your tea house, with its … exceptional magic, reveals all truths. But it does not. The only knowledge you possess of my son comes from rumors and the salacious tales that circulate through Bloomhaven's drawing rooms."

"That is not *all* I know of him," Lady Rivenna replied, her words weighted with unspoken meaning.

A pause stretched between them, taut as a drawn bowstring.

"I certainly hope," the High Lady said slowly, dangerously, "that you are not attempting to leverage my secrets, Lady Rivenna. For I would wager the confidences I hold of yours carry equal weight."

"I threaten nothing. We have guarded each other's secrets for years. That shall not change now."

"Good." The High Lady's tone softened marginally. "Now that we have dispensed with that unpleasantness, allow me to speak plainly. I realize my maternal bias, but I know my son far better than any collection of gossip birds and loose-tongued society matrons. I have observed him closely since the Crown Court commenced. His feelings for Lady Aurelise are beyond question."

Aurelise pressed both hands over her mouth. Though she knew this to be true already—she'd heard the words 'I love you' from Ryden's own lips, after all—hearing someone else declare it made her, somehow, want to giggle.

Fabric rustled as one of the two women shifted position. "I thought we had reached an accord regarding this matter, before the Crown Court even began," Lady Rivenna said. "You harbored concerns about the unsuitability of her magic, while I worried over the mismatch of their … temperaments, let us say. We both decided there would be no match between them."

A jolt of indignation pierced Aurelise. How easily these two women had spoken of her and the prince as though they were mere pawns to be arranged.

"We were in agreement, yes. However—"

"Then I am here to remove my granddaughter with immediate effect. The things I have learned of that are taking place within these walls—"

"Things?" The High Lady's voice sharpened to a blade's edge. "What precisely have you learned? And through what means?"

"Surely you did not imagine I would send Aurelise here unaccompanied, without some method of ensuring her safety?"

What? Aurelise's mind reeled in confusion.

More rustling, and then she heard the High Lady's voice, pitched with incredulity: "What exactly did you dispatch with her?"

Silence.

Then an incredulous laugh escaped the High Lady. "You sent one of your plants. Those tea house vines that excel at—"

"Very well, yes," Lady Rivenna interrupted, a note of defensiveness creeping into her tone. "I presented it as a gift, a reminder of home. But indeed, the vines have been whispering their observations, and what I have heard has been most—"

The High Lady let out another laugh, a sound caught somewhere between astonishment and reluctant admiration. "Oh, Lady Rivenna. You are truly something extraordinary."

But Aurelise barely heard her. Heat flooded her veins, and her breath came quick and shallow as she pictured the oversized teacup with its trailing green-gold leaves—the gift she'd cherished as a piece of home. It had been *observing* her? *Spying* on her?

Before wisdom could intercede, she'd bolted upright and spun to face the two women, her hands clenched into trembling fists. "Grandmother! You have been *spying on me* the entire time I've been here?"

The reaction was instantaneous and, under any other circumstance, might have been amusing. Lady Rivenna gave a startled shriek—an undignified sound Aurelise would have sworn her grandmother incapable of making—and clutched a hand to her chest. Beside her, the High Lady, wearing only a nightgown and wrapper with her pale blue hair tumbling loose about her shoulders, seized both arms of her chair, eyes going perfectly round in disbelief.

She recovered first, however, her eyes narrowing as she took in Aurelise's presence. "What," she asked in a voice that could have frozen flame as she slowly rose to her feet, "are you doing in here? How did you even enter? The enchantments on this room should have prevented it."

"Prince Ryden gave me permission," Aurelise managed, lifting her chin despite the trembling in her limbs. "He said I might come whenever I wished. And I … I needed somewhere to think, to process certain matters, so I was … hiding."

She drew a steadying breath, hoping to call on that elusive courage Ryden seemed so sure she possessed.

"But I find I do not particularly appreciate discovering that you both have been manipulating and orchestrating my life behind my back. I would like to request—politely and with respect—that you cease your meddling at once."

The High Lady's eyebrows rose nearly to her hairline. "Oh, would you now?"

"Yes." Aurelise dropped into a hasty curtsy, then straightened and raised her gaze once more. "With respect, Your Grace."

"Aurelise, dear." Lady Rivenna rose to her feet, apparently having recovered from her shock. She lifted her chin, striving to recover her usual formidable composure, but after a moment her shoulders lowered, and a flicker of embarrassment crossed her face. "I apologize for … well, manipulating and orchestrating, as you put it. I admit," she added with a sigh, "it must have seemed an unforgivable intrusion. And perhaps it was. But I swear to you, my dear, it was done only out of concern. I was merely trying to look after you."

Aurelise searched her grandmother's eyes for some trace of manipulation and found only weary truth. She felt the edge of her anger begin to ease. "I understand, Grandmother. But I've learned I'm not nearly so helpless as everyone seems to think."

"Well, be that as it may, I still believe it would be wise for you to return to Rowanwood House with me tonight. Regardless of whatever … spark might have developed between you and the prince, this is a matter of magical compatibility, not mere affection. Your magic remains fundamentally unsuitable—"

"Actually, it is not," Aurelise said at the exact moment the High Lady declared, "I believe you'll find we were mistaken on that account, Lady Rivenna."

Both women turned to stare at each other. "If you had not insisted upon interrupting earlier," the High Lady continued, "I would have explained that Ryden and Lady Aurelise have discovered her magic provides precisely the calming influence we had hoped to find."

She turned to Aurelise, her expression softening somewhat. "I apologize for dismissing your magic so readily at the start of the Season, though I hope you understand I sought only what I believed best for my son. As the days have passed and I have observed you, I find that you remind me greatly of my own mother—gentle and shy, yet so beloved by everyone both here at Solstice Hall and throughout the Shaded Lands."

Heat bloomed across Aurelise's cheeks at the unexpected praise. "I—oh. Thank you, Your Grace. That is most kind."

She took a breath and turned to her grandmother, drawing strength from the High Lady's support. "Her Grace speaks truly of the calming influence my magic appears to have developed. Moreover, I've consulted with Kazrian, and he believes he can craft an enchanted cuff that would allow the prince to carry a measure of my magic with him always, providing stability whenever needed."

"Well." Lady Rivenna appeared to brighten somewhat at that. "How remarkably convenient. Then there exists no requirement for you to marry the prince after all."

"No requirement, no." Aurelise kept her voice steady despite the emotions roiling through her chest. "But our feelings for one another—"

"Aurelise, dear," her grandmother interrupted with that particular tone of condescension that suggested she knew best, and Aurelise quickly discovered that perhaps her anger had not ebbed after all. "These feelings shall pass. I know what is best for you, and that young man is certainly not—"

"No!"

The word rang out with such unexpected force that Aurelise shocked even herself. Both older women stared at her as though she'd suddenly transformed into something unrecognizable.

She opened her mouth to apologize, then forced herself to swallow the words. She took another steadying breath. "With all due respect, Grandmother," she said, "you do not. The High Lady is right that you know nothing of what the prince is truly like. He is thoughtful and patient and possesses far greater depth than anyone realizes. And even if you do not believe a word either of us says, this still would not be your decision to make. The prince has made his choice clear, and—perhaps more importantly, where you and I are concerned—I have made mine."

The truth of it struck Aurelise even as the words left her lips. She had made her decision. *She had made her decision.*

The feeling that had nearly consumed her in this very room the day before—when Ryden's fingers had slid into her hair and his hand had closed around hers, when the world had seemed to blur into music and heartbeat—hovered now at the edge of her awareness, beautiful and terrifying in equal measure.

I swear to you that I would never let you drown.

You will not be swept away.

The High Lady regarded Aurelise with unexpected warmth, the subtle shimmer of tears evident in her eyes. "I had all but surrendered hope that my son would marry for love," she murmured. "How glad I am to be proven wrong."

Then, as though catching herself in an unseemly display of emotion, the High Lady straightened, composing her features into their usual regal mask. She turned to Lady Rivenna with the air of someone delivering a final verdict.

"Well, Lady Rivenna. You have heard your granddaughter's wishes." Then her voice dropped, though not so low that Aurelise couldn't hear. "It appears you and I shall soon be connected by more than merely our mutually guarded secrets."

Dearest Lise,

I love you.

Yours, with every part of me,

Ryden

Chapter Twenty-Seven

THE NIGHT AIR CARRIED THE SCENT OF JASMINE AND WONDER AS Aurelise stepped from the palace doors into the transformed gardens of Solstice Hall. She paused at the threshold, one hand pressed to her heart, the other clutching the silver moonflare token she'd been turning over in her fingers all day. Above her, the sky had become a canvas of impossible beauty.

Dozens of paper lanterns drifted upward on invisible currents of magic, each one glowing from within. Some burned with the warm gold of summer afternoons, others shimmered in shades of rose and lavender, while a precious few gleamed silver-white as they ascended toward their celestial destinations.

Guests inscribe wishes on enchanted parchment, Ryden had told her the night they had sat beside the lake, *then fold them into lanterns. When released, they rise into the night sky.*

Above her, the lanterns rose in graceful spirals, dancing around one another in patterns that seemed almost choreographed, as though the wishes themselves knew how to waltz. It made her want to lift her hands and trail her fingers through the air, calling forth an accompanying melody.

She had spent most of the day sequestered in her chambers, alternating between pacing the length of her room and sitting frozen on her bed, staring at the letter that had been waiting in her enchanted box when she'd woken that morning.

She wanted to write the same words back to him. She also wanted to say them out loud, in person. But minutes had stretched into hours, and now the festival was well underway, and it seemed she had yet to find her courage. So she had clutched the moonflare token to her chest, taken a deep breath, and finally ventured forth from her chambers.

The gardens were filled with the soft murmur of voices and gentle laughter. She could see the Crown Court ladies in their finest gowns, their faces tilted skyward as they watched their wishes attempt to find their matching stars. The High Lady presided over it all from an elevated pavilion draped in silver silk. And somewhere among them all was Ryden.

Her stomach performed a series of acrobatic maneuvers that would have impressed even the palace performers. After everything that had transpired, she knew exactly where they stood. She knew he loved her. She knew she loved him. She knew she'd already made her choice.

So why did the thought of actually seeing him, of looking into those eyes that knew all her secrets, make her feel as though she might dissolve into a thousand glowing fragments? In a good way, of course. In what she was beginning to suspect might possibly be the *best* way.

"You remember the plan?" Aurelise whispered as Thimble darted past her in a pink and purple blur.

Thimble twirled midair before darting back and hovering at eye level, her whiskers practically vibrating with excitement. *Oh yes, my lady! We locate the prince, create a spectacular distraction so everyone looks elsewhere, then Spark and I shall ingeniously maneuver him behind the rose bushes where you may FINALLY kiss him senseless!*

Heat flooded Aurelise's cheeks. "Well. Yes. Something like that."

WONDERFUL! Thimble declared, spinning in a delighted circle. *This is the most romantic mission we've ever undertaken! Oh! But my lady—* The mouse's eyes went perfectly round. *Your gloves! You've forgotten them!*

"Oh dear," Aurelise said, knowing perfectly well she'd left them in her chambers with deliberate intent. She'd spent the better part of the afternoon imagining what it might feel like to slide her bare fingers through a certain prince's beautiful blue hair. And truly, out here in the garden's gentle darkness, who would even notice the absence of proper hand attire?

A disapproving puff of glittery smoke drifted past her ear.

"What?" she asked innocently, turning to find Spark perched on a nearby garden statue, his golden eyes narrowed with suspicion.

I am merely observing, came his telepathic drawl, *that for someone who claims to have 'forgotten' her gloves, you seem remarkably unconcerned about retrieving them.*

"Perhaps I'm embracing spontaneity," Aurelise suggested, beginning to walk deeper into the gardens. "Is that not what you and Thimble have been encouraging me to do all Season?"

There is spontaneity, Spark replied, gliding alongside her, *and then there is scandalous behavior designed specifically to facilitate the touching of royal persons.*

Aurelise's already warm cheeks heated further. "I haven't the faintest notion what you mean."

Thimble giggled. *Oh, Spark, you're such a tremendous fussbudget! This is romance! True love! The culmination of—OH!* Her squeak could have shattered crystal. *I SEE HIM! I SEE HIM!*

Aurelise's heart attempted to flee her chest entirely. "Oh stars," she breathed, pressing both hands to her stomach. "Is love supposed to make one feel quite so … ill?"

According to the academic literature, Spark intoned, *the physiological symptoms of romantic attachment often mimic those of mild food poisoning. Elevated heart rate, occasional lightheadedness—*

"How wonderfully reassuring," Aurelise managed, though she was already moving toward the rose garden, drawn by an invisible thread.

Ready, my lady? Thimble asked, practically vibrating with anticipation.

Aurelise nodded, though readiness seemed an entirely foreign concept at present. She slipped between the tall rose bushes, their blooms releasing perfume into the night air, and tried to quiet her thundering pulse.

Behind her, she heard what could only be described as theatrical chaos. Thimble's squeaks rose in what might have been an attempt at mouse-sized operatic performance, while Spark contributed several dramatic roars that wouldn't have frightened a kitten. There was a crash, startled exclamations, and what sounded suspiciously like Lady Ellowa shrieking about her hair.

Aurelise pressed a hand to her mouth, stifling a laugh—

"Well," came a familiar voice, warm with amusement and accompanied by the sound of stumbling footsteps, "that was certainly subtle."

She spun around, and there he was. Prince Ryden came to a halt before her, looking slightly disheveled, definitely startled, and absolutely perfect. His jacket bore evidence of what appeared to be tiny paw prints on the shoulders, as though he'd been physically herded into the roses.

"Hello," she breathed.

"Hello," he replied, and his smile was so tender, so full of unguarded affection, that her knees went rather uncertain.

"Hello," she said again, which was ridiculous, because she was fairly certain she had just said that.

His smile stretched wider. "Hello … L."

They stood there for a moment, simply looking at each other, twin smiles playing at their lips. The sounds of the festival seemed very far away, as though they'd stepped into their own private world where only lantern light and roses existed.

This was him. R. The man whose words had lived in her thoughts and threaded through her daydreams for so long stood before her now—real, tangible, *hers.* Could her heart possibly bear so much happiness?

"So," he said finally, his voice carrying that teasing quality she'd come to adore, "I heard rumors of someone completing a certain dare list. Or very nearly completing it."

"Oh?" She tilted her head, finding her courage somewhere in his familiar warmth. "What might you have heard?"

"Only that a certain lady—who previously insisted she could never stand up to anyone who frightened her—boldly confronted none other than the High Lady herself."

"And Lady Rivenna Rowanwood," Aurelise added, lifting her chin with a touch of pride. "Who I would argue is perhaps even more terrifying than your mother."

"Oh, without question," Ryden agreed immediately. "Mother merely rules a kingdom. Your grandmother could reduce grown men to tears with a single raised eyebrow." He paused, his expression softening. "My mother is well aware of this. She told me that if she hadn't already been impressed by you, watching you stand your ground against your formidable grandmother would have convinced her entirely."

"Your mother is … impressed by me?"

"Indeed she is." He offered another of those disarming smiles, the sort that left her knees unreliable and her pulse quite incapable of behaving itself.

She looked up at the lanterns drifting overhead, needing a moment to gather herself. "The festival is beautiful," she said softly. "I can understand why it's among your favorites."

"Have you made a wish yet?"

"Not yet. Have you?"

"Mmm." His smile curve up on one side. "It might have contained a word beginning with L."

She quirked an eyebrow, finding refuge in their familiar banter. "Lamentable liar?"

His laugh was rich and genuine. "Actually, it was rather shorter. Four letters. Begins with L-I and rhymes with 'fleece.'"

She glanced down before daring to look up at him through her lashes, a shy smile ghosting across her lips. "You know you do not need to wish for me," she murmured. "You already have me."

His gaze flared—warmth and adoration blazing into something bright and unguarded. "Stars," he breathed, "if I did not love you so completely already, that would undo me all over again."

The raw honesty in his voice sent heat blooming across her cheeks.

"And I shall never tire of how beautiful you are when you blush," he continued. "Is that too forward? I'm saying it regardless. You blush frequently and it's utterly enchanting and I adore it."

A laugh bubbled up from somewhere deep in her chest. "You sound like … him. You. The way you write in your letters."

"Well, yes. We are, as it happens, the same person."

The reminder made her feel shy again, the magnitude of it all—that her secret correspondent and this wonderful, maddening prince were one—threatening to overwhelm her.

She remembered the moonflare token still clutched in her palm and held it out, the silver moth catching the light. "If I could wish for anyone," she said quietly, "I would wish for you."

For a moment he didn't move, didn't speak, and she glanced up just in time to see him swallow before he stepped closer. He reached out and enclosed both her hand and the token within his larger ones. The warmth of him seemed to encompass her entirely, and she found herself swaying toward him.

Then he stopped, shaking his head. "Wait. No. There is something I must say first."

He released her hand, and every part of her wanted him to take it back. But his expression had changed, his usual confidence seeming to waver, replaced by a raw, unguarded honesty.

"I need to apologize," he said, taking a steadying breath. "For not revealing myself sooner. I know how it must have seemed—a deception, a betrayal of the trust you placed in me through our letters. I felt as though it was the only way for you to come to know me, but that does not excuse keeping the full truth from you for so long, letting you think you were corresponding with one person while growing close to another, when all along we were—"

She stood on tiptoe, gripped the front of his coat with both hands, pulled herself toward him, and pressed her mouth to his.

For a heartbeat, they both froze—he from pure surprise, she from the shocking realization that she hadn't the faintest idea what came next. But then his arms came around her, drawing her against him, and her uncertainty dissolved into something far more overwhelming.

The moonflare dropped from her clenched hand as her fingers slid upward, threading into his hair, soft and warm beneath her trembling hands. His palm traced a path down her spine, settling at the small of her back, where it spread and drew her closer still until there was scarcely space for breath between them. His other hand tangled in her hair at the nape of her neck.

Her lips parted on a trembling breath, and his met them again, surer this time, a rush of warmth and need that made her pulse stumble. *"Stars … L …"* The sound of her name, half gasped against her mouth, carried such raw longing that it sent shivers racing through her, heat unfurling beneath her skin.

Her magic broke free in a rush of sound, a thousand threads of melody unfurling at once. Music tangled over itself in scattered harmonies, swelling and spilling outward until it became everything: air and heartbeat and breath and light as the world tilted and all she could feel was him. His breath, his touch, his heartbeat thrumming against hers. The sensation broke over her like a wave, dizzying and all-encompassing, flooding every thought until she was lost in it—overwhelmed, undone, yet utterly unwilling to draw back.

He tightened his grip on the back of her neck, further angling her face upward. His mouth moved against hers with growing certainty, drawing her closer, drawing her under, until the world itself seemed to bend around the space they shared.

And she was drowning. She was flying. She was coming apart at the seams and being remade with every thundering beat of her heart. But she did not let go.

Gradually, the rush softened. The fierce rhythm of the kiss slowed, faltered, until they were simply breathing the same air, mouths barely apart, foreheads almost touching. Her pulse raced wild and uneven as he murmured, breathless against her lips, "Are you still with me?"

She nodded, her nose brushing against his, her hands now fisted in his jacket, as though he were the only thing holding her upright. "I … yes."

The rush had not fully left her; it surged and receded in turns, a tide of heat and light that threatened to take her under. But as she breathed him in —his warmth, his steadiness—she felt it settling. The tide was easing, and though she still felt the pull, it seemed she had not been swept away after all.

"I promised I would not let you drown," he whispered, knowing where her thoughts lingered.

She nodded again, eyes still closed, and then it turned into a side-to-side motion as she gently dragged her lips back and forth across his, because—stars above—the soft brush of his skin against hers sent the most wonderful tingles throughout her entire body.

"Are you enjoying this?" he asked, and she both heard his smile and felt it against her mouth.

"Yes." Her laugh was soft and breathy, and this was without a doubt the most intoxicating thing she had ever experienced. Even more entrancing than the driftshade.

He kissed her again, the soft, sweet press of lips on lips. "L …" he murmured. "L for Lovely …" Another kiss at the corner of her mouth. "L for Luminous …" The next kiss on the curve of her cheek. "L for Literally Everything I've Ever Wanted." His lips brushed over the delicate skin of her closed eyelid as a breath of laughter escaped her.

He drew back slightly. After another few moments, her eyes fluttered open, the world slow to return, only to find his gaze already waiting for her—steady, reverent, as if he'd been memorizing every breath she took.

She lifted one trembling hand and let her thumb trace the curve of his lower lip, soft and warm beneath her touch. The motion drew a faint hitch in his breath, and for a heartbeat she forgot how to breathe at all.

Then she met his eyes again—so close, so impossibly full of everything she felt—and the words slipped out on a whisper, fragile but certain. "I love you."

He stilled at her words. For a moment, he only looked at her, eyes shining in a way that made the breath catch in her throat. Then, very softly, he said, "I love you, Lady Aurelise Rowanwood, more completely than I ever knew one heart could hold."

Her lips curved, trembling between laughter and tears. "Now that I've been brave enough to say it aloud, writing it in a letter should be easy." She paused. "That is … if we'll still be writing letters to one another?"

"Of course." His eyes sparkled with mischief now, the solemnity giving way to familiar playfulness. He leaned in, his mouth close enough that she could feel the smile in his words. "Dear L," he murmured, "you kiss nicely."

A surprised laugh escaped her. "*Nicely?* That's all?"

"Very nicely," he amended solemnly.

"Dear R," she said, chin tilting up in mock offense, "your compliments could use work."

"Dear L," he countered, lowering his forehead to hers, "your wit remains as dangerous as ever."

"Dear R," she whispered, her voice softening again, "I dare you to kiss me again."

"Oh, a new dare? How positively *bold* of you, my lovely Lise."

"I believe it's only fair if I write a few of them now. You've been monopolizing all the dare space in our letters. And now that I've completed the original list, it seems we are in need of a new challenge."

He smiled then, that slow, devastating smile that made her heart trip over itself. "I would be delighted for you to write as many dares as you'd like. For now, I shall gladly accept the first one."

And with that, he brought his mouth down to meet hers again.

Epilogue

Dear R,

It is nearly midnight, and tomorrow I will marry you.

I should be sleeping. My lady's maid has already scolded me twice for still having one of the faelights glowing, warning that I'll have shadows beneath my eyes tomorrow. But how can I possibly sleep when every thought is of you? When tomorrow, after all this time of letters and longing, I will finally be yours in every way?

Do you know what is strangest of all? I'm writing to you from the very same room where I penned that first letter, thinking I was pouring my heart out to enchanted paper. The room where I first called you 'Not-So-Imaginary' and you called me 'brave' when I felt anything but.

I hardly recognize her now, that terrified girl who wrote to an enchanted box, convinced she would shatter under the weight of her own magic, convinced she could never love anything as much as her music.

But you were right, weren't you? (Yes, I know, you are R for almost always Right About Things.) That day you asked if there might not be room for different kinds of joy, different colors of the same light. I was so certain nothing could shine as brightly as the feeling of my own musical creations flowing through me.

I was wrong.

You shine brighter. You shine so bright sometimes I can scarcely breathe for the wonder of it And tomorrow I am going to promise to spend the rest of my life basking in that light. I will walk toward you—not run away, not hide, not flee to the kitchens or the music room or the gardens—but walk steadily forward to take your hand.

With my whole heart,

L

P.S. My mother insists on an elaborate hairstyle tomorrow with approximately three thousand pins. I do hope someone will be available to help remove them all tomorrow evening. Someone patient and gentle, with clever fingers. Any suggestions?

My Dearest Soon-To-Be-Princess L,

Midnight finds me equally awake, sitting at my desk composing a reply to the woman who altered my very existence with a single letter, whom I can scarcely believe I will have the right to call my wife by this time tomorrow.

And speaking of this time tomorrow—you asked for suggestions regarding the hair pin situation. I might know someone. Devastatingly handsome fellow. Legendary charm. Has been dreaming about running his fingers through your hair since approximately the sixth letter you sent him. I could make introductions if you'd like?

But perhaps I should stop there before this letter becomes entirely too improper for an unwed lady to receive. Though after tomorrow … well. After tomorrow I'll be able to write all manner of improper things without your roses' disapproval. They'll have to accept me as family.

And while we're on the subject of family—how scandalized do you think they would be at this somewhat unconventional addition to my vows: 'I promise to kiss the honey from your fingers whenever

Ah. I was just interrupted by Spark lifting his head long enough to fix me with a look of withering disapproval and a most judgmental puff of glittering smoke. I swear, he knows precisely what I'm writing. Nearly as bad as Horatio. Thimble, on the other hand, would no doubt approve—if she were conscious. She's currently collapsed against Spark's side like a fallen courtier after too much wine, one tiny paw flung dramatically over her face.

There. Spark has gone back to sleep now, Thimble has begun to snore, and I'm left sitting here imagining that first glimpse of you tomorrow—the hush of the hall, the swell of music, and then you, radiant and blushing and beautiful. I make no promises about remembering how to breathe.

Yours (in only a few more hours),

R

Dear R of the Legendary Charm and Clever Fingers,

I think I have forgotten how to breathe already.

But I'm glad to hear that Spark and Thimble have made themselves at home in your study. They did look rather forlorn when I left Solstice Hall. I shall be delighted to see them tomorrow at the ceremony (though that excitement pales in comparison to the breathless, heart-pounding thought of seeing you).

And as for that devastatingly handsome fellow you mentioned … an introduction won't be necessary. I believe I'm already quite well acquainted with this gentleman. Though I must warn him that I was not exaggerating about the number of pins (all right, perhaps I was, but only a little). It might take considerable time. He should probably clear his schedule. I'm thinking I shall likely require his services … all night.

Boldly yours,

L

My Darling, Daring Soon-To-Be Wife,

I … have no words.

Speechlessly yours,

R

P.S. All right. I found some words. You are going to be the absolute ruin of my composure, Lise. Fortunately, I look forward to the devastation.

P.P.S. Schedule cleared.

My dearest blushing (you, blushing!) R,

Who could have known, at the beginning of all this, that I would one day be the one to ruin YOUR composure?

Delightedly yours,

L

I did, L. I knew.

Would you like to know what else I knew?

I knew I loved you before I knew your name.

I knew I loved you when you started teasing me in return.

I knew I loved you when you suggested that first outrageous prank at your grandmother's tea house.

I knew I loved you when you admitted I made you blush.

I knew I loved you when you said our letters made words come as easily as breathing.

And I will love you for every heartbeat this world allows me.

Ryden …

I love you.

I love you, I love you, I love you.

Thank you for being real.

Thank you for waiting while I learned to be brave.

Thank you for loving me through ink and paper, through silence and distance, through all my anxieties and insecurities and overthinking.

P.S. I LOVE YOU.

P.P.S. That last one was just in case you missed the previous four.

My darling Lise,

I am perilously close to committing a royal scandal by stealing a carriage and racing through the night to you, because the thought of waiting even a moment longer to hold you in my arms feels intolerable. But I'll attempt restraint. Barely.

I LOVE YOU!

(That was me exercising truly heroic restraint.)

For now … sleep, my love. Dream of tomorrow. I'll be there waiting, trying my best to look composed and failing utterly the moment you walk in.

All my love,

Ryden

My love,

Sleep well. I will be dreaming of that first quiet moment after the final note of celebration fades, when the world grows still around us and it is only you and me at last.

Bravely, boldly, entirely yours,

L

Next in the series …

Don't miss the fourth book in this delightfully whimsical and romantic series!

Once upon a time, in a land not so far away, a young science graduate named Rachel found that the real world wasn't a place she wanted to inhabit all the time. So she decided to escape into the magical realms that had occupied her mind since childhood.

Armed with a vivid imagination, Rachel spends her days conjuring up fantastical worlds filled with adventure, romance, and plot twists, where readers can escape the real world along with her.

Rachel lives in Cape Town, South Africa, with her husband, two little wildlings, and three fur-babies.

www.ingramcontent.com/pod-product-compliance
Lightning Source LLC
Chambersburg PA
CBHW020458310726
48979CB00016B/2708/J

* 9 7 8 1 9 9 8 9 8 8 3 4 1 *